PRAISE FOR THE BALLOONIST

"This is a real tour de force a stylish and brilliant conjuration of a 19th century inventor's world. Memorable characters against a vividly realised background. This one is masterly."

—Mary Renault

"There can no longer be any question whatever that MacDonald Harris is one of our major novelists."

—*Los Angeles Times Book Review*

"The author's unruffled direction-finding in the cross-currents that he loosed, his command of language (languages, too: French, German, and Swedish, plus some confident echoes of Greek and Latin) and his avoidance, perhaps excision, of the obvious made me follow his tragedy (yes) happily and without pity or terror."

—Richard Usborne, *Times Literary Supplement*

"Metaphysics, science, sex, the romance of ballooning, turn of the century charm, all combine in a lyrical, deliciously comic and moving novel. Wonderful entertainment in the very best Jules Verne tradition."

—*Publishers Weekly*

"Chilling and comic…carefully fashioned…an unusual mixture of Arctic Adventure and Parisian love story…told with fin de siecle elegance…ingenious…as highly polished as an antique machine on view in a glass case."

—*Kirkus Reviews*

The Balloonist
MacDonald Harris

Foreword

by

Philip Pullman

THE OVERLOOK PRESS

New York, NY

This editon published in paperback in the United States in 2012 by
The Overlook Press, Peter Mayer Publishers, Inc.
141 Wooster Street
New York, NY 10012
www.overlookpress.com

For bulk and special sales please contact sales@overlookny.com

First published in the US 1976

This edition © 2011 The Estate of Donald Heiney
Foreword © 2011 Philip Pullman

Cataloging-in-Publication Data is available from the Library of Congress

Printed in the United States of America

1 3 5 7 9 8 6 4 2

ISBN 978-1-59020-980-6

Donald Heiney (MacDonald Harris was a pseudonym) was born September 7th 1921 and died July 24th 1993.

He wrote 16 novels, a non fiction book on sailing, and a large number of scholarly books on Comparative Literature. In 1982 he received the Award in Literature of the American Academy and Institute for Arts and Sciences for the sum of his work, and in 1985 he received a Special Achievement Award from PEN Los Angeles Center.

His interests included sailing, arctic exploration and music.

OTHER FICTION
BY MACDONALD HARRIS

Introduction by Philip Pullman

MacDonald Harris (1921–1993) was the author of sixteen strikingly intelligent, interesting, and original novels, of which *The Balloonist* was probably the most successful. What amazes me, and has done since I read this book when it came out in 1978, is that he's not far better known.

I can think of two reasons why this might be so. In the first place, the public loves a writer who produces the same book year after year. They know where they are with an author like that; they can buy their new books with confidence, secure in the knowledge that nothing surprising will disturb the placid tenor of their habit. The parties to this unwritten contract value consistency above every other quality. Every one of Harris's novels, however, is quite different from those that came before it. To his publishers, it must have seemed as if he was trying to start a fresh career with each new book.

If the first reason for his comparative neglect is that each of his books is different, the second might be a particular quality they all have in common. A writer can't help a certain continuity of *something*, even if the subject matter and the setting of his novels varies as much as Harris's: from late eighteenth-century Venice to wartime Japan, from the early days of the film industry to terrorism in modern France. And what is continuous in his novels is a curious sort of stance towards the world, a quite un-American stance, if I can put it like that: the position of an intelligent adult confronting the tragi-comic absurdity of existence. There is little that's heroic about Harris's protagonists, but a great deal that's ironic and witty and sympathetic, with an acute sense of the ridiculousness of things. And while this is very agreeable to a certain kind of taste, as it certainly is to mine, it's not a *popular* taste.

But all his novels are extraordinarily _interesting_. And gripping, too: he knew how to arrest the attention and keep it, how to time the events of a narrative so that we can't help turning just one more page.

And another quality that remains constant in his work is a superbly flexible, elegant and witty prose. It's the work of someone who attends to every aspect of the words they're using, not least their weight, their rhythm and their colour. Once I open any of his novels at any point I find it almost impossible not to turn and read on, so delightful is the sensation of a sharp intelligence at work.

In _The Balloonist_, we see all of his qualities at their best. Typically, he sets the story in a part of the world he hasn't written about before, and equally typically he evokes it with a marvellous feeling for the whiteness of white, the coldness of cold. We're in the Arctic, towards the end of the nineteenth century, and our narrator, the Swedish Major Gustav Crispin, is setting out with two companions to fly to the North Pole. The _Prinzess_, their balloon, sponsored by a German brewery, is fitted with all the latest gear and the finest instruments, including a rudimentary radio with which Major Crispin is very pleased. Since no-one has invented broadcasting, though, he has nothing to listen to but the hissing and crackling of the atmosphere itself, which tells him, he believes, the direction from which a storm can be expected.

The Major is a delightful character, a little pompous, a little impatient, but impulsive and passionate too, and, like other Harris heroes, utterly helpless when it comes to love. Harris is quite superb at love, especially love between difficult, prickly, unlikely people. The love affair in _The Balloonist_ is richly comic and sexy and ultimately very moving, and he never invented a lovelier heroine than the beguiling and exasperating Luisa.

The technical background of this book is immaculate – which is to say, it feels solid when the characters pass in front of it, and it convinces me that it's all real. That does matter: we want to feel that the world we're reading about does exist, or could exist, or did exist, and technicalities and details of clothing and behaviour and speech as well as of machinery are all part of what makes it seem real. There's a danger in research, which is that the writer is likely to be so pleased with what he or she has discovered that they can't bear to leave it out, and it's a fine judgement to make, whether you're deepening the perspectives and pointing up the chiaroscuro or just overloading the story with more information than it can carry. A research principle I've found useful is to read enough to enable me to make up convincingly anything I don't know. MacDonald Harris convinces me in *The Balloonist* that if he's made any of the background up, I can't tell. It's all fascinating. And what's more there's just the right amount of it, and it comes to us convincingly in the voice of our narrator, who is fascinated by mechanical devices and the problems of mathematics, and it's all there to serve the story.

The character-drawing in this book is particularly skilful. One encounter with Luisa's timid mother, perpetually grazing on pastries ("Do you know Mifeuya?") and I never forgot it. And the admirable Waldemer, his "American and pragmatic head screwed squarely on his shoulders" – who could wish for a better companion on a dangerous expedition? By the end of the story, Waldemer still has not realised what we more acute companions of the Major in the little gondola below the vast and gaudy swell of the *Prinzess* twigged some time ago. But his bravery, his cheerfulness, his way with a kerosene stove! The ingenuity with which Waldemer boils their coffee without setting fire to the hydrogen in the balloon is delightful.

And one small technical point: much of the story is told in the present tense. I've complained many times about the present-tense habit, which has now become almost the default setting for any narrative with aspirations towards the literary. In the hands of most novelists it's a pointless affectation. But if there was ever a novel in which its use is justified, in fact necessary, it's this one.

I hope that in this second voyage of publication *The Balloonist* finds as many admirers as it deserves, and that we shall see some more of this singular, elegant and witty novelist's work restored to print. MacDonald Harris is too good to be neglected.

•

12 July 1897

At four o'clock Alvarez comes to tell me everything is ready. I immediately arise and go to the door of the shed. The air is clear and tepid, the sun hangs motionless in the east. The wind is still blowing gently from the south. It is not as much wind as I had hoped, but perhaps it is enough. Turning my back to it, I pause for a reflective moment to look northward in the direction of our hopes. Before me a beach of brown gravel stretches away a few hundred metres to the sea, a flat and endless grey surface wrinkled only slightly by the wind. At the edge of the water, bound to earth with a complicated system of ropes, is the Prinzess on which all our schemes and efforts have concentrated for so many months. Beyond her, only a mile or so across the strait, the shape of Amsterdam Island is clearly outlined in this crystalline morning light, and along to the right is the larger mass of Vasa Peninsula. The temperature, I note, is five degrees centigrade.

Alvarez is standing at my elbow, and without turning to look at him I know he is watching me with an expression I have come to recognize not only in him but in the other members of the supporting party, from the doctor to the last cook and carpenter in these final days as our preparations have drawn to a climax. They look at us as though we were dead, or more precisely, in the way one might look at men who are to perish in some bizarre and complicated way previously unknown to human experience, men who are to be executed perhaps by some new and intricate apparatus whose effects are unknown and might involve some unexpected and unimaginable ecstasy before the final annihilation. It is not exactly a sympathy. The experience that lies before us is so unprecedented that they, the men who observe us, have no sense of participation in our fate, knowing it is one reserved exclusively for us and not, like death from an ordinary illness, something that they themselves may be eventually destined to experience. And so their glance is one of curiosity rather than sympathy or envy, and is quite distant and detached in its regard; it is a speculation as to what we might be experiencing in our thoughts and sensations in this thing that is already beginning to happen to us and will soon separate us inexorably from all the other men of the earth. It is the look one might give to men who were about to voyage to the moon, or be mated to goddesses or wraiths. Perhaps we are, although I am not quite sure which I mean, or what I mean by that. I would do better to avoid fanciful metaphors and concentrate on the task at hand.

Alvarez, the crew chief, is an Argentine and knows neither English nor Swedish. Since I know no Spanish we communicate in the French which is the working language of the base camp. In any case Alvarez is not loquacious; he works with his hands and his brain and speaks only when necessary for the job at hand. After a while, still watching me out of his tanned face without expression, he merely inquires, "Ça va?"

He means the wind. I tell him it is adequate, perhaps. "And there are disturbances to the southeast. In a little while there may be more wind than we can use or need."

"Then we should start preparing the Prinzess?"

"Of course. Immediately. Remove what is necessary. Leave only the three ground ropes if you like."

"D'accord, Commandant."

With barely a nod to me, his face still expressionless, he disappears in the direction of the workshed. After only a moment I can hear his sharp voice through the walls of the shed. "Allons les gars—a l'éveillée! Tout est rassemblé—où sont les couteaux? On part!"

Most of the preparations have been completed for several days and what remains to be done is a matter of twenty minutes or so: removal of the lashing ropes, checking of instruments, loading of the final equipment. Out of habit, although I know almost precisely what it will say, I glance at my watch: a little less than ten minutes after four. Then, after a last appraisal of the wind, I go back into the sleeping shed to wake the others. Waldemer is already up, busying himself seriously and a little sleepily with the personal possessions he plans to take with him. When I touch Theodor's shoulder he says nothing, only looks at me with eyes that from the moment they open fix me steadily without so much as a glance at the other objects in the shed. Then he comprehends and pulls himself out of his sleeping sack without a word. The sleeping sacks are of reindeer leather with the fur inside, warm, but I can predict that the hairs they shed will be an annoyance. Theodor efficiently rolls up his sack; he seems as wide awake as if he had never been asleep, although he is still not very talkative. So much the better! We have not come to this place to talk. We should emulate Alvarez.

I quickly dress and collect the few instruments I have not embarked the night before: field glasses, the level sextant, the two pocket chronometers. (I speak of night only from habit since at the latitude of Spitsbergen the summer sun is always skulking around the horizon like a kind of friendly and stupid animal.) With Waldemer I walk down to the edge of the water and verify for myself that the instruments are carefully installed in the gondola. Waldemer stows his photographic apparatus, which except for the folding tripod fits neatly into a kind of leather portmanteau with a handle at the top. We have time for a final check of the chronometers Kullberg 5566 and Kullberg 5587. Still two minutes and thirteen seconds apart; the rates are constant. Then we go back to the sleeping shed where Theodor is lacing up his boots, his mouth set in a little crease of seriousness on one side. The doctor, alerted by Alvarez, has come ashore from the Nordkapp anchored in the bay and is waiting to examine us one last time. Except for Theodor and me he is the only one who knows—as inevitably he must know—the oddness that rests at the centre of this trio of us. A bear of a man with unkempt grey hair and whiskers, he applies a stethoscope to our chests in a rather perfunctory way. We have no fevers, palpitations, or visible fungi that would prevent us from carrying out our folly, as he regards it.

"Do you have dreams, Major?" he asks me unexpectedly.

"Dreams? What kind?"

"Of flying, for instance. Or climbing mountain peaks. *Odd* dreams, as they seem to you."

I might have told him that even my waking existence seems rather odd to me, but we have no time for a pleasant conversation on epistemology. "Do you ask in the interests of science, or merely to verify my health?"

"Both, I suppose."

"I'm perfectly healthy. I'd be glad to engage you in Indian wrestling if you like, but some other time. Are you done with us?"

"I am speaking to you now not as a physician but as a man. It would be too much to say that I am fond of you. I am not. But I am concerned over what you are doing to yourself, and to others, as I would be for any human being."

I simply meet his glance and look back at him, politely but without any expression. After a moment he takes me by the elbow and we move toward the door of the shed; outside he draws me a little apart from the others.

"Flesh has its limits, and different flesh has different limits. What you are concealing in this matter is more than an indiscretion, it is a crime. Besides I think you will find that this mischief you have made will defeat your own purposes."

"Are you sure you know my purposes?"

"I would have thought they were fairly clear."

I smile and might have remarked that he knows more than I do, then. But I only say, "If I am a criminal you ought to have told the authorities."

"I have sworn to you to say nothing, and you know that I will not. But you are taking a life in your hands—three lives, although I hold you more greatly responsible for one of the three."

"I am grateful for your advice. Goodbye, Doctor."

To my surprise he doesn't reject my hand and responds almost warmly, it seems to me, to the pressure of my fingers. But there is no smile of sympathy on his face, only an immobility—not of disapproval, one has the impression, but of indifference—that contrasts oddly with the cordiality of his grasp. He turns and without a word goes back toward the ship, not waiting to witness the crucial moment of this enterprise for which we have prepared for so many weeks.

For the second time this morning I make my way down the shingled beach to the water. The great roundness at the water's edge, stretched upward as though by the force of some mysterious and insubstantial gravity, curves at the bottom into a kind of dimple or extrusion resembling the mouth of a chemical flask. The net of light cord stretched over it is another geometry of reticulation imposed on this sphere. I am struck for the first time with the beauty of the form: the Prinzess strains upward, the ropes downward, and in their blind logic these forces have created an ellipsoid of exquisite feminine roundness. The alternate segments of red and white silk, tapering to points at the top and bottom, are each of them perfect shapes according to the laws of spherical geometry, yet when glanced at again they disappear as separate entities through a kind of optical trick and merge into this rounded whole to which nothing could be added and nothing taken away. The whole gives the impression of something ethereal in its substance and yet perfect in its concept, like the thought of a mathematician. As the breeze touches it, the shape trembles, dimples here and there, and then resumes its geometric curve. The red and white stripes, which are functional and intended to increase the visibility of the Prinzess at long distances, seem an intrusion, almost a frivolity in the barrenness of the surrounding landscape. Everything else is grey or brown, the sea is the colour of iron. The wind is holding constant at eight knots from the south.

At the water's edge a considerable crowd has collected: workmen, cooks, sailors from the Nordkapp, old Captain Nyblom, whom I have known from the time of the Greenland expedition. Alvarez is on top of the gondola checking the guide ropes and verifying the screw mechanism that detaches them in case of entanglement in the ice or for some other reason. My two companions stand by the gondola with their hands on the instrument ring, waiting for the word to mount. Theodor is elegant as usual in a fur-lined German officer's greatcoat, a peaked cap, and boots which came from Foirot in rue Saint-Honoré. I glance at his face for a sign of emotion, but he seems completely self-assured, with the faint touch of arrogance or contempt that is part of his nature. He has trimmed his hair short and neatly cleaned his fingernails, I see, in preparation for the flight. Waldemer is wearing a thick padded shooting jacket and a hunting cap with flaps, and you sense rather than perceive that there is long woolen underwear beneath, the American kind with a door at the rear, a most practical arrangement. As for me, I am clad in the outfit made for me by the Greenland Eskimos in 1882;

a coat of reindeer skin with a hood, breeches of the same material, and sealskin boots.

Alvarez comes down from his inspection of the guide ropes; he has checked the manoeuvring valve carefully and verified the ballast. We haven't bothered with breakfast; there is no time to lose if we are to take advantage of the favourable wind. The lines that hold the Prinzess to earth have been removed except for three stout ropes of Manila fixed to stakes. Three workmen are standing by these with knives we have been careful to sharpen the night before. There is a certain amount of conventional handshaking, which makes everyone concerned feel rather silly. Alvarez is the enemy of all sentiment and does not participate in this ceremony. Not looking directly at me, his eyes fixed on the lower part of the gondola, he merely says crisply, "Bonne chance, Commandant." Captain Nyblom, for some reason, shakes his head slowly, without altering his wrinkled Norwegian smile.

Somewhat impeded by our heavy clothing, we climb up into the gondola. Because of the bulky shooting jacket Waldemer has some difficulty crossing the instrument ring, and is immobilized for some time with one leg on one side of it and one on the other. No one shows even the faint trace of a smile at this (and again I think of condemned men who are being adjusted into some execution machine which malfunctions slightly so that there is a delay in the proceedings; it is with exactly that combination of detached silence and curiosity that the spectators watch us), and by unbuttoning his coat at the bottom I manage to help him across and in. "Thanks, Major." He is puffing a little at this incident. But he is smiling; if he can climb so smartly over the instrument ring then surely he, and all of us, can do the rest! Theodor shows no sign that he has observed this little playlet. He has swung over the ring as though it were an exercise he has performed a thousand times, and now he stands quietly waiting for the next order, with his gloves resting on the wicker of the gondola. I notice that his earlobes are already grey, and I wonder if he will be able to endure the much greater cold we are soon to encounter.

Now that we are aboard, the mechanic Eliassen and his helper attach a spring scale to the bottom of the gondola and pull it down a little to measure our buoyancy: eleven and a half kilos. Alvarez is waiting for a lull in the wind. The ropes creak, at my feet the pigeons supplied by a Stockholm newspaper coo softly in their wicker case. There is a faint and not unpleasant smell of kerosene to the south in the centre of the island, some round grey knobs of hills are watching us like a circle of spectators. Slightly to the east of north lies the larger mass of Spitsbergen, mountains we can't hope to climb over and must skirt with the help of this wind which we hope won't turn fickle. In the other direction, a quarter of a mile away, the Nordkapp with her tall narrow funnel and her squared foreyard rests docilely at anchor in the bay. It is too far away to see if the doctor is watching, but I'm sure he isn't; he is no doubt in his cabin writing up the notes of the examination. The time, a minute or two after five. I can no longer see Alvarez because he is directly under the gondola, but I can hear his voice speaking French with its brisk consonants, asking for the last time if everything is ready, warning all hands to stand clear of the guide ropes. At the last moment Eliassen comes running across the gravel with something in his hand and I catch the word *dagboken*: I have forgotten the pocket diary bought only two weeks before on Drottninggatan in Stockholm in which I am to record my notes of the voyage. The diary is handed up amid jokes about absentmindedness. From under the gondola the telegraph-like voice continues to give orders.

"Attendez un moment . . . calme . . . attendez."

There is a pause, so silent that we can hear the ticking of the two chronometers and the sound of the air in the rigging, and then the note of the wind drops a little.

"Coupez! Coupez tout!"

At the same instant I feel the gondola stir, lurch to one side, and rise slowly. The white faces below are a clump of strange flowers, damply pale against the brown of the beach, following our motions as sunflowers follow the sun. Everything below us, the sheds, the camp, the white faces looking upward, dwindles and shrinks as if pulled to a centre by invisible lines of force. I look over the side to be sure the guide ropes are trailing property. They slither over the beach and enter the sea, where they follow behind us leaving three snaky furrows on the water. Slowed by their drag, the Prinzess begins to tilt sideways. We begin to descend toward the sea, slowly at first, then dropping lower at an alarming rate. As the wave tops come up I see quite clearly, not more than two metres below us, something gleaming on the water: a piece of tinfoil or silver paper, probably a wrapping of a photographic plate from the pictures we took yesterday. Waldemer has his hand on the ballast string. But we must not release ballast too soon; if we do we will also have to release gas in order not to soar too high, and we will need the gas later. At the last moment he pulls the drawstring and a stream of fine lead shot slithers downward with a hiss. Almost at the same instant the gondola strikes the water with a heavy, almost metallic sound. We are thrown sideway against each other and keep our balance only with difficulty. Waldemer gropes for the ballast string again but I reach for his arm and restrain it. The gondola touches the sea once more, not quite so heavily this time, and this last contact with the terrestrial sphere seems to lend it force. The Prinzess lifts a little, hesitates and descends, and then begins to climb again. The guide ropes lift evenly up until only about a third of their length is still trailing in the water.

Waldemer catches my eye and shakes his head, smiling now, but still panting a little from the excitement.

"The vixen! She almost gave us a bath before we were decently off!"

Theodor says nothing. The camp behind us and the semicircle of watchers are almost invisible now. On the beach we can make out the sheds and, barely detectable in front of them, some pinpoints and variegated spots, our last glimpse of human beings. The ship in the harbour is a toy. To the northeast I see land I have previously known only from the chart: the end of the Vasa Peninsula, Vogelsang and the other outlying islands. Waldemer suddenly remembers something. He opens the leather portmanteau and unlimbers his photographic apparatus: a large oaken box with a goggle on the front of it, the tripod, and a number of plates with their holders. He unwraps the tinfoil from a plate and throws it overboard, and it sinks downward with an odd slowness like a silver bird. The plate snaps in and out of the slot. Like all specialists he grumbles at his tools. "At that range of course . . . And from a moving platform." What will show on the plate are some flyspecks. But his journalist's instinct is satisfied and our departure is recorded for posterity, insofar as posterity reads the *Aftonbladet* and the *New York Herald*. Theodor has mounted the theodolite and is taking a final bearing of the camp to verify our course. He inclines the tube downward, adjusts it to align exactly on the camp, reads the bearing of the azimuth ring, and makes an entry in his notebook. It seems incredible that we are off at last. I open my own pocket diary, find the page "12 juli," and write, "0501 GMT. Ascent from Dane Island. Wind S. 8kt., sky clear."

•

My emotions are complicated and not readily verifiable. I feel a vast yearning that is simultaneously a pleasure and a pain, like a desire for a woman. I am certain of the consummation of this yearning, but I don't know yet what form it will take, since I do not understand quite what it is that the yearning desires. For the first time there is borne in upon me the full truth of what I myself said to the doctor only an hour ago: that my motives in this undertaking are not entirely clear. For years, for a lifetime, the machinery of my destiny has worked in secret to prepare for this moment, its clockwork has moved exactly toward this time and place and no other. Rising slowly from the earth that bore me and gave me sustenance, I am carried helplessly toward an uninhabited and hostile, or at best indifferent, part of the earth, littered with the bones of explorers and the wrecks of ships, frozen supply caches, messages scrawled with chilled fingers and hidden in cairns that no eye will ever see. Nobody has succeeded in this thing and many have died. Yet in freely willing this enterprise, in choosing this moment and no other when the south wind will carry me exactly northward at a velocity of eight knots, I have converted the machinery of my fate into the servant of my will. All this I understand, as I understand each detail of the technique by which this is carried out. What I don't understand is why I am so intent on going to this particular place. Who wants the North Pole! What good is it! Can you eat it? Will it carry you from Gothenburg to Malmö like a railway? The Danish ministers have declared from their pulpits that participation in polar expeditions is beneficial to the soul's eternal well-being, or so I read in a newspaper. It isn't clear how this doctrine is to be interpreted, except that the Pole is something difficult or impossible to attain which must nevertheless be sought for, because man is condemned to seek out and know everything whether or not the knowing gives him pleasure. In short, it is that same unthinking lust for knowledge that drove our First Parents out of the garden.

And suppose you were to find it in spite of all, this wonderful place that everybody is so anxious to stand on! *What* would you find? Exactly nothing. A point precisely identical to all the others in a completely featureless wasteland stretching around it for hundreds of miles. It is an abstraction, a mathematical fiction. No one but a Swedish madman could take the slightest interest in it. Here I am. The wind is still from the south, bearing us steadily northward at the speed of a trotting dog. Behind us, perhaps forever, lie the Cities of Men with their teacups and their brass bedsteads. I am going forth of my own volition to join the ghosts of Bering and poor Franklin, of frozen De Long and his men. What I am on the brink of knowing, I now see, is not an ephemeral mathematical spot but myself. The doctor was right, even though I dislike him. Fundamentally I am a dangerous madman, and what I do is both a challenge to my egotism and a surrender to it. To the doctor then I am a criminal, to the Danish ministers some kind of prophet or saint. Or I will be if I succeed. Succeed in what? I had forgotten my own arguments on the pointlessness of my goal.

I don't note any of this in the diary, of course, nor do I confide it to my companions. I have already come to realise that this little book only a few centimeters square, with its prim calendar in Swedish and its toylike printed phases of the moon, will be totally inadequate for transcribing the true record of what is to come. For what is to happen can only happen inside our three minds, and will be recorded there in the infinitely complicated system of fibers and electrical charges that we call the memory, without understanding very clearly what we are talking about. The outward events become instantly nonexistent except insofar as they are fixed by this mysterious organ. The important events that happen to me in the next few days will therefore be those that take place inside my own mind. I hardly propose to communicate these complicated cerebral events to my companions and even less to the world at large, even if it were possible to do so, which it is not. The contents of the mind are infinite in their convolutions and at any given instant couldn't be encompassed by a hundred encyclopedias, let alone by a small pigskin booklet costing two kronor. So it is clear that like Columbus I must keep two diaries, the pigskin booklet devoted to what are crassly called facts, and the other a Mental Diary in which the true events of the next few days are recorded. The log that Columbus showed to his crew was a lie; all the positions in it were false and designed to allay their fears that they were about to fall off the edge of the world. And the pigskin book too is destined to lie, although not

quite in the same way. It is destined to lie because the outward events
of our lives bear little or no relation to what is really happening to us.
The pleasures and pains that come to the body from the outside are
pinpricks; the intelligent mail regards them with contempt. It is not
the body but the mind—this monster, this tyrant—that must be tricked
and deluded into thinking that its lot is a happy one. The outer world
exists only in my perception of it, and this perception is bent always by
the shimmering lens of my consciousness. So it is clear that the Mental
Diary must concern itself both with inward and outward events. And it
is clear too that in this odd document the past and present must mingle,
like layers of warmer and colder water merging gradually in a sea. Each
sensation, in the instant it is perceived, becomes a recollection. And
between near and far recollections there is little to choose. Luisa in the
drawing room in Quai d'Orléans, Theodor only a metre away from me
in the gondola—one is real and the other only a kind of ephemeral
Magic Lantern projected on those brain fibers crawling with electricity.
But which? I have only to close my eyes and they blur and merge,
the profile at certain angles of the head is the same, his contempt is
her pale chastity, his courage her quickness to anger. Do I know for a
certainty—I ask myself—that this feel of the instrument ring under my
gloved hand is a fact, and that the smell of a sun-warmed cab horse, the
clop of hoofs on an avenue in the Bois, are memories? For the feel of
the instrument ring too becomes a memory, in the very instant that I
seek to grasp and comprehend it.

•

Probably not everybody shares these little difficulties. It is my strength
and my weakness—I have finally come to realise—that I have a strong
sense of the presence of the invisible, that forces unseen by others are
quite real and present to me. Certainly Waldemer has no difficulty
dealing with the external world. He himself is a part of it, solidly three-
dimensional against the whitish background of the horizon. There is
no question whether he is in Paris or here in the gondola. Just now
he is developing the plate from the photograph he took at the time of
our departure. Although he is only a recent initiate to the mysteries of
photography, he is already adept at it and speaks knowledgeably of its
chemistry, preferring for development the recently discovered alkaline
process using pyrogallic acid, which permits exposures of a fifth of

a second or less. Just now he, or at least his head and shoulders, are underneath a little tent of black cloth which he has erected over the opened portmanteau and its contents. Inside, he is carefully sloshing the plate in a tray of pyrogallol with potassium bromide, then fixing it in a solution of hyposulphite of soda, then meticulously washing it for several minutes in fresh water. Now he emerges into the daylight with the plate gripped carefully by the corners, holding it between himself and the sun in order to look through it: but the pose, a hieratic one, suggests that he is holding it up to this solar deity for inspection or perhaps for commendation.

"Ha! Well, the range was a little extreme, as I thought. Still—"

He hangs it up in the rigging by a pair of clips provided for the purpose. He is not quite satisfied with it, yet he is satisfied with it. Just doing something requiring this quantity of apparatus, and this degree of specialized knowledge, is a satisfaction to Waldemer. Like many or most Americans—undoubtedly the reason for the success of that remarkable nation—he feels obliged to be doing something at all times. A sigh or two of satisfaction, a glance around the horizon, and he is squinting into the theodolite which Theodor has left mounted on the instrument ring. He puts the canvas cover back on the instrument.

"I make out our course to be north by east a half east."

"Very good."

"Hard to tell now though, because the guide ropes are out of the water and you can't sight along them. The sun has come up out of the mist and is warming the gas, and that's made us rise. We could use that handful of ballast we threw away now.

This is self-evident.

"Hallo, it's eight o'clock. About time for a little breakfast, I think. I'd be glad to fix it."

He is right on all counts. The sun has climbed out of the hazy ring around the horizon and is glowing more warmly now, with a kind of swimming on the surface if you look at it directly. Penetrated by this energy, the Prinzess swells and rises. The three guide ropes, which were previously streaming behind us in the sea, now hang directly down with their ends clear of the water. We can no longer estimate our course by the snaky trails they leave in the water, and from now on we must depend on the sun compass. Waldemer is correct as well about the time, which he has derived from his reliable pocket watch, manufactured in Massachusetts. It is true that it is about time for breakfast, and even more true that he would be glad to fix it. He is always happy to do anything of immediate and practical benefit to himself and others, especially if it involves the use of any sort of mechanical apparatus. Breakfast not only involves the primus stove—a simple but admirable machine in its own right—but the contrivance which Waldemer has invented to prevent the stove from igniting the hydrogen in the immense silken bag over our heads. First the coffee pot is filled with water and charged with the proper amount of coffee. Then it is set on the stove and held in place by a clamp, and the whole affair is lowered below the gondola on a rope some ten metres long. Waldemer carefully jerks away at two strings, one attached below to a patent English stove lighter and the other to the lever controlling the fuel. Finally, after a number of failures there is a yellow flicker underneath, along with the odour of burning kerosene. The flame turns blue; the stove is operating properly.

"Ahah," sighs Waldemer. He is pleased with himself. I smile too and am happy for him that the stove lighter has worked properly. He is really a splendid fellow, a hero of our time. Even though he is a journalist by profession, his true mission in life is to preside over his stove lighters, firearms, and all the other clever mechanical devices that an overbred civilization has come to regard as necessities. He is an emblem of our century, and even more of the century to come, the era of self-propelled carriages that will eventually do away with legs. He prefers tinned roast beef to a cow, not because it tastes better, but because the manner of its containment in the tin is ingenious. He is free from sentiment about nature. An animal to him is something to be looked at through a gun sight, something that falls down and turns into meat when the exquisite mechanism of the trigger is actuated. He has no hostility to animals, he simply regards them as somewhat inferior machines, smelly, you know, and prone to brucellosis and other mechanical maladjustments. Waldemer is an old companion of my adventures. He is necessary to me because without him I am only something more than half a man; I am incapable of taking an interest in a stove lighter. Together we are at least a man and a third. Machines are not perfect of course and neither is Waldemer. Occasionally things do not work out as he plans. This is fortunate, because if he were as infallible as machines are in the dreams of their designers he would not be human and I would not care for him as I do. Machines turn; their wheels turn, and with each turn of the wheel a minute atom of substance is worn away and the machine is no longer the same. Besides, there are—imponderables. This Waldemer has never understood. Sometimes a machine of this sort, believed to be perfect but actually possessing a soul, will turn on its maker with a quiet treachery far more dangerous than that of any animal. But—

In a reverie I imagine that it was my ancestor who invented fire and Waldemer's who invented the wheel.

•

The first glimpse I ever had of him was emblematic of the whole man: he overtook me one summer day on a country road in Pennsylvania, borne along on a bicycle, that ingenious device that man has contrived as an extension of his locomotor apparatus. A bicycle is interesting to a mathematician. It deals with the well-known difficulty with legs, that there are only two of them. One being constantly brought forward into position for the next step, the weight of the body is left on the remaining one, a precarious condition which results in lurching and inefficient motion. For this reason nature has evolved the horse and other four-legged animals, so that a sufficient number of legs will always be where they are needed without an undue effort. But the wheel is vastly superior to the quadruped. By a well-known mathematical principle, the number of legs is increased until it approaches infinity; analogically speaking, the polygon is extended to the circle. Now there is always a leg—that is to say a mathematically infinite point of the wheel—under the progressing body. The rider can relax his own legs at will, for short periods, and it is not even necessary for him to mind very carefully what he is doing. The wheel in its dumb perseverance will take care of the physics for him. His progress is assured, and he can add momentum or subtract it as he pleases by working the pedals or the brake in turn. Regarded purely as a locomoting animal, he has converted himself into a greatly improved one by combining himself with the product of his thought. Thus Waldemer, appearing behind me on the outskirts of Harrisburg on that bucolic summer day, waved cheerily, braked on the dusty road, and fell flat in front of me along with his machine.

Only a little less cheerful, he extricated himself from the bicycle, slapped the dust from his clothing, and introduced himself. He was about thirty in those days, a stocky young man with a handsome head, horizontal eyebrows, and a soft but bushy mustache shaped like the handlebars of his bicycle. He resembled exactly one of those clean-cut heroes in the American dime novels I had read as a boy in Stockholm, those who smile but only with a little wrinkle-of-taking-life-seriously between their brows, and this was prescient, because it was exactly one of those boys' adventures that he and I were setting out on together. He was irrepressibly good-natured and there was no question whatsoever about his intelligence. He had just begun work as the central Pennsylvania correspondent of the *New York Herald*, and he regarded his encounter with me as his first *opportunity* (he was fond of the word opportunity, quintessentially American as he was) to move from his small-town origins into the realm of world events. After he had explained the circumstances, he helped me onto the handlebars of his machine, and together we went on down the road in search of Woodlawn State College and Professor Eggert.

Cuthman Eggert was at that time a leading authority on aerostatics. I had come to him ostensibly out of curiosity, but at a deeper level no doubt because some demon inside me sensed that balloons were to play a part in my destiny. I had known he was interested in the problem of dirigibility because of his papers, which I had read in the library of the Royal Institute of Technology in Stockholm, and he in turn had taken note of my own publications on aeromagnetics. We corresponded, exchanged opinions, and agreed to meet—I because what I was interested in lay up in the sky too high to be reached with ladders, and he because he hoped, perhaps, that my knowledge of magnetic phenomena might be of some use to him in solving the problem of the dirigibility of aerostats. He proved to be a humourless man with a bony frame, a little smaller than ordinary size, intensely devoted to his researches and scarcely aware of the practicalities of daily life around him. He had no small talk. He proposed an ascension for that very afternoon, and together we went out to his apparatus, which he kept in a shed at the edge of the college hockey field. His balloon—the only one of the three he owned that was currently in working order—was a rather small one, capable of lifting about a hundred and fifty kilograms, including the basket. It was made of a single layer of ordinary silk, varnished after stitching, and no doubt leaked abominably. His methods of gas production were also primitive, although conventional for those days. He was obliged to produce his hydrogen on the spot by adding iron filings to a large earthenware flask of muriatic acid, and then to remove all traces of acid and other moisture from the product by passing it through a system of filters. The gas was then piped to the filling tube of the balloon, which had to be held in position by the three of us as it swelled and gradually assumed form. The whole process took a matter of three or four hours, broken by intervals in which it was necessary for Professor Eggert to uncap the flask and add more acid and filings. At last the balloon stood up like a soufflé with the basket underneath it, the whole prevented from rising only by the weight of a couple of bags of sand. The hockey players on the field, when they saw that preparations were imminent, stopped to watch us.

Then occurred an extraordinary and, as one looks back on it, quite childish confusion. It became clear only at this point that the balloon would carry only two persons, and the Professor had not thought out the practical arrangements to the point of deciding who these two were to be. He invited me to climb in, and climbed in himself, leaving Waldemer standing on the grassy field, still polite, still cheerful, but holding the basket firmly with one hand. Waldemer pointed out that he had come all the way out from Harrisburg on commission from his newspaper to describe the sensations of a balloon ascension and would suffer a monetary loss if prevented from doing so. This seemed reasonable to me and I climbed out. Waldemer mounted into the basket, whereupon the Professor climbed out and stood on the ground beside me; not out of any kind of displeasure or petulance, but simply because it seemed to him better, until these practical questions had been settled, for everyone to get out and discuss the matter calmly with both feet on the ground. Waldemer, however, was not easily persuaded to come down. Cheerfully, doggedly, and intelligently, reinforcing his position with logic, he clung to the basket of this celestial bicycle, which was soon to solve for him another of the anatomical flaws of man, his lack of wings. His well-modeled chin was set and it was clear he was not going to get down. What benefit could this ascension or any other ascension possibly have for mankind unless mankind became aware of it? And how could mankind become aware of it unless modern journalism disseminated its notice over the world? If this ascension was worth undertaking, it was only in that it might become part of the annals of man's progress, and the custodians of these annals were those who converted ephemeral events into the permanency of print, i.e., himself, Waldemer, the other employees of the New York *Herald*, and their colleagues throughout the nation and the world.

It might be thought that Professor Eggert gave in to him out of weariness, but this was not so. In the end Professor Eggert was persuaded by his argument. In spite of his abstruseness, his scientific reclusiveness, he was not insensible to the benefits and even the necessity of publicity. He invited me to climb in, I took my place beside Waldemer, and Waldemer pulled the cord of the bursting valve in the belief that it was the rope that released the ballast. The silk bag gave a gasp, doubled inward at the centre like a man who has been stabbed with a dagger, and quite slowly began to sink down over us. The hockey players gave mock cheers. We had plenty of time to get out of the basket and join Professor Eggert before the balloon lay like a heap of discarded clothing at our feet.

Of iron filings there was a copious abundance, since central Pennsylvania is freckled with iron mills, but muriatic acid was expensive. I was forced to resort to my own pocketbook to buy another demijohn, which had to be brought out from Harrisburg in a wagon. In any case, the ascension was postponed until the next day, when everything in fact worked faultlessly and Waldemer and I soared for an hour over various neat farms divided into rectangles, landing finally in a rye field. Professor Eggert followed us in a shay drawn by an intelligent mare that had learned a good deal about the movements of balloons and was able to trace out their landing places with hardly any guidance from the reins. Waldemer proved to be a valuable and useful assistant on that occasion. He soon learned to tell the bursting cord from the ballast rope, and we made many ascensions together over the Pennsylvania hills. Eventually we surpassed in our knowledge the bony and devoted Professor Eggert who was our teacher and learned things about balloons that even he didn't know. In fact, although erudite and assiduous, Professor Eggert was in the final analysis somewhat deficient in imagination. His obsession was the discovery of a means for the direction of motion of gas-suspended aerostats, to free them from the whimsy of the winds. He had tried vanes of various sorts, and here he was excruciatingly close to the solution, although he didn't know it himself and this approach was generally scoffed at by theoreticians of the time. Giving up vanes as a bad job, he turned to pedal-actuated airscrews and to devices emitting jets of gas. I have no opinion on these expedients, although it is possible that they may prove workable at some time in the future. Some of his experiments were highly perilous, and while ready to trust his own life to these untested devices, he was unwilling to risk the lives of others, and frequently used animals as subjects in his researches. This led him into the complicated and exasperating difficulties of training cats to actuate gas valves and so on, a distraction which in my opinion interfered with the more important course of his discoveries. During my association with him, his thinking processes became completely stuck on the possibility of using aeromagnetism for steering purposes. He knew from my publications and others that electromagnetic lines of force curved symmetrically around the earth from pole to pole like a graceful feminine garment, and also that these fields were related in some elusive way to the electrostatic forces that produced lightning, St. Elmo's Fire, and other paraphenomena of the atmosphere. I had many discussions with him on this matter. He argued that since the magnetic field consisted of lines of force, or at least was commonly spoken of in that way, there must *be* a force involved, and if a force existed, then there must in theory also exist the possibility of harnessing it for a useful purpose such as steering a balloon. I tried to convince him that the so-called lines of force lacked absolutely the power of pulling any object either north or south, and at the most they were capable of *aligning* elongated ferrous objects into a position parallel with themselves, as they did with a compass needle. But he contended, first of all, that if a compass needle is twisted, then a force has been applied to twist it, and this same force might at least in theory be used to twist a balloon. I pointed out that twisting a balloon was not the same thing as sending it off in a direction contrary to the wind, that he might twist the balloon until it spun like a top and it would still drift exactly with the wind in accordance with a dumb and inevitable law. Yet he could not give up the idea that the solution of dirigibility lay concealed somehow in the problem of turning the balloon at various angles to the wind.

Here again—as my subsequent discoveries proved—he was prescient but insufficiently imaginative. He did, during the time I knew him, reach the point of sending up magnetized iron bars in balloons, on one occasion adding a barnyard fowl which he had trained to operate a mechanism locking the bars into place when the alignment was correct. Unfortunately, this experiment took place in the late fall on the verge of a storm, and a westerly gale blew the apparatus, as far as anyone could tell, toward the Atlantic coast and out to sea. It is possible that in an earlier age, the age of Franklin and Lavoisier, let us say, Eggert might have achieved a name for himself in the scientific world. But in the nineteenth century technology moved too quickly for him, and he was unable to surmount the problem of specialization that is the genius and the curse of our epoch. I felt a great sympathy for him, and I owed him a great debt and still owe him one for the tutorship he generously and quite selflessly offered me in aerostatics. Where is Professor Eggert now? Probably still at his state college, sending up ducks, kittens, and lady students in the antiquated airships of twenty years ago, and pursuing them over the countryside in his shay.

•

"Major, what are you thinking about so quietly there? Always falling into thought, you are. It's your Scandinovian mysticism." This is his American form of humour, a badinage consisting mainly of jolly and bluff insults. "A metaphysical lot, you Swedes. Look at Swedenborg. You have too much time to think in the winter, that's your trouble. Take the Norwegians. They have the same climate, but they spend the winter sliding around their hills on skis. They never think a bit. Look at 'em, bursting with health."

Actuating the string attached to the fuel valve so that the stove hanging below goes out, he pulls in the rope hand over hand and retrieves a perfectly brewed pot of coffee. This he pours into cups of a thick unbreakable variety selected by himself, and passes them to us, along with slices of coarse bread and butter.

"Ah." He exhales contentedly. "Is the breakfast all right, Major?"

In actual fact I drink the coffee but find I have little appetite for the bread and butter. Not noticing this, he spreads his own bread thickly with butter and falls to. "Better than a poke in the eye with a sharp stick," he comments in another widely applicable phrase of his. Still chewing, he gropes in his clothing for a handkerchief, removes a few crumbs from his mustache, and continues with the meal. Now and then he washes the bread down with a swallow of steaming coffee that produces another sound of satisfaction.

"There is something in what you say," I admit. "But you oversimplify as usual. Swedes are quite possibly metaphysical in the winter, but they are hedonistic in the summer. Around Easter a transformation takes place. From then till autumn they're as free from metaphysics as you Americans. They develop enormous appetites. They become amorous. I can assure you that in the summer a Swede never thinks at all."

"But it's summer now. Therefore, if your theory is correct, you shouldn't be falling into thought."

"Ah. But you see, it's precisely from summer to winter that we are journeying. In Stockholm the air is balmy, on Dane Island it was brisk but still hardly cold, and now we are headed for ice and snow. In short, my dear Waldemer, space and time are interchangeable. Ordinarily it would be necessary to wait for several months for my metaphysical phase to come on, but we can produce the same effect at will by a geographical displacement."

"Too deep for me. One of your paradoxes, I imagine. What's this, Major, you're not eating your breakfast."

"I might, if we were headed south."

"Very witty. Here, give it to me, I'll finish it off."

What is left of my bread and butter, the greatest part of it, to tell the truth, disappears into Waldemer. Then in a systematic way he sets about his morning ablutions. First it is necessary to answer the call of nature, which he accomplishes by means of the door in his underwear and a sanitary apparatus we have brought along for the purpose. Theodor finds something to look at in the other direction during this process. Then, after carefully washing his hands in a minimum of water, Waldemer turns to shaving. He fills a teakettle, puts it on the primus stove, and lowers the whole affair over the side again as in the business of coffee making, Following the rule prohibiting inactivity at any time, he brushes his teeth while waiting. The water is soon hot and the kettle below, with a kind of snoring noise, begins emitting a plume of vapour. He pulls it up, fills the shaving mug with hot water, and in a trice he has covered his face with foamy soapsuds. His straight razor he removes from a walnut case, tests for sharpness with his thumb, and holds poised over the waiting cheek.

"Ah."

Something is troubling him. He looks in the toilet case, turns everything over, and assumes an expression of concern mingled with annoyance. "Drat it, I don't seem to be able to find my pocket mirror. I was sure it was here." He turns to me hopefully, apologetically, expectantly. "Major, I wonder . . ."

No, unfortunately I have not brought any mirror. I don't intend to shave on this expedition, I explain, and I predict that he won't either when he sees how difficult the process gets as we go farther north.

He turns to Theodor, but Theodor politely and regretfully shakes his head.

"Ah."

Waldemer is perplexed. His face is covered with shaving soap, which is rapidly drying. The water in the teakettle is returning to the temperature of the atmosphere.

"H'mm."

He takes a teaspoon from the provision basket, a bright and shiny new one, and tries unsuccessfully to catch his image in it, even the reflection of a small part of his cheek the size of a postage stamp, which he might shave and then pass along to the next piece.

"Bother!"

The spoon is far worse than those distorting mirrors at carnivals that send us back images of ourselves as dwarfs with three-foot foreheads. Waldemer is genuinely troubled at the lack of a mirror; if the expression were not out of character for him, I might say that he is metaphysically troubled. It is clear, if one observes him carefully, that his anxiety cannot be accounted for by his mere inability to shave. He could shave blind, by feeling with his fingers, or it would be possible for him not to shave at all. If he hurries, the water in the teakettle will still be warm enough for him to wash the soap from his face. No, Waldemer's perplexity at the moment goes beyond shaving. What troubles him deeply is that there is nothing in the universe—since the universe for the present consists of the airship and its contents to reflect his image back to him and thus verify for him his own existence. If one looks in a mirror and finds an image reflected back, *something* must be generating the image, and this something is one's self. It is not enough merely to feel your knee with your left hand, or bump your head against a wall. This sort of thing only proves that you are having sensations. But *what* is having sensations? Perhaps the sensations exist in themselves, hanging in a void, pretending to themselves that they belong to a person. A mirror represents confirmation from the external world. Naturally Waldemer if he chose could ask one of us whether he exists. "I say, old man, I am still here, aren't I, and just the same? Or just about the same." Thus the women who are continually asking if we still love them, or if they are pretty today, or if we like their dress. But it is typical of Waldemer that he has come to rely on a machine—since a pocket mirror is a tiny and simple machine—for a need that others satisfy through human relationships. Waldemer is troubled and I am not quite sure what is taking place in my own soul either. For I stole his mirror from his toilet case, last night in the shed, and hid it under the crate that served as our chair. It's still there in the shed, no doubt, where Eliassen will find it as he found my pocket diary—which I left behind quite inadvertently, incidentally; no metaphysical motives there. "Ah, pity, Mr. Waldemer has forgotten his mirror. How will he shave?" How indeed? Why indeed have I been so furtive and so perfidious? I don't know. Waldemer doesn't know why he misses the mirror so profoundly and I don't know why I stole it. I conclude—I prefer to conclude—that it was playfulness on my part. A mirror is a trivial thing and to be annoyed because one has no mirror is petty. It is a little joke, like cutting off a fellow's suspender buttons. Without suspender buttons his pants fall down and he has no dignity. It is really an American form of humour, like Waldemer's jolly bantering. Also, it gives me pleasure to know that there are no mirrors in the airship. What do I mean by that? I'm not sure. Perhaps that I have no need to verify my existence with a little machine, or perhaps that I prefer not to verify my existence. This little trait of mine, which I have just discovered, is perhaps dangerous, I am not sure. Perhaps not.

"Major, I wonder if I might borrow your sextant. The fact is that this infernal soap is drying at a dizzy rate. If I don't get it off soon I'll be caked with the stuff, like a Grand Guignol actor, for the rest of the trip. Drat me for being so stupid as to forget my mirror."

The sextant is essential to our navigation in this enterprise, that is to say, to our survival. It is a Koerner of the latest model, modified through the addition of a mercury level for the purpose of establishing the horizontal plane in the absence of a horizon. Taking it carefully from its wooden case, I hand it to him. Waldemer has respect for the sextant. There is no danger that he will break it. Carefully—most carefully—he takes it in his left hand while holding the razor in his right, and shaves himself by observing the tiny piece of his cheek which is visible in the index mirror. Man, contriving instruments to measure the world, succeeds in taking the measure of himself. Or more simply: Man as Reflected by His Instruments. When Waldemer is done he returns the sextant to me and I put it back in the box. Then he pours the rest of the water, which is still slightly warm, into his hands and vigorously rubs over the shaved places. To finish he dries himself neatly with a towel and hangs the towel in the rigging to dry. It immediately freezes.

•

Through all this Theodor has said nothing. He has eaten his breakfast with dignity, retrieving each crumb and wiping his fingers afterward with a linen handkerchief, but all rather absentmindedly, as though he were scarcely noticing what he is doing. Now he has set the coffee cup aside and is gazing with intelligence off into the horizontal plane, where there is nothing whatsoever to be seen. Theodor has many fine qualities but he is not quite sure yet who he is. He fancies himself a poet, and in fact writes fairly decent poetry when he is able to surmount the influence of Heine, but he is also fond of military clothing. His parents—the parents of Luisa—consist of an American father, now deceased, and a mother who was born of mixed blood in the Portuguese colony of Goa on the coast of India. The two came together somehow in Paris, but this is a whole story in itself. The mother in many ways is an interesting person, although I can't say I care very much for the Goans I have known. The combination of bloods, in my experience, produces little more than a medley of Portuguese excitability and Oriental sloth, the least attractive side of both races. The mother's main contribution to the world has been to bequeath her complexion to Luisa. Or to Theodor; I forgot for the moment that I was thinking about Theodor. His complexion is a translucent olive, pale like the moon and yet in some way at the same time dark; exactly—come to think of it—like the moon, which also gives this impression of darkness. But unlike the moon, which suffers from various pockmarks, this complexion is flawless and of a single substance, like a fine china teacup. Moons, china, there are too many metaphors in all this. But persons like Theodor demand metaphors; they evoke them, so to speak, from the ambient atmosphere. His voice is clear and rather high, a voice that would be almost a soprano if it were a woman's voice, but since it is his voice it merely sounds refined. Theodor is a person of considerable culture, particularly in science and in languages. In addition to English and Portuguese he speaks French flawlessly, Swedish only after wrinkling his brow a little, schoolbook German, and the Italian of a Swiss hotel clerk. With his dark eyes and long aristocratic Silva e Costa face he is strikingly handsome, especially when he is speaking French or Swedish. Why have I brought him along? Because he has studied aerostatics and can sight through a theodolite, and also, no doubt, because he can regale us with some poetry if things get dull. I am beginning to see that, in spite of careful plans, there are many doubts and ambiguities in what I have brought along on this expedition and what I have left behind; for example, that I have deleted a mirror, which is useful, but have brought Theodor, who is vulnerable to the accusation of being merely decorative.

Still, it is better not to be confused about anything so fundamental as the sexes. Theodor is a man among men, the beau ideal of a young adventurer, and in spite of his complexion he is inured to the common hardships of cold, discomfort, and fatigue. I have climbed the Aletschhorn with him over the glacier and he never asked for quarter, although my legs after a while pounded like hammers. He is as contemptuous of the needs of his own body as he is of other human beings. What does he love? I hardly know. Perhaps his clothes, perhaps his dead father, or even me, in his contemptuous way. It is curious that for all his beauté he never looks in mirrors. How does he confirm his existence? His existence is inside himself. He is indifferent to the fact that his complexion and his dark eyes were never made for these latitudes. There is something Persian about him, a languor of oases, an indolence, which he subdues or ignores with the contempt for physical discomfort inherited no doubt from his frontier father. His only delicacy is a modesty about the needs of nature; in these things he is almost girlish and retreats behind a canvas stretched across a corner of the gondola. Although Waldemer hasn't noticed it he, Theodor, hasn't shaved yet this morning and yet his cheek is as smooth as it was yesterday. There are some things to come still in his manliness.

•

This Prinzess, the third to bear her name, is enormous. She is at least four times as big as any airship I have ever had anything to do with. Or so it seems now, when the clutter and distraction of the preparation are behind us and we are left to ourselves in the gondola. It is almost two metres from where I am standing to where Waldemer is checking the bolt of his light .256 Mannlicher rifle. Two metres is not very much in a ballroom, but under these conditions it is unbelievably and luxuriously commodious. We stand on a light floor of laminated wood, fabricated according to a new American process, which is removable in sections and under which provisions and spare gear are stored. Circling the gondola at shoulder level is the instrument ring, on which thedolites, magnetometers, and other paraphernalia may be mounted as needed. Between the instrument ring and the gondola itself a set of canvas windbreakers may be fitted in bad weather; in fine weather some or all of these are removed. Everything is stowed neatly; there is room for the pigeons and even for Waldemer's miniature darkroom. If we stretch our hands upward we can touch the bearing ring, a small but intensely strong circle of steel to which the converging cluster of rigging from the gas bag is attached, and from which, in turn, depend the guys that support the gondola. To the bearing ring are fitted the long bamboo poles which serve as yards for the sails, at present furled or rather drawn in on their rings like curtains through a system devised by myself. The gondola of wicker and Spanish cane, the bamboo spars, the hempen ropes stretching up over our heads give the impression of an antique sea vessel, a fantastic craft out of some print of the sixteenth century. Everything is stowed neatly under our feet or in bags attached to the bearing ring. The ballast of fine lead shot hangs to the outside of the gondola, each bag with its drawstring for releasing. A carefully planned and well equipped expedition, the whole paid for by the estimable and well-merited firm of Prinzessin Brauerei G.m.b.H. in Bremen, in return for the privilege of naming our craft and driving therefrom a beneficial notoriety; although this policy may turn back on them if our venture goes badly, so that the product of their brewing is associated in the public mind with doom rather than with the intoxication of success.

I have in my pocket a clipping from an Austrian newspaper which I have carefully cut out and saved in my billfold, for what purpose I am not sure, perhaps to amuse myself in dull moments: 'Jener Herr Crispin, der mittelst Luftballon zum Nordpol und zurück fahren will, ist einfach ein Narr oder ein Schwindler." Probably I am a fool and a swindler, Herr Oesterreichischer-Zeitungsschreiber, but what business is it of yours? I am not swindling you. At the most the hardheaded German brewers, who understand precisely the risks they are taking. On the whole, to this heavy-handed Teutonic invective I prefer the humour of the American polar explorer who told a reporter, at the time of my visit to New York last year, which was attended with a good deal of publicity, "People who wish to arrive at the Pole by means of airships, steam carriages, trained polar bears, etc., are attention seekers rather than serious explorers." Touché! He has me there! Peary himself, it seems, is planning an expedition to the Pole using dog sleds in the dozens guided by whole villages of Eskimos, probably because he finds it easier to train Eskimos than to train polar bears. He is right that I am not serious, I wish I could be, but blast! We will see who gets there first. If he does I will drink to him cheerfully. I forgot to mention that the managers of the Prinzessin Brauerei G.m.b.H., in addition to paying for the expedition, have also made us a gift of two dozen of their best bock packed in a hamper full of straw. We will drink these in time and so they too will serve as a kind of ballast, the bottles and eventually the liquid going overboard to compensate for the gradual loss of hydrogen from the bag. Our lives waver on these handfuls of gas and grams of weight.

•

I take the Koerner sextant from its case and point it at the coppery disk hanging in the east. Theodor watches the two chronometers, waiting for me to call out the exact moment of the observation. Looking through the sighting tube and slowly turning the screw, I bring the image of the sun in the index mirror down exactly to meet its twin floating in the mercury. Since the sun is still rising the two disks keep persistently trying to creep a hairline away from each other. Wait . . . wait . . . Now I've got them: "Allez . . . houp!"

Theodor writes down the time: 09h 06m 52s GMT. So on until five altitudes have been taken. I average these, discard one altitude which seems to contain an error, and set to work with my logarithms and almanac. In twenty minutes, with fair confidence, I am able to draw a position line on the chart, locating us at 80° 40' north and 11° 32' east, or some forty-seven nautical miles north-northeast of Dane Island.

I write this formula on a slip of paper, adding, "All hands well. Altitude 200 m. Proceeding north. Prinzess expedition, 0906 GMT 12 July 1897." Then Waldemer unbuckles the wicker case under our feet and thrusts his arm in. There is a soft fluttering, some alarmed coos, and Waldemer's arm emerges holding a grey and white pigeon with a pink bill. The pigeon twists his neck and flaps one wing a little, whether in alarm or in eagerness for the coming flight is not clear. I pass Waldemer the slip of paper and he rolls it tightly, screws it into a tiny aluminum tube, and fixes the tube to the pigeon's foot, managing to do all this while holding the pigeon softly pressed against his chest. Then, with the pigeon perched on his right hand, he raises it and transfers it to the instrument ring in front of him. The pigeon looks around brightly with little jerks of his head and pecks at something on his shoulder. He seems content on the instrument ring and shows no inclination whatsoever to fly.

But Waldemer has learned something about the functioning of this particular mechanism. "Now then, darling." He carefully extends his gloved forefinger and touches the bottom of the pigeon, about halfway between his virile parts and the place where his legs are attached. Like a clockwork bird whose lever has been touched, the pigeon soars into the air, his wings slapping loudly until he gathers speed and flies more smoothly. At first he dips lower; then he circles the Prinzess at a medium distance, climbing with white flashes of his wings, which beat faster and faster until they are too rapid for the eye to follow, a kind of optical twittering. Finally, gaining speed, he slides off on a tangent and soars away to the south. Smaller and smaller he becomes a dot, a winking pinpoint—and then he has disappeared. Waldemer, with an air of satisfaction, continues to stare in the direction of the pigeon for some time after he is no longer visible. This tiny speck of life, we hope, will make its way some eleven hundred miles to its home in Trondheim. No pigeon has ever flown so far or over so deserted and forbidding a sea, but perhaps this one will. There in the Norwegian fishing town the honest watchmaker and pigeon fancier who is his owner will find him huddled on the sill of the cote, trembling with fatigue. He will give him food and caress him, and he will pull the tiny slip of paper from the tube and take it to the telegraph office. Electrical currents will carry the words to the *Aftonbladet* offices, whence they will be disseminated by other wires and cables to Waldemer's own newspapers, the London *Daily Mail* and the New York *Herald*. In this way the world will learn our exact location at nine hours and six minutes Greenwich mean time, provided the pigeon reaches his destination and a whale has not eaten the transatlantic cable. Sometimes a Physeter macrocephalus, or sperm whale, scooping krill from the sea bottom with his long jaw, will encounter a submarine cable and snap it like thread without noticing what he is doing. Sometimes, on the other hand, this swimming elephant gets his jaw tangled in the cable and drowns. This of course has nothing whatsoever to do with the Prinzess expedition and the pigeon on his way to Trondheim; it is simply one of many indications that the struggle between nature and civilization is not yet quite decided.

"Well, Major?"

"Well?"

"Thinking again, I see. And I can imagine what you are thinking about."

He carefully does not make a roguish smile, but the signs of its suppression are visible behind the mustache.

"Can you?"

"The sight of the pigeon flying off. You know. Makes us think of . . . our—loved ones."

"Loved ones?"

He thinks it is rather dense of me not to get the drift by this time. "Miss Hickman. Eh?"

I glance briefly at Theodor to see his reaction. No reaction at all. To judge from his face he might not even have heard; but of course he has heard. I decide to follow a mock-dignified and slightly offended line, calm but my chin raised just a fraction of an inch.

"You forget we are still travelling north. And the farther north we get, the less my thinking concerns itself with such—carnal matters."

Waldemer really *is* embarrassed. The roguish smile emerges from behind the mustache; his defence is to treat the thing as a joke. "Well, Major. I wasn't really referring to—h'mm. Carnal matters. It's just that, you know. One's more tender sentiments . . ."

"Whenever I notice any such, I go to a doctor. He gives me a medicine for them."

"Ahah. Bravo, Major."

•

Theodor, by way of ignoring this whole conversation, or pretending to, has been studying the chart, checking our course with the parallel rules and verifying the distance run by stepping it off with the dividers. His glance is intent on this crisscrossing track of pencil lines that begins at the camp on Dane Island, passes between Amsterdam Island and Vogelsang until it clears the Spitsbergen group, and then verges off northward onto the blank part of the chart. Finally, sensing I am watching him, he looks up.

"Well?"

For a moment he hesitates, afraid perhaps that with his lack of experience he has made some blunder in the calculations. "You can check whether I'm right, Gustavus. It seems to me our speed has averaged eleven and a half knots instead of eight. And we're being deflected a little to the east."

Standing in absolute silence at his side, so that our elbows touch, I pretend to check his figures. But I know without looking that he is right. I frown over this for a moment with my finger on the chart. After a while Waldemer notices that I have fallen into thought again, my Swedish vice.

"Something up with the weather?"

"I think so."

"Still looks lovely. Not a cloud in the sky except for this infernal haze."

"What is happening would be a long distance away. Invisible to your mortal eyes, I'm afraid."

"Ahah. Perturbations in the ether. Well, you'd better consult the Spiritual Telegraph, Major."

This is said in his usual tone of good-natured banter, but it is exactly what I plan to do. With a quickening excitement that I seek to control, or at least to conceal from my companions, I bend down and unstrap the lid of the leather case stored under our feet. Inside is the apparatus that has occupied my private thoughts for so many months, the climax of my investigations into the relation between aeroelectricity and geomagnetism that go back as far as the Greenland expedition of 1882. It consists of a coil of fine wire wrapped precisely around a fiber cylinder, a condenser made of tinfoil and waxed paper, and a crystal of galena over which is poised a tiny hairspring. The crystal is connected through a pair of insulated copper wires to the magneto-auditory converter, which to tell the truth is an ordinary telephone receiver manufactured under the Bell-Edison patents. Finally, there is the aerial coil or catching basket, consisting of more copper wire wound around a frame and rotatable through a pair of pivots. I erect all this and verify that the connections are tight. Then, holding the receiver to my ear with one hand, with the other I gently touch the hairspring to various points on the galena crystal.

The scrap of mineral is very tiny, no bigger than an English farthing, but over the months I have come to know every detail of its surface as the husband knows the body of the wife. There, next to that double ridge and in the pit no bigger than a flyspeck, is a particularly sensitive spot. The end of the hairspring descends with a tremble into this concave triangle, and in the earpiece I hear sounds until recently never apprehended by the ear of man. A rustling, rushing, crackling, hissing, rubbing, muffled cracking noise, like celestial bacon being fried. Adjustments of the coil and condenser slightly increase the volume of these sounds. What am I hearing? No one is quite sure. What is certain is only that these cryptic sounds have coursed through the atmosphere from the beginning of time, but have been audible to the human ear only in the decade—less, in the five or six years—since the development of the detection apparatus. Where they come from—what intelligence or blind force it is that sends them crackling and hissing on their way to us—is an enigma. But I think I have begun to guess. I have guessed that the cracklings are produced by the agitations of the atmosphere that we ordinarily refer to as weather. Weather consists of various collisions between airs of different sorts. Some masses of air are dry, some are wet, some are compressed and others rarefied. In this way, following the laws of physics, they drift about in relation to each other and shift their respective positions. The wet masses, becoming rarefied, lose the strength of their grip and release rain. The dry masses, becoming warm, ascend upward, and others rush in to take their place. The atmosphere is the battleground of invisible monsters. This is well known. But what is not well known—if my guess is correct and my discoveries are not the product of a disordered fancy—is that these lumps of warm, cold, wet, dry, and other kinds of air, by dint of rubbing against each other like huge animals, produce electromagnetic vibrations exactly similar to the cracklings and sparkings that result when sealing wax and fur, or silk and a lump of amber, are rapidly frictionated. Further, that these emanations are directional in nature. Should there be, for example, a rarefied air to the westward, the prevailing wind will be from the south. It is to the area of low pressure that the lumps of air rush most vigorously and begin circling in cyclonic pattern, causing the most collisions and therefore the most cracklings in the electromagnetic apparatus. It is possible that this is only a metaphor. Nevertheless, like those well-known metaphors that men in some ages have called gods, it works and can be understood if a man studies the manner of its interpretation. I believe it was Goethe who said, with a prescience only possible in a scientist who was also a great poet, "Nature is infinite. But he that will take note of symbols will understand all of it. But not altogether." Or he said something like that; I haven't the text at hand and have to rely on my memory.

Leaving poetry out of it, what are we to think of these emanations that seem to speak to us out of the invisible emanations that have all the attributes of occult phenomena and yet are detectable only by the latest scientific apparatus? Perhaps this is the sixth sense that men have pondered over in all ages, from the ancient to the modern, without understanding very clearly what they are talking about. Supposing you had no sense of smell—the idea of such a sense would hardly occur to you except through a sort of mysterious intuition. And this thing I have found is mysterious all right. I remember that August day in a pasture in Varmland when I first heard lightning—I don't mean that I heard thunder, but that a half-darkened shed with the Edison receiver pressed to my ear I heard the crash of fire striking from a cloud still a dozen miles away, a full minute before the sound of thunder reached my ear. The lightning bolt had signaled its existence through certain mysterious vibrations; but vibrations of what? *Something* had vibrated, some fine gas our organs are too crude to detect had trembled at the stab of the bolt. What purpose can this shimmering of the ether have? Has it waited patiently, over the billions of years, for the moment when I happened to connect up my earpiece to the crystal of galena and became the first to hear it? If so its accents are a little cryptic. Perhaps I have only intercepted a message intended for someone or something else.

I will confess that this thing I have stumbled across fascinates me to the point of ecstasy, and also that it seems to me vaguely dangerous. Dangerous how? I don't know. It is simply that there is an element of necromancy in all this which, in the privacy of my own mind, I quite candidly regard as ominous. If you go sticking your finger in nature's private parts you do so at your own risk, and at the risk of all humanity. In the Middle Ages the alchemists, without understanding what they were doing, groped about with their cauldrons and retorts in an effort to turn lead into gold. Instead they discovered the principle of chemical combination, which in turn gave birth to gunpowder, and an entire civilization of castles and cathedrals crashed to the ground, the alchemists bleeding under the ruins along with everybody else. (It is true that gunpowder was invented by the Chinese, but I am speaking analogically.) It is characteristic of man that he is annoyed by secrets, that as soon as he is aware there is something to be known that he does not know he wants to know it, whether or not the knowing will make him happy. In the end it is perhaps this that will destroy him.

In the meanwhile, however, it is likely that we have a century or more to be happy or unhappy before this development takes place. Particularly in the case of aeromagnetic waves, it is unlikely that they will destroy us in the near future. On the contrary, it is probable that for a time they will be of great practical use. I am perfectly well aware of the investigations being conducted in this sphere by Hertz, by Signor Marconi, and by others. In my opinion these endeavours have every chance of succeeding. Consider: if static electricity is made to leap from one brass ball to another, the spark will cause a compass needle to be deflected in the room below, as much as thirty feet away. The fact was noted by Trowbridge as early as 1880. This being the case, there is no reason why, if the electric spark upstairs is interrupted in accordance with the system of Morse's code, a message cannot be read downstairs on the compass, even though no wires connect them. Could such a contrivance work in an airship? Undoubtedly. Over long distances? Possibly. In no case am I going to hint of this to Waldemer. He has quite enough to occupy his mind as it is. If he ever suspected that the apparatus in the leather case might be used to send messages to the outside world, he would be composing drivel for it night and day. Including, no doubt, our "sensations," such as the fact that our noses are cold and we are enjoying our dinners, and also our delight at the efficient functioning of the apparatus. This has already happened in the case of the ordinary telegraph worked by wires. A man sits in Chicago and taps out, "How well this telegraph works." And the operator in New Orléans replies, "Yes, the telegraph is a great invention." No, decidedly, the practical possibilities of aeromagnetism must be concealed from Waldemer.

In prophesying the weather, however, a great deal is possible even with my limited understanding. Having tickled the galena crystal with the hairspring, I satisfy myself that a normal amount of bacon frying is going on in the carpier. Now comes the difficult part—detecting the direction of the chief mass of the emanations. Ahah, Professor Eggert, we are back to directions! Your suspended iron rods and your duck didn't quite work, but you were on the right track. By listening to these ethereal scratchings I will send this airship not in the direction it wants to go but in the direction I want it to go. This is made possible by a modification to that part of the apparatus called by some investigators the aerial wire and by others the antenna, through analogy to the fragile erections attached to the brains of certain insects for receiving emanations, no doubt, of their own sixth sense. This wire—and here my invention is unique—I have wound into a flat coil mounted on a frame that can be rotated, so that it intercepts the maximum amount of aeroelectricity when facing toward it and none at all when it is turned on edge. In this way the bearing of a meteorological disturbance from the operator can be precisely determined. Turning this contrivance back and forth, I establish that the direction of the loudest cracklings is east-northeast. Out with the chart again. There is undoubtedly a region of rarefied air in the direction of the cracklings. The wind turns dumbly about it in accordance with the well-known laws of rotating bodies, and the Prinzess, like a bemused lover, just as dumbly follows the winds. I dismantle the apparatus, put it away in the case, and strap the lid shut.

Neither of my companions says anything, but clearly they are waiting for my prophecy from the invisible world.

"There's a mass of fluxuous air—here."

I draw in a rough oblong on the chart, to the east and somewhat to the north of us.

"This is bending the wind in a slightly oblique direction. Consequently our course is taking us a little to the east of north."

"Ahah. H'mm."

He looks at the chart, a little troubled.

"Never get to the Pole that way."

Here Waldemer is right, but in a far more complicated way than he thinks. In a pedagogical spirit only slightly tinged with malice, I decide to offer him a little lecture in mathematics.

"On the contrary, an airship moving north-northeast will in the end—*must* inevitably—reach the Pole."

I look about for a scrap of paper and, not finding any, sketch rapidly on the edge of the chart. A rough polar projection: circles for the parallels of latitude, radials for the meridians.

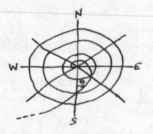

"If the airship continues to move north-northeast it will, by definition, cross all meridians at the same angle—the angle θ that I've indicated here—amounting to twenty-two and a half degrees." With a winning but treacherous little smile I lead him into this logic. "Thus, viewed from directly above as I've drawn it, the course will describe a spiral around the Pole, coming closer and closer to it according to the formula for asymptotes as presented in the theorem of Geminus. After a time it will be only a mile from it. Then a foot. Then an inch. Then a millionth of an inch."

Waldemer knows there is something wrong here but he is not sure what. He is not attuned to these abstractions—asymptotes, theorems of Geminus, spirals that approach infinity.

"Come off it, Major. You and your paradoxes of Zeno. I'll settle for a millionth of an inch."

Theodor at this point gravely intervenes to demonstrate his own competence in mathematics, not so much at Waldemer's expense as at my own.

"Excuse me, Gustav. There is a slight error in your assumptions. The problem is not really geometric but trigonometric."

He takes the pencil himself and begins sketching on another part of the chart.

"Let *r* indicate our distance from the Pole, V our forward velocity, and θ our course, or angle to the meridian. Now we may break down our velocity into two components.

$V_r = \cos \theta = const$
$V_\theta = \sin \theta = const$

"The linear velocity at which we approach the Pole is constant and we must inevitably reach it in time. But what you have neglected is that the *angular* motion—the rate at which we are whirling about the spiral—becomes infinite as the airship approaches the Pole, so that the centrifugal forces involved will either destroy the airship or the laws of physics, one or the other."

Congratulations, Theodor. You are correct and have beaten your teacher in an open demonstration, even though the audience may not appreciate it.

"H'mm."

Waldemer regards all these hieroglyphics and insect tracks with increasing sheepishness, suspecting now that both his legs are being pulled in different ways and feeling that it is hardly fair ganging up on a fellow in this way.

"D'you know what I think, Theodor? I think the Major's paradoxes of Zeno are catching. You're as big a wag as he is. I would never have suspected it of you. I thought you were a more serious young fellow."

Waldemer's American and pragmatic head is screwed squarely on his shoulders. Now that he has caught the expressions on our faces, he isn't going to buy either of these theories. He grins a little himself. Actually, of course, the spiral isn't a paradox of Zeno but a chimaera, a mythical beast existing only in the world of abstract mathematics. This wind if it continues to blow will bring us to somewhere in the neighborhood of Wrangel Island on the eastern coast of Siberia, an unattractive itinerary. But I know too that the cyclonic system to the east will very likely deepen and pass south of us, so that in a day or two this deflection in our course will be self-correcting. Still, I will leave Waldemer to wrestle in his mind with the spiral, even if he suspects—knows now—that it is only a joke. I have to confess that another of my vices (the first one is thinking) is that I am not candid by nature. In order for me to feel quite myself there must be something in me that I have not confided to my fellow human beings, even one I am as fond of as I am of Waldemer. For my *self,* to me, is simply—what I know and the others do not. Waldemer is afraid that if he can't see himself in a mirror he will cease to exist, and I fear that if I tell all I know, I will cease to exist. I am aware of course that such a stance is petty and insincere, and also leaves me open to a charge of being unscientific. For a scientist—is he not?—is one who seeks selflessly for the truth in order to share it with his fellow men. If you discover secrets in your alembics and don't publish them in the accepted journals, instead hug them to yourself and use them to carry out the schemes of your private will, then you are not a scientist but a sorcerer. Give us the truth! they clamour, like children pestering for candy. Well, probably they are happier without it. And what would they do with it if I shared it with them, this poetic and intoxicating thing I have discovered? Make a toy out of it, or a weapon.

My two companions, at least, are content to leave these mysteries of the ether to me. "The wind may change tomorrow; if not we may decide to do something about it." Waldemer nods, Theodor silently studies the penciled sworl I have drawn on the chart. It is getting somewhat colder now. The thermometer on the instrument ring reads minus four degrees centigrade. Perhaps this is due to our altitude, perhaps to the disturbance approaching from the east. I put up the hood of my reindeer-skin coat and remove my arms from its sleeves, hugging them over my chest. The coat is roomy enough that, taking out the arms in this way, it is possible to turn around inside it as though it were a small tent. Waldemer has pulled down the flaps of his hunting cap and buttoned them under his chin. I can see that he is cold but resolved to say nothing about it even if his nose and ears fall off. The end of this first organ has already turned a faint violet, the colour of the wax used to seal hermetic instruments in laboratories. Theodor is impassive. His ivory skin has only assumed a slight grey cast, as though the blood has drained out of it. His military cap has no flaps and it is his ears, I predict, that will be the first to be frostbitten. It is curious that the sun gives so little heat. It has now risen almost to its maximum altitude. But it has not seemed to rise very much; instead, it only gives the impression of trotting around the horizon from east to south, as though it were following us at a distance and trying to get a glimpse of what we are doing. It is absolutely disk-like, giving no impression of sphericity at all. It has another quality I have noticed all morning and which seems to me significant. Perhaps through some kind of physiological reaction, an irritation of the retina, its surface gives an impression of crawling slightly, the areas of deeper red shifting slowly to this or that part of the disk. I am deeply attached to the sun. I regard it as divine, life-giving, and ominous. That I am deliberately fleeing from it now, I the sun-devout Scandinavian-that in the middle of summer I should be fleeing northward to hide from its warmth around the bulge of the earth-is in itself significant. Does the sun know what I am doing? Undoubtedly. There it is, crawling redly, immobile, watching.

13 July 1897

An hour or two past midnight. In the polar twilight, a hazy and indistinct grey with tinges of pink, I am asleep or am I? it doesn't matter, I am aware perhaps of the creaking of ropes and the gentle breathing of my companions and yet at the same time another part of me moves in other places, unreal and yet far more solid in their myriad form and texture than this insubstantial particle of reality in which I am suspended half-asleep from a globe of hydrogen in a sea of frozen air. In this other consciousness into which I slip deeper now and then as one might descend lazily into a bath of tepid water, a bath that calls and attracts with its warmth and yet to which one cannot surrender totally and immerse one's being for more than a few instants since breathing is not possible in that violet and soporific fluid, in this deeper consciousness the objects are hard, vivid, piercing, all the more hard and vivid for their very unreality. The word *sleep* is greatly too simple to describe this state. At one end, toward the surface, it merges into daydreaming; at the deeper extreme, if one were to sink to the bottom, it is death. But the soul knows how to preserve itself. It drifts at a nice depth, now descending a little and now rising to touch the surface, in the manner of those sea creatures who must breathe air and yet whose nourishment lies deep. I hope I shall not snag myself on a telegraph cable down there. Inside the skin coat, when I awaken and only drowse a little, there is a smell of reindeer hair and tar, a comforting pungence, I am quite warm in this tent I have made by pulling my arms inside the coat. Doubled until the knees approach my chest, the hood over my face, I am enclosed in animal content. In the moments when I sink lower, toward full sleep, a curious phenomenon takes place. A part of my body, mistaken about the circumstances or perhaps responding to some private reality of its own, awakens and stirs toward a goal. In the vividness of its imagination this part of me thinks of, invents, or conjectures its mirror image in another similar and yet importantly different organism, a concavity to match its convexity. The stupid brutal thing is not a whit discouraged at not finding this concavity; it goes on yearning in its stiff and mindless way, exciting itself with its own thumping heart. In my moments of half wakefulness I am inclined to be ironic about this delusion this fifth limb of mine seems to have fallen into. And yet is it not strange and curious that a part of me, a part of my consciousness even though a lower and coarser part, should mistake a portion of reindeer skin in this way for the embrace of a yearned-for and beloved companion! And stranger still that only a single scrap of membrane, of all the animal substance in the universe, should be the one this fine nerve of mine should desire to touch—that it should be so exigent, so obsessedly selective, and yet so easily deluded. It is only in the wakened state that the body makes fine distinctions. Asleep or half-asleep it is ready to settle for the shabbiest simulacrum. Fold of reindeer hide or whatever, beloved one, this blind snake tightened in an arc is your adorer! What twaddle, a plague take it. It would be better to stay awake and put an end to such foolishness. I am not very sleepy anyhow. I turn over inside the warm skin bag, settle my limbs into place, and doze off or half-doze again, but this time with a difference. Through a trick I learned long ago as a boy, and practice now and then as other men practice with dumbbells or playing cards, I enter fully conscious into the storehouse of my dream matter and select exactly those pictures that I choose rather than those that blind seeking of the blood happens to stumble over, so that sleep becomes something like one of those stereopticon viewers that fasten on your nose and enable you to see with a vivid roundness, more powerful than life, whichever of those cardboard images you choose from the box on the table. In short, it is possible to dream what one will, although it requires some effort, just as it is possible to remember *what one will,* a street number or the formula for saltpeter.

But it is necessary to be hard, as hard as an angel. Steely, gripping the memory in my will's fingers, I pierce downward through layers that shimmer as they part and close again behind me, their soft torn edges clinging to my limbs. In a stratum not far from the surface I encounter a yellow room in a villa, Stresa. Then a carriage on rue de Rivoli, a balloon flight over Suomi, an angry white face in the twilight in the Bois. Finally, deeper than all these and a good deal more vague and evanescent, there comes into focus the hall of the Musée Carnavalet on the occasion of the Fifth Congress of the Paraphysical Society in 1895, where I was lecturing on electromagnetic phenomena in the atmosphere. I had just embarked on the possibility of extraterrestrial sources of the waves when I caught sight of an extraordinary face in the audience. A rather long, pale, and absolutely motionless visage with eyes fixed intently on me, a lofty brow, a mouth that gave the impression of being held in place only by a conscious effort of the will so that two little creases formed below it on the chin. Immaculately groomed, gown from Worth's, soft hair gathered into a knot at the back. Incredibly enough, at that time she was only nineteen. Following the lecture she presented herself at the podium and engaged me in a discussion of the Female Question.

"Captain" (I was a captain in those days), "these matters, emanations or whatever you call them, do you believe they are susceptible of investigation by women?"

I looked up from my notes and hardly knew what to answer. Was this an attack or some kind of an overture of friendship, of admiration?

"Why? On the other hand, why not?"

"It seems—I mean—I gather from what you say that they are an ethereal kind of thing." Did she always speak this rapidly, and not quite looking at the person she was addressing? "C'est à dire, subtle, and perhaps women, being creatures of intuition and especially good at invisible things, might be particularly fitted to investigate them. Also they can be studied in one's own home with very little apparatus, and they don't get one's hands dirty."

Or she said something like this, I don't remember exactly. I do remember that she spoke with a great assurance and even a challenging air, a faint touch of contempt, and yet that she blushed as she did so, a kind of pink spider forming on her throat and moving upward into the paleness under her chin. The little speech on feminism evidently came from one part of her being, the vascular reaction from another.

"In fact, a good deal of apparatus is required," I countered as moderately as I could, "electrostatic generators, coils of wire, Leyden jars, and things of this sort, many of which are expensive. Not only do they get your hands dirty, but frequently there is danger involved; for example, a good many observations can be made only from airships. I hardly think you would like that. As for the tasks men and women are adapted for, you make too much of the difference. The parts of the human body that distinguish the sexes"—(second appearance of the pink spider; I plunged on)—"are the most ephemeral. In skeletons they are hardly discernible except to an expert. Whereas, comparing man with ape, the skeletal difference is apparent even to a layman. I wonder where you get your opinions about intuitions and such things?"

But one of her qualities that I learned immediately was that she never answered questions. To frame a remark to her in the form of a question was to distract her instantly into another subject, as though by an invisible system of switches. "Do you know the dramas of Strindberg?"

"I have never been to a play in my life."

"So much the worse for you. You talk as though you had read him. He is mad of course. I can assure you I am perfectly able to afford Leyden jars and coils of wire, and I would adore ascending in an airship. I have a book of engravings about the frères Montgolfier. It's a pity you haven't read Strindberg. It might have armed you against me. As it is, you are my victim. Captain, please come to tea at my aunt's. It is perfectly proper, she belongs to the best society of the Île Saint-Louis. You can explain your emanations to her, and perhaps you might give me a list of the apparatus I ought to buy."

I said that I would or I wouldn't, I don't know what I said, but the outcome was that I actually presented myself at the house on Quai d'Orléans on the following day, dressed like an idiot in a white shirt and patent-leather pumps. The aunt maintained a curious establishment. It was hard to say whether it was respectable or not. Luisa in stressing its propriety had perhaps slightly overemphasized the point, since what was the purpose of mentioning this if there wasn't some slight doubt about it? The whole family had a characteristic quality of raffishness combined with the greatest kind of dignity, a juxtaposition that reappeared in the various members in various disguises but was always recognizable once you were familiar with it. Perhaps it owed this to its ancestry, which tended toward the mongrelish, although in a highly aristocratic way. The American father by this time was of course not on the scene, since he had gone back to his own country through some complicated circumstances that I didn't quite follow and had died in an attack on an Apache camp in New Mexico in 1875. This exotic demise was evidently not considered comme il faut in the family, since he was never spoken of. In addition to his debts he left to his family only the quintessentially transatlantic name of Hickman, which everyone concealed as though it were an unfortunate secret. His widow, Luisa's mother, evidently lived as a kind of dependent and companion of the aunt, wore saris and even a caste mark on her brow, although she was three quarters of European blood, and did nothing in particular except drink tea and eat sticky Levantine pastries. She was not held in very high regard among the Silva e Costas, perhaps because of her marriage to the handsome but penniless American frontiersman. The aunt was a spinster. Her long face tended slightly to the equine and her eyebrows sloped a little outward, like the eaves of a house. She shared the ivory family complexion, although in her case it had been marred by a childhood smallpox that had lent it a kind of lunar and irregular texture like weathered alabaster, or satin from an old wardrobe. She also suffered slightly from a chorea-like affliction that caused slight and almost imperceptible movements of her face: the chin, fixed as it were by effort, nevertheless tremored to the left a fraction of a millimeter or less, once or so a second, returning immediately to its former position, in a movement so subtle and so faint that it was to an ordinary twitch as the pulsing of a tiny insect's heart is to the beating of a clock. The beholder, in fact, did not necessarily notice this movement upon first meeting the aunt, it was so slight. Once you had become aware of it, however, it lent a faint negative quality to everything the aunt said and did; whether she praised your poem, invited you again to tea, agreed with your politics, the imperceptible vibration of her head seemed to reiterate constantly, "Nay, nay. It is all nothing, I deny all." She dressed in long gowns of the Empire period and wore her hair in ringlets, although the effect was somewhat marred by the gold-rimmed spectacles that gave her a kind of Voltairean air. It was said she was very wealthy. I believe she disliked men on principle, and perhaps this is where Luisa got her suffragism, although the connection was a little tenuous. In any case she was very polite to me. She spoke French in an accent of her own that involved distinguishing sharply between the vowels, with a different shape of mouth to go with each. "On voit," she told me calmly and not unkindly, "que vous z-êtes un vr-rai é-rudit." I forgot to record that one of her breasts had been removed in an operation and she wore a padded appliance in its place.

In addition to the aunt there was an uncle in Pondicherry, another aunt in Palma de Mallorca, and a female cousin in Poland with whom Luisa exchanged violet-scented letters. The house on Quai d'Orléans remained something of a mystery to me for a long time. There it was in the middle of the Seine, neither on the Left Bank nor on the Right. It was ambiguous. It may have been true that the family "belonged to the best society of the Île Saint-Louis," although such judgments are of course a matter of taste. Certainly they had nothing to do with those old Bourbons and Bonapartists who hated each other so cordially in their seventeenth century town houses on Quai d'Anjou and rue Saint-Louis-en-l'Île. The aunt's teas were frequented by a coterie that ranged from the fringes of Faubourg Saint-Germain to the more dubious elements of Montmartre. There was a young professor of art history from the College de France, a pedcrastic English poet, a Brazilian naval doctor of impeccable credentials. I was introduced to M. Lugné-Poe, the director of the Théâtre de l'Oeuvre, which impressed me only negligibly since I had never heard of the place. The inhabitants of the house were all women, the guests all men. Except for a lady physician, a friend of the aunt's, who had a frame like a stevedore and specialised in nervous afflictions. Perhaps it was she who treated the aunt's trembling. There were other ornaments: a fashionable photographer, a teacher of geology from the École Normale, and once the Greek poet Jean Moréas came to sip tea and recite his verses from under his soft mustache. I will say that the principles of the place were thoroughly democratic. On one occasion I was introduced to a street paver, on another to a retired customs inspector who painted in his spare time, a rather stupid fellow he seemed, named Rousseau although he was no relation to the philosopher. I went there a score of times perhaps, and in addition escorted Luisa occasionally to places like the Café Royal or an exhibition of Etruscan artifacts. It was perfectly proper, since we were accompanied at all times by her dog and sometimes by the footman from

Quai d'Orléans, a gloomy and red-faced young Breton with pimples. In fashionable afternoon attire Luisa made a remarkable effect. Her dark hair in medium length with a simple knot at the back was not the fashion just then but it suited her admirably. Her gown of black moire was cut to the level of the breastbone, and the coat she wore over it she had a way of throwing back over one hip with her hand. It was clear to the spectator that she was an extraordinary young woman, that she was thoroughly at home in this city, and also that she was not French. If her complexion were not enough, there was the shape of her face: in her case the genetic Silva e Costa elongation, instead of assuming equine form as it did in the aunt, gave a long-nosed, patrician, even-eyed, ruminant, self-contained, faintly supercilious expression; she looked something like a llama. Her dog was a pug, naturally, and she carried too many things in her purse. She was one of those marsupial women whose security lies not in a home but in this little portable womb they carry about with them, filled with pocket combs, handkerchiefs, vials of cologne, foreign coins, hair ribbons, smelling salts, unread novels, stubs of pencils, dinner mints, scent, tweezers, ends of theatre tickets, mascara, tiny powder boxes that play Swiss waltzes when opened, even a china egg. Her favourite of her bags was a kind of reticule made of Bayeux tapestry, exquisitely beautiful, I have to admit. When we went to an exhibition or musical event she would comment on things in her controlled, slightly artificial voice, a little disconnectedly perhaps but frequently with considerable insight. There was no question that she was intelligent and even that in her way she took the things of the mind seriously and was capable of applying herself to them assiduously when she chose. Once, simply to play a joke on her when she asked what I was reading, I lent her an abstruse philosophical treatise in German (it was on the theory of irreducibility in irrational numbers) and contrary to all expectation she understood something of it. Her scent was one I have never encountered elsewhere: a thin, barely perceptible violet like the fragrance that plays round the poles of electrical apparatus. She preferred Gérard de Nerval to Goethe, Schumann to Bach.

I had come to Paris that spring with the idea of working in the Bibliothèque Nationale, but for one reason or another I rarely got around to it. At Quai d'Orléans at five o'clock I would find myself mesmerized into conversations with Luisa which I had not chosen and which surely had not been organized by her, since she was scarcely capable of organizing the contents of her handbag. Did I care for Rilke? He and I were almost perfect strangers. She informed me that he had invented "la poésie des choses." Bully for him. She wondered if I liked riding. She rode every morning in the Bois, very early when the world was asleep (by "le monde" she meant six hundred people out of a population of two and a half million, and probably she was speaking of nine o'clock in the morning). And: she would drop casually that it was this very evening that a diva only rarely heard was to appear in recital at the Salle Meyer, and she was curious if I planned to attend. I would reply that I never went to such things, and she would say "Ah!" in her most interested and yet distant manner. There would be a silence, which I would have been wise to leave alone, but deuce take it all! In spite of myself I would end by inquiring politely, "Are you?" Oh no, she would explain in a kind of dreamy sarcasm, you see it wasn't considered fashionable for young ladies to make their way about a large city alone, it might subject them to insults or other embarrassments, a stupid prejudice but for the present at least society was organized in this way, que voulez-vous? Naturally I would end by offering to protect her from ruffians, amorous cabmen, etc., and find myself presently sitting in the Salle Meyer listening to a plump Milanese soprano trill her way through the Mad Song from Lucia. It was not long until she was clearly taking me for granted, a thing I abominate. "À demain, n'est-ce pas?" she would remind me mellifluously as we parted. "Chez ma tante."

At the aunt's the next day a hungry Balkan violinist played czardas, the conversation was of Rodin, the gloomy footman served loukoumi and tea. I learned quite by accident that Luisa was engaged. Her fiancé was a young Spanish officer of artillery who, it seemed, was considered a family joke. His name was Alberto but for some reason he was called the Peninsula. Perhaps it was because he was Spanish, or because he was only semi-attached to the family. I never actually encountered him at Quai d'Orléans, although there was a photograph of him on the piano: a self-satisfied young man with a strong jaw, something like a bulldog, and a meaty nose. His eyebrows met over the nose, so that he really only had one of them. I cannot say why I found this last detail repugnant, or amusing. I don't know what I expected eyebrows to do. The aunt's sloped outward and I found this eccentric too. The aunt never did ask me about my emanations, as Luisa had promised she would, but on my final visit to Quai d'Orléans she did interrogate me about my position in life. I told her that I was attached to the Royal Institute of Technology in Stockholm and had every expectation of becoming its librarian in due time, and in the meanwhile I was devoting myself to my researches, which had won me a modest recognition along with membership in an international society or two. This crass little speech was pompous but so, I felt, was the question.

"Luisa tells me you are interested in spiritualism."

"Not at all."

"Well then, in electricity or something. It's much the same thing."

"It's the furthest thing possible from the same thing."

"Is it true that, with electricity, one can tell what people are doing in the next room?"

"Only if they are sending out waves with a coulomb apparatus."

"What is it exactly that you are discovering then? I am sorry that I am such a stupid old woman." The head vibrated back and forth, denying all, as she smiled and made this apology.

By this time I was feeling quite arrogant, not to say hilarious. "I believe that intelligences on the stars may be attempting to send us telegraph messages. If so, it is a question of the greatest importance. Are you interested in such matters?"

But, like her niece, she countered all questions by changing the subject. "Do you know, I wonder if you have noticed that Luisa is a remarkable young person. We expect extraordinary things from her. Extraordinary. Do you know that she reads Dante?"

I agreed that she was educated beyond the common sphere of woman, but my phraseology here was unfortunate and evoked a blank stare.

"These spheres of which you speak, my dear Captain," she informed me, "are of a bygone era. Persons of advanced thought, these days, no longer believe that half the human race is confined in one sphere and the other half in another, or rather free to wander around and do exactly as it pleases. Apropos, tell me something, dites donc, why is it that you are a military man and yet you don't wear a uniform?"

"Primo," I explained, "I am on detached duty; secundo, the container ought to indicate the contents, and taken apart from or inside my clothes, I am not very uniform."

"Inside your clothes you are not the same?"

"Profoundly different."

"Ah." A skeptical look came into her eye, but she said nothing, only waggled her head.

I forget what else happened at this last tea. A good many idiocies. I talked for a little while to the mother, or attempted to, but it was thick going. For one thing she stood slightly too close to me for the conversation to be comfortable. It was about an arm's length, or three quarters of a metre. As inconspicuously as I could I would back away about a hand's breadth, she would follow me by the same distance, and so on. This has happened to me before and it is a futile exercise at best. Such a ballet can describe large circles around a fashionable salon. Perhaps, I thought, I ought to get over this nineteenth-century aversion toward the mere propinquity of other flesh. On the other hand, perhaps there was something deep in my blood too Lutheran and Nordic for these tropical birds. At any rate, the mother, Madame Hickman née Silva e Costa, stood too close to me in a sari and caste mark and holding a saucer with a pastry on it, conversing with me in a thin timid voice slightly below the threshold of audibility, glancing about her now and then rather apprehensively as though to see whether anybody was observing. It was only with the greatest attention that I could make out what she was saying. I had the impression that at any moment she might whisper, "I have been abducted by these people. Please rescue me." She smelled of musk and nervousness, like a small animal. She spoke a mixture of French and what she imagined to be English, so that understanding her, in addition to a physical feat, was an exercise in comparative philology.

"Do you like Paris?" I at length detected.

"Very much."

"Have you had many new experiences?" Or perhaps she said, "Have you made very many new experiments," since the French word is ambiguous, even at normal loudness.

"Experiences? How?"

Glancing around again, she hazarded, "Do you know Mifeuya?" or so it sounded to me. I was not sure how to respond. Who or what? A Japanese painter? A seaport in Turkey?

"How?"

"Millefeuille, a pastry."

Ah. "Certainly, madame," I told her with as much respect as I could muster for the subject, "I know it very well."

While waiting for me to answer she had taken a tiny bite of the confection on her saucer, and now she chewed it with a timid rotary motion of her jaw while she tried to speak at the same time. "C'est ra-vi-ssant," I finally caught. It was not clear whether she meant the millefeuille or what she was now enjoying. For her it was probably the same; her mouth was full, of the word, of the thing, and it was ravissant. Talking to her was very simple now that I had caught the trick of it; you had only to pretend that you were talking to a very small child, perhaps three, who had just discovered bonbons and wanted to know if you had heard about them too. You had only to assure her, with a gravity proper to the subject, "I do indeed, and they are very good."

The mother melted, evaporated into the collection of guests, or perhaps merged into the Astrakhan carpet. I found myself in a bay window looking out over the river with the fashionable photographer from rue de la Paix, whom I hoped to interrogate about the possibilities of using photography in an airship to record meteorological phenomena. But it was difficult to talk to him when he was continually glancing around and over my head, probably in search of someone who was wealthier than I and more likely to pay a large sum to have his visage recorded on a glass plate. These swervings of his nose were held in place by a tense jockey, a pair of gold-rimmed spectacles. Finally he noticed me. "You are an artist?" he inquired.

"Hardly."

"Not an artist?"

"I am a natural philosopher, more or less."

"Odd, you profoundly resemble an artist. Believe me, in my profession it is necessary to make a study of physiognomy and I know what I am talking about."

"Perhaps a naturalist is not very different from an artist, physiognomistically speaking."

"Profoundly different. Profoundly different." The gold spectacles controlled the nose now and held it exactly in my direction. "Art is permanent; nature is in flux. Nature is dust and vapors, noxious. What we see about us, these fair prospects"—the nose bolted briefly toward the decolletage of a lady a little distance away—are in reality a constantly degenerating panorama of corruption."

"How long will a photograph last?"

"With good care, fifty years or even a century."

I was about to comment that the same was true of a man, but we were interrupted by the aunt, who took him away to waggle her head at him in a corner.

The whole collection, for some reason, affected me that afternoon as a nest of madfolk; I could hope for little better from the pederastic English poet or the professor of art history. I found myself filled with a powerful desire to escape, but in the vestibule I encountered Luisa, who was looking bright, wistful, and a little flushed from the stimulation of society. "Ah . . . then . . ." she articulated tentatively.

"And so it's farewell," I told her with a conventionally regretful smile.

"Surely only au revoir. You were going to give me a list of apparatus, and . . ." She didn't finish, she trailed off.

And what? Oh, those three little dots at the end of her sentences.

"To begin with, all that is needed is a head, my dear lady. And a library full of books."

"You are pleased to mock at me. It is only your male conceit. At least you might tell me the books to read."

"I am very pressed, I leave Paris for Stockholm tomorrow."

"And what is it that calls you back?" she inquired sweetly.

"Another affection, perhaps?" (*Another,* I noted, was a very interesting and perhaps even slightly presumptuous locution on her part.)

"Only a balloon ascension, to tell the truth."

"I would adore a balloon ascension. You must take me with you."

It was difficult for me to explain to her why, given the mores of our time, it was impossible for a well-bred young woman to remain for fifteen or twenty hours suspended in a basket with a man without recourse to the amenities of civilisation. "I am sorry. It is not some sort of a picnic, you know. It's a serious scientific venture, involving hard work, boring details, and so on."

"I am not afraid of hard work and I am not easily bored. Surely I could be useful. I could take readings of your barometer or something."

"Goodbye, mademoiselle," I told her, smiling and offering my hand.

"Au revoir," she corrected me, smiling just as conventionally.

·

Immediately upon my return to the Royal Institute I began preparations for the flight I had projected from the Stockholm district to southern Finland, the purpose of which was to try out in practice the steering apparatus I had finally devised after a good many years of thought. The route I planned was suited to this end because it lay mainly over the sea, where the guide ropes were less likely to become entangled in the landscape or otherwise damaged. I had written to Waldemer before I left Paris to invite him to accompany me on this flight. Unfortunately, I explained, I would be unable to pay his transatlantic expenses, since the flight was supported only by a very small appropriation from the Institute, but I hoped that his newspaper would finance his voyage to Europe in return for exclusive coverage. When I came back from Paris, however, I found a letter from New York on my desk. Waldemer was unable to extract the travel money from his editor and besides, a thousand regrets, he was occupied with another assignment which would keep him busy for several months, a comprehensive series of articles on the tinned-food industry, which was on the point of bringing the highest refinements of the palate to the masses. It was clear from his letter that he genuinely regretted not to be with me, although this was not because he preferred my company to that of the soup magnates; it was because he regarded aeronavigation as a more important technical development than the preservation of food. He would have and *did* prefer my company to that of soup magnates, let it be clear; it was just that his personal pleasures were always a secondary consideration with Waldemer. He was a dedicated and consecrated professional, a hero of modern journalism. It was too bad, because to tell the truth I enjoyed *his* company (I was not quite so consecrated), and besides, he was an invaluable assistant and one I had taken a great deal of pains and effort to train.

The aeronautical side of this particular flight, however, would not be excessively demanding, and in a pinch I could always manage the newly invented guide ropes by myself. What then did I need a partner for at all? I answered my own question: the balloon was designed to elevate approximately a hundred and fifty kilograms, and lacking this weight it would be necessary to carry along sandbags or something else to make up for it. Surely some human being could be found who was at least more useful than a sandbag, if only for reading the barometer. How had that example got into my head? Why did I telegraph Luisa? It was a folly. I think more than anything else I did it to challenge, through a definite and quite concrete proposal, her feminine whim of the kind she was always expressing without any notion of the practical entailments, declaring her readiness to be hypnotized, to go down into coal mines, to be present at a dissection, etc., simply to indicate that she was as sturdy and as reckless as any man. After a while you felt a malicious but irresistible impulse to say, Here is the corpse, dear lady, take up the scalpel yourself and find the hypogastric nerve, climb into the coal basket, and don't blame me if you soil your gown. This was a dangerous tactic with Luisa. If I had known her as well as I did later, I would not have tried it.

To cut the matter short, I telegraphed asking her to join me on the flight to Finland and received an answer almost with the speed of the electrical impulse. Her reply was precise, orderly, and substantial, detailing exactly which train she was taking in order to arrive at the Kungsholm Station on the following Monday, and adding that she was bringing along dust-proof travelling clothes and a salt reputed to be specific against altitude. Why dust-proof? Did she imagine the balloon was dusty? Probably she had noticed the clothes in a ladies' magazine. As for altitude, the steering apparatus I proposed to try out depended on the balloon remaining quite close to the earth and it was doubtful that we would rise even as high as the Vendôme column, but I didn't bother to send a counter-telegram explaining all this to her. Instead, I instructed the workmen to prepare the balloon for an ascension on Tuesday, weather permitting, and then busied myself collecting the instruments and charts I needed.

On Monday at three o'clock in the afternoon I met her at the station. She was impeccably clad in a surcoat with blue fox fur at the hem, the same fur at the tops of her boots, and a muff to match, and she was followed by a porter pushing an enormous wagon full of luggage. The portents were not good. Removing one hand gracefully from the muff, she offered it to me and then restored it to its warm place. It was an ordinary day in May, the temperature was quite mild. "Sweden!" she exulted, tossing the hair from her high forehead. "Comme c'est charmant! I love the air, it smells of something like ship's tar. And those fillettes, the little girls with the riding crops—" (I had no idea what she was talking about)-"elles sont délicieuses. Where do you live?"

Without responding in any precise way to this question, I told her I had arranged lodgings for her for the night in a small hotel near the Institute. "Ah," she replied, delighted with everything. "How very thoughtful of you." Just as graciously she followed me to the end of the platform and smiled winningly at the porter while I tipped him, and allowed herself to be put into a cab. It was mean and curmudgeonly of me to reflect that if I had been meeting Waldemer it would not have been necessary for me to tip the porter for carrying *his* baggage. Contrary to my expectations, it was possible to affix all her bags in or on the cab in some way, top, sides, and rear. We went off. It was five minutes to the hotel.

What in the blazes was I to do with her? I had other things to occupy me during the evening—the final adjustment of instruments, a call at the weather office to look at the maps. She was charming, fragrant, feminine, flattering, accommodating, cheerful, and quite imperious in her need to be entertained or otherwise done something with at every moment. At the hotel, which was a modest affair without a lift, she signed the register in a fine baroque hand and then followed the ill-humoured hotel servant as he bumped and battered his way along a narrow corridor with a portmanteau in each hand. "Oh dear. I'm not sure this will do at all," she murmured from the depths of the corridor. And I too had begun to fear that the hotel would not do for such an elegant person and wondered what I had had in mind in selecting it. In actual fact, when we arrived at the room it was not excessively squalid. There were hunting prints on the wall and a vase of roses, even a square piano. From the window it was possible to catch a glimpse of the Kungsträgård. She sat at the piano and played a fragment of Schubert, then sprang up and pulled aside the curtains.

"And that park?"

"The Royal Gardens."

"Ah. Everything is fascinating, it is so different from Paris." Everything she had seen so far was exactly like Paris, unless she meant the smell of tar, or the fillettes with the whips. "But you will take something?" she suggested with a small gasp or intake of air as though she had abruptly thought of it. "Some tea, brandy, liqueur? I don't know your customs."

Declining ceremoniously, and thanking her, I took my departure. Outside, the afternoon was growing chill. Perhaps she had been right to bring a muff. The Fiend carry her off! I slapped my hand on my forehead and left it there, the fingers working in the hair. The flight was ruined. I went to the rented room where I lived on the square facing the Institute, found on my bureau a chronograph watch I had meant to have checked at the jeweler's that afternoon, took it in my fingers, and almost threw it at the wall. Then I checked myself; it was an expensive timepiece and it had always run perfectly with a steady rate. Instead, I seized the bell rope and ordered something from the servant; tea, liqueur, brandy, what the blazes was my custom?

I changed into a dress coat, at seven o'clock I called for her and we went to dine at Stallmästaregården. Shellfish on ice, potage au cresson, and roast beef in the English manner. With claret and French coffee the whole came to a hundred and fifty kronor plus gratuities to waiters. Luisa, radiant from the claret, expressed a desire to go to a café concert or some equivalent entertainment. She was infected with the tourist mentality; she was entranced by the difference of the new country from her own and at the same time she wanted to do in it exactly the same things she would have done in Paris. I consulted my wits. There was a chamber-music concert and the Royal Ballet, but these were too stiff and formal. My own pleasure in the evening when I had nothing better to do was the Chess Club. Usually, however, I studied. This particular evening it was imperative that I call at the weather office, which had promised to remain open for me until nine. At length I bethought myself of a kind of café and music hall in Apelbergsgatan where, if I heard correctly, beverages could be procured and persons sang foreign songs to the accompaniment of a piano. We went there in a cab. The interior of this establishment, I found when it was too late to escape, was so triste as to inspire one immediately with the idea of suicide. In a white-painted room lit with oil lamps we listened to a portly baritone sing lieder, while a female, perhaps his wife, thumped the piano along quite other lines. Luisa inquired as to the "boisson du pays" and out of malice I ordered two tumblers of our native akvavit.

She drained hers off perhaps under the impression that it was white wine, and even drank another when I replaced it, although at a slightly lower rate. The baritone had embarked on "Röslein, Röslein auf der Heide," insisting on the refrain as though he hoped to subdue the piano through reiteration. Luisa had changed her dress of course and was now totally ravishing in a persimmon-coloured gown that rose from her feet to her bosom, quite simply and without a wrinkle, and then dissolved in a froth of lace. Her shoulders were bare. She did not seem to be cold. Everyone in the cafe naturally could do nothing but look at her; all conversation had stopped. Luisa was enchanted with everything. The waiter provided her with a bowl of nuts, and she found this charming, cracking filberts with a silver nutcracker and delicately placing the kernels between her lips, offering me a morsel (I declined politely, with upraised palm and a smile), and sipping her akvavit. "Stockholm, c'est un délire." She would be delirious if she drank very much more of that stuff. What on earth had I intended anyhow? With some difficulty I persuaded her it was necessary to go to bed early, and we departed, leaving the other patrons with the impression that Frenchwomen (or was she some kind of Hindoo?) drank akvavit in public and lived on cracked filberts.

At her hotel everything was dark; we had to ring and wake up the boot boy. "À demain, my brave aeronaut." She lifted her hand and held it at shoulder level with the palm open toward me, smiling, in an oddly touching gesture. "Your crew will dream of you." I walked home. It was a quarter to eleven, too late to go to the weather office.

•

In the morning, at the station again, she appeared in the thin light of dawn in the prophesied dustproof costume, which consisted of a long linen coat of fashionable cut, black stockings, practical walking shoes, and a hat secured with a veil tied under the chin. She carried her favourite tapestry reticule, which no doubt contained the famous smelling-salt specific against altitude (our altitude of one hundred metres), and for further baggage only a small leather traveling case sufficient to hold a change of dress. It was necessary to take a local train to the small town of Bergshamra, a journey of an hour or so, where the ascent field was located on a promontory overlooking the sea. At Bergshamra all was prepared. The workmen had been at their task since the evening before and the Prinzess, the second of her name to be financed by the generous Hamburg brewers, was almost fully inflated. The wind blew steadily from the west with a little more force than I would have wished; the ascent would be precarious, but once in the air we would make good speed. A small crowd had gathered to watch the ascension: a journalist or two, a few curious countryfolk. Our baggage was put into the by no means large basket hanging under the globe of hydrogen, we ourselves mounted, and preparations began to release the mooring ropes. Luisa appeared quite unperturbed, a little paler than usual perhaps but collected and dignified, even when managing the difficult clamber over the rim into the wicker car. She asked a minimum of intelligent questions about what she did not understand and, collecting her duster together in one hand, tried to keep out of my way as I moved about the car adjusting my instruments. So far well enough. Still, the vain creature had prevented me from visiting the weather office, and I could only trust that this west wind would not fail us completely or on the other hand turn into some sort of a gale. My consolation was that the clerks at the weather office seemed to know approximately as little about these matters as I did. The mooring ropes were cut, we lurched violently sideways, the wicker car banged into a tree stump, and we rose away from the earth, swinging like a pendulum. First crossing of the Gulf of Bothnia! The two journalists had their notebooks out and were already composing leaders.

Immediately I turned my attention to the matter of weights and ballast. In the eddies over the promontory it was impossible to tell whether the Prinzess intended to go up or down, but as soon as we were over the sea it became apparent that she was excessively light. She would sweep along horizontally for a minute or two, then, as though she had suddenly remembered something, she would ascend approximately the height of a flight of stairs, continue awhile again her level flight, and then go up another flight of stairs. The guide ropes hung down quite uselessly with their ends above the sea. I estimated our excess buoyancy at ten kilos or so, and set about releasing a corresponding amount of gas by means of the maneouvring valve. But perdition take it! I had done this fifty times and this was the first time I miscalculated. An excessive amount of hydrogen whistled out, as my senses instantly detected; we began to descend and we were probably now eight or ten kilograms heavy. Well, blast it. Luisa could hardly do worse than I. I showed her how to release the ballast, since she was so anxious to perform some useful function. It consisted of sandbags of twenty kilos each, hanging on the outside of the car, and each bag had at the bottom a releasing flap worked by a drawstring. The whole thing was perfectly simple, she easily grasped how to work the drawstring, but for some reason failed to shut off the flow, so that the whole contents of the bag fell into the sea.

This accident was so exactly the correlative and opposite of the blunder I had just committed—its other sex, so to speak—that it exasperated me precisely for that reason. "Blazes!" I burst out. "Didn't you understand what I said?"

"I understood perfectly what you said."

"I said to release half the bag."

"Ah! that detail you neglected to mention. You explained how to pull the cord, and I did exactly as you told me."

"I said half the bag."

"You said nothing of the sort. I took particular care to pay attention to exactly what you were saying, so I would not make a mistake."

"Nevertheless you made one."

I was angry, she was angry, she faced me across the wicker car proudly and whitely, totally without expression, the pink blush appearing at the base of her throat and spreading slowly up the neck. It was our first quarrel. "If you are saying I am lying you are a contemptible cad. If I were a man you would not dare charge me with that, or else you would have to answer for it. If it pleases you to insult your crew, you ought to confine yourself to your own sex."

"Very well. An interesting point. Let us discuss this. In the first place, if you were a man, you might not have botched the first very simple task you set your hand to. In the second place, if you were a man, it would not be quite so easy for you to refer to me as a contemptible cad, or else *you* would have to answer for *that*."

"In short," she concluded, "simply because we are of the opposite sex, we are behaving toward each other like two strange animals instead of cultivated and well-bred human beings."

"Precisely."

"Then I suggest that you treat me with at least the decency you would observe if I were not a woman, and I will do the same. In the meanwhile, what practical damage, *if any*"—(she almost burst out, she was still angry)—"has been done by my alleged clumsiness?"

"We are ascending much too fast, and in a minute you will need your smelling salts."

"What will you do about it?"

I could feel the bristles of my mustache settling slowly again; they always prickled when I was angry. After a pause of five seconds or so I told her quite calmly, "Work the mancouvring valve again." Doing so, with great care this time (in order, perhaps, to convey to Mademoiselle by pantomime that we were getting low on ballast), I released enough gas to bring us into level flight and even to incline the course of the Prinzess slightly downward toward the sea. We still had a hundred kilos, more or less, of sand left against further blunders.

And now I had no more time for the mysterious complexities of the feminine soul, because the moment had come to test the construct of my imagination on which everything depended, the sole reason for the flight and all its elaborate preparations. The west wind was carrying us steadily in a direction which would miss the end of Finland by a few miles and bring us after two or three days to St. Petersburg, if Luisa had not lost all the ballast by that time. St. Petersburg was perhaps an interesting place, but it was not in my plans and our visas were not stamped for Russia. It was necessary, therefore, to deflect our course leftward, or slightly to the north, in order to cross up to the Finnish coast and arrive at our destination. In short, to sail *across* the wind, something that no one else had ever done before. First I worked the maneouvring valve with delicate tugs (if that contraption should stick the gas would all fly out and we were doomed) in order to release just enough gas to bring us downward toward the sea. Then the drag ropes, or guide ropes as I preferred to call them, came into play. These were three in number, long and quite thick, made of coco fiber impregnated with oil so they would float on the surface of the water. When the Prinzess rose high they hung below it in a kind of graceful Doric column. But as we descended and they began to trail in the water, a complex set of interworking reactions followed. The balloon slowed, first of all, and tilted a little in the direction of its movement like the head of a charging bull. Simultaneously a slight wind was felt, not so strong as the real and natural wind we had felt at Bergshamra, but a wind all the same. This wind was the secret of everything! All those who had sought the dirigibility of balloons, Professor Eggert included, had despaired of sails or wind vanes, since the balloon by its nature is deprived of wind. It rides on the wind and is part of the wind, and therefore no wind impinges upon it to be put to any useful task. Anyone who has ascended in a balloon has remarked this wonderful windlessness, the absolute silence and stillness of the craft. But at last I had found a way to interfere with this sterility. An important principle lay at the bottom of it: progress when unimpeded is uncontrolled. Only by slowing down the creatures of our wit can we steer them in the direction desired. If your object is to get somewhere, anywhere, as quickly as possible, then you can simply harness nature and let her drag you along willy-nilly without worrying very much about the direction. But if you have a destination in mind, then mere progress is not enough. It is necessary to have direction, even if this results in slowing down.

The guide ropes were now trailing in the water for perhaps a third of their length, leaving three snaky wakes behind them. We slowed perceptibly. There was a stir and touch of coolness on our cheeks from this breeze I had contrived, and it was time to set the sails. These were hauled out on the bamboo poles by lines running through light blocks at the ends and controlled at the lower corners by other lines. Here Luisa could be of some help. It really required three hands, or better four or five, to handle all these sheets and outhauls.

"Now then, dear lady, that cord in your left hand—if you please— and in your other—" It was really quite complicated.

"I don't see the reason for this. What is it exactly that we are trying to do? Unless you explain the principle, it is utterly impossible for me to pull all these strings and cords in the way you want."

She was perfectly right. It was my own fault for choosing a bluestocking and person of culture as my crew. If I had taken along a simple blockhead who was accustomed to obeying orders, I could simply have said "Pull this!" and "Slack that!" and he would have done as I said. But once having made the decision to allow in the balloon a woman who had read Dedekind's *Stetigkeit und irrationale Zahlen,* I was obliged to go into principle, in lack of which the cultivated mind is paralyzed and invariably pulls the wrong string. I would have felt the same myself if someone had asked me to manipulate something complex without explaining the reason behind it. In short, I first had to explain to Luisa how sails worked in order to enable a vehicle such as a ship to proceed diagonally into the wind. Then I proceeded backward into the principle of guide ropes, the impeding of velocity, and dirigibility in general. She listened to everything with that same seraphic attention I had observed when I first caught sight of her face during my lecture at the Musée Carnavalet: motionless eyes fixed on me, mouth held firmly with the two little creases at the sides. Then, she following my directions, the two of us set the sails and trimmed them at an oblique angle to the wind; or, more precisely, we worked an iron handle attached to a pinion gear until the wicker car with its sails was turned at the requisite angle to the guide ropes. The wind now came diagonally. The three snaky trails in the water behind us began a long and mathematically precise curve to the left.

The exertion left me a little short of breath. I sat on a packing case and contemplated what we had done, not without a certain satisfaction. A glance at the compass showed me we were heading east by north, exactly toward the Finland peninsula. It was a good moment. But instead of enjoying this sense of accomplishment at my leisure, unfortunately, I was obliged to turn my attention to a peculiarity of my personal physiology that had put me to some pains before on occasion, although not in such delicate circumstances. Under conditions of particular tension or suspense, such as our precarious ascent from Bergshamra that morning, my organism accelerated the pace of its fluid-rejecting processes and, after only an hour or two, required a subtraction of moisture in unmistakable terms. The sensation had been present for some time while I ignored it, but now it had become imperative. There I was, suspended over the Baltic Sea with this femme savante, and the thing that had to be done, that nature cried out for in inexorable accents—the thing that if not done would result in physical torment and eventually in my death—was forbidden by every convention and decency of the society that produced us both. Patently it would be done; I was not going to be tortured and slain for a convention.

"Mademoiselle," I requested (I was still calling her mademoiselle at this point, even when I spoke English, out of a no doubt slightly ironic politeness), "mademoiselle, might I ask you to turn your head for a moment and observe, precisely out there on the horizon where I am afraid there is really nothing to see, to tell the truth, but you have an imagination," etc., etc., and without very much formality the thing was soon done. Whew! When out of gratitude and sheer physical relief I offered to do the same for her, she simply stared at me without a word. Very well, plague take it, perhaps my suggestion was in poor taste. To cover the confusion of the moment, and also because in my new lightness I felt full of vigor, I busied myself with my instruments to verify whether the system of guide ropes and sails was still working. Mounting the theodolite on the edge of the basket and sighting backward along the wakes left by the ropes, I satisfied myself that we were still moving in a northeasterly direction. "Next stop, Finland," I reported with some satisfaction.

"Then with this contrivance an airship might go anywhere?"

"The wind permitting."

"How, the wind permitting?"

"It is possible to cross the wind diagonally, but not to butt directly against it."

"Could one go, for instance, to the Italian lakes?"

I burst out laughing. "You are a hopeless sentimentalist."

"And you are an arithmetic barbarian."

"Why is it we always quarrel?" I asked her quite cheerfully.

"It is something in your character. What good is a balloon or anything else if one can't go to pleasant places in it?"

"What's wrong with Finland?"

"It's cold there, for one thing, and all the inhabitants speak Finnish."

"It was you who wanted to come," I reminded her, "on the pretence of devoting yourself to scientific inquiry."

"I am quite ready to inquire scientifically into something. What is there to inquire into?" I showed her how to take readings of the simpler instruments, and soon she was doing it by herself. There was no doubt she had character. Her own character, of course, but character.

•

The sea was a greyish blue, streaked here and there with foam that left long scratches on its surface. The wind had mounted now; the sails, tugging obliquely, pulled us at an exhilarating speed toward the invisible

Finnish coast, the guide ropes leaving three foamy trails in the water. The Aland Islands appeared ahead and, anxious to avoid tangling the guide ropes in habitations or trees, I altered our course slightly to clear them by twisting the pinion ring. (Ordinarily I would have risen over the islands by releasing a little ballast, but now, since Mademoiselle had left us short of sand, I preferred to conserve ballast by steering around the obstacle. Or, to be perfectly honest, I might have released ballast of which we had a quite adequate reserve, but I preferred quite childishly to put her in the wrong by pretending that we were short of it.) The islands were a cluster of low-lying shapes like weasels, with here and there a house or a patch of green woods. The surf broke on the outlying rocks. We passed only a half dozen miles or so from the harbour at Mariehamn; I could see the ships lying at anchor in the roadstead and a large bark under full sail working sideways across the wind toward the town. Almost directly below us a fishing smack, with a lugsail sticking up out of it, pitched into the waves and seemed to remain exactly in the same place. We swept over it, the guide ropes missing the craft by a few metres or so, and at that moment the young fisherman in oilskins raised his head and caught sight of us: an incredible apparition, a gentleman and a smartly clad young lady rushing past him overhead in a basket. He made no sound, only his mouth opened, and he followed our path by slowly rotating his whole body as the sunflower follows the sun. As he disappeared from sight, still watching, his mouth still open, his arms went mechanically back to pulling up the trotline hand over hand. A mechanical doll, a toy worked by springs.

Gulls flew around us, observed us curiously and concluded we were not likely to throw out fish, and swept away in long curves. There was a muted crashing sound from the whitecaps below, along with the brook-like plashing of the guide ropes. On the horizon ahead there appeared some scattered brown lumps with patches of mist clinging to them: the islands along the Finnish coast. In the course of an hour we threaded, swerved, and curved our way among them with the agility of a dancer, I turning the iron handle and hoping that these long and rather shallow arcs would be enough to miss all the obstacles. Then the coast itself appeared, with some rather frightful surf smashing away at a granite cliff. The game of turning the handle was over for the day. It was too risky trailing the guide ropes across the countryside; if the ropes should catch in a farmhouse roof, first the roof would go up, then both roof and balloon would come down again, and everyone would be displeased, both farmer and aeronauts. I released a half bag of sand. We rose by increments until we were barely high enough to clear the hungry cliff, which (it seemed to my imagination) lunged up slightly to snap at us with its jaws as we passed. Now the Gulf of Bothnia was added to my accomplishments. Some specks no larger than midges appeared and plunged around the Prinzess in circles: land birds, swallows.

It was late afternoon; the sun was beginning to dissolve in a body of mist over the sea. Now that we had turned off the mechanical wind we had invented, the Prinzess hung absolutely silently in the greyish air. We furled the sails. Below us, like a canvas landscape in a museum, the countryside unrolled evenly and placidly from the east. There was a scent of plowed earth and greenery. The land consisted of meadows and mysterious-looking woods, with a scattering of lakes. Here and there were farm buildings with red roofs and sides and white trim. For some reason not a single human being was visible. It was about five o'clock on a Tuesday afternoon, and what all the Finns were doing at that hour I had no idea. They had been spirited away by invaders from another planet and the land belonged to the cows, who cropped away at the yellowish grass and scarcely looked up as we soared by two hundred metres over their heads. No, there was a man out hacking at weeds with a scythe. He was up to his knees in a ditch, cutting the weeds at the side of the road, and he failed to notice our passage. As we passed overhead he stopped for a moment, transferred the scythe to his left hand, and wiped the sweat from his brow with a handkerchief. In the silence we could even hear the patient exhalation of air he made as he turned back to work. Then the rhythmic swish of the scythe again. Would he look up and see us disappearing? No, he was intent on his work.

Here were more lakes. The countryside that had been one fifth lakes was now two fifths lakes, and according to the chart I had spread out on my knees it would soon be four fifths lakes, transmogrifying itself from a countryside with lakes into a kind of huge freshwater sea with islands. This, according to the laws of probability, meant that the farther on we drifted the less likely it would be that we would land with dry feet, and the Finnish lakes looked as though the Finns had somehow found the secret of reducing water below the temperature of ice. It was time to bring this particular adventure to a close. It was almost dark now. I had expected the wind to die away as evening came on, but it was still blowing away with its idiot enthusiasm. I would have preferred this canvas panorama to stop rolling by underneath, just for a moment, so we could settle gently onto it. No matter, we would have to come down as best we could, before the landscape became even more watery. Without bothering to explain things to Luisa, I made dexterous preparations.

"What must I do?" she asked finally in a small voice.

"Take care of the instruments. Take the barometer in one hand, the theodolite with the other, and with another hand hold firmly to the gondola."

Without a word she set her teeth and somehow produced three hands and did as she was told. She was determined to blast once for all the myth of feminine weakness. The devil with the instruments; I only hoped she didn't fall out on her head. Attention! It was time to grasp the nettle. I seized the cord of the maneouvring valve and pulled it gently. There was a gassy hissing from above. The balloon, we, the wicker car, everything settled delicately, with a dreamy slowness that contrasted markedly with the speed of the landscape racing by underneath us. Blast! I had forgotten the guide ropes. They would snag in something, or at the very least they would tilt us sideways and spill something important out of the car, perhaps Luisa and the two instruments she was still clutching to her bosom. Clambering up to the bearing ring, I rapidly detached them and watched them fall one by one into the meadow below. A large red farmhouse staggered toward us but managed to squeeze by under the car. Then a clump of trees; we managed to clear that too, but now we were sliding rapidly down an inclined plane and presently bumped into an elder bush. Luisa clung for dear life with her third hand, and in spite of the swinging of the car I successfully groped for and found the cord of the bursting valve. There was an enormous sigh overhead. The balloon folded in the centre and fell sideways. The car bumped twice more and by some miracle came to rest almost upright, supported by another elder bush that had providentially sprung into place. We were a stone's throw from a large lake. If I had delayed another ten seconds in pulling the bursting valve we would have been in it. Where in thunder had that lake come from?

I had never noticed it until this moment. Well, no matter. I clambered out and sank up to my ankles in the sodden ground.

The thing to do, quite evidently, was to make my way backward toward the farm buildings that had passed underneath us only a few minutes before. Luisa insisted on accompanying me, although I persuaded her to give up the two instruments she was clutching like babies and leave them in the car. A light rain had begun to fall. Ahead of us I caught a glimpse of a human figure, whether male or female it was impossible to tell, fleeing under the cover of the shrubbery. It was farther than I thought to the buildings, a good half a kilometer. The figure appeared briefly again, then split in two and revealed itself as an old woman and a boy, a fair distance ahead of us and running as fast as their legs would carry them to a kind of shed on the outskirts of the farm. Reaching this building, they disappeared into the door, which instantly shut again.

We followed on behind them, panting a little, Luisa laughing over her own dexterity at skipping over the puddles. The building was more of a lodge or large storeroom than a shed. The door, built out of stout planks, was barred from the inside. I knocked, rattled the door, and called out in four languages, not however including Finnish, which I had never bothered to learn. Nothing. They were in there, the bucolic trolls, but they were not very hospitable. More pounding. I got a rock and pounded more efficiently. "Hey, mother! Friends. Telegraph hereabouts? Aeronauts from Sweden."

Silence. Little shufflings and bumpings from inside, but nothing more. The rain pattered gently but steadily on the roof of the lodge, on the grass with puddles, on ourselves.

"Hey, mother. Young fellow. A bowl of soup would not be amiss. Paid for on delivery, of course; you could use a little cash, hey?"

Bang, bang with the rock. This treatment was not good for even so stout a door as this collection of planks, but it couldn't be helped. "Hey, mother inside. Open. Are you Christians or some kind of Turks?"

This did it. A shutter near the door swung slightly and the old woman's eye appeared. It was a red eye, with an eyebrow on top and a not very clean area of skin all around. "Who are?"

She could mumble a few words of Swedish. The masters hereabouts were Scandinavian and the peasants Finnish. "Aeronauts," I reiterated. "An expedition of friends."

"Are man?"

"How, are man?" Thunder take her!

The eye disappeared momentarily and appeared again, looking even more dubious than before. "Are not maybe—" and she added a Finnish word I did not recognize but which signified, no doubt, some demon or hobgoblin common to the neighborhood. What did she require me to do? Cross myself? Remove my trousers to show I had no tail?

"No spooks. We are not that what-d'you-call-it I can't pronounce, instead just common folk like yourself, balloon voyagers."

"Ballong resande?"

"Yes, yes," I exclaimed in my four languages, "friendly folk, in a balloon from Sweden to visit your land, and we're getting cursedly cold out here, and so are our feet."

Well. At last the door opened and the old woman appeared, tremoring in most parts of her body, and behind her the boy with eyes like teacups. Luisa reassured them; I don't mean that Luisa said anything, she only stood there looking cold, but it was precisely this quite concrete apparition of a pretty lady holding her elbows that convinced them that we were not malevolent spirits of the atmosphere or some kind of genii. "Master and Lady," babbled the old woman, "come in to the fire."

"First, where is the telegraph?"

This was totally beyond the old woman, who had probably been born sometime in the eighteenth century, but the boy understood and told us, speaking his first words, that the telegraph was in Helsingfors. Blast it, I knew the telegraph was in Helsingfors! It was precisely to Helsingfors that I wanted to telegraph. The point is, where was there a nearer telegraph, so we could send a message to Helsingfors and thence to Stockholm, and eventually to Paris, to assure our associates as well as Luisa's mother and aunt that we had come to earth in good condition? The boy, wanting very much to be helpful, suggested that Timo might ride a horse. It was not clear who Timo was, perhaps a grown-up farmhand, or perhaps the boy was speaking of himself in the third person, and it was not clear besides where Timo would ride the horse to: all the way to Helsingfors, or was there a telegraph station at some intermediate point? A plague take the whole thing. Making oneself understood was too difficult. Let the chattering instrument be silent until tomorrow. Until that time we would cease to exist, we would hover in a limbo that was neither earth nor air, since nobody knew in which element we were. Where was this famous fire? Could it be used to dry one's stockings?

It could do better than that. In fact, the lodge was far too humble for Master and Lady, in the opinion of the locals. A strong young man with flaxen hair appeared, perhaps Timo, or if the boy were Timo then Timo's father, and led us to a rustic cottage at a few hundred metres' distance. It was no doubt a guest house they kept for visiting ballooners. Meanwhile, the boy ran off, his legs rotating like spindles, to get our bags from the balloon. The cottage had a low roof and decorations cut in scrollwork, and a large stone chimney at one end. It consisted of a single room with a low-roofed alcove, at one side of the chimney, to serve as a kitchen. A fire was laid instantly and a yellow tongue of flame began to creep through it. The revolving boy shot through the door with the bags. Would Master and Lady, inquired the old woman, still quavering slightly against the possibility that we were supernatural, like a supper, a bit? Yes, we would like supper a bit, and also something to drink, strong drink, at least Master would, and the opportunity to dry our clothes before we were seized with phthisis. Everything would be provided for, Master and Lady had only to request, the whole thing went on wheels. While the three of them, old woman, strong young man, and boy, revolved in and out of the door like figures in a Swiss clock, useful things appeared: a jug of ale with two pewter mugs, a bottle of spirits for me, a cold haunch of mutton, a Herculean cheese, along with bread, potatoes which the old woman shook up in a pan over the fire, and a jar of what appeared to be elderberry preserves. Towels which the old woman warmed in the same manner as the potatoes. And, I swear by Odin and Freya, a pair of slippers, and for Luisa soft felt boots of the kind worn by Lapps in the frozen north.

Did Master and Lady find it good enough for their supper, this coarse fare that they ate themselves? Quite good enough, in fact luxurious. Did Master and Lady want more of something or anything? Nothing. What was provided was utterly sufficient. She would cause Timo (it *was* Timo, the strong young man with the flaxen hair) to bring an oil lamp, to see by. Unnecessary; the fire provided quite sufficient light. Thanks on all sides. A surplus of hospitality, but still with tremors. We are not spooks, old woman. Mortals like you, chilled by rain and warmed by fire, fond of cold mutton and cheese. The old woman was gone, but the boy lingered on for some reason. Finally he worked up his courage.

"Flyga morgon?"

What?

"Soar again tomorrow?"

Well, perhaps not tomorrow, but we would soar again in the future.

"Take me with?"

It was an even draw which was harder work for him, his courage or his Swedish. One or the other, or both together, made the sweat stand on his brow and his eyes blink, but his dream of soaring held him rooted there before us, in spite of the peril of mysterious retributions he could only guess at. Good night, Finn boy, dream of soaring, bide your time, the air is full of hydrogen and all the worms in China are making silk as you sleep. He was gone. We were alone. The rain pattered constantly on the shingled roof.

Seated at the rustic table in the firelight, we ate the mutton and the cheese, drank the ale, and finished it off with elderberry preserves on coarse peasant bread. Luisa rose from her chair and wandered around the room, pausing finally before the fire. She held out her hands to the warmth. "Oh, I am wet. I am soaked to the skin." She said this not as though reporting a physical discomfort but absently, dreamily, in the tone of one who says that she is sleepy, or that her tiredness is good. With the utmost simplicity she raised her arms to feel under the soft mass of hair behind her neck and unfasten certain snaps. Then, reaching lower along her back, she opened other fastenings. The traveling gown slipped down to reveal some expensive linen. As a gentleman I naturally looked the other way. I sat at the rustic table, turned up the ale mug and found it empty, and stared at the door. Presently I heard her voice inquiring where the trolls had put the bath towel. It was at the end of the table, neatly folded.

"Well, bring it here, foolish fellow."

Amid a great silence I did as I was told. When I turned with the towel I saw with a certain surprise that the expensive linen, all of it as far as I could tell, had arranged itself over the chair by the fire. She was still facing the fire with her back to me, one hand supporting herself on the back of the chair, a knee bent and resting on the chair seat. In the gloom of the half-lit room there was visible a slender back of a quite unbelievable paleness, the shadows of the vertebrae faintly visible along it. Petulantly she looked around to see if the towel was coming. The long brow was still calm (the hair had come down in some way, how the devil had that happened!) and the mouth was as usual held together with those two creases that signified, perhaps, the irritation of a will confronted with the intractability and rebelliousness of substance, its own included. The towel was put around her with a gesture like enfolding wings: holding the corners in my two hands I placed it onto the pale back and passed the corners around the shoulders to her waiting hands. But through a clumsy accident, a fumbling, these hands took not only the corners of the towel but my own fingers as well and drew them downward. The towel had escaped me and in place of it I felt two soft and warm prominences designed by a malicious ingenuity exactly to fit my hands, with something like two tiny fingers in the centres that stiffened to press against my own. For a second or two she remained motionless. Then, turning about so that the towel half fell from her, she pressed her forearms weakly against my chest to defend herself—herself! who was defending me?—while the pink spider mounted upward toward the pale shadow of her throat. "You . . . that is not what I meant . . . that is not what I meant you to do." The flush continued over her face, her elbow dug into my chest, she really was angry or a part of her was. Yet all these struggles and twistings, these ostensible and ineffective efforts to escape that for all I know were quite sincere, were in evident conflict with another part of her being that she was powerless to influence. She was helpless against the thing and so was I. *That is not what I meant . . . that is not what I meant you to do*, she was whispering with her face close to mine. *You are . . . oh, dearest beloved, that is not what I meant you to do.* But her limbs seemed now to move quite for themselves, in ways she had not intended. Her last faint objection was muffled, crushed under the softness of her lips. When her mouth was freed again she had nothing to say. This femme savante, this reader of *Stetigkeit und irrationale Zahlen* had become phenomenally wordless, there was only the patter of raindrops on the shingles and the soft sputtering of the fire. Through some legerdemain we sank into a yielding abyss consisting of a bed from the previous century with an enormous feather quilt, along with some fresh bed linen smelling of lilac. The mouth erstwhile held so firmly was now seeking and tremulous, a flower with pale edges. How had this transformation taken place? It was magic too that resistance and softness could mingle so ingeniously, that a point of coral so delicately gathered on the faintly pendulous hemisphere, almost too fragile to touch, was the key when brushed ever so lightly of the power that drew us together in a soft convulsion, downward and ever downward, while we swam feebly, the motions of our limbs only carrying us farther from the surface and deeper into this sea of warm and fantastic shapes until the deepest and most secret shadow parted and drew to itself, by some miracle, exactly that seeking part of me that yearned so heartfeltly to be enclosed in exactly those pulsating rings of hot honey that quickened and tightened about it, in a manner almost alarming, until at last it—she, I, everything, I am not sure exactly what—burst into its cataclysmic and astonishingly prolonged expostulation of surrender. The storm passed, we lay finally half-tangled in each other's limbs, knowing neither ourselves nor each other and having become a single oblivion. The fire went out, that Finnish cottage grew terribly cold, thank God for the featherbed.

Asleep. One eighth awake. Half awake. Then asleep again, yet awake enough to be aware that I was sleeping so that I could feel the white slithering of the linen along my limbs as I turned, now and then the contact of a warm and columnar softness against my knee. I am aware finally that I am not in Stresa but in another part of the world. An embracing silence, no sound but the faint creaking of the ropes that hold the silk to the gondola, as though the Prinzess herself were stirring in her sleep. In my half-waking state I feel an odd dread, a premonition of some watchful and waiting thing that is hostile in a diffuse and unclear way and yet a thing that is most deeply craved. If this thing is awake, I tell myself, it is better for me to be awake too. I crawl out of the sleeping sack of reindeer skin (perdition take the contraption, it leaves hairs all over you just as I expected) and fasten the hood of my coat tighter around the neck against the cold. As soon as I rise to my feet I am struck by the beauty of the scene. The sky is barred with stripes of thin clouds through which the sun, almost on the horizon now, shines weakly and indistinctly, its outline soft as though melted. The sea is an immensely hard and reflecting pewter. Because the sun has sunk into the cloud bank and can no longer warm the balloon even slightly, it has descended until the guide ropes touch the surface of the water. Still the sun is there, now whitish, now greyish, picking its way along the horizon sideways and beginning already to curve imperceptibly back into the heavens again. It was no doubt this white unsleeping sun, at two o'clock in the morning, that filled me with that odd premonition of something not as it should be, of a watchful presence. That and the sinking of the Prinzess so that the three guide ropes, dropping below now in a shallow curve, touch the pewter surface and carve onto it three arrow-shaped marks, not plashing and lacy like the wake of a ship, but as hard as the surface of the sea itself. In some way I had sensed this closer presence of the sea, perhaps because the guide ropes, even though they made no sound detectable by the outward ear, had spoken in some mysterious way to a sense in my inner self. Or perhaps the very slightly greater heaviness of the air itself, as we sank lower, had wakened me. If there are liquids which can detect the coming of a distant storm, shrinking and trying to hide in their tubes of glass, then perhaps in some infinitely tinier capillaries of the body the fluids may respond in a similar way to the lower altitude, imperceptibly, but enough to stir the consciousness already on the needle point of waking. When the föhn sweeps over central Europe the suicide rate triples; the soul is sensitive to the minutest changes in the air around it. The question is not to invent new detectors for the messages of nature, it is to learn to listen to the detectors that are already with us. Well, bother! enough of this philosophising. I should have been a schoolmaster; I rap with my ruler and tell those in the back row to wake up. "Tell us more facts!" they cry out. You are already breathing facts; they pass into your blood and pulse in the hair tubes of the brain, demanding only that you awaken to listen to them. Perdition take it! they would have driven me to an asylum in a week, those inky-fingered boys with their smell of porridge. Which direction are we going? The wind is south again. So much the better. We are headed keenly and willy-nilly toward our destination, that mathematical point where a lot of invisible and quite arbitrary lines converge.

At my feet my two companions are humped furry rectangles, indistinct in the grey light. Their heads are totally hidden. One of the shapes stirs slightly, a foot flexes and extends in the bag of hide. It is not Waldemer but the other; I can recognize the slenderer form even though the sleeping sacks are identical. Detecting in some way that I am watching, perhaps by a capillary intuition analogous to that by which I detected only a little while before that the sun was watching me, this form stirs, rolls over, and finally a head protrudes from the opening of the sack. Theodor emerges, in absolute silence puts on his cap and winds a woolen scarf around it and over his ears, and then stands up to look at the pewter sea. He is cold. He shifts from one foot to the other and his elbows press against his sides. We converse in low tones in order not to awake our companion.

With the scarf around his head he resembles a bedouin, an effect enhanced by his dark Persian eyes and his paleness. "I dislike that sun," he remarks calmly.

"Because it ought to go away at night?"

"Not for that exactly. Because in staying up at night, it tries to fool us by looking like the moon. That milkiness."

"You don't like milk?"

"I detest milkiness and snow, everything white. It suggests things clammy to the touch. Corpses, winding sheets."

"In that case I'm afraid you are taking your vacation in the wrong direction. Ahead of us everything is white, the sea as well."

"I'm not on my vacation." Stiffly. "It isn't a complaint. I am simply remarking my preferences."

The well-concealed but unmistakable feminine trace in this temperament comes out now and then in these intuitions, these preferences for one landscape over another. In making it clear he is not complaining, however, he is at his most manly. Theodor is more complicated than he seems, or than he would like to reveal. Bands of India rubber stretch through him on the inside, their tension creating the perfect symmetry of his exterior. I refrain from reminding him that on the Aletschhorn, only a few months ago, he told me he liked white things; but that was in another existence, in another universe, it happened to other persons.

"Ahead," I point out, "you can see iceblink." It is faintly visible on the northern horizon, a band of white against the iron grey of the clouds. "The white sky is caused by reflection of light from the ice beneath it, which is also white. On the ice white animals prey on each other."

"And their blood when it is shed is white also?"

"No, it is red just like ours. Their eyes too are various colours, such as black or cobalt. There are exceptions to the whiteness, but in general the region we are approaching is white."

"We don't seem to be approaching it very fast."

"We are, as a matter of fact. We would go even a little faster if we rose a bit, since there is no need for the guide ropes to be in the sea now that the wind is from the south."

Together, fumbling a little in our mittens, we work to release ballast. Theodor manipulates the ballast cord with precision and makes no mistakes. A quantity of lead shot, stretching out in a long and indistinct line, falls in absolute silence into the sea. The Prinzess stirs, a little unwillingly (she is sleepy too), and at last lifts her guide ropes out of the water, trails them down to touch it once again briefly, and begins a slow climb. When the sun warms the gas again it will expand, and we will have to release a little of it. In this the balance between these globules of lead and the infinitely finer molecules of hydrogen—our lives lie cupped like moths in a boy's hand. If we could hide under the fog bank ahead it would protect us from the sun and thus from the loss of more hydrogen, but we will have to climb over the fog bank, otherwise it would be impossible to take observations.

"What time is it?"

"After two."

"In Paris the cafés are closing, and yet I'm not sleepy. It was strange that the ballast fell so silently." Did he expect it to ring out on the metallic sea? And yet it was so strange.

14 July 1897

At eight o'clock we catch sight of a white gleam below through a rift in the clouds—the pack! This plain of ice stretches away endlessly to the Pole, and on most of it no human being has set foot. In this latitude it is still soft; many crevasses and open leads. Occasionally there is a line like a seam in a fractured and partly healed skull: a pressure ridge. For a few minutes we chatter about this, pointing out to each other features of the pack and estimating its thickness. When we stop talking an extraordinary thing happens: we can hear the ice below. A grinding, a growling in the throat, scratchy coughs, a kind of heave as though someone in the next room were trying unsuccessfully to vomit. It is the sound of a great flat animal lying stretched from one horizon to the other, too weak to rise and too strong to die. July is not a good time for the pack. It feels its mortality. Let us hope it can hang on for a few more days; we may need to walk on it.

The sun has climbed up out of the mist and glows redly again, its outline a little rubbery. It gives out a feeble warmth, not enough to thaw our faces but enough to heat the Prinzess and cause her to rise. We are drifting at an altitude of perhaps four hundred metres over a low-hanging sheet of clouds with many holes in it. Through one of the larger openings I catch sight of something and point it out to Theodor: a red stain on the ice, the remains of a bear's dinner. He gazes at this with some interest. After it is far behind us he still looks back now and then, thinking perhaps to catch a final glimpse of it. The bear is an untidy fellow, a successful Darwinian who has no table manners because he has no enemies. If he scatters blood and entrails around, never mind, there are plenty of other seals, and nobody is likely to interrupt him at his repast. Besides, his tablecloth is self-cleaning. Presently it will melt and everything will fall through into the ocean, the bear too; he always forgets this and has to swim stupidly toward the north in search of something solid to clamber onto.

All this is mere conjecture. I really don't have very much experience of bears and leave such things to Waldemer. He, as it happens, is too busy to concern himself with these aesthetic and metaphysical contradictions. He has lowered his cook stove down and is manipulating the cords; the familiar odors of kerosene and hot coffee drift upward into the gondola. We breakfast on coffee and pieces of bread which we thaw by holding them against our coffee cups. After breakfast a sun sight fixes our latitude at 84° north, or about two hundred and forty nautical miles from Dane Island. A little more than three hundred and sixty to go. If this wind holds—and everything indicates that it will—we have a chance of reaching our destination in another forty hours, that is sometime on the early morning of the sixteenth. Afternoon, night, morning; these are only habits we carry with us from the Green World. Here everything is oblique, the sun goes sideways, the night is made out of milk, and morning and evening are diagonal tendencies, so to speak, that converge at a point slightly out of the picture so we can't see how it is done. What nonsense! This is a strange diary I am writing; or am I writing or only thinking it? I don't understand it very well myself and I have the impression of another consciousness a little distance away, perhaps looking over my shoulder, for which it all makes better sense, but which does not choose to confide in me what it is all about, and it is for this watching thing that I am writing. (I am writing, damnation take it, here is the small pigskin notebook on my knee, but what I am writing is only our morning position and a few other naked facts that could interest only a positivist like Waldemer). It is possible that cold affects the wit, causing certain neurons in the cerebellum to miss their connections. A harmless aberration, no doubt. Perhaps on the other hand I have merely discovered a new literary form. The frozen diary, or network of irrelevancies, as untidy and inevitable as a polar bear's meal.

I am recalled from these numb but interesting musings by the practical voice of Waldemer. "Major. You know . . ."

"Ah. It's time to send another notice of our progress to a breathless and expectant world."

I scrawl the morning position onto a scrap of tissue paper, and Waldemer adds a few descriptive details for readers of the New York *Herald*. I can't see what he is writing in his fine precise hand, but I catch a glimpse of "...northward...progress...hopeful..." The paper is screwed into the aluminum tube and we open the wicker case, which we have covered with a quilt to keep these small flying machines warm. Still, these are Norwegian pigeons and the climate here in July is no more severe than it is in their home in Trondheim in the winter. I notice, however, that they have eaten little or none of the Indian corn we put into the case the night before. They seem nervous and evade the hand that penetrates the case from the top. Waldemer manages to grasp one— evidently one of the less agile—and removes it from the case. Bird and tube are assembled, and Waldemer places them on the instrument ring as before and touches the invisible lever between the legs. But this pigeon is not very energetic. His wing droops shabbily, his eye lacks luster.

"Come now, Jewel. It's away to the south and home."

The pigeon contemplates him out of a dull eye. Waldemer, insisting on his view of the pigeon as a mechanism that can be made to function once the design is grasped, scratches him encouragingly in other places, and the pigeon raises each foot in turn and puts it down. Would like to go back to sleep apparently if Waldemer would stop bothering him. Homing instinct is lacking or totally paralyzed. Finally Waldemer takes him in two hands and tosses him outward into the void. The bird comes to himself, staggering and flapping, and manages to fly in a ragged circle back to the instrument ring again. Waldemer is still cheerful but a determined set is forming on his mouth. He flings the bird out with two hands again. This time the poor creature is too weak, or the gondola no longer seems an attractive place to him. He attempts a kind of caricature of flying, mainly with one wing, but sinks constantly lower. Finally it turns into a soft fluttering ball, the single wing still beating convulsively. Waldemer declares that the pigeon was not well, that it was suffering from an illness of some kind. "It certainly was an ill-bred bird," I agree. "Probably not a homing pigeon at all but some loafer from the public square that the dealer has palmed off on us." But the

sight of this soft ball plummeting into the cloud has depressed us all—
Waldemer especially, although I too for some reason am affected by the
weight of this omen—and there is no talk of trying again with another
pigeon. The incident is closed. Yet by watching Waldemer covertly I can
see he is still pondering over the thing. He doesn't like maladjustments.
Does the tiny machine need oiling, is there a screw that needs to be
tightened? By God, he will give it oil. He will adjust its ball bearings
until it sees the light and does its proper duty, by heaven, he is not going
to be outwitted by a cooing thing no bigger than a glove. Well, at least
the stove works. The stove is a wonderful contrivance, Waldemer. It
doesn't blink and coo at you, and when you jerk the string it cooks the
coffee, every time. That is because you made it and not God. Waldemer
stamps his feet to warm them and is soon cheerful again. Foolish to be
put out of sorts by a clockwork bird!

•

A sharp crack from below, like a rifle shot. A particularly brittle piece
of ice has split under the pressure from the sea. Extraordinary how
something so unsubstantial as water, even in congealed form, can make
so metallic a sound. The cloud layer below us is a little thinner now and
the pack is visible most of the time, only hidden now and then by a veil
of gossamer-like mist. But behind us, to the south, something important
is preparing to happen. The white clouds are huddling together in a
wall around the horizon, this wall is darkening along its lower edge,
and ragged streamers are detaching themselves slowly from the wall and
drifting away in fragments. The disturbance I overheard on the Spiritual
Telegraph on Monday has deepened into a storm, as I expected. This is
certain to be good news for us. It will produce a strong south wind, and
if the laws of rotating mechanisms are still in operation, the wind will
later veer into the northwest and north for our return journey. And in
fact, after only half an hour or less, the Prinzess leans a little to the first
puff of wind, swings gracefully and slowly for a few moments like an
enormous pendulum, and begins to accelerate her pace.

Theodor and I secure all the loose gear and rig the canvas
windbreakers against the snow that is sure to come now. Then we busy
ourselves with the instruments. By triangulation with the theodolite
we calculate our speed at eighteen knots. It is a strange sensation to
have the storm come upon us and yet feel no wind, since the Prinzess is

carried along in the air and moves evenly and silently with it. Only now
and then, when a random gust a little stronger than the others strikes
her, does she shudder slightly and sway until she has adjusted herself
to the new velocity. This pendulum swinging is a pleasant novelty.
The motion is dignified and very slow, requiring perhaps three or four
seconds to sway to one side, pause, and swing back to the other. Now
and then for some reason the Prinzess begins very gradually to rotate, as
imperceptibly as the hands of a clock, so that when the next gust strikes
her the result is a circular or elliptical motion, the gondola tracing slow
conoidal patterns in the air. The wall of nimbus to the south moves
toward us with surprising speed. Tatters and fragments of it are already
overhead, and our speed over the ice has increased to twenty knots or
more. This a piece of luck; we had not expected to career north so fast.
But there is a disadvantageous side to this useful storm. As the clouds
cut off the sun the gas in the envelope cools and contracts, and its lifting
force is reduced. Furthermore, a plaguey rime begins to form on the
balloon and its rigging, and this adds a further weight to the load the
diminishing sphere of gas can scarcely lift anyhow. Theodor sights down
at the ice to estimate our altitude, knowing that the guide ropes are a
hundred metres long. "A hundred and twenty metres. A hundred and
ten." We scud along at an astonishing pace, a velocity that seems even
greater because of our closeness to the ice. Now and then the guide
ropes brush the surface of the pack, sending the Prinzess into more
graceful swayings and circlings, until she manages to rise a few feet
again.

The others glance at me.

"Lighten."

We jettison a good deal of our ballast, more than I would really care
to if I had my choice, so that the next time we are in this predicament
something more useful and necessary than lead shot may have to be
dropped overboard. But this does the trick; the Prinzess is reinvigorated,
she strains upward against the ropes, we rise to three hundred metres
again and rush along to the north. A consultation with the Spiritual
Telegraph confirms that we are dealing with a large and vigorous storm
that will go on blustering for some time. Lowering the hairspring
carefully into the crystal, I hear cracklings emanating from all directions
from southwest to southeast. With the Bell receiver held to my left

ear, my right hand delicately manipulating the hairspring, I gaze at my companions, who are watching me with that peculiar idiotic and half-embarrassed silence of modern man who has given over his fate to a few scraps of metal and is now wondering what the machine is going to do with him.

I lower the receiver from my ear. "South winds. The prognosis is favorable."

"I've watched you do that a dozen times, Major. I wonder what you hear in that thing."

I let him try. I hold the Bell receiver to his ear, he listens, and an intelligent, respectful, but not very enlightened expression comes over his face.

"Odd," he comments finally.

"Mother Nature is scratching herself."

"Leave off with your metaphors, Gustavus. They only make Waldemer nervous."

"Of course they don't make me nervous." He hands me back the receiver. "It's just that—he's always making jokes about these things, even though it's he himself that's invented them. Sometimes I wonder if he—what the devil am I talking to Theodor for, as if you weren't here—I wonder if you really appreciate the—h'mm. Tremendous significance of—all these developments. I mean, specifically, what we're doing here. Because, don't you see, if we can make our way to the Pole and back, using the winds as a highway—"

"You see, he uses metaphors himself. Journalism is nothing but metaphors. Cabinets falling, the Sick Man of Europe, and so on."

"Veils of silence drawn over questions," Theodor joins in. "Tides of humanity. Gathering storms on the political horizon."

But he waves aside all badinage and his intelligent expression is at its most earnest. "If we can make our way to the Pole and back, as I say, using the winds as a highway, then enormous balloons four times or ten times the size of this one might be constructed to carry goods around the world—why, as early as the Paris exhibition of 1878 they made one a hundred and seventeen feet in diameter, which had a carrying capacity of twenty-eight thousand pounds and ascended with forty passengers. Imagine!"

He is competent at his profession and he has all the facts and figures. It is also quite possible that he is right. He goes on in this vein for some time, envisioning airships laden with English woolens crossing the Atlantic with the trade winds, transported by railroad to Nova Scotia and reloaded with American horse collars, patent apple peelers, enameled or brass doorknobs, wooden nutmegs, and so on, which they will carry rapidly back to Europe under the influence of the westerlies prevailing at that latitude, firing his own imagination as he talks and beginning now to write in his head the article which he will beyond any shadow of a doubt publish when we return to the crowded warrens of skyscrapers and printing presses, an article in which the phrase "using the winds as a highway" will certainly figure. His thoughts are still on the World of Cities. In spite of his outdoorsmanship, his strong-jawed love of guns and nature, he is par excellence the civilized man and draws his strength from these ant heaps where men work so assiduously at their machines and go home each night to send their millions of identical plumes of chimney smoke into the air. Through invention and change, he sincerely believes, mankind will be transformed. A new kind of human being will be created to use and inhabit the wonders that will come from the laboratories and factories of the future. What was England two centuries ago? he demands of us. A lot of meadows and elm trees. The whole thing would scarcely support ten million people. Then came the steam engine and the spinning jenny, and the face of the land was transformed, a new landscape was created and along with it a new species of creature, modern man in his frock coat. Look at England today—instead of a lot of meadows there are factories, smokestacks belching out prosperity, villas in the suburbs. The population has trebled and quadrupled; the whole country teems with Englishmen who work happily in the factories and go home at night to replenish the population. And so on. He has found a way to keep warm, lucky fellow, through agitating his lungs and making the air hum so vigorously through his larynx. He is eloquent and convincing when he speaks of the poetry of cities, even though he would not put it in those terms.

Cities! I find to my surprise that his evocation of chimney smoke, even, produces a twinge of something like regret in me. Drifting over this unpeopled vastness gives one a malaise of emptiness. This is nature— this is the planet devoid of men! This endless-stretching expanse of white—featureless, immense, silent. After a while the soul hungers for voices and warm rooms, even for smokestacks. The very purity of this antiseptic plain stretching away from horizon to horizon makes one long for squalor. After a day or two of it one would willingly lie in a London gutter and savor its aroma, the reassuring stench that drips from life. New York in August, horse cars and frying grease. The slightly putrid fragrance of Paris, with its flavour of wines and coal smoke. Stockholm: herring, leather, sailor's tar, boiling linen. Perhaps because the sense of odour has nothing to grip in these sterile latitudes, as soon as one closes his eyes it turns inward to the pungencies of recollection, which spring to mind with a startling vividness. The perfume from a fat cab horse's back, jogging through the Bois in the autumn sunshine. Thin acrid sweetness of horse chestnuts. Sun-warmed leather, faintly perspiring cabman, whose back is almost as broad as that of his beast. Clop of hooves on the pavement, intermittent light through the elms, roughness of my tweed cuff against my wrist, her visage serene and confident yet with the pink spider beginning to climb on her throat again (she was still only a girl really—a child!), not quite looking at me but at the air at one side of my head, the faint smile at one side of her mouth. "And why has it taken you so long to come back? Six months! You are cruel."

"No doubt I am. But I have work to do, you know, an existence is not only composed of sherbets and cab rides in the Bois."

"You still think I am trivial. How can I persuade you that I am serious about these things?" (She meant magnetism and electric sparks.) "I would have thought that after Finland . . ."

Another of her eloquent trailings off! But I refused to follow these oblique feminine subtleties, they amused or irritated me, and I pressed her maliciously. "How, after Finland?"

This really made her blush. She had not meant that at all, she insisted, but the blush gave her the lie. She had really meant both at once, the poor thing, her deftness with the barometer and theodolite and the folly afterward in the stone cottage. And so she turned the conversation smoothly (yet still blushing) to exhibitions and recitals, compliments on a gown, the bright and fashionable surface of her Faubourg world. How, after Finland? Bother! After Finland there was blessed little, to tell the truth. I worked hard at the Institute, writing a paper on dirigibility

through guide ropes and maintaining my contacts with New York and
Hamburg. When after six months of violet-scented letters and even a
telegram I presented myself once again at Quai d'Orléans I found myself
transformed by some sort of infernal legerdemain into a kind of suitor,
one whose loyalty and continuous presence in the house were taken for
granted and who was expected to subsist indefinitely on expectations
of some vague and idyllic future. Although I had come from Stockholm
with the idea of burying myself in a dusty laboratory with my papers
and emerging only now and then to consult the Bibliothèque Nationale
or purchase scientific supplies, I found myself moving into not exactly
elegant but by no means squalid rooms in rue de Rennes, I could hardly
afford them, and even buying myself the striped morning coat of a
swain. I accompanied her to fittings at Worth and Vionnet, to Boissier in
Boulevard des Capucines for a kind of bonbon that could be obtained
only there. On the lake in the Bois de Boulogne we drifted elegantly
over the lilies in a rented skiff, I in my frock coat, she in a gown from
Worth: a scene from Watteau. The devil! This was not working out as
I had planned. One would have thought that after Finland (how, after
Finland?) things would have been much simpler and more natural, that
a major obstacle in our friendship (shall we call it) would have been
surmounted so that one would not be confronted by this same obstacle
again and again and our little intimacy, so necessary to man and beast,
might be repeated again from time to time. But no; here on her home
ground there was another Luisa, or rather there were several Luisas who
merged and divided, slipped tantalizingly out of reach or dissolved in
myriad forms like characters in one of Herr Strindberg's plays. (I had
read something of this lunatic now and devilish hard going it was.) She
seemed to hold me to account in some way for the Finnish cottage,
although God knows I had fallen into her clutches as innocently as a
child. Where was that pale and moonlike back in the firelight with its
curve of shadows? In Paris she seemed indifferent, even slightly ironic
about these mergings of our hands and ardours that took place now
and again behind doorways, as though she regarded them as a means
of verification of the attachment rather than as a pleasure or end in
themselves. The miracle of the restoration of virginity, disputed warmly
by theologians, Luisa performed daily and without effort. Any given
day's gain was lost overnight, so that the aspirant had Sisyphus-wise to

begin his task constantly anew, a discouraging prospect even for a young man, which I was no longer. In this unlikely chastity she was defended most of all by the Bayeux reticule. In order to make love to her it was first necessary to distract her attention from this portable museum; otherwise she was capable at important moments of turning to search in it for an almond dragée or a pin to catch up her hair, finding en route a letter from her Polish cousin Gela which she insisted on reading to me. Let us put the reticule over here, dear Luisa, behind the armchair or preferably outside the door in the salon, and get on with our business. I would manage finally to unfasten one snap at the top of her dress in the back. You cunning gypsy! she accused. She considered it degenerate of a man to understand the workings of female clothing, yet left to herself she would never unfasten it in a million years. (In Paris, that is; in Finland the dress had come off entirely by itself through sleight-of-hand.) Entry of the Breton footman. Mademoiselle had wished to be reminded when it was three o'clock, so she could go to see the Monets at the Luxembourg. Had Mademoiselle! The demons carry her off! In the vestibule this lout of a Breton would appear with her paletot, but she would gesture to me with a patrician motion of her head. And I, subfootman under immediate command of the Breton, would take the coat and attempt to get her into the thing. The mass of moire, silk-lined, was a feminine conundrum. While her arm waited, I searched for the place where it was to go. Where was that blasted opening? And once found, the arm was too limp and in its fumbling the passage through the silk was lost, or the sleeve hole was the wrong one and would result in a serious confusion if pursued. The Breton stood by with thumb clasped behind his back, too well trained to offer suggestions. This would provide good telling belowstairs. At last Luisa took the coat from me and slipped into it herself, with an elegant deftness. "Thank you, Gustav dear." It was not necessary for the Breton to run after a cab; I was capable of that. Or not run after it at all; simply wave in the direction indicated with my hat, a pearl-grey homburg that went with the frock coat. To the Luxembourg! Luisa was placid, sibylline, her irony if any showing only imperceptibly in the faint shadows below her mouth.

And yet Finland! Could those sighs and urgencies, those unmistakable pyrotechnics of ardour, have come from a person who was only partly enjoying herself? (Pricked by some demon of scepticism, I remembered that in French fireworks are called feux d'artifice.) No matter, I attempted to convince myself with at least some success, the simulacrum of bliss was the same as bliss. Love is a disease according to the Viennese doctors. Take away the symptoms of a disease and what do you have? Yet she seemed cured. She seemed to have forgotten the episode, as though it had not happened or had been the unimportant lapse of a friend whose conduct she hardly approved and yet was prepared, in the end, to regard with a cosmopolitan indulgence. It was terribly hard work, this thing of embracing behind doors; it was fraught with obstacles that she surely laid deliberately in my path. Should a door be shut, the Breton would appear and open it. Were we alone in a dark and curtained cab, she would require me to light matches while she searched for something in her reticule. And my work was suffering! I had come to Paris, I was barely able to remember in my more lucid moments, to verify the work of Neumayer and Fritsche which was to be found in manuscript in the Bibliothèque Nationale and apply it to my own researches on atmospheric phenomena. In rue de Sèvres an instrument dealer was still waiting to demonstrate for me a bifilar magnetometer. Do you know what that is, dear Luisa, a bifilar magnetometer? It is what you swore to be so richly interested in, that day when you interposed yourself into my life at the Musée Carnavalet. Yet she did manage to read the barometer over the Gulf of Bothnia. Drat the Gulf of Bothnia! On the other side of it was Finland and the stone cottage. Well, and was I not happy in the stone cottage? In any case, half the people in the world were women and they were hardly a novelty. What precisely did I wish anyhow, and why did I not ignore her and go on exactly as I was before I met her? Because I was a blithering idiot whose glands were more powerful than his brain. Now and then I found time to glance into a book or twiddle briefly with some instrument in my rented room. Chiefly in the morning, since Luisa, as I might have guessed in spite of her stories about rides in the Bois at dawn, rose late in the morning, while my habits were thoroughly diurnal. From the Bibliothèque to Quai d'Orléans to the instrument dealer to the room in rue de Rennes I coursed or plodded wearily, wearing out quantities of shoe leather. It was impossible to do both these things well. I was like a man playing kettledrums and having constantly to turn his attention from one to the other. And now and then some perfidious angel of betrayal would whisper at my elbow, "You will never have your freedom until you effect matrimony with this remorseless creature, so that you can go off and leave her each day as all men do, busying yourself with the truly important questions of the world, while she prepares the downy nest of night. This is the way of the world."

•

This I was not quite prepared to do. I was a certain kind of creature and could be no other; as soon as I felt any heart flowers growing in me I uprooted them mercilessly, or else I faced the risk of having her or some other beseech me, pale-faced and tears in eyes, not to go off and do what I wished to do and what my whole soul and being called for me to do, simply because there might be danger attached to it: "Think of me." No, dear Luisa, my need for you is tremendous, cosmic, and fundamental, but it has its limits. Besides, the matter was more complicated than that. It was by no means certain that an honourable proposal from me would even be greeted favorably by the powers that governed in this household, even though unmistakable suggestions were applied to me in this respect, not only the questioning of the aunt about my prospects, but the behavior of Luisa herself in certain circumstances usually public, and embarrassing to myself, such as the occasion six weeks or so after my arrival in which she stood by the piano and recited Goldsmith to the assembled guests, with speaking glances in my direction at the end of the more meaningful lines:

> *"When lovely woman stoops to folly*
> *And finds too late that men betray,*
> *What charm can soothe her melancholy,*
> *What art can wash her guilt away?"*

Well, it was a question. What art indeed? If there was an art she had it; she had been very well educated by somebody or other. There were actually tears in her eyes as she embarked on the second and even more pathetic stanza.

> *"The only art her guilt to cover,*
> *To hide her shame from every eye,*
> *To give repentance to her lover.*
> *And wring his bosom—is to die."*

There was a tinkle of applause, and from the corner the sari-clad mother sighed, "Oh, la pauvre." Luisa soon brightened up and spoke no more of suicide, and indeed it was not necessary for her to take such radical and irreversible steps to wring my bosom; she could do it simply by reciting a poem while concealing a piece of onion in her handkerchief. Who had coached her in this playlet? I began to see that in order to grasp Luisa, in any sense in which the verb might be taken, it was first necessary to understand something of the functioning principles of this household, and it was a study almost as formidable as that of aeromagnetism. The aunt dominated all. Yet like all tyrants she herself understood only a part of what she dominated. As for my understanding of her, it consisted of a chasm in which two great mysteries yawned: primo, how she regarded me, and secundo, what it was exactly that she intended for Luisa. On my first encounter with her, when she had interrogated me about my military rank and suchlike, she had seemed only an amusing if faintly ominous doll, her head vibrating while she pronounced her thinly veiled hostilities. But as I studied her more she acquired complexity and I understood her less. I began to compile a stock of information, mostly from conversations with other guests, in the hope that this would lead me to the clue that would eventually enable me to understand the aunt and the others in the family, especially the aunt. She had been born in Goa but brought to Europe as a tiny infant, it seemed. Somehow she had inherited the family fortune, acquired the seventeenth-century hôtel particulier on the Île, and assembled this menagerie of Peruvian ambassadors, poètes manqués, and unattached young officers who rotated around her like a planetary system. One had the impression that there were invisible forces supporting this household that had not yet been detected, that the aunt lay under the protection of an eminent political figure, or that the economics of the house rested on hidden and lucrative vice that was revealed only to initiates. One thing was certain, and that was that there was a powerful sexual element in the energy that the aunt radiated to the external world. Never mind that she was a spinster! That this part of her nature had never been conventionally fulfilled was the centre and secret of her power. She was an allegorical personage, one of those virgin-goddesses from mythology who punish infractions against their will by excruciating and picturesque torments, like being trampled by stags. "How is it, Captain," she asked me once, "that we never see you any more in the house?" (I had come only once that day.) "No doubt there are things more fascinating that keep you in your rented room." I could not seriously convince myself she was referring to a bifilar magnetometer. "We know what men are, overgrown boys who must have their toys. Be careful, Captain, that some toy or other does not break in your hand. They are expensive, I am sure."

What in the collected works of Aeschylus did she mean by that! Did she have a Roentgen-ray telescope, this vibrating matriarch, or did she wring confessions out of Luisa with thumbscrews? This second was not likely, since Luisa herself seemed to have forgotten about Finland almost as soon as it happened. Perhaps, in spite of all probability, she was referring to a bifilar magnetometer. And the mother! She was another study that grew more profound as one attempted to penetrate it. I also learned something of her biography, but it threw less light on the matter than one might have hoped. She had remained in Goa, it transpired, when the infant-aunt had been brought to Europe—the why of all this was an unfathomable mystery, whether the imperious father had decreed this out of whim, or whether some economic or other consideration determined the separation of the sisters—and she had spent her girlhood there in that heap of ruined churches and monasteries on the Indian coast, inhabited for the most part by priests banished from Portugal for misconduct, a town looking back with comatose nostalgia to the days of its glory in the seventeenth century—a steamy odorous backwater, cut off from India by the river Terakhul and from all civilization and hope of culture by the sea. There, eating curry and attended by ill-humoured servants, she had spent the seven thousand hot and identical days between her birth and her adulthood, and longing in her secret thoughts for heaven knows what, although hardly a cabbage could have been satisfied with the existence she led, and she must have grasped some hint of what life was like from the servants. Was she really an imbecile or was this the role that life had taught her to play? Perhaps the sun had scrambled her wits like eggs, or perhaps the aunt had been quicker from the beginning and this was why she had been taken off to Europe and the younger sister left to stew in those odorous miasmas where nothing ever happened.

For whatever reason—death of the father, total decline of the family fortunes in Goa—this deprived creature found herself at the age of twenty suddenly commanded to transfer herself to Paris by order of the aunt. And there, after only a few short weeks, she encountered the dashing and laconic American, Mr. Hickman, whose father had just died and who had chosen, rather foolishly, to spend his patrimony on a Grand Tour of Europe in the eighteenth century fashion, rather than on improving the small New Mexico cattle ranch that was already mortgaged to the hilt. Why in the name of Thomas Jefferson the slim-hipped, long-jawed cowboy ever fell in love with and married this sloe-eyed Oriental moron was beyond me to say. Something in his soul lacked and yearned for exactly that languor, perhaps; it was the attraction of opposites. What was certain was that the aunt received this news with a maenadic fury, turning from the messenger speechless and white-faced and retiring to plan her counterattack. Nothing could be done, the cowboy had galloped off with her on his pony or otherwise abstracted her, and the marriage was solemnized in Bougival. Shortly afterward they sailed on the Cymric for New York. For what was there for them to do in Paris? Both of them were out of place there, whereas on the cactus-strewn mesas of the Far West she would at least be a rare object standing out against the landscape, an exotic flower. (And indeed this was perhaps precisely why he had come to Paris, to seek out and marry a Goan of Portuguese ancestry who spoke no English and would be the only bride in New Mexico to wear a sari.) The marriage lasted only a few weeks or a few months, but here I am only guessing. Why did she come back afterward? Probably, I imagine, because the bridegroom had left her entirely penniless after he galloped off to be slain in the attack on the Apache chief Victorio near Blanco, New Mexico, an event which is referred to in footnotes in the more complete histories but which was eclipsed by the more spectacular demise of General Custer at the Little Bighorn the following year—a year in which, as it happened, I was working as a janitor in the Swedish exhibit at the Centennial Exposition in Philadelphia and saving my money to study natural philosophy at Johns Hopkins.

At any rate the return of the young widow to Quai d'Orléans is not hard to imagine—the sloe-eyed beauty contrite but seraphic, the aunt slashing at her with little chops of her head: "Miscreant! Betrayer of your proud race! Debased plaything and slave of the five-limbed! Put on your sari, dab the vermilion of purdah on your forehead, and henceforth eat my bread in sorrow! You will leave the house only accompanied by servants. And woe to you if the pentapod has implanted a child in your womb!" Crushed by this curse, and yet perhaps with a faint demi-smile something like Luisa's at the corner of her mouth, the sloe-eyed one retired to her room to spend the rest of her life as a kind of heirloom, a grandfather's clock or an old family retainer. And when her abdomen swelled, the aunt's wrath (I could imagine) turned to sarcasm, tempered only slightly by the eventual revelation that the cause and consequence of the swelling was a female child. There she stood, the aunt—in my mind's eye—with her own sideways and merciless smile of derision, remarking with faint judders of her head to the servants or perhaps to the sloe-eyed one herself, "I know how to prevent conception with an ordinary five-franc coin. Grip it between your knees and hold it there constantly in the presence of the opposite sex."

•

Yet there were dislocations of fact here, mysteries surrounding mysteries and others inside them. For instance: I learned quite by accident that there was a brother in the family whose existence I had not suspected, un nommé Theodor. Luisa referred to him quite casually one day, apropos of her plans, rather vague ones, to spend a few days on the Italian lakes, either alone or with persons unnamed. "Possibly Teddy will be there," she remarked abstractedly. At this point I had not put things together sufficiently to realise that Theodor's existence was inconsistent with my whole theory or web of conjecture about the marriage of the mother with the cowboy and his almost immediate massacre by the Apaches, and it merely seemed to me a wonder that she had a brother who had never been referred to before. "Why is he never around?" "Oh, he comes and goes. He is attending a military school. He is studying to be an officer." "Like me?" I suggested, faintly jealous perhaps and also a little amused. "Oh no, not at all, he is going to be a real officer, who will fight in wars and kill people, and be decorated for bravery." Bravo for him. Back in my lodgings, of course, it soon penetrated to me that the existence of Theodor required a much longer conjectural marriage of the mother and the cowboy, a pair of years at the minimum, it seemed to me in my male obtusity about such matters, or else a second and

quite inconceivable escapade of the mother (with another person? With
the ghost of the demised cowboy?) some months after the first. By the
principle of economy this last was a poor story; one elopement was an
adventure, two verged on the farcical. Perhaps then the two children
were twins; but Luisa had implied she was the older, or had she? Once
when I was talking to the aunt about something quite different, I found
my attention wandering because a part of my mind, as I discovered,
was still pondering over this enigma. Realizing I had lost track of what
the aunt was talking about anyhow, I asked her impulsively, "And your
nephew—is he older or younger than Luisa? I am sorry that it is so
stupid of me to forget."

"Who?"

"Theodor."

Her eyes narrowed on me keenly. "And who told you of this?" Like
an eagle she fixed me; nay, nay, nay quivered her chin.

"Luisa."

"Pay no attention to her. It is only her vapours. What nonsense!"

And that was the end of it. Luisa might be vapourous, this I was
willing to concede and perhaps even had evidence for it that was
not at the disposal of the aunt, but surely this did not affect the fact
that she was either older or younger than her brother? Or a twin; I
had forgotten this alternative. The plague take these sibyls and their
dithyrambs! Yet that mysterious and improbable wedlock of a generation
ago still held my attention and puzzled me, for reasons I could identify
only obscurely. For example: in those brief weeks, months, or pair of
years of their idyll, however long it had lasted, what language did the
newlyweds speak? The sloe-eyed one was reared in Portuguese, with a
substratum from the servants of whatever the indigenous language is in
that part of the world, Urdu, I imagine, and received no education at
all. The cowboy spoke American and no doubt some twangy French.
But what use was this in abducting a Goan beauty from a seraglio?
Sign language goes well up to a point, but in the long evenings alone
there are serious matters to be discussed. I imagined her articulating to
the ardent bridegroom, timidly, "You know mifeuya?" And in a flash of
insight, probably erroneous, I saw in this business of language the key
to her secret existence; the mother I mean. Suppose for the purpose
of argument we have a person of normal intelligence, reared by bad-

tempered servants in no language at all or in baby talk, and suppose we imagine this person flung at an age of twenty into a multilingual society of bewildering complexity—a society which commonly substitutes speech for action—this person, struggling to express herself in three words of Urdu and badly pronounced French, might well be regarded by universal agreement as lacking in wit; a term which, especially in its French version esprit, is frequently confused with the ability to express oneself in well-constructed epigrams. An individual widely regarded as an imbecile will end by sharing the opinion. And so the mother, no doubt, totally withdrew herself from this world of salon intellectualism where the play of minds was rigorously verbal and the failure to recognize an allusion to Henri de Régnier a disgrace, and limited her satisfactions to the realm where language was superfluous, i.e., the world of the senses. She operated so successfully in this sphere that she was able to capture the slim-hipped and legendary if somewhat impecunious hero of the Far West—simply, no doubt, by keeping her mouth shut and directing her sloe eyes to advantage—and thus accomplished what the aunt was probably incapable of even if she had not regarded it as beneath her contempt; that is, reproducing herself in the normal female way. As for the frontiersman, we can believe he died happy, content with his own reckless courage and knowing his progeny assured, even though in an odd kind of household. The mother then retreated to the only other kind of sensualism available to her, gluttony, and who can blame her? She might have taken up drugs, or young footmen. Judgments of one's fellow human beings are very complex. Perhaps in time I would come to understand the aunt too, and forgive her for being what God had made her.

Whether or not I was correct about all this, it was clear that the mother had found a way of life only moderately damaging to the health and not requiring complicated sentences. A certain mythology existed about her in the household, according to which she was supposed to have no opinions and was not to be told anything shocking. Her soul was supposed to be covered with a neat and shiny coat of varnish, which nothing could penetrate. Yet occasionally a spark of personality asserted itself in unexpected ways. She was never actively drawn to anything, except food; her days of passion were behind her. But her organ of repulsion was still vigorous. She "took dislikes," as Luisa said. Sometimes a ray of sunlight striking her in the eye, or an unfortunate remark of a guest, would produce an embarrassing reaction. There was the bluff English consular official, for example, who was pleased to be amused at her caste mark. "I see you've got your sealing wax on," he told her with British joviality. "Ready to be posted." She smiled at him timidly. She was holding a teacup, and in an odd gesture, almost as though she were offering a toast, she raised it to the maximum height she could reach in the sari she was wearing, about the level of her head. Since she was short and he about six feet tall, this brought the cup to the level of his chest. He observed it with perplexity, and she told him rather anxiously, "Moment," as a sign that he should not go away but remain exactly where he was. Going to the sideboard, she set down the teacup and bent over the ottoman from a nearby sofa. Struggling under this weight, she brought the ottoman to the Englishman and set it before him, a little to one side. Then she returned to the sideboard for the teacup, mounted with it onto the ottoman which raised her almost to the same level as the Englishman, lifted the cup with the gesture as before, and poured the contents over his head. Then, getting down from the ottoman, she turned to the spectators and remarked quite calmly and more or less apropos de rien, "I hate a fool." It became necessary to lead her out of the room. "Mother is singular," Luisa would say smoothly at such moments. It was an accurate Dickensian adjective and the more patient observer perceived what he ought to have seen long before, that the mother was thoroughly in command of her behavior and that very little happened to her in the world that she had not chosen to happen. This life of hers was singular, from the simple syllables she pronounced only after some thought to the systematic manner in which she ate toast, afterward moistening her ten fingers at her lips in exact order, then wiping them on the napkin one after the other in the same sequence. If it were contrary to all likelihood that her emotions were so violent, it was even more extraordinary that she controlled them with such precision. Regarded in this light her abduction or seduction by the frontiersman turned in the mind's eye into a positive act and one that she had willed herself, and even Luisa herself became more plausible. All members of the family, I was beginning to see, shared certain traits; tempered in Luisa's case by the laconic and graceful recklessness of the cowboy.

•

"The wind is veering. South-southwest now. It's come around more than a point."

Theodor, the scarf still bound around his head, is standing by the theodolite watching me with his dark bedouin eyes. For a fraction of a second I fail to grasp what he is talking about. Then I sight into the instrument, check the compass, and see that he is correct. Had I been asleep? No, my eyes were only closed for the five minutes or so I had allowed myself to rest them briefly from this whiteness.

"A little woolgathering, eh, Major? Looked as though you were in the Land of Nod."

Not feeling in the mood for bluff repartee, I ignore Waldemer and address myself to the meteorological question.

"More wind now too. Must be thirty knots. A gust from the east would be helpful. We're already off course to the right. But the wind will back as the cyclonic system passes over us. And then come around to the north, in a day or two."

With the cold stiffening my lips this is about as long a speech as I care to make, at least on technical subjects. The temperature is steady at minus ten centigrade. The wind scours along the pack below us, sending streamers of cake flour sliding along its surface and making a sound like a dull hum. That slightly sharper grumble is the noise of the ice grinding and splitting against itself. Strange that in this cutting gale we feel no wind at all and have the impression of floating in a calm. We are even sheltered from the snow by the swelling girth of silk overhead; it is as though we were suspended under an immense umbrella. In the well-equipped gondola there is a feeling of safety, a coziness, as though in this tempest, in this most inhospitable part of the world, we are somehow immune to all the worst that nature can contrive. This immunity is an illusion; the weight of snow is accumulating on precisely that upper hemisphere of the silk we can't see, and down here below, a thin and crystalline rime is slowly forming on everything, the ropes, the wicker of the gondola, the balloon itself. This sugar candy will eventually weigh tons and destroy us, if something isn't done about it. Yet for some reason I am unable to feel any sense of peril, and probably my companions are the same. We are conscious only of cold, and of an immense and absolute isolation.

While I was resting, curled up in a corner of the gondola with the hood drawn over my face, Waldemer has busied himself by making lunch. It is four o'clock in Greenwich, but we pay heed to the clock only for navigation purposes and eat whenever we have the chance. The fragrance of beef stew rises from below us. If it were quiet we might hear the hiss of these large snowflakes falling into the hot pan on the stove, but it is not quiet; constantly in our ears is the vague and muffled rumble from the pack below.

Theodor is still watching me reflectively, with the same expression on his face that I saw when I opened my eyes only a few minutes before. It isn't at all an anxious expression and there is even, it seems to me, a trace of irony in it.

"And the weight of this snow on the balloon. What will we do about it?"

"This is only a squall. It will pass quickly."

"And the rime is forming on the rigging."

"Knock it off with a mallet if you want something to do."

But his mood isn't active, only observant and reflective, with tendencies even to the metaphysical.

"Do you know, I think I used to dream of this place as a child. You've brought me to a strange part of the world, Gustav. This whiteness . . . this space with no walls, no horizon, as though we were floating in a universe without matter and only white space around us . . . and this kind of white thunder coming from a distance. Do you think it's possible to dream of a place—a real place— you've never seen, and then later find that your dream was real?"

"When I was a child I used to dream about America."

"And what did you dream of?"

"Buffalo, and prairies."

"And when you came to America, did you find the buffalo and the prairies?"

"No, when I came it was to Philadelphia. All I saw were horse cars."

Waldemer looks up curiously when I mention his native land, but returns his attention to the stew as soon as he realises our conversation is metaphysical.

"And what do you dream of here in the gondola when you sleep?"

"Paris, at times. At times, other places."

"So much? But you've hardly been asleep."

This is true; it strikes me too as a little curious. But if this whiteness continues, this sphere of milky ether that surrounds us on all sides including above and below, it won't be necessary to sleep in order to dream; the mind itself will fix on its own images for lack of anything outside it to grasp. I open my eyes: whiteness. I close them: blood veins and sparks, symptoms of mild irritation from cold and white light. It is important to fix on something, in order for the consciousness not to be spread out, dissolved, lost in this dimensionless milk. I try to recall in my mind the exact dimensions, the plan, the furniture of my lodgings in rue de Rennes, the salon with its dusty brocade hangings and its window that looked out on a white enameled sign across the street saying BOULANGERIE PÂTISSERIE and next door to it VILLE DE PARIS SERVICE MUNICIPAL DES POMPES FUNÈBRES in gold letters on black, the little hall that led to the bedroom one way and to the W.C. the other, the parquet floor that became as familiar to me as my own hand as I pondered there, staring at it for hours, at grips with the baffling enigma of constructing a wave detector for aeromagnetic emanations which would produce an audible signal for the operator. That white waste of the unknown, filled with invisible mathematical formulae, was as formless and frustrating as a storm in the arctic. The crux of the problem, I grasped finally, was the rectification or filtering of these electrical tremblings in the air, so that what remained of them would move in only one direction and thus have the capability of activating a magnetophone. I had rejected Signor Marconi's "coherer," filled with metal filings, as too delicate and too easily disturbed by joggings for the use I had in mind for it. Instead, my attention was caught by several papers of Krobenius in which he described the properties of certain mineral crystals which allowed an electrical flux to pass through them in one direction but not in another. These papers— unpublished and existing only in manuscript form in the Bibliothèque Sainte-Geneviève—I studied with some care, although they were less enlightening than I had hoped. In them Krobenius was reticent about the identity of the minerals used in his investigations, describing them only as "certains sels cohésifs de la famille plombière." I then wrote for and obtained an appointment to visit him in his studio in Neuilly, but this interview was somewhat unproductive. Krobenius, an eccentric octogenarian in a long grey smock, denied having worked with crystals and pretended to be deaf when I referred to the manuscripts I had found in the library. As I was being ushered out of the studio with a rather perfunctory courtesy, however, I did catch a glimpse of an envelope on the table: a bill from a well-known dealer in gems and minerals in Place Saint-André-des-Arts. It was a simple matter to go to this dealer and request, "I have just come from Professor Krobenius, and would like samples of the same cohesive salts of the lead family which you sold to him, I am sorry, the name slips my mind."

The crystal in question proved to be galena. Provided with a dozen small grey and gleaming chips of this substance, I hastened feverishly back to my lodgings. The antenna wire I had draped out the window, to the great disapproval of the concierge. The filter or wave sieve of Signor Marconi, which allowed only waves of a predetermined length to pass, I was already familiar with and had built several. It consisted of a coil of fine wire wound around a cylinder and operating in conjunction with a spark condenser of tinfoil and paper. The coil was provided with a sliding contact that enabled me to vary the wavelength at will. To one of these contrivances I now hastily connected a crystal from the dozen in the envelope. The only remaining step was to wire the Bell magnetophone to this arrangement in such a way that the rectified pulses would activate its diaphragm; I was not sure how to go about this and a good deal of trial and error would be necessary. Unrolling a length of high-quality silver solder, I had just begun to heat the soldering iron over a spirit lamp when the pest of a concierge knocked on the door. Under ordinary circumstances this individual left me alone, having learned that I was a person of solitary habits with a tendency to ferocity, and she ventured as far as my lair on the fifth floor only when she had something of importance to communicate, like a telegram.

The door being unlocked, I called for her to enter, still preoccupied with the task of heating the iron.

"Pardon. A monsieur to see you."

"What kind of a monsieur?"

"A foreigner."

"Well, I am a foreigner myself. What else?"

"A military person, young, of good manners."

"Well, show the infernal nuisance in." I still wasn't paying complete attention. I tried the heat of the iron with a wet forefinger.

There presently appeared in the doorway a very young man, hardly more than a youth to judge from his smooth cheek, with a long-faced and dark-eyed sort of handsomeness, improbably clad in the uniform of a German military academy. The cap seemed almost too heavy for his slight neck to support, but he did not take it off.

"Monsieur Crispin?"

I nodded, undecided whether to put the iron down or to go on with my work.

"I have the honour to present myself. I am Luisa's brother." Definitely, although reluctantly, I put the iron down. "Ah, you are Teddy!"

But he was cool, nodded only faintly, and evidently would have preferred a more formal mode of address. I picked up the iron again, examined it, and wondered again if I might not go on heating it as he talked. "And so—to what do I owe the honour?"

"As you know, our family is without a father. So it seems I am called upon to function in a parental locus. It is not a role I would have chosen. But my obligation in the matter is clear. In short, I am the tutelar head of a family, and one to which you stand in an ambiguous relation."

"You seem to make a great deal of rigmarole about it. Why don't you sit down?"

While he spoke he fixed me with an unmoving and very determined paleness, exactly like Luisa. "It isn't customary under the circumstances. I must make it clear that my intentions in this matter are purely formal. I have no animus against you personally. But, in my function as head of family, it is necessary for me to call you formally to account for your actions."

He spoke well, this lad. They trained him in rhetoric, perhaps, in the German military academy.

"What actions are you speaking of?"

"I am not here to relate anecdotes, which you know better than I. What are your intentions in regard to Luisa?"

Hurrah! Here we come to it! The whole business, including his nervousness and his rather amateurish hauteur, gave the impression that he was acting in a school play set in the eighteenth century, Schiller's *Don Carlos* perhaps. There was something incongruous about his standing there with his hat on and making this speech in the epoch of railway trains and coulomb apparatus. He wanted to know my intentions in regard to Luisa! Thunder and consternation! What were her intentions in regard to me? From all appearances he was capable of calling me out to fire pistols at each other over a handkerchief, this fragile youth with the determined set at the corner of his mouth, simply because through sheer accident (to oversimplify very greatly) I had passed a night with his sister in a Finnish farmhouse.

He spoke in a birdlike but level, well modulated, even slightly menacing voice. He was hardly more than an adolescent. "Might I ask how old you are?"

"That has no pertinence whatever to the matter at hand. I am eighteen."

"You look sixteen, if you will pardon me for saying so, in any case too young to burst into rooms calling people to account for matters you can hardly understand. Have you much experience of women?"

"That is even less pertinent," he said, stiffening. "I visit the establishments provided, as necessary for hygiene."

"Bravo! Your hygiene seems excellent, as far as I can tell. In that case, what the devil business do you have interfering between two mature people who have contracted a friendship?"

"Do I have your word as an officer and a gentleman that your relations with Luisa may be described by the term contraction of a friendship?"

"Absolutely."

"I have information that they are more."

"Your information is erroneous."

"You are aware that there is a fiancé?"

"So I have heard."

"You don't regard yourself in that role?"

"I hope not."

"You are aware that, in polite society, it is improper to offer attentions to a young lady to whom one's intentions are not serious?"

"My intentions are very serious."

"And they are?"

"To instruct her in science." I was not quite without malice in this. He was putting me out of sorts.

"My information is that, last Tuesday at a quarter past three, you were affectionate with her behind a doorway."

"I will never do so again! Bother take her and her kisses!"

I was firm too now and getting quite angry. I stood facing him and holding the soldering iron. I was at my most leonine; the points of my mustache bristled, no doubt, and the short stiff hair over my temples rose as it does on such occasions. We confronted each other; he turned even paler than before if that were possible, but he did not retreat an inch.

I waited for him to say, "A friend will call upon you this evening. Please provide him with the name of your second." And what would I do then? Pack my baggage and go back to Sweden with my tail between my legs? No, by Thunder, not for this stripling! I would meet him in the Bois and no doubt end with a bullet in my pancreas or some other uncomfortable place, since they undoubtedly taught him to shoot at his Militärische Hochschule whatever else was on the curriculum.

But instead of pronouncing this formula he hesitated for an instant, his mouth gathering faintly at the edges as he met my glance, and in that moment his chance to be a Schiller hero slipped away from him. He wanted to live too, perhaps, and for all he knew I was a real officer instead of a fraudulent engineer-cum-librarian who lived on a diet of paper and had never been near an academy. His dark eyes never flinched, however.

"And so you affirm that your intentions in regard to Luisa are honourable?"

"Absolutely," I replied in an almost gentle voice. I might have responded that Don Juan or even Jack the Ripper, possibly, were honourable men according to their lights and you achieved very little in the world by going around asking people to their faces if they were honourable, but perhaps he would find this out for himself in time, and I decided to leave the matter with this single word.

"Then I must be satisfied. I have nothing further to demand. I am sorry to have disturbed you."

"You haven't disturbed me at all. It was a pleasure to make your acquaintance. And now, if you will excuse me, I will go back to my crystals."

"You are a crystallographer?" "I am a magneto-electrical aereographer, and just now I am using this silver solder to affix these copper wires to an octahedron of galena. Stay and hold the wires in place for me, and afterward we can go to lunch."

"That is not called for in my function," he said, stiffly as before, but with a slight trace of regret I thought. We parted amicably. He had called upon me with a quite spurious challenge and been satisfied with a blatant lie. What nonsense, to lose one's temper at a schoolboy! I had the impression that at a certain point in our interview—when I had managed to lower my voice and respond quite candidly to him as one human being to another, even though my candor was only partly sincere—he had in spite of himself felt an impulse of admiration or attraction to me—he was very young. In spite of his lack of prominent maleness, or perhaps because of this, he seemed to long vaguely for a friendship with me on equal and male terms, a friendship that would be the symmetrical opposite of that scene of antagonism in which we had confronted each other as officer to officer and he had called me to account for my actions. The young idiot!

I went back to my apparatus. The soldering was soon done, although the spirit lamp hardly got the iron hot enough, and I busied myself bending the hairspring of a watch into a tickler to probe on the surface of the crystal, as described by Krobenius in his paper. With growing excitement, forcing myself to slow down and verify each step as I went, I connected the magnetophone and put the receiver to my ear, then began scratching cautiously on the surface of the galena with the spring. Nothing. Some connection must be insufficiently soldered, or perhaps the arrangement of crystal and coil needed to be altered. Plague and perdition! How could I do any serious work with all these interruptions? I would do better to crate this whole bundle of rubbish and take it back to Stockholm, where I could work under excellent conditions in the laboratory of the Institute. And why didn't I? What in the name of electromagnetism held me in Paris, this city of women and perfumed puppets in top hats? Reasons of hygiene, no doubt.

•

And what did Luisa want exactly? Did she want a list of apparatus? Did she want to hold the wires while I soldered them to the galena? No, she wanted me to take her to the opera. A cape with a red velvet lining rather appealed to me, but I had never worn an opera hat in my life and I did not propose to begin now.

We had it out in her boudoir, so-called, furnished with a dressing table and a certain number of armchairs, and connecting with her chamber, where I had not yet been so fortunate as to set foot. "Voyez, ma très chère amie," I reminded her firmly but with a formal and even elaborate courtesy, "I am not here in Paris to enjoy the opera, or even cafe concerts at the Royal. I am here to do serious work of a scientific nature, work which in all modesty I believe to have some slight importance." (It was not for her to ask why I couldn't do it in Stockholm, and a good thing it wasn't, because I would have been at a loss to answer.) "But at the very brink of what seems to me an important advance in knowledge, I am distracted by the necessity of escorting you to all these café concerts and other frivolities which—it seems you cannot attend alone without the danger of being violated in the streets. And if that weren't enough, now it seems there is this plaguey young idiot of a brother who visits me to pose these quaint medieval questions of honour, which I am at a loss to respond to even if I had the time."

She seemed not at all surprised that he had come to see me. "Ah well, Teddy," she said negligently. "He's a child, he likes to play at tin soldiers and imagines he's one himself. He is quite harmless and we are all fond of him."

"I might be fond of him myself, blast take it, but the point is that all these interruptions and botherings are distracting, it's not the proper mental atmosphere for serious thought. Worth, the Royal, the Salle Meyer! *Your* existence is delightful no doubt, but what about mine? We've come a long way, it seems to me, from the Musée Carnavalet! It would be pleasant, I have no doubt, to be two butterflies flitting together over a sunlit meadow, but . . ." Well, she knew what I meant. I stopped talking.

"Ah, my existence," she said with a little sigh. "It's very fine no doubt. Oh, how I envy you, my friend. You're a man, you can come and go as you please. And when you are a foreigner, no one knows you in Paris, and you can ignore what people think."

Her manner of reasoning was helical, turning round and round a subject while rising in vehemence, but never quite getting to the point. If I could ignore what people thought, I might have responded, it was because I spent all day shut up in a rented room with a lot of wires and crystals so that no one had the slightest interest in what I did. If she meant my being affectionate behind doorways, as Theodor put it, that was at least as much her fault as mine. And what was the point about foreigners, since she was a foreigner herself?

"Evidently you can come and go as you please too," I pointed out, "since you were able to come to Stockholm without visible damage to your reputation."

She gave me one of her firm, searching, slightly hostile looks. But there was no irony in my manner, or none showed, and she decided it was not tactical to take umbrage.

"And even to Finland, you might have added."

"Even to Finland.""You were pleased to be sarcastic, once, about the Italian lakes," she reminded me.

"But Stresa is a very pleasant place."

"No doubt. And this is apropos of?"

"Nothing, except that my Pondicherry uncle, who never comes to Europe, owns a villa there."

"Thank you very much for the invitation, but, as I have tried to explain in my stumbling way, I have researches that unfortunately keep me in Paris."

"Oh, you are a *thing*," she declared, her mouth tightening in vexation. "I haven't made you an invitation."

"And had you intended to?"

"Yes, I had, in due time, but you force a person into the most awkward situations, crudities even, through this ill-mannered habit of yours of leaping to the end of a speech before one has got there."

"I am sorry. Please start over again and deliver the whole speech, and I will listen attentively."

"What might have been a delightful sojourn you have now made impossible."

"It is impossible anyhow, because my work keeps me here."

"You can bring your wires and crystals to Italy. No one will disturb you."

"I'm not quite sure I understand. *You* will not disturb me?"

"You take me for a frivolous woman, I know. How can I convince you that I am interested in serious matters? If fashionable young men were all that is needed, I can assure you, there are plenty in the offing."

(This an allusion, no doubt, to the mysterious and Peninsular fiancé.) "But if you will make only a slight effort of the memory, you will recall that our friendship began initially because of my deep interest in your scientific work. J'ai une telle envie d'être sérieuse!"

"In that case, you can come to rue de Rennes and hold the wires while I solder them."

"Then you won't come to Stresa?"

"What is it exactly that we can do in Stresa and cannot do here?"

"Oh, bother!" she burst, exasperated, and turned to the window.

•

It is impossible to shut out this marrow-piercing cold, but the whiteness at any rate can be excluded by shutting the eyes. At least one of my senses, thank God, is voluntary. The whiteness is an illusion, and so is the blackness, or rather the deep charcoal grey that replaces it when the eyes are closed. This light filtering through the lids ought to be pink; has my blood too turned pale in this penetrating milkiness, am I exsanguinated? I ought to have eaten my beef stew, and perhaps I have, I muse vaguely from my vantage point somewhere just on the verge of consciousness, since its odour is no longer apparent. Or perhaps I forgot to eat it because my mind has involuntarily rejected nourishment, although why it should do this is an enigma I am too far from an objective and rational state just now to examine. The human head, that undiscovered planet. There is a lot to be explained yet by somebody, Dr. James or perhaps Charcot, about how this fine machine works. For instance, I am almost entirely awake now but the words from the Paris boudoir still ring in my head as though they had been spoken only a moment before. "Oh, bother!" Bother indeed. It is a bother to be cold, to be hungry, to be driven by this imbecilic impulse to entangle one's limbs ardorously with other persons with whom one may not have very much else in common. It is a bother to rush off to unlikely parts of the globe for purposes that, when regarded calmly, seem quite unnecessary. "All the trouble in the world," I believe it was Pascal who said, "comes because men will not remain quietly in their own rooms," or something like that. With the steely effort of will I have mastered now through long practice, I force myself back to sleep, not to sleep but to slip out of consciousness and into a realm of myself where I know a certain happiness lies, to *dream true*. For a while what courses through the brain filaments comes partly from the epidermis and retina, partly from more mysterious telegraph stations in another country, places we are forbidden to go when awake. I know where I want to go, but to go there I must take a journey. Since it is necessary, I abandon myself to these consecutive, vivid, and yet disconnected impressions of a tiresome trip over an entirely unnecessary number of Alps. The pictures are all in the right order but tilted to one side or the other and wavery; some small boy has scratched or bent the stereopticon. Dijon. A lake with poplars. Dôle, a square church steeple. Cinders and rushing air, rattle of carrosserie, the odour of coal-burning machinery mingled with that of some hygienic Swiss disinfectant, then via wuerstel & mustard, a humble but nourishing Teutonic smell, to the chemical odour of soap (I remember that the soap had the legend KROEBER impressed into it) and so to Milano Stazione Centrale, an enormous crystal roof full of steam and noise, with the odour of hot rolls, Libri, giornali! Portabagagli! Outside a broad piazza in the sunshine. Carrozza, signore? Subito, subito, ecco! Creak of harness and wheel grit on dusty road, and so on to the villa on the hillside. A view over the lake, with some vineyards around it, and here and there in the middle distance a peasant tying up the vines. November; the sun warm but an autumnal chill in the air as the shadows grow longer.

All this is banal and might have been expected from a perusal of tourist brochures. But abruptly, in an absolute silence broken only by the faint cries of birds, a portrait by Vermeer appears in the doorway. A composition so fixed in its outline and every nuance of colour that it can be examined months or even years later with each of its qualities intact. The frame an arched doorway of greyish stone; behind this a quantity of mimosa and a marble balustrade. The light as in all Vermeers from behind and to one side, illuminating the subject diagonally. A long gown of pink brocade falling to the floor, drawn in to a high waist under the breasts. The forearms in the full sleeves crossed lightly over the waist, ending in a pair of finely modeled hands with fingers absently twined together. Hands, shoulders, and gown turned partly away, since she had come from the courtyard still illuminated with the fading daylight into the darker salon and turned to face me so that the soft mass of hair was drawn back over the shoulder. The singular visage with its pale llama-like brow and long lip, the mouth that tightened only slightly at the corners, contemplated me with a seraphic calm. And everything, it seemed to me, lay in this expectant and mysterious apparition of pastel tapestry, lay concealed and yet eloquent, its existence promised only in the white reality of the hands and face. I didn't move, neither did she, and our very motionlessness and failure to speak was oracular, announcing to both of us that something wordless and transcendent was about to manifest itself, perhaps something powerful and pagan concealed in the green and tepid involutions of these wine hills. In the silence I heard the unmistakable, grating, violin-like note of the evening's first cicada.

In some way my cigar was put out, she moved about eluding me playfully down the corridor with her demi-Gioconda smile, and we were transported weightlessly into a yellow room full of angled evening shadows. High-ceilinged, painted in vivid Pompeiian ochre, shuttered windows facing the lake, which through the narrow horizontal openings could be seen below and not very far away, wrinkling in the evening breeze. When I turned from these shutters the brocade was in the act of slipping from—in contrast to its own elegance and stiffness—an astonishingly fragile shoulder. The fiendish craft of that gown became apparent—under it the eye expected a pink analogous to the brocade, but the reality was so far finer and paler that the soul received a little shock, a spasm of unbelief. She was adept at prophecies; the Vermeer glance had foretold the yellow room, the brocaded gown her complexion. It had been cold in Finland, it was warm here, so that this demonstration could be as prolonged and intricate as she liked. In such a climate she evidently did not feel that any clothing other than the gown was necessary. Standing with her feet a little apart on the marble floor, she removed a white carnation from the bouquet at the bedside and turned to me for a moment with the flower held at her throat in a kind of misdirected pudeur, then laid it with a slightly exaggerated theatricality on the linen expanse of the bed. There it lay, that plaguish virginal blossom, long like her American legs and rather self-consciously symbolic. The hypocrite! It was not in flower gardens that she had learned this thing of standing with her feet slightly apart and one foot turned out in the boyish grace of a dancer (perhaps that was it, the aunt had sent her to ballet classes), so that at the place where the legs finally came together a space of yellow wall was visible between them; nor this gesture of loosing the hair ribbon with both hands raised to the left, the hardly more than adolescent breasts inclining at an angle and causing a faint and corresponding crease to appear in the waist at the right; nor the candor of the forward-held hips, the apex of the triangle between them shaded in the exact texture of the dark mass that fell over her shoulders: in short, was this the would-be balloonist and magnetographer? Something was seriously in disparity here.

I was in no mood or state for puzzles, however; I postponed cerebration and surrendered myself to the passing moment. Our limbs fitted ingeniously; as in Finland no doubt, although there in the tumult of the occasion I had not noticed it. So nicely were these arms, legs, and so on suited to interweave that they seemed to find their way to each other by themselves without our paying very much attention to how it was done, so that these arrangements and the resultant ecstasies took place, so to speak, quite separate from ourselves and we were free to mount, soul joined to soul, to higher places than we had anticipated or thought possible, cherubim drunk on light in our spheres of grace and harmony. That yellow room! Its ochre was the colour my veins had hungered for. Did they know what they were doing, these arteries pounding in their excessive way? They would do themselves some harm. At last this pulsing that had before seemed generalized throughout my circulatory system, and hers too for all I knew, gathered to a single place, trembled for what seemed an infinitely prolonged instant on the brink of overflowing, and then sprang out arclike and keen in, I was quite certain as I examined the catalogue of my experiences, a totally unprecedented intensity. This phenomenon grew fainter, but only very gradually, like waves dying on sand after a storm.

•

We lay for some time like exhausted swimmers, able to reach the beach but not to rise or crawl entirely from the water that still lapped at our ankles. When at last we extricated our slackened limbs and drew apart on that canopied Empire bed, she had the air of being pleased with herself. Pushing back with one hand the mass of soft hair that had fallen over her face, she revealed once more the keen intelligence behind that serene and lofty brow. She was curious about everything. What was that extraordinary large vein here, the one she almost touched with her forefinger? I explained that a man required, at certain times, a copious supply of blood just there. Ah. Might from my point of view this miracle be repeated after a suitable interval? All things would happen in the plenitude of time, I assured her abstractedly. (If she kept pointing things out with her finger this way they surely would.) Whether they would be miracles would depend on the circumstances. She was blithe about the probability. "You know, it's my jour de fête today, I'm twenty."

"Incredible."

"How? You would have expected me younger, or older?" I didn't know what I meant exactly. Perhaps just that it was incredible she should have any age at all.

At a certain point it was (I felt) my turn to be curious. "How is it that your elders permit you, not yet having reached the age of majority, to go wandering off in this way across the map of Europe so freely?"

"Who would prevent me?"

"Your aunt for instance."

"Ah, ma tante." And she explained that the aunt for all her obdurate bosom (one was obdurate, the other cotton wadding) was indulgent toward female peregrinations, believing that the frailer sex should be accorded at least the same freedom of movement permitted to the male. And if a young gentleman of good family should take it into his head to travel via Wagon-Lit from Paris to Stresa, who would gainsay him?

Who indeed? "Still, I was under the impression you had certain attachments."

"I don't understand to what you are referring. Your way of speaking is so abstract sometimes."

"If I am not mistaken, you possess somewhere, although you may temporarily have mislaid him, a fiancé."

"Ah, the artillerist!" She burst into peals of laughter. He was a clumsy fellow to whom one sometimes gave sweetmeats, pour s'amuser. She would introduce us sometime and I would see for myself that he was not to be taken seriously. Except by himself; he was of the sort that took everything seriously, to the point where he was a bore. And full of vanities, over matters for which he could hardly take the credit. It was the aunt herself who had christened him the Peninsula because of—how should I say? How had Luisa herself put it?—because of the diameter and span of his young manly powers. The mother too was privy to this joke. "Mother is singular. She never liked Alberto because of his chin." Neither had I, and now I knew why. The eyebrows too! I was not sure how I was supposed to respond to confidences of this sort. What pitiless and obscene name would these Valkyries devise for me? The Pipestem, perhaps, or the One-Round Revolver. In wiser ages they had burned old women who were too prescient. And was the Peninsular Campaign likely to continue? "Don't be crude. I have already told you he was a nonentity." How, crude? It was I who was crude? It was too feminine for me.

In this whole expedition through tunnels and over Alps and culminating in the villa and its yellow room, I had been aware of a vague feeling of apprehension, or restiveness, that I was gradually able to identify as a suspicion that I was on my honeymoon. Of all the roles that fate in its malice might set in my path the character of bridegroom, I felt, was the one that suited me least. Now another thought struck me, or a variation or subtlety, and an even more disquieting one: that I was on my honeymoon and she was not. She had chosen to accompany me, perhaps, to tell me amusing stories. There were invisible and probably sinister forces working here against which it was necessary to be on one's guard. To this caution the vigorous sap of life in me responded that what had happened had made me rapturously happy. But this was just the point. On this joy, to strangle it, I leaped deftly like a wild beast. My very being and what it called me to do were in peril here. Because, if matters continued this way, I knew for a certainty that the day would come when she, the plucky adventuress who had accompanied me on the Finnish flight and pulled the wrong ballast string in the wicker car, would end by begging me with tears in her eyes not to risk myself and instead to remain by her side here, there, in the yellow room or some other place, in the bliss of domestic intimacy. And that every fibre of my being opposed; it was precisely because it tempted me, this happiness, that I struggled against it so fiercely.

It was not really she, I knew now in a kind of prescience, but those two witches in Quai d'Orléans who had spun this spell about me in their war against an enemy who was not even properly aware he was being attacked. It would be necessary to oppose them with all the power of my own being. The trouble was that such a defence required technique and skill, and my understanding of woman, I now began to see, was imperfect. My vanity of a healthy male had led me to the delusion that, from a dozen or so adventures in my native city, I was adept enough at dealing with a sex which (I believed) was either hopelessly disarmed by its innocence or rendered accessible by its very lack of this quality. But those well-bred Ingrids and Kristins whose hands one clasped in their wealthy fathers' orangeries, those ineptly rouged wenches in dockside taverns, were mechanisms of a misleading simplicity. With sighs to one, and small sums of money to the other, one might do as he wished. What one wished to do, of course, was not the same with the one as with the other. But with the one and the other, from time to time, it passed the hours when one was not busy in the library. Then in recent years my scientific investigations had demanded more and more of my attention. For months at a time I forgot to visit the dockside, and the maidens gave up and married law students. I had reached the age when one's illusions are at least partly behind one, and my prickly short hair, my mustache with its wiry points, and the tuft under my lip were grey at the edges. Now, in my full and ironic manhood, I had somehow fallen into the clutches of this pack of maenads who had begun by clouding my wits and would end by destroying me as they had destroyed Orpheus. I was an autumn crocus, a subject for satire. "Crispin in Love," or better "Crispin Furioso," mad for ardour. This belle sauvage—and I had expected to entertain her with my superior wisdom! And it was not only she, the long-lipped, pale, and faintly contemptuous focus of this delirium that periled me (it was still a mystery how on the one hand she could resemble a llama and on the other hand exert such a powerful spell of desire, when llamas were not considered beautiful and conventional beauty was arranged along quite other lines) but the aunt and mother as well, the wistful Stockholm virgins and the waterfront strumpets, the whole race of cloven tetrapods who inspired man to his most powerful and exalted dreams and then stifled him to earth when he attempted to carry them out. Beware, Crispin! It is your five limbs they envy, and they will not rest until they have made you like themselves.

And yet how cunningly this peril was made! These pale fragilities and corals, these darknesses that drew one's being like a magnet, were the creation of gods who were powerful even though malevolent and must be sacrificed to, else they would destroy. Tomorrow I will leave; no, tomorrow and tomorrow. Wednesday, Thursday. The climate still being mild, and we better acquainted now, the brocaded gown had given way to a mauve peignoir fastened in the front only with a pair of ribbons. Luisa in the baroque doorway, the mimosa in the background, was Delphic against the marble balustrade. The knee appearing in the garment's opening as she turned, leading the eye inevitably upward to the shadow faintly visible in its translucence, was probably only an accident. It was time for tea, the sibyl pronounced. So it was.

"On peut le prendre dans la chambre jaune. Tu veux?"

I wanted. Why tell foolish and unconvincing lies? On the ochre wall the late sun from the lake shimmered imperceptibly. In the distance a voice called in Italian, the evening's first cicada vibrated in the vines. Dear Luisa, why does the peignoir slip from your shoulder when you have not even poured the tea? Soft darkness of hair falling; that Empire bed, with its lilac-flavored linen, is a magnet and a tomb. The tea things are scattered on the bed, the teapot overturned, her faint voice supplicates in my ear, "Oh sweetest one, my love, my cruel Viking, *now*." Slightly moving my foot, I brushed the teacup to the floor and it broke with a tiny tinkle.

16 July 1897

If the wind gods are aware of us at all they must be amused at these efforts we have made to bore a peephole into their secrets. Three overgrown infants swinging in our crib full of toys: popguns, coils of wire, tubes with flat beans of glass in them which we stick to our eyes. The gale, which is only now beginning to weaken, has been pushing us along before it for thirty hours. In which direction? More or less north, I think. The blowing snow almost obscures the surface five hundred metres or so below us, and without a fixed point on the pack to sight in the theodolite we can only roughly estimate the direction of our drift. That magic and not-existent point can't be far now. A red sun full of blood manages to appear fuzzily through the clouds again, and with quick work I am able to take a sight. Theodor has written down the times, I read the altitudes from my instrument and enter them. My cold fingers in the mitten manipulate the pencil clumsily, making the large figures of a child in which the nines and the zeros do not quite close. Have I made a mistake in my calculations? Several no doubt. This frozen piece of paper that I am covering with chicken scratches should be preserved for posterity as an example of human fallibility. Trusting in myself, and in the conviction that five eighths of the way from .10012 to .10048 is .10036, I determine that our latitude is 89° 54' north. And the longitude? What on earth difference does it make only six minutes of arc from the Pole?

I sight back rather carelessly along the compass and see that in the dying wind we are still floating along more or less to the north. A sky full of tattered clouds, the pack below only partly visible through a veil of whitish mist. The drift I estimate at six knots. This wind that has made its last confession and is breathing only feebly must hang on for another hour. Then it must die, and even turn and blow the other way, but only then. The sight was taken at 0118 Greenwich. What's the time now? The time! Time is everything now, there will be no more sights taken and time is our only distance. First I take off my mitten, then without unfastening the toggles of my reindeer-skin coat I reach upward inside it, downward to the trousers pocket, and grope around for the watch. The instrument is finally after a certain fumbling brought to light. One forty-seven Greenwich. Of the six miles to the Pole, I guess roughly, we have covered half. Waldemer, to the maneouvring valve!

"I say now, Major, are you sure of those figures? A fellow wouldn't want to make a mistake, you know."

One fellow wouldn't, perhaps, but the next one might not be so concerned. "Leave the higher calculations to me, and stand by the maneouvring valve!" And if you pull the wrong rope, you lovable blockhead, we are dead.

We sink. Imperceptibly that crinkled and fractured plain of ice comes up through the mist. Damnation! I have forgotten to put my mitten back on. The hand is turning the colour of a granite church in Oslo. My face is probably the same, but I form it into an icy imitation of a smile and remark to Theodor, "Facilis descensus Averni-you know your Virgil?"

"Easy is the descent to Avernus," he finishes for me, "through every day and night the gate of Dis stands open, but to retrace the steps, to return to the upper air, that is the task and the trouble."

"You can see that a classical education, even in a Militärische Hochschule, is of some practical use in the world. It gives advice on handling a balloon. Look sharp now, Waldemer, that stuff below is coming up fast. Leave off spilling gas and spill a little ballast instead!"

A grey rivulet of lead streams down; the ice below is only a hundred metres away now. We are descending far too fast! With a pocket knife I cut away a bag of shot entirely. After a delay of only a few seconds we hear a faint thump from the ice below. Our plummeting has been slowed by the dropped ballast, but now I am concerned about sideways drift. I turn and look north in the direction of our motion, where clumps and uneven blocks of ice are streaming toward us and passing underneath at an alarming rate. Five knots at least! Thunder and tarnation. Unfortunately, we can't pull the bursting valve as we land, because we have a use for the balloon later. At an altitude of ten metres we race over a ridge made of jaggy hillocks. An extraordinary phenomenon—that this lazy drifting, as it seemed when we were higher in the air, has turned into the violence of a charging buffalo as we settle toward the ice.

It would be nice if one could think over in a leisurely manner the best way to handle this maneouvre. But since no human being before us has ever done what we are doing now, we will have to grit our teeth and trust to our instincts. Attention! Achtung! The guide ropes behind us are slithering over those jagged teeth we just missed, slowing us a little. The bottom of the gondola makes contact with snow or soft ice, lifts free again, then strikes more heavily. The gondola tilts sideways with a lurch and the enormous spherical shape over our heads moves on, away from us, with the wind. Is the Prinzess going to go off and leave us? She sways, strains, drags the gondola another bumping metre or two, but Theodor with great presence of mind has dropped to the ice, run back to the guide ropes, seized them in his gloved hands, and pulled backward, digging his boot heels into the soft and crystalline surface under him. The bulk of the gas bag overhead still wishes to travel on but seems content to stop for the moment, straining only slightly.

We can breathe easier.

I pass Theodor the ice anchor and he digs a hole for it and sets it firmly. The only trouble is that the Prinzess, deprived of the weight of both Theodor and the ice anchor, now wants to go up again as well as sideways. Theodor, bending his knees, pulls down at the ropes. He can't keep that up very long. The Prinzess is sixty kilos light. In all my calculations I never anticipated this very obvious problem. We have come safely down on the ice but we can't get out to stand on it, since the weight of a handful of lead shot is enough to make the balloon go up or down. Should we step out of the gondola, the Prinzess would fly off and leave us. And yet that is precisely what we have come here for, to step out. Theodor, his boot jammed down onto the ice anchor, stands waiting.

For a while, a minute or more, the situation seems an impasse. We don't even discuss it since no one can think of anything to say. Valve off more gas? Impossible. We will never leave here unless we conserve every handful. Subtracting our weight from the gondola, in order to get out and take some steps toward mooring the Prinzess more securely, would undoubtedly result in the anchor tearing out of the ice. We are two metres from our goal but have no means of reaching it. Except for Theodor who—it occurs to me only at this moment—is the first to stand on this long-sought-for mathematical point.

In the end it is Waldemer who thinks of the solution. Theodor is brought back into the gondola, giving the ice anchor a final jam with his foot before he leaves it. Then Waldemer gets out onto the ice with certain implements of iron, including a saw and a long-handled axe. He is almost as skillful with these as he is with a rifle or a cook stove. In only a few minutes he has cut out of the ice a squarish lump two metres long and the width and thickness, approximately, of a man. Since it is blockier than a man it probably weighs even more. We struggle to get this thing into the gondola with our mittened hands. The Prinzess very slowly rises and falls, threatening to pull the anchor out of this rotten July ice at any moment. The block of ice falls once onto Waldemer's foot, but we manage to wrest it upward over the instrument ring and into the gondola.

"Ila." His panting makes him steam, coating his mustache with rime. "Another two like that should do it."

In half an hour the three Ice Men have taken our place in the gondola and we are able to get down onto the stiff, very faintly heaving surface of the pack. Waldemer is exultant. Theodor is still breathing a little hard from our struggle with the blocks of ice and if he has any emotions he doesn't bother to indicate them. The air is oddly still now, only a faint breeze on our faces. A thin but curiously opaque frozen mist hangs over the ice. Horizontally we can scarcely see farther than we could throw a stone; vertically the view is clearer and we can see clouds overhead, the sun appearing occasionally in some fracture in the white blanket. The temperature is minus twenty centigrade, the barometer low but steady. I might take another sight to confirm our position, but to what end? It would be impossible to move now that we have come down where we are. And so this place is the place we have set out to come to, I so declare as commander of the expedition.

Although I have controlled my excitement externally, it has had its usual physiological effect on me. I wander unobtrusively around to the other side of the gondola and perform a much-desired discharge of bladder contents. There is a good deal of steam. Some of the golden droplets solidify before striking the ice and roll across it like tiny amber pearls. When I come back around the gondola I see that Waldemer has set up his photographic apparatus on the tripod fifty metres or so away from the Prinzess. Theodor and I are obliged to stand in negligently heroic attitudes by the gondola while he slips several plates in and out and reaches around to trip the shutter by hand. (The rubber air bulb is frozen and breaks at the first touch.) Then a shot in trio; the apparatus has a delayed-exposure device that enables him to trot over and take his place by our side before it clicks. He folds everything up, the tripod over his shoulder and the oaken box clasped in his arms like a baby, and carries it back to the gondola.

And what is the fantastic fellow doing now? Up there in the gondola with only the Ice Men for company he has found one of those bits of tissue paper we use for pigeon messages, and for five minutes now he has been covering it with endless sentences in a script as minute and meticulous as fine needlepoint. The task warms him up; the pink comes back into his face, the rime on his mustache disappears. The ink freezing, he continues with a pencil sharpened to a needle point with a bit of sandpaper. At this distance I can't read his dispatch and probably couldn't read it even if I held it to my eye, but I can imagine what it says. Alert! *Herald* and *Aftonbladet*! Stop presses! Valorous polarnauts report from the earth's axle bearing! An impressive triumph for mankind and the rubberized-silk industry. The heroes tired and cold but in good spirits as they stand on the peak of our planet. Thinking of loved ones. Report some difficulty in going to the bathroom and in keeping fingers warm but otherwise in good health. Could not have made it without help from Divine Providence. And so on. Oh, he is covering that tissue with a lot! Can the pigeon carry it all? I climb up into the gondola to see if he has really turned it over and is writing on the back now.

"Major, you know, I have here . . ."

"Yes, I know."

"Just a few words. Later, of course, I thought . . ."

You will write a book and stand on platforms from Durban to Ketchikan, recalling this moment. The photographs will be projected by a magic lantern. Here are my two companions, Major Crispin and young Theodor. And here are the three of us together. Perhaps you wonder who is operating the shutter. A polar bear? No. Ha, ha! As it happens, the photographic apparatus we had with us was fitted ...

The slip of tissue in his fingers, he is bending now over the wicker aviary.

"Allow me, Waldemer. I've anticipated you."

With some difficulty due to double mittens, I have removed the quilt, opened the wicker case, and extracted a pigeon. He is already perched on my wrist. A little dull and stiff he looks, poor fellow, he probably didn't expect it would be this cold at latitude ninety. And besides, all the pigeons are off their feed for some reason; the Indian corn is hardly touched. Waldemer rolls the small square of paper and passes it to me. I insert it into the aluminum tube on the pigeon's leg and in removing my hand I surreptitiously extract it again with my fingernail and slip it into my mouth. The thin tissue dissolves like a sacramental wafer and it is hardly necessary to swallow it. The tossed pigeon flutters indecisively, recovers himself, and begins to flap his wings more efficiently just as he is about to settle on the ice. He circles the Prinzess once or twice and then flies off in the wrong direction, but it is not a serious error. Waldemer is not aware of it, the pigeon is not aware of it, and only I know there is no dispatch in the aluminum tube. Another little dishonesty, one of my typical crimes. I hide Waldemer's shaving mirror, I extract his prose from the pigeon tube and eat it, and so on. Why do I behave in this way? Perhaps because of this perverse impulse I have, a totally indefensible quirk of my makeup, to withhold whatever I know from the common and vulgar fund of information, my secretiveness of a medieval alchemist. And perhaps too because I am anxious that the world down there below should not become too infatuated with progress. Our coming to this place was at least in part an accident, a whim of the winds, but mankind would only believe it was done with its machines and become even more puffed with pride than it already is. But won't the secret be known, won't my companions talk when they come back again to the World of Cities? Perhaps they will, or won't. Perhaps we won't come back.

In any case, the pigeon flew off in the wrong direction. What is this talk of directions anyhow, since at this mathematically peculiar place where we are, there are only two directions, pole-hither and pole-hence? It is impossible to go farther north, there is no east or west, everything is south. I walk pole-hence a few steps to contemplate the scene. My two companions are working efficiently. They have got the tarpaulin out of the gondola and stretched it up on a pair of bamboo poles to protect us from this frozen drift mist, and Waldemer has lighted the primus. Theodor is unwrapping from butcher paper the chateaubriand we have brought along to celebrate the occasion. And in fact we are hungry! Great God, in our excitement we haven't eaten for twenty-four hours! A few metres from them, as they crouch behind their canvas, the gondola is wedged at a slight angle against a ridge in the ice. From it, diverging upward, the skein of rigging rises until it embraces finally the gigantic mass of the gas bag, its higher curves—latitudes I almost said—beginning to soften in the mist. And in truth there is a curious symmetry here. I stand on the very peak of the globe, mottled in its way with continents and other features, and on top of it, bolt upright, stands the balloon—this other soft planet with its own markings, the tapering red and white stripes that correspond to the meridians of the larger sphere. The thought of man has unwittingly contrived a metaphor of the planet on which he whirls through space. And powerfully I feel that just as I am a passenger on this balloon so am I on earth, a black speck in the immensity of space; and whoever is guiding it, the Great Nobody, is not very sure of his navigation.

Another of my vices: abstract thought. Twenty more steps backward, incidentally, and I will be permanently lost in this directionless mist and my ruminations will become even more metaphysical, since they will no longer be hampered with a body. The danger always lurks for the transcendentalist that he will achieve his goal, to be united with nature, and so cease to exist. Back the other way, then, polehither, to rejoin my companions.

Waldemer has got the cooking machine working with great efficiency. A blue flame hisses from the burner, the warmth is perceptible on the face even at a distance. Theodor ceremoniously produces the chateaubriand, a thick piece of Norwegian flesh from the tenderest part of the ox. This is soon crackling in the pan, but because it is frozen solid it will be some time before it is edible. I had expected a delicious savor to arise from this cooking, after our long hours of fasting, but for whatever reason the steak gives forth almost no odour.

"That pigeon—ha!" conjectures Waldemer, bending to adjust the primus to an even hotter flame, "is probably well on his way to Trondheim now. What part of the way would you say, Major?"

"Oh, well on his way. Not halfway perhaps, but well on his way."

Turning the steak with a pocket knife and not looking up, Theodor says simply, "The pigeon is dead."

"Ha! Theodor. You're revealing yourself for a pessimist just like the Major. Here we have arrived, haven't we? Where no man before us has set foot—even though the Major was full of gloom and doom and talked about the pack ice drifting, difficulty of navigation, and so on. So let us look on the bright side of things and imagine the pigeon well on his way." Waldemer in his mind's eye sees not only the pigeon flying through the air toward Trondheim but all those printing presses, gigantic, waiting for that little slip of tissue paper to fall into them, whereupon they will begin spewing out extra editions like Niagara.

"Gustav, I think this piece of meat might be done now."

He removes it from the pan and cuts it into three pieces. In fact, it is crisply carbonized on the outside and a pale pink in the interior, a perfect steak in the American manner.

"Named after a poet. Did you know that, Waldemer?"

"No," jovially. "I thought it meant, 'Your hat's on fire.'"

"That's chapeau brûlant." Theodor and Waldemer have at least one thing in common, they like to make bad jokes together. "The poet was Francois René de Chateaubriand. Who came to America and observed the redskins singeing buffalo flesh over their campfires."

"Did he?" Waldemer considers all information valuable, even when it doesn't interest him personally. "H'mm."

"Did you see that on the prairies, Gustav?" "I've already told you, I never went west of Philadelphia."

Waldemer stops chewing and puts down his pocket knife. "Ah."

"Ah?"

"The bubbly!" With a smile.

He is an incurable sentimentalist in spite of his conviction that he is a practical man, and he gets up with enthusiasm, hugging his sides against the cold, and goes to the gondola for the champagne. He is quite right in doing so, since the champagne has been brought along for exactly this moment. It is packed in its own narrow basket, padded in straw, under the floor of the gondola. He returns, holding the wire-wrapped bottle by the neck and a look of insufficiently suppressed satisfaction on his face.

"Ha! Almost forgot."

The wine is Veuve Clicquot of the best quality. "And properly chilled too, you can be sure of that." Waldemer sets the bottle down on the snow. We look at each other. Waldemer looks at us.

"The glasses, drat it."

He goes back for them, and Theodor says, "I'll bet we forgot them."

"Everything has been checked by Alvarez. There is a list as long as your arm. The glasses are aboard, and Waldemer will find them."

He finds them in the provision case, packed carefully in excelsior, and comes back carrying one in one hand and two in the other, and this is not easy to do when one is wearing double mittens. Sets them in the snow by the bottle, in a neat row. Twists the cork deftly like a man accustomed all his life to opening champagne, his expression set with the effort of doing this precisely, and exhaling a good deal of steam.

"Have to watch out—ha ha!—pesky cork may pop out and hit you in the eye—this stuff has a way, you know."

"If you are blinded by a champagne cork, old fellow, never fear, we'll guide you back to New York."

"Ha! Just takes a knack, that's all."

The upshot is that the cork comes out in perfect silence; even an ominous silence.

"H'mm."

The hollow-stemmed glasses are arranged in a row in the snow. With jovial ceremony he tilts the bottle's mouth over the first. Nothing. Increases the angle. Shakes bottle lightly. Inverts it totally over the glass. But even upside down it declines to give forth its contents.

"Well, I'll be dratted. What do you suppose? The stuff is defective."

Theodor takes the bottle from him and examines it for a moment. Then, abruptly and with considerable force, he breaks it against the ice anchor. The bottle comes apart quite easily; the middle third shatters, the bottom and the top can be removed like hats from the molded form of substance contained within. Theodor patiently picks off the few remaining crumbs of glass.

"Ha! Well, there's a predicament. Did you ever hear of the like? What should we do now, d'you suppose?"

"Eat it, I imagine."

The steak is a succulent meal, even though the morsels, as we cut them with our pocket knives, get cold before we can bring them to our mouths and will freeze if we don't work quickly. As for the champagne, we divide this up too with our pocket knives and eat it with our mittened fingers. It consists of clusters of sharp needle-like crystals, pale white, with the taste of a sherbet made of apples. As it melts under the tongue a faint tingle sinks downward into the palate, merges into the substances of man. It's quite good, really.

Having melted the wine in our metabolism, and begun at least to digest the steak, we gather up the paraphernalia of our picnic and put everything back in the gondola. The tarpaulin we spread over the instrument ring to keep out the light, and as much of the frozen mist as possible. We are snug in our miniature habitation, a remorseless nature outside held back by wicker and canvas. Before we throw the Ice Men out onto the snow to make room for ourselves, I go outside one last time to be sure the Prinzess is well secured and that everything is as before. The wind has died completely. In the absolute calm the Prinzess stretches precisely upward, the hoarfrost beginning to whiten the red silk of her stripes. Before my face the particles of frozen mist hang fixed like tiny needle points. In the silence I can hear a muffled complaining and grinding from the pack ice under my feet: pushing, slowly buckling, its edges chafing and crumbling.

"What does it mean?"

Theodor has come out of the gondola behind me. He stands with the shawl tied over the top of his peaked cap, almost enclosing his cheeks and face.

"The calm? It means there is no wind."

"And will there be wind again?"

"In time. Perhaps tomorrow. Perhaps in a month."

His glance studies me, and he smiles faintly.

"Did you know that before we came?"

"That there might be no wind? Of course."

He says nothing more. His mittened hands in the pocket of his greatcoat, he contemplates the place where the horizon would be if it were not obscured in this white atmosphere. The sun can barely force its rays through it. It—the sun—has crept around in another direction now, moving imperceptibly sideways with no inclination whatsoever to rise as the sun does below in the Cities of Men. It looks more like a moon than a sun, a moon of red liquid metal, but totally cold. We are conscious only of cold, and of an immense and absolute isolation. The gondola fifty metres away is barely visible. It is clear that, to all purposes, the two of us are alone in the universe, and under such circumstances convention can be dispensed with. This being so, I am free to concede at least to a Mental Diary that what I feel for Theodor is love. I admire the recalcitrance of his flesh and the keen, faintly contemptuous profile of his face folded in the enwrapping shawl, his soft and almost baby-like skin spotted with frostbite, but sufficient in himself and making no complaint. I think, for some reason in French: Il sait se défendre. We are perhaps a metre and a half apart and remain so. Neither of us speaks. What separates us is only the ten thousand years of complication in which we have hopelessly enmeshed the naturalness and simplicity of our actions, that is to say, everything that humanity calls civilization. Is it possible after the ten thousand years to feel a natural sentiment? And how to tell the natural from the perverse? And yet, half-frozen as I am, I feel myself capable of leaping like an armed warrior into this abyss God has dug with His hands between man and the animal. Perhaps this is a delirium, a malicious and nonexistent notion playing on the brain fibers as false images sometimes play on the inside of the retina. Malicious and nonexistent? Malicious because nonexistent. We are both tired; we are all three tired. We go back into the gondola and the Ice Men are politely evicted from their places; they seem content lying in a row on the snow outside. Then we unroll our sacks of reindeer hide and I lie down chastely with my two companions.

•

It is cold and only partly dark. I slip downward and am no longer aware of my body, then rise a little toward the surface again. I am very comfortable and at peace with myself, with the world, with everything. Some sun warms me, a sun that is probably inside me, since the real sun could hardly pierce through the shutters. And also because, since the hillside on which the villa is built faces north, toward the lake, the sun is rather late in making its appearance in the morning. Even at seven o'clock the light that comes into the room is a faint greyish blue, the light of pre-dawn. Luisa sleeps soundly with a pillow over her head and only a portion of her white shoulder showing. I, face downward with one knee drawn up, hover somewhere in a region where the body is asleep and the soul only conscious enough to be aware of the fact. What my half consciousness ponders about, in a way far too imprecise to be described as thought, is the mysterious dynamic that draws my body toward that other one I can sense only thirty centimeters away from me now in the canopied Empire bed, but only at certain times and in certain ways. And it is she who chooses, it is clear to me even nine tenths asleep, not only the ways but the times. Usually it is at sunset with the faint reddish reflections from the lake coming through the shutters. Just as the time we live in is called the fin de siècle, so our lovemaking belongs to the fin de jour; there is something crepuscular about it. Never late at night; at night she talks. In the daytime also she talks. At other times even when not talking she is quite distant, at the dressing table brushing her hair or standing by the crumbling marble balustrade with her back to me idly adjusting a flower at her shoulder, and the power that is still there somewhere inside her is directed elsewhere or not energized at all. At such times, even if she should happen to turn so that our glances meet, her intense consciousness and the quick irony of her intelligence, the wordy flow of conversation that comes out of her at the slightest impulse, are chilling to ardour if there should be a question of any. At other times (it's sunset now, blood shimmers on the lake) she might turn, speaking quite casually of indifferent matters or not speaking at all, and a hesitation as her glance or voice lingers an instant longer than necessary, some magnetism she seems to be able to focus at will, radiates toward me and permeates instantly every last nerve and vein, so that the calm glance fixed on me and the whole power of her body say quite simply: you. And obediently my desire responds with a dumb and animal urgency, I have no power over what I might do or even say, the aching clench in me is pulled to that elusive darkness as by a magnet. It is as though (I muse, still to all purposes asleep although aware of the dawn trying to come in through the shutters) the power of her femininity radiates from the frontal aspects of her body, and when she rotates this mechanism only a quarter turn away from me the effect ceases or is wasted on an empty wall. I imagine that she might call me—in fantasy—from a distant room and through many walls, simply by directing toward me this mysterious electrical emanation she was able to focus, when she chose, toward any given goal. Her power was directional; it was important (if you wished not to be rendered powerless and foolish) not to stand in its path. Then I was all at once awake, with a tingle running up and down my epidermis and culminating in my scalp.

I slipped out of bed and went into the salon. But there was nothing to write on and I had to go back into the yellow room, cautiously and with one eye on the bed, to steal some sheets of Luisa's mauve and scented notepaper from the writing desk. Likewise a pen, a frivolous and feminine one with a long plume on it, but no more suitable one could be found. At the great table in the salon I drew various diamonds and spirals on the mauve paper and tried to recall Stone's experiments on directive emanation of aeromagnetism. These two elusive and invisible forces, the power of Luisa's body and the shimmer of Hertzian waves, had intersected somewhere in my half-sleeping mind to form a kind of metaphor. I saw or half guessed now that there might be an apparatus that would be sensitive frontally to the oncoming waves, so to speak, but not laterally. But Stone's antenna wire, like the form I had left under the bedclothes in the yellow room, was concerned with the sending out of power. It was for the receiving apparatus I had already built—the coil, condenser, and crystal that rested neglected in my rented room in Paris—that I now cogitated feverishly to devise a directional aerial wire. The pesky ostrich plume tickling my chin, I covered several pieces of paper with sketches. I quickly grasped that, if my theories about the conversion of aeromagnetism were correct, a simple pair of horizontal wires would suffice. But in order to intercept a suitable amount of energy they would have to be several hundred metres long. In short, impractical to carry aloft. Yet might not the length of antenna wire be coiled around on itself into a flat shape like a bedspring? And this, mounted on a pivot, could be rotated easily by hand. Yet, if it rotated, how could wires be connected to it? Bah! it was a simple mechanical problem, one for a first-year engineering student. I drew bedsprings, rug beaters, and fly swatters, and settled on a kind of loop in the shape of a flat diamond with two wire leads coming out of it at the bottom, where it swiveled. The hearing ear would be sensitive to the waves only when facing flatly toward them; turned on edge it would hear nothing. It would work!

Blast and a thousand thunders! By bad luck the idea had come to me in this bucolic Piedmontese backwater with no apparatus at hand and no place within a hundred leagues to procure any. What time was it? Impossible to determine, because I was still in my nightshirt. Creeping back into the yellow room again (the form under the covers stirred very faintly, then stretched back into quiescence), I lifted my clothes in a single bundle from the chair and carried them, sleeves and trouser legs dangling, into the salon. The watch when extracted from the trousers showed it was nine o'clock. I had been squiggling with this ridiculous plume for two hours. The serving woman, Garofana, had left some hot water on the hob, which I hastily made into coffee and drank. Then I got dressed and bolted out into the piercingly clear morning.

In the village of Stresa (for it was really little more than a village) there was naturally no dealer in electromagnetic supplies of the rather special kind I required, or even an ironmongery. Wire above all. It was wire that I must have! If needed it could be wound around an embroidery frame or any pair of sticks. At the Caffè Garibaldi, where a lazy boy was sweeping out last night's sawdust, I learned of a blacksmith in the nearby town of Pallanza. It was not easy to procure a carriage in that sleepy lakeside town at nine o'clock in the morning, but with bribes and a few shouted threats I achieved it. Along the lakeshore we went, on a pleasant stone-paved road, past the most charming scenery in the world, which I could have wished at the bottom of the Atlantic. The coachman pointed out the Isola Bella to me, the idiot. Presto, presto! A Pallanza! Don't bother me with your stupid bellezza! He muttered something like "Pazzo," grumbling to his horse or to himself. Yes, I am, you blockhead, but there are all kinds of madmen and I'm the kind that's looking for some wire. We arrived in Pallanza, but the blacksmith was not in Pallanza and instead in its outskirts. Finally we found him. He was already at work, the gods be thanked, thumping dumbly at a red-hot horseshoe. Wire, wire! It was with difficulty that he could be persuaded to let that scrap of metal get cold and turn to listen to what I was saying. Che tipo di filo, dunque? Some heavyish wire for an antenna, and if he had some very thin and hairlike copper wire, I would take that too. Copper no, but he had some heavyish wire of iron which he would show me. Exploring massively and with exasperating slowness in a junk heap he kept in the back of his hut, he produced a tangled bundle of rusty filament the size of a small haystack. It was American, he said, and of the finest quality. It was of a new sort invented for making fences, and at intervals it was fitted with little daggers of sharpened wire that were intended to keep the cows from breaking it. Bah! it was Hertzian waves I wanted to catch, imbecile, and not cows! It was of the latest design, was all he argued, and he would not charge any more for the barbs. I turned away in disgust. The coachman had gone down to the lake front, perhaps to answer a call of nature, and I had to retrieve him before I could go back to where I came from.

Copper wire! Copper wire! Well, there was none to be had in Stresa and environs. In the villa I found Luisa up and putting pins in her hair, in a dressing gown that fell to her feet in Roman dignity.

"Have a nice walk?" She said this absently, hardly looking at me. "Be a dear and bring me my coffee, will you?"

"You wouldn't know, I imagine, where one could obtain fine or heavy copper wire in this rustic place of exile?"

"Please don't ask me difficult questions. I haven't had my breakfast." It was almost eleven o'clock. Having arranged her coiffure in at least a provisional way (it curved to one side and fell along her throat, charming), she moved gracefully into the salon and found the floor littered with my notes.

"You might have mentioned it, dear heart, if you wanted to use my paper. It's from Laurrison's and quite expensive. What on earth have you been scratching and scribbling about anyhow?"

I wasn't in the mood to explain to her the whole thing. "I must have some copper wire, because an idea has just come to me which can be held down and made captive only if copper wire is wrapped around it. Also some condenser foil and waxed paper." There was probably not to be found such a thing as a piece of galena even in Milan! And the soldering iron! And the spirit lamp to heat it!

"What's the idea about?"

"Hertzian waves, aeromagnetic rectifiers, antennae, and directionality."

But it was too early in the morning for her to assume or even simulate, with any degree of enthusiasm, her role of femme savante. "Can't it wait?"

'No."

"Why not?"

"Because my brain won't wait. It's like that. I make no apologies for it."

"I wish you had brought me my coffee. The fact that I have not had my coffee is making us both cross. It was not really to concern ourselves with aero-Hertzian antennae that we came here, you know."

"What we came here for would surely take, at the most, only a half an hour of each day."

"Don't be crude."

"The rest of which, it seems, you devote to your hair. And to your gowns, which are charming."

"Now we are quarreling. Why can't you send for your apparatus from Paris?"

"It would take months."

Her manner changed abruptly. You could see her working the little wires that changed the look on her face. She became placid, knowing, regret in her eyes, a promise in her smile, with a little crease under it almost like a pout. "It isn't true I spend all day on my hair and my gowns. We can have a nice breakfast à l'anglaise, and then we can go for a carriage ride along the lake." (I had already done that.) "You can telegraph to Paris for your apparatus, or you can go to Milan for some copper wire. You can be back in the afternoon." Both hands on the soft coil of hair lying along her throat, making some final nuance of adjustment to it, she turned to me with a hopeful, a significant smile. The dressing gown, which she had put on carelessly, was hardly fastened at all in front. "Tu veux? But you must hurry, because I miss you."

"Primo, there is no galena in Milan, and secundo, there is probably not any condenser foil either. Tertio, the conditions are not right here for one to think of any serious matter consecutively for more than five minutes. And don't point that body at me! It isn't sunset! It's only eleven o'clock in the morning!"

"Oh, you!" She tore away and fastened the dressing gown up to her very neck, furious. "You take everything wrong! I exhaust myself trying to be pleasant and charming, I try to bring some sweetness and light into our existence, and you spoil everything by reducing it to the—to the—animal."

She stormed away into the kitchen to find her coffee, and I followed. Now I tried to arrange *my* face. No chance of making it affectionate, let alone seductive, but at least I could behave in a civilized manner and make it clear to her that I appreciated her efforts even if they only succeeded in arousing the animal in me. It was a quite harmless animal really, liked a sugar lump now and then, and appreciated being stroked.

"There's no chance of finding what I want in Milan. You can come back to Paris with me. I can go on with my work, and you can come to rue de Rennes and hold the wires while I solder them. You know," I added recklessly, "the sun sets in Paris too." As soon as I said that, I wished I hadn't, because if the sun ever set in rue de Rennes I would never again be able to do any work there, her perfume and her invisible feminine necromancy would permeate the place and I would never be able to think of anything there but *that*.

"We've been here only five days."

"How long did you expect to stay?"

"Five weeks. Or five months."

I snorted.

"You didn't find it pleasant then?"

Ha! Stresa was already in the past tense. "I find it pleasant as can be. It's only that—to be perfectly candid—after a time it is necessary to get back to the serious business of life."

"Thank you for your *exquisite* candour. And what might that be—the serious business of life?"

I was a little at a loss. It hardly seemed convincing to tell her that it was some wire wound around a pair of sticks. "May I beg to remind you that it was you who originally initiated our relationship, and on what grounds? That you wished to improve your mind by devoting it to difficult and intellectual matters, you could scarcely control your enthusiasm for aeromagnetism in those days and you begged and pleaded that I would give you a list of books to study, whereas as soon as you had enticed me into that den of she-serpents in Quai d'Orléans—"

I paused, and after a moment she said almost calmly, "What?"

"It was *you* who began to turn *me* into something else, and with a fair success—something that was not what I am and must be, something that interfered with and in fact made impossible the very work, the very intellectual lucubrations that had caused you to admire me so fervently in the first place—a Lovelace, a Parisian coxcomb, an escort to café concerts and a wearer of frock coats . . ."

"Go on, go on."

"That's all." '

Then *go!*" she burst out, actually stamping her foot. "I notice that you always become intellectual, for a few days, just after your affections have been satisfied. Later perhaps you will come back with that moony look in your eyes, and want another bonbon so that you can be gratified and go back to your soldering iron. I don't care for the bargain. Garofana, get out! Vai! Vai! Vai al inferno!" (The serving woman had come in.) "You speak of the way I behaved at the Musée Carnavalet. What kind of a spectacle do you think you provided? As soon as you caught my eye you were smitten all over with lechery. I could see it from ten rows away." (Could this be true?) "And your pretence that you could take any interest in my mind! It was, 'Come to my hotel, mademoiselle, and I can give you an, um, list of books.' " (I had said nothing of the kind.) "I can tell you that I've had enough of the whole business! J'en ai marre! Go, go, I tell you. Take your lofty intellect, your Hyperborean erotomania, and your stockings, which smell, incidentally, and go back to playing with your copper wires. Go! If you hurry you can catch the afternoon train for Paris. There might even be one for Stockholm, that would even be better."

She followed me around, pointing out my shortcomings to me as I jammed everything in my valise. For example, she reproached me for leaving her. "You're just like all men! As soon as you get what you want it's adieu without so much as a glance behind you! Why don't you leave me some money? You can put it on the mantelpiece. Five francs, I believe, is the customary sum. And be sure to relate all the details to your gentlemen friends." (I didn't have any gentlemen friends except for Waldemer, who was terribly straitlaced and would refuse to listen to anything of the sort.) "You don't even know how to pack a valise! You're wrinkling everything. You're a ridiculous puppet, and a stupid one besides, a Punch, you need to be beaten by a policeman."

The valise and I were finally in the carriage, going down the road. It was a cool clear day and I felt better, even good. This was probably the end of it, I expected. There are some things that, once having been said, cannot be taken back. For example, "I don't love you" can be taken back, but not "Your stockings smell." So much the better! I longed for my rented rooms in rue de Rennes, for my solitude, for the clean and chaste intoxication of thought. Milan was rather gloomy with the grey haze of November hanging over it, but it didn't matter because I wasn't staying there. Vetturino, Stazione Centrale! The crystal roof over the station was black with soot, I noticed now. It is possible to be much more observant when one is alone and the thoughts unclouded. I drove off a porter who wanted my valise by threatening to dismember him. "One ticket to Paris, second class."

"By way of Domodossola?"

"I don't care! Parigi! Parigi!"

•

The first thing I did after leaving off the valise in my lodgings was to go to Pertuis et fils in Avenue du Maine and buy a roll of number 36 annealed copper wire, which I insulated myself by dipping it into shellac with a roller device I had contrived. Then I set to work to build the frame for the antenna basket, which took me several days because I wanted it just right, and because I was a natural philosopher and not a carpenter and had to compensate for my lack of skill with infinite pains. It was to be not only a laboratory model but also, I hoped, a serviceable instrument sturdy enough to be used in the field and even taken aloft. The upright consisted of a stout dowel of oak, and the cross bar made of a batten of the same wood was set into the upright through a mortise. Tiny holes were bored in these two members (the wire was only five mils in diameter) and a hundred and eighty metres of wire, enough to reach from the room where I was working to the Luxembourg Gardens, was wound through the holes and tightened into a flat diamond shape. That part of the cylindrical upright extending below the antenna basket was held in two oaken bearings and provided with an azimuth ring and a handle so that it could be turned conveniently. Then came the problem of transferring the waves from this rotating antenna to the Marconi rectifying apparatus. As I had promised myself in Stresa, this was a simple engineering problem. I had to go out for more materials, once again to Pertuis: two brass slip rings of the kind used in electrostatic apparatus and a pair of thin graphite bars to make contact with them. The theory of this part of the work was rudimentary but the mechanics were exacting. I had to fabricate two little boxes of mica to hold the graphite bars, with tiny springs in them to apply pressure to the slip rings. This, along with the business of mounting the bar holders on the apparatus and aligning them exactly in place, took several days. I had just begun connecting the lead wires to the springs inside the mica boxes when the concierge knocked on the door. It was the first time she had taken notice of my existence since Theodor had paid his little visit of honour on me several weeks before. Without looking around I called for her to enter.

"Pardon, monsieur. Y a une dame." "What kind of a lady?"

"A foreigner."

"Well, I am a foreigner too. What else?"

"Well dressed. Enfin, c'est une dame."

"Well, show the internal nuisance in."

She disappeared and Luisa metamorphosed in her place. She was well dressed, it was true, but in a different manner now, a woolen skirt and jacket in the English style, with a simple shirtwaist and mannish tie. Her hair seemed to be shorter. It still ended in a soft coil hanging to one side, but now it came only a little below the ear. Her face was even paler than usual, and she seemed thin.

"Am I disturbing you?"

"Yes, but come in."

Her manner was different too, not the fashionable young lady of the Île Saint-Louis and not the sibylline enchantress of the yellow room. It was a third Luisa. She was smooth, cool, intelligent, polite, and even a little distant, while at the same time she made herself thoroughly at home. Everything inside the English clothes corresponded exactly to the clothes themselves. Her yellow gloves came off and she put her umbrella in the stand herself so as not to disturb me. Her voice was controlled and lower than before. She addressed me in the formal second person when she spoke French and called me nothing at all in English, thus avoiding the intimacy of the first name. We talked amicably for a quarter of an hour while I went on working.

"It's been so long since we've seen each other." (It was about a week.) "You know, I'm afraid I behaved frightfully in Stresa. Of course your work is important. I was a silly vain thing to object to your coming back to Paris. You were quite right; it was originally to help you in your work that I became your friend, and not to hinder you. And I'm afraid that in the heat of discussion I said some rather—unkind things about your character."

This was noble of her. She probably expected me to reciprocate by taking back the things *I* had said about *her* in the heat of discussion. But I didn't feel that the fact I had told her she was a nincompoop was really equivalent to the remark she had made about my stockings. However, all this seemed behind me now—behind us. There was a kind of intimacy we could never enter into again and perhaps it was all for the best, since it had produced in her the English suit and a new and more intelligent manner—and if I made no apologies I refrained from stirring up the coals of old conflagrations, confining myself to polite small talk as I went on connecting up the wires. I even made conventional inquiries.

"And your aunt? And your mother?"

"Well, thank you."

"And your uncle in Pondicherry?"

"All well." She looked around the room, smoothed her hair, and said briskly, "May I make you some tea?"

"Please do."

"No," she reflected on second thought, "I won't. These—roles, you know. Are so conventional. You might make me tea if you like, later, when you're not working. What is it that you are doing, please? And might I not help you in some way?"

"I've just finished soldering the lead wires onto these springs, which in turn make contact with these two bars of graphite, which as you can see slide back and forth in their holders."

"Bars of graphite?"

"Yes." Carefully I mounted the mica holding boxes into position before the two slip rings. "You see, in order for the Marconi rectifying apparatus to receive impulses, it is necessary for the waves to pass from the antenna basket—hereto the condenser and coil—here. The two can't be connected directly, because the antenna basket must rotate. And so I'm arranging this system of graphite bars and slip rings, in order to collect the waves from the antenna and direct them to the receiving apparatus."

"Why must the antenna basket rotate?"

"In order to determine the direction from which the Hertzian waves are coming."

"But what is sending the Hertzian waves?"

"The clouds! The clouds bumping and grinding together produce electricity exactly like the static generators you are undoubtedly familiar with from your excellent education."

"And why do you want to determine their direction?"

"Primo, if aerostatic phenomena are taking place in the atmosphere, in order to study them it is first necessary to know where they are. Secundo, I am interested in constructing a directional receiving apparatus for its possible use in prophesying the weather. Tertio, scientific knowledge of any sort is an end in itself."

She addressed herself smoothly to the antenna basket, examining it carefully for the first time, and yet as though it were something she was not going to be intimidated by and which her mind was perfectly capable of mastering. "

And the Hertzian waves strike on—which side?"

"On either side."

"Then—it seems to me"—she was still thinking—"the apparatus will be incapable of differentiating between sides. Because a wave striking the antenna from the north—let us say—will produce exactly the same effect in the apparatus as one striking it from the south."

Brava, Luisa. This problem of reciprocality was the one that still bothered me, although I was thinking about it and considering a number of solutions. She had walked up to the thing, looked at it without even touching it, and instantly I perceived its chief limitation in its present form. I might have found this intuition a little annoying, instead I chose to admire her.

"In a single observation this might be a handicap. With several observations from a moving platform, however, a vector may perhaps be established which will make it possible to determine a unilateral source for the waves."

"Ah . . . since the deflection caused by the motion of the platform itself would be unilateral—to the left, let us say, if the motion were to the right—and this would be inconsistent with a reciprocal wave coming from the rear of the observer."

"Exactly." Thunder take it, there was also a mind here in addition to intuition.

But she showed no signs of being pleased with herself; she was still cool, crisp, and detached. Having clairvoyantly seen through to the chief flaw of the antenna basket, she now permitted herself to touch it, setting her well-manicured fingers onto it lightly, with care not to bend the wires or damage their shellac insulation.

"I can hardly believe that the clouds send out waves you can hear in such an apparatus."

"If you would like to wait, you could hear some. With good luck I'll be finished in a half an hour. There's a storm building up in the direction of Rambouillet."

"I would adore hearing some. But I would prefer not merely to wait for a half an hour. Surely there's something I can do to help."

She was so brisk and intelligent, so businesslike in her cambric shirtwaist, that in the end I let her do it. I showed her the problem of shaping the ends of the graphite bars to the curvature of the slip rings, a task for which at least three and perhaps four hands were useful. "The bars must fit snugly onto the slip rings, otherwise electricity from the waves will be lost. The bars are flat and the slip rings curved. I will wind fine emery paper around the slip rings—thus and hold it with my fingertips. Then, as I rotate the vertical shaft of the antenna basket, you must press the graphite bars firmly onto the rings. The tension of the springs is not enough. The emery paper will grind away the ends of the bars in the exact shape of the rings. You see?"

"Very well." She grasped the bars with her thin fingers and pressed them inward. With her hands stretched out, the sleeve of the cambric shirtwaist fell down over one wrist, and she removed the other to push the sleeve up. A black smudge appeared on the cambric.

"Why is this messy black substance necessary?"

"Graphite is self-lubricating, and is an excellent conductor of electricity."

She examined her fingers briefly and went back to the task. I turned the shaft with one hand and held the emery paper with the other, she pushed on the bars. The graphite was hard and it was slow work.

"Have you noticed, we both have long fingers. I can't stand people who have short fingers. There's a woman who comes to Quai d'Orléans, her name is Lucienne de Portoriche but I call her Madame Gecko. She's an impossible person, really. Darting at you with little chops of her head, almost as though she had a tongue a yard long and were catching insects."

I didn't know Madame Gecko, so I made no comment.

"Have you ever noticed that each person you meet, if you look more closely, resembles an animal?"

"Which animal?"

"That's it, you see. Each person resembles a different animal. One is a camel, another a hedgehog, someone else a flitterbat. Chauve-souris is a funny word. In Italian it's pipistrello; I like that better."

This chattering, or demonstration in comparative linguistics, was not really necessary to our task. However, she was so smooth and helpful in other ways that I decided to take it in good grace. To remain silent in the face of such an elegant effort at conversation would seem curmudgeonly.

"And I?"

"A lynx." She almost smiled here, caught herself, and resumed a grave intensity of expression, with her mouth even drawn a little together in her concentration on the task. I examined myself in a mental mirror. The rather high brow and slightly outstanding ears, the bristly hair at the temples that would not lie flat, the somewhat prickly mustachio with the corresponding tuft under the lip. If I had been younger and less experienced I might have reddened. I decided not to tell her what animal she reminded me of, because I suspected she wouldn't appreciate it, although why she thought I would appreciate being equated with a slinky marauder of the forest I didn't know. Getting a little impatient at the task by this time (my left hand was at an awkward angle and getting tired), I rotated the shaft more rapidly. Just at that moment she moved her hand to get a better grip on the graphite bar, and the fragile substance broke under her fingers.

"But it's *brittle.* "

"Of course."

"You didn't tell me."

"I didn't think it was necessary for me to give you a lecture on the physical properties of various elements and compounds before you helped me in a simple task."

Her lips tightened. But she didn't say, "Are you going to commence that again?" Instead, still calm, she said, "What must we do now?"

"Nothing."

"Nothing?"

"Pertuis is closed for the day. I can go there tomorrow, at ten o'clock in the morning, and buy another bar of graphite, if he has one in stock."

"But it was you, you know, who jogged the apparatus."

Ah hah. In the first place I hadn't accused her of any ineptitude, although this thought may have been in the air. In the second place, she was supposed to be holding the bars firmly in her two hands, and even if I had begun rotating the shaft a little faster, this was no reason to break one off as though it were a stick of celery.

"I jogged nothing."

"In short, it is I who am guilty of bringing your valuable scientific investigations to a standstill until ten o'clock tomorrow, just because I am a silly woman who doesn't know that graphite is brittle."

"I expressed no such conclusions."

"But you don't deny them. Isn't that right? You don't deny that in your mind I am a bungling, vain, loquacious, imperseverant, flighty, wrongheaded, illogical, vaporous, self-indulgent, sentimental, and impractical creature, just because of my sex."

"Why should I have to deny it? I've never affirmed it."

But she plunged on, not listening.

"While you of course belong to the magnificent race of pentapods, identical to the rest of us except for a certain appurtenance about which you are terribly vain, and which serves no useful purpose in the world as far as I can see."

This was really unfair. And—how could I put it?—flighty, wrongheaded, and illogical. I might have cited evidence to her, but it would only enrage her the more. Although oddly enough she was not really showing any symptoms of rage. She was still cold and contained. The mouth was held like a small soft vise. She didn't speak another word; there was no need for her to, the ones she had spoken were quite eloquent and made the matter clear. only a liquidity about the eyes, a moisture that trembled and seemed about to fall over the lash but never did, showed that something was happening inside. She looked around for some means of cleaning her blackened fingers. There was a pitcher and basin on the commode across the room, even something that passed for a bar of soap, but to utilize these would have been too domestic a gesture, too intimate and too sharing of the tools of my personal housekeeping, for her mood of Corneillian abnegation. She rubbed her hands on the woolen skirt and thrust them into her gloves. Then, taking her umbrella, she went out. She did not "flounce," or "storm," she left with perfect dignity.

And I? what had I done? I had spoken only facts: "Graphite is brittle," "Pertuis is closed until ten o'clock in the morning," and so on. I had even let her call me a lynx without responding. I was not responsible, I felt, for what took place in her soul. Yet how clairvoyantly she had seen the problem of reciprocality! If she had insisted on my telling her frankly what I thought of her—there at that moment, in her English suit and cambric—I would have said that I found her admirable but not desirable, except perhaps at the very end when the balance between the two qualities was evened a little. Wasn't that what she wanted? I was guiltless, I told myself as I faced my useless evening. It was shortly after this that a new epoch began, that of her musical career.

•

Still as she is fixed there in the photographic dream apparatus behind the retinae, it is often in that guise— bent over that odd harp of oak and copper wire, her glance intent not on me but on the invisibility of electrical currents coursing—through the thin filaments—that I see her. For the serious business of life ("And what might that be?") one wants companions. So if I have predilections for one or the other of Luisa's temperament—I tell myself—it is more useful to me in its brother form, a transformation in which the body no longer radiates distracting energies and the dark eyes, having been in their time exotic and sibylline, become knowing in another and more masculine way, watching, reflective, stoic. His glance turns from the apparatus mounted on the provision case to me.

"But you can't tell whether the waves might be coming from the reciprocal."

"True."

"Still, if a deflection could be established through vectors—"

"For that it would be necessary for the platform to be moving. And, for the present time, we are fixed in one place."

The eyes half hidden in the bedouin shawl go back to the slowly searching antenna basket. In the silence the graphite bars squeak faintly on the slip rings. The antenna rotates first in one direction and then in another, hesitates, and settles on a bearing on the left. I get out the notebook and write down, "1320 GMT. Disturbances along 95° east," since in our present predicament, where all directions are south, we are obliged to use meridians of longitude for directions.

"Still, you've settled on a unilateral bearing."

"I am guessing." "And what are you guessing?"

"That the storm that brought us here has left an area of high pressure behind it. And that another cyclonic system is forming off to the left, in Siberia."

"So there will be wind?"

"Perhaps. Perhaps not. In any case not much."

"But see here, Major. Suppose there isn't any?"

"Then—we will stay here."

Theodor and Waldemer exchange a glance. Waldemer is—earnest. That is the only word for his expression. A little crease has formed in his forehead, exactly between his eyes. It is the first intimation he has had that his optimism about the expedition, about life itself, about everything, might not be justified, that I might not bring him through after all as he has always bluffly and cheerfully expected—that he himself might be mortal. It lasts for only a moment. Theodor is expressionless.

"What must we do?"

"Persuade the wind to blow."

"You mean we must pray?"

"Bah! We must *will* it, force it out of those Siberian hills. Give it no rest, wake it up from its sluggish sleep." And, afraid I may have alarmed him a little with these necromantic ravings, I add practically, "In the meantime, we can think how to lighten the Prinzess."

In this cold the hydrogen has contracted, the rigging sags passively and the gondola rests on the ice. Even if the wind should come now (and I am by no means sure it will) it would be impossible to ascend. In the dead calm the fog has lifted a little and is now a bed sheet of milk hanging a few hundred metres over our heads. If we could ascend through it the sun would warm the bag and restore its buoyancy. But to get up there we must throw away something heavy. We can begin with the hoarfrost and rime on the gondola.

Waldemer is ready to start on the rigging with a mallet. But first it is necessary for him to answer a call of nature. He climbs down out of the gondola, removes mittens, unbuttons hunting jacket, and strives at the openings of his trousers and the practical undergarment underneath. A surprisingly robust cylinder something like a Philadelphia breakfast sausage appears and emits a vigorous stream of gold.

"Have to do this fast. A fellow could freeze off hiswhatchamacallit. Ever get frostbitten there? It's not very jolly, I can tell you."

Theodor watches him steadily, calmly, without comment. He himself has never been seen performing this action. His modesty, or his pride. Perhaps he prefers to take care of it when Waldemer and I are asleep, which means being uncomfortable for long periods of time. No matter! each of us has the right to be odd in his own way, and Waldemer and I have our own oddities. Waldemer has his clothing adjusted now and climbs back into the gondola. Resolutely grasping the mallet, he mounts to the bearing ring and begins banging on the skein of frozen ropes. Shards of ice, like whitish broken tubes of glass, fall on our heads. Theodor and I gather them up in our mittens and throw them over the side, then he finds a pan in the provision basket that will do a better job. I take the hatchet and work on the ice on the gondola itself, chipping carefully in order not to damage the beautifully handworked Spanish cane.

In an hour the three of us have removed, perhaps, thirty or forty kilos of ice. Theodor, the lightest of us, climbs on up higher into the rigging to dislodge the thin crust of rime clinging to the balloon itself under the net. Waldemer and I get out to collect the miniature camp we have set up a few metres from the gondola: the stove, the cooking pan, a can of kerosene, a few spoons and implements. We abandon the tarpaulin as too heavy but save the bamboo poles.

"That fellow. He's really bully, you know."

I say nothing and he goes on.

"I had my doubts at first. Seemed to me a thousand people we might have brought along who would do better. I told you so quite frankly, as you'll remember. But—"

Expressionless, I stop him with a negative motion of my head and a gesture upward to the round gas bag. In the frozen air the slightest sound carries far. Ten metres or more over our heads Theodor, his boots jammed into the net and clinging with one hand, is tapping steadily and patiently at the crust of rime. Flakes of white and brittle debris fall with each blow. And it is this, finally, that seems to wake up the wind. With each blow of the mallet a molecule of air seems to stir, over there, in the direction of the great sleeping Russian beast. We don't feel it in our faces, since these are virtually frozen, so much as sense it in the stirring of the great soft sphere hanging in the air over our heads. The ropes creak very faintly. The wind! Not a wind really but a breath, a reluctant and preliminary zephyr that we hope is a portent of more to come. The direction isn't ideal for our purposes but perhaps it will do; we only want more of it.

Theodor climbs down the net, swinging the last few feet with his legs free, and drops into the gondola. He seems tired but elated; his teeth are set perhaps against the cold or perhaps against a youthful impulse to smile. Rather hastily we make preparations to ascend before the wind dies. The Ice Men, who have taken our places again in the gondola while we break camp, are thrown overboard; they live here so they won't mind, and they wouldn't last long in the World of Cities. Theodor, curiously energized in spite of his fatigue, drops down with an ax to free the ice anchor. But he is unskillful with the tool and it ricochets off the hardened ice. Waldemer moves to help him.

"Never mind. Leave the anchor there."

"You don't think we'll be using it again?"

"It's not that. It's the weight."

And in fact, even with the anchor and ax abandoned, the three Ice Men thrown overboard, a bag of ballast sacrificed, the Prinzess is reluctant to leave this place. She rises a half a metre or so, drifts slowly in the direction of Franz Josef Land, and soon begins to bump on the ice again. Climbing out and hanging to the side of the gondola, I stretch my leg down and shove upward with my boot. It is surprising that this immense machine, stretching over our heads as high as a church steeple, can be moved in this way with a small shove of the foot. Very slowly, with a kind of clocklike grace, the Prinzess rises and then slows as though something heavy in the air were pushing her down. Soon she is settling again and only a hand's breadth from the ice.

"Another bag of ballast?"

"Not yet. What else is superfluous?"

I am in favor of deleting the pigeons, which with their wicker basket must weigh eight or ten kilograms, and my two companions agree. The two rifles we keep for the present. The last of the Prinzessin Brauerei bock goes overboard in its hamper, also the photographic apparatus. I expect Waldemer to object to this last but evidently the candid discussion of our predicament this morning has gone home to him; the little furrow is still there in his brow. He says nothing. Finally the shovel, the floorboards of the gondola, a kerosene tin, and a novel of Barbey d'Aurevilly which Theodor has brought along to read. This does the trick. The Prinzess, still reluctantly, continues her upward slant toward the low-hanging whitish clouds. I estimate: lateral drift four knots, ascent ten metres a minute. The last we see of our long-sought-for and finally attained mathematical point is a small diagonal line in the ice: the handle of the abandoned axe.

Waldemer has cheered up again now. "Drat it, I wanted to bring a flag. The axe will have to do. A surprise for the next fellows who get here."

Theodor has tied the scarf under his chin again and is holding it against his ears with both hands.

"That will be Peary and his village of Eskimos, probably. Imagine their dismay. What's this? An axe made in Connecticut. They've beaten us, fellows."

"You forget that, according to De Long, the pack is drifting at fifty metres an hour or twelve hundred metres a day. So that in a year the ax will be four hundred and thirty-eight kilometers from here."

"Ah well, Major. You and your paradoxes."

This rude good fun warms us a little if nothing else. But I observe a nuance in Theodor's joke about Peary that Waldemer hasn't noticed: his acceptance not only that the pigeon we sent from the Pole is dead but that in no other way will those in the World of Cities ever learn what we have done. I think this myself but have said nothing. Only Waldemer, evidently, still believes in the happy outcome we have so blithely predicted to ourselves and to others, even though it is possible that in a deep part of him a doubt may have crept in now. Theodor is perhaps aware that I have noticed what he said, perhaps not. I remain silent and let the two of them chatter.

Before the ax handle disappears from sight we mount the theodolite and take a bearing on it to establish our course. We are moving a good deal more to the east than I would have hoped—to the east, I can say now that we are no longer at the Pole and are back in the world of directions. This wind will never take us to Spitsbergen. Never mind, there are plenty of other islands strewn along the eightieth parallel between Greenland and Siberia. And the wind is holding, we are still rising and in the cloud bank now, it is thin and we are soon through it—the sun! It is somewhat behind us and to the right, pale pink like a melon, swimming faintly at the edges in its arctic way, and it gives out a slight, barely perceptible warmth that we can feel through our clothing but not on our frozen faces. The Prinzess feels it too; after half an hour the gas has expanded enough that we have climbed to eight hundred metres. Even a little too high. I hope we won't have to use the maneouvring valve. The hydrogen is constantly seeping in tiny quantities through the seams and stitches, even through the fine rubberized web of the silk itself, and what we have left is precious.

We have a discussion about navigation. Our present course will take us to somewhere near Franz Josef Land, but we can't expect the wind to hold in this direction. The cyclonic system sucking it in toward the continent will gradually bend it leftward, pulling us into that awkward gap along the eightieth parallel where there are no islands. And I don't expect we can go all the way to Siberia with the Prinzess day by day getting flabbier as her gas seeps out.

There is the chart: first there is Spitsbergen, then leftward along the parallel Franz Josef Land, then a long space with nothing in it, then the islands of the Siberian Archipelago.

"Spitsbergen is only a little to the right. If we set the sails to steer across the wind . . ."

"We'd have to drop low enough for the guide ropes to drag. And to do that—"

"We'd have to vent gas." Theodor is warming a little now from this pallid sun and no longer holds his mittens over his ears. He still seems exhilarated from his feat of knocking off the hoarfrost. He is cheerful and his dark eyes are watchful and interested in everything. He is like a quick and confident bird, fragile in some places and strong in others, not unhappy to be looking out at the world from the cage of the gondola and its supporting ropes. Waldemer is busy overhauling his heavy Martini rifle, he has the bolt out now and is anointing it with whale oil, which does not thicken at low temperatures, and Theodor seizes the opportunity to move closer to me and to do an odd thing: watching or pretending to watch something outside the gondola, the sun or the nonexistent horizon, he brushes my thickly jacketed elbow with his own and I feel my hand grasped in a soft but firm enclosing touch. This lasts for only a few seconds and is quite formal; interdigitation is impossible because of the mittens. When I glance at him he is watching me with a placid smile that has something in it—how shall I say? encouraging, reassuring.

I permit myself to smile slightly too. Without speaking I form my lips silently to tell him: "Va-t-en. C'est fou."

But Waldemer notices nothing. And indeed why should he notice anything when I noticed nothing myself for so many months? This face with the military cap and greatcoat, like a white dahlia in the muzzle of a gun, is an odd enough contrast itself that nobody would think anything odd of its behavior. In other clothing there is something firm and resolute about the face, virile in spite of the smooth paleness of the chin, but the uniform throws into relief its very delicacy of modeling, the grace of antique marble, a Cyprian hermaphrodite. Even on his second visit to rue de Rennes— he only dropped in for a chat, nothing like the stiff call of honour the previous fall—I was struck not so much with his youth as I had been the other time but with his mastery of the youth, his control of what for others of his age would have been perfectly spontaneous and unconscious gestures. That second time he simply knocked and came in himself without bothering to be announced. Perhaps because he preferred to visit informally and sans façons, perhaps because the concièrge had given me up for a hopeless lunatic by this time and no longer had anything to do with me.

I had just finished working, as a matter of fact, and was feeling about as sociable as I ever do. "Why don't you take off your cap?"

"We're not supposed to. It's a rule of the school."

"And why aren't you in the school now?"

"It's a holiday. I'm home for a few days."

"And where exactly is this famous school anyhow?"

"Oh. Là-bas. Somewhere beyond the Rhine."

I could get little more out of him about his mysterious Prussian education. He asked me about my work—in his thin, rather high but controlled voice—and I showed him the directional antenna basket, which was finished by this time and had enabled me to plot the course of several winter storms moving across the Île-de-France. Whatever else they taught him at the Militärische Hochschule, he had a modest but sound grasp of electrical theory. I gathered from a reference he made that he had studied Vogelweide, an excellent textbook at least for an introduction to the subject. "And what about the problem of the reciprocality of the antenna system? Have you solved that yet?"

I showed him a plot I had made the day before of a disturbance moving from Pontoise in the direction of Versailles. "The wind being from the north here in Paris, I can assume it would be almost the same only a few kilometers away. Since the bearings move in a clockwise direction—as you can see from the plot—the disturbance was necessarily to the west."

The watchful eyes took in everything as though it were not very difficult.

"In observations from a moving platform, of course—"

"In a moving platform the problem would be different. The displacement of the geometric centre . . ."

And so on. Until I became aware, after a half an hour, that we were getting along famously. I did what I seldom do for visitors, I connected up the Marconi apparatus and allowed him to listen to the distant crackling of a disturbance somewhere off over the Morvan. He himself, taking the dividers and parallel rule, plotted its bearing on a large-scale map of France I kept spread out on the table.

It got to be five o'clock.

"I usually take a cup of tea about this time. Would you—"

"I would. Thank you."

He didn't offer to help; perhaps we were not yet on such intimate terms. While I made the tea he sat watching me, slouched in the armchair with one leg over the side. I dug some English biscuits out of an old tin box and we sat for an hour or so talking about various things, among them Luisa. He no longer threatened to shoot me over her or reproached me for being affectionate behind doorways.

"You know she's studying voice now."

"No, I didn't know."

"Of course she had voice lessons before as a child. But now it's serious. She practices several hours a day, and she goes for lessons to an excellent teacher in Passy. She has a range of three octaves. It's difficult at her age to take it up again. If she had professional ambitions she ought to have kept it up and not dropped it."

"Then she has professional ambitions?"

"So I imagine." "Do you think she has talent?"

"Undoubtedly she has talent. But at what?" He made a little smile at me—not of amusement, but to indicate that the subject was serious and at the same time not serious. "This, I think, is what she wants to find out. She is determined to be somebody and not just an ornament. To occupy a post of strenuous responsibility in the world." (How well he expressed himself.) "And then too, you see," he added smoothly, "the whole thing is connected with you."

"With me?" I frankly was surprised, or had to pretend to be. After the incident of the broken bar of graphite I had imagined (for the second time, the first was Stresa) that I was banished totally from her life and thoughts and our relations had come to an end.

"Yes. You've been a great influence on her, whether you realise it or not. You've inspired her to want to make something of herself—to become better. And, you see, in the realm of science—even though she takes a great interest in the matter and is not without a certain understanding, I believe—she must leave the position of predominance to you—she can't hope to compete."

All this was rather stiff and formal; he frowned and held my glance as he talked. "It's only lately, I think, that she has understood that. And so now she has turned to music, a realm where she has a certain talent, or so she believes. And a talent that you don't share, if I'm not mistaken."

"You're not mistaken. I don't know the first thing about music, and I have an ear of solid twenty-gauge tin plate."

"If determination can do it she will succeed. She's a remarkable person, don't you think?"

I began to see the possibility of regarding this interview in another light. Was he an emissary? From the aunt—or from Luisa?

"You seem to know her wishes and plans very well." "We're very close in some ways. In other ways, different."

"What does the aunt think about all this?"

"The aunt? Ah, Ma Tante. She is in favor of each person fulfilling himself in the manner in which he or she is best fitted, regardless of the conventions of society."

This muddle over genders was the first flaw in his beautiful English.

"I too am not very much interested in the conventions of society. The trouble, of course, is that it is sometimes difficult to tell what he or she is best fitted for, until he or she has tried a good many things."

"Exactly." He got up to go now, abruptly but still courteous and correct as always. "Apropos, why is it that we never see you in Quai d'Orléans any more?"

I might have told him that I had never seen him there in I my life and could hardly believe he ever went there, instead I left the oddity of his life untampered with (to tell you the truth I didn't believe he went to a Militärische Hochschule at all) and simply remarked that I had been very busy.

"We are at home every afternoon to friends." (Which I knew.) "Ma Tante has asked about you. And also Luisa."

He smiled, clasped my hand briefly, and left. It was six o'clock and I felt unsettled, with a sense that I had nothing to do for the rest of the evening, although I had enjoyed his visit. The fact was that this talk of Quai d'Orléans had made my life in this room surrounded by coils of wire and pencil scratches on paper seem dull. Thunder take it! And what had Ma Tante asked about me? If she wanted to know anything about me she could ask Luisa.

18 July 1897

A frozen white haze fills every nook and crevice of the air; the sun penetrates it only dimly. This phenomenon extends immensely high into the air and it is impossible to climb out onto the top of it. Under these circumstances our altitude is simply what we can defend, and this is not very much. We can tell from their curve that the guide ropes are dragging on the ice below, although the ice itself is invisible. The Spiritual Telegraph still reports disturbances to the southeast, and it is this region of rarefied air that is sucking us back, even though slowly, toward the World of Cities No sights for forty-eight hours. We have only an approximate notion of where we are. The Prinzess is getting heavy with rime again. Wherever the white haze touches her a substance like fine sugar collects, hardening finally to ice. For every particle of it that forms, a particle of something else must be thrown out of the gondola. All the ballast has long since gone. Yesterday we threw over a cooking pan and an empty kerosene tin, spare clothing, our remaining books, one of our two pairs of field glasses, the provision case emptied of its content, the heavier Martini rifle. And yet we are still sinking, as I verify by periodic readings of the barometer. Waldemer seizes the hempen rigging and shakes it, and a few pieces of white crust fall on our heads. A half a kilo perhaps. But it consoles him to collect these fragments painstakingly in his mittened fingers and drop them into the whiteness below. Furthermore the exercise will keep him warm.

I decide to try to sleep a little, but this whiteness we are suspended in penetrates even the closed eyelids. For some reason I have the impression of an immense, white, cold, frozen anger, a universe bent on destroying us not by blows but by the absolute silence of its wrath. In the sleeping sack with the hood pulled over my head, I manage to achieve something close to darkness. In this way too I am reasonably warm and in time become drowsy, although I doubt whether true sleep is possible under these conditions. In the silence I can hear my companions moving about in the gondola and, occasionally, a distant crepitation or grumble from the ice below.

"Hello, here's a bag of white beans. Forgot we had brought those. They'll be first-rate boiled with a bit of bacon."

"Takes too much fuel."

"Right! Takes a lot of kerosene, and takes water too, boiling beans. Takes beans too. More weight to get rid of. Otherwise we'll be throwing it overboard soon."

From ten metres below the gondola I hear the little clicking of the starting mechanism as Waldemer attempts to light the stove. He is having some difficulty; probably the burner is clogged with rime. Here in the half darkness under the hood, my body braced against the curve of the gondola, my head motionless, I can feel the imperceptible sinking of the Prinzess. Something in my blood is aware, quite precisely, of each centimeter of space that we pass through in our slow descent, as though a rule or scale marked with altitude were slipping silently and harmlessly through my body. No question, I have some kind of barometer in my capillary system. Voices are still discussing beans. Click, click! Drat that infernal contraption. Should he risk pulling up the stove and trying to light it in the gondola? Waldemer wonders. If he does he will surely blow us all up, but for some reason I cannot take this danger seriously. Lighting the stove anyhow, by what technique I am not sure (perhaps I have dozed off for a few moments and woken up at a later stage in the difficulties), the two of them turn to discussing the macabre ethics of jettison. For, when we shall have thrown everything out of the gondola to lighten it, what will be left to throw over but ourselves? We'll draw lots, ha ha! No, we won't draw lots. That's a stale joke. Wolves pursuing the Russian bridal sleigh, lifeboat running out of water. Who is the Individual Least Useful to Humanity? A long discussion on this matter, in a jocular vein, some of which I doze through. When I become aware of the dialogue again, they have decided it would be better for each of us to cut off, say, part of one limb, so that we might return to civilization three one-legged men instead of two men hale and whole but guilt-ridden over the deletion of their companion. Beans bubble now; or perhaps that distant mutter is the ice grinding its teeth. And lower, lower, the measuring stick slips through the blood. Now I can, by leaning only slightly and encouraging her to rotate so the bustle doesn't hamper, extend my hand to reach the ankle, that complex mechanism of convexities so supple—working in its silk that it seems, in some way, autonomous. Or do I mean anatonomous? Above this wonder the silk cylinder tapers to its narrowest point, then gracefully begins to acquire diameter again. This infernal taffeta constitutes an impediment; hurrah for long arms. I arrive at a second articulation as functional and as aesthetically satisfying in its way as the ankle. "Attendez un moment, calme!" cautions Alvarez. There is no need to rush matters in the least. The ascent can wait for a moment when the wind is just right. In the meantime, it would be well to verify the apparatus, particularly the manner in which these two tendons arise so ingeniously behind, in the articulation of the joint, and rise into the unexplored regions above. Between them they enclose a hollow where we can remain snug while waiting, the knee pit. That's the jocular vein, running just along the femur. You can feel the pulse there, pulsing faster as the blood works faster in the heart, shall we call it, a convenient shorthand for the centre of feeling. Reluctantly I leave this harbour; perhaps unwisely as well, since how can one expect a smoother, rounder more pleasant concave place? A return to verify the perfection; it is the same—ah well, a pity! our goal lies farther north. The unknown calls with inexorable voice. Coupez! coupez tout! We rise, our companions below us dwindling like a clump of black flowers. En pleine mer, first voyage to Bothnia! This journey is possible only under favourable atmospheric conditions. Such silken weather can't keep up, luck has lasted too long, and in fact the smoothness ends; at the eightieth parallel we reach a zone of elastic, convoluted into tiny pressure ridges, firm enough to press into the surface beneath it. We descend, cross the zone, and rise in a smooth curve on the other side of it. The mathematics of this are cunning: pressure inward plus soft resistance outward equals the grace of a conic section. Beyond the confined parabola there is the curve of an unknown planet. The white terrain, as we venture on, shows its contempt for us with an icy motionlessness. Northward of the boundary, for a surprise, the silk ends, but the gaiety of this discovery is only temporary. For, if taffeta and a petticoat of mousseline were not enough, I must now reckon with drawers! Fluted linen, ribboned, tight at the thigh and as cunning as Carcassonne; might withstand even a prolonged siege. O tempora, O dix-neuvième siècle, and when the goal seemed so near at hand! Such obstacles are not to be forced, instead taken by stealth, obliquely. An oddity of this progress is that my shoulder now rests where my hand was once so elated to be, my elbow in the concavity of the knee. Reasoning thus, by a process of primitive addition, it is easy to see that the hand is nigh unto the neighborhood of the Elysian Fields. Once under the linen it rushes even too hastily, so that, coursing past the fine ravine where limb is joined to torso, it falls in confusion onto a grassy mound somewhat beyond its aim, but never mind, it is only necessary to retrace the path a bit through this pleasant dell into the descending slope where—what in the infernal blazes is this? the Fiend carry off such jokes! whence comes this obscene Vendôme Column where touch expects concavity? is there no respect for distinction any more? ugh! blast! it even has this stupid pair of withered prunes dangling beneath it! out of this place! and as fast as possible!

"You're so smug about it—that's what I mean; all of you. Little boys with your toys. As if they were really useful for anything such as bettering the lot of humanity, or discovering profound truths . . ."

Who was it, exactly, that was angry here? I thought I was angry, but she froze whitely, the small creased places forming at the corners of her mouth, her eyes even darker in the pale face. Yet it was she who had bought this India-rubber joke for ten francs, no doubt, in some low shop. And she became imperious, in such moods she was superb. She stamped her foot and commanded, but grandly, without a trace of petulance. "Pentapod! meet my glance, don't turn away. These fleeting millennia of your dominance I ignore, do you hear? I reside in the eons, I've forgotten nothing. My strength is of the earth, yours is words. Do you know who I am?"

"I think so."

"You're wrong. I am before arithmetic and squeaking poets. I deny cities. The earth is round and encloses us, we live in it and not on it. You've forgotten, but I have not."

"That odd aunt of yours put all this in your head, I suppose."

"There is no aunt! I am she! There is only one! And I offer you a challenge—divest yourself of your stiff shirt and your electricity, your *Stetigkeit und irrationale Zahlen*—no, you can't do it, you're afraid!" A touch of contempt showed on the white visage with its two compelling shadows. "There are other magnetisms, more ancient. You know about them but pretend to forget. In chess, from game to game, the players change sides from Black to White. Do you dare?"

"Regarding it only as a game, why not?"

"Ha! And all your coils of wire and balloons, your honours and societies, aren't they only a game? I dare you! It's you pentapods who are supposed to have the courage!" In her white contempt she was magnificent: tyrannical, commanding, her face vibrating faintly almost like that of the aunt. And she was relentless: "Players, change sides! I condemn you to tetrapodicity!"

With surprising strength she pushed me sideways, into the open door of the wardrobe. I lost my balance and very nearly fell. In clouds of taffeta, of linen, of satin, wool, brocade, muslin, silk, velour, lace, cambric, poplin, alpaca, gauze, I was almost stifled; but there was an odd luxury—about sinking into this scented and pastel mass, tepid like a bath. In some manner the tubes of black serge enclosing my legs had become removed, perhaps through an adroit prestidigitation on her part, perhaps only in the friction of my falling into this soft place. More by feel than by sight, since I was virtually blinded by these flounces and ribbons pressing me from all sides, I located a particularly fine example of drawers and donned them. I had expected some difficulty in this, but they mounted neatly about me and smoothly covered the area of my bifurcation with hardly a wrinkle. There seemed to be a poker in her curse, I reflected; in truth I had become four-limbed. The contrivance of whalebone and stiff linen that came next to hand nipped my waist rigorously but not unpleasantly. These silken snakes that rolled so smoothly up over the legs were a novel sensation, a refinement of sorts after the coarse cylinders of black that had covered them before. A satin gown in somewhat severe Empire style and a pair of ball slippers with narrow heels completed the transformation.

"Well?"

"Well?"

"Are you going to come out, or hide in there all day?"

"You know we always linger at these matters. Our tardiness is a tradition."

"A silly one." She hardly glanced at me, and in fact there was nothing remarkable in the slightest about the appearance I presented. My hair was rumpled but I brushed it downward, toward my bare shoulders, with a gesture I was so familiar with from observation that I performed it almost with a sense of habit. As far as I was able to determine without feeling it, merely from the sensation inside my face so to speak, my imperial—a neat tuft that I cultivated under my lower lip—seemed to have gone the way of the fifth limb, and along with it the short-clipped and stiff mustachios. Turning in a brisk motion, I felt the satin clinging lightly as it rotated on the lower part of my person. At the rear, just over the rising of the hips, the stuff was gathered into a kind of knot or flat protuberance falling away into pleats, and although this contrivance was visible only with difficulty, I was constantly aware of it, reminded by its contact and slight weight of my own binary protrusion just under it which the bustle in its bland hypocrisy pretended to conceal and to which it only succeeded in drawing attention, my attention as well as that of the spectator. With a humorous appreciation I admired the slimness of my fingers, the neatness of the silken feet in the ball slippers. I felt suave, smooth, and clean of impediments. If the corset thrust the softer parts of my chest upward and outward into divided swellings of characteristic shape, it only brought the most sensitive parts of these shapes lightly into contact with my clothing, another curious sensation.

"Shall we take something? Tea?"

"Why not?"

She pulled the bell cord. For the first time I glanced at her. Well-tailored tight trousers, a smoking jacket, a tie of Byronic cut. A pair of elastic-sided pumps completed the masquerade. Raising both hands to her hair, she pushed the mass rearward and at the same time upward, to the back of her head. Then, coiling the loose ends forward again above her temples, she pinned it so that it resembled a kind of turban that went perfectly with her dark eyes and the paper whiteness of her face. She resembled a Persian prince, fragile, blasé, visiting Paris and negligently adopting its mode. The clothing removed she had evidently kicked under the wardrobe or otherwise abstracted from view. There was a discreet knocking at the door to the room.

"Entrez."

It was the Breton footman, the short-legged, swarthy, and sullen one, with the tea service on a tray and the napkin on his shoulder. He set the tea service down on the round pedestal table in the corner of the room, a table provided with two Louis Quinze chairs upholstered in tapestry.

"You may pour, please, Yves. Two lumps for me and only lemon for Madame. And then leave us alone."

The brute said nothing at all, nor did his face show any expression; probably like the other bovines he was incapable of it. He served the tea with a minimum of clumsiness, dropping a lemon pip into my cup and almost, but not quite, reaching in to pick it out with his fingers. Then he departed. I understood now that the ceremony of ringing for tea was only in order that Yves might be a witness to our little masquerade. And why not? He was probably used to such things.

I drank my tea and then, impelled by a feminine prescience, went back to the wardrobe to look at the things. It was a large structure of polished mahogany, almost a room in itself, and there must have been three hundred garments in it. At the end, a very logical place, was the German military coat with its metal buttons, and the cap hanging next to it. The label inside the cap was authentic: Lindevarius Hutmacher, Wiesbaden. There were several pairs of trousers, not counting the ones worn at the moment by the Persian prince. At the end of the wardrobe there was even a smell of tobacco. I went back and sat again at the little round table.

"And if you had called me out? I might have killed you, damn it."

"I've taken pistol lessons. It's not very difficult."

I turned away to the window. Tea was over; the Persian prince stood up impulsively, came around the table, and enclosed my chest from the rear with two arms of velour. "Tu es charmante ce soir. N'est-ce pas?" The adjective with its feminine ending fell naturally from a voice that was now a light tenor, only slightly thin in timbre.

•

Now even more than before she was charming and ingenious, versatile, Protean, leading me onward like a slightly mocking will-o'-the-wisp in the shadows, and in Paris at least unseizable; the French insaisissable is better, because the sibilants suggest something serpentine and supple slithering out of a grasp. I was busy with the preparations for the long-

anticipated polar expedition which was to take place the following
summer; in a few weeks I would go to New York to confer with
Waldemer on the details. In the meantime, I defended myself with a
certain manly skill; for example, I refused to see her in the daytime
and in this way I even managed to get some work done. After six a
magnetism—which had become a habit now—drew me inevitably to
Quai d'Orléans. I wasn't a fiancé any more (and never had been, that
was left to the Peninsula) but an odd kind of family friend, one that no
one in the family had anything to do with but Luisa. And she in fact
little enough, because she was busy herself. The voice lessons in Passy
continued, mornings from nine to eleven. Meanwhile, she must learn
Swedish, because one of the rules of this lunatic game we were involved
in was that she must master everything that I knew, or attempt to,
while there were things that she knew (feminine things) that I was not
allowed to know, or was admitted to only in tiny stages. Her attempts
to try her Swedish on me, or communicate with me in that language
(I never responded to her in it on any occasion) were curious: rather
pointless remarks that might have been those of a madwoman, not that
they were at all violent, but they seemed to proceed from an internal
logic having an insufficient connection with the events outside in the
external world; or, more precisely, they seemed to proceed from a mind
that lurked quite patiently in its lair until the exact event presented itself
that seemed to make a given remark appropriate, and then pounced on
it. For example, the menu between her two gloved hands at Maxim's
(where, the Baedeker cautioned the English tourist, "Ladies are not
admitted"), she pondered with imperial condescension and presently
inquired: Vad dricker du för vin? I am sorry, Luisa, I only drink wine
in French. And after a moment, when I didn't answer: Hör du mig,
Gustav?

Yes, I hear, but I choose not to respond. I gave her an objective
glance, silent and quite long, and returned to my own study of the
menu. But she persisted, not at all disconcerted by my failure to answer,
her chin or the part of it visible over the menu still raised in that slightly
imperious way: Jäg försöker lära mig svensk. I could *see* she was trying
to learn it, but I remained deaf, out of rudeness perhaps or my own
kind of insanity, but also to signal that any effort on her part to turn
me into her Swedish tutor was condemned to death in the womb and

that I did not intend to allow this or any other language, including that of mathematics, to become a plaything between us which she would then use to entangle me even more firmly into her bonds of knitting wool and embroidery silk, which would eventually lead to my total domestication. Attempts to speak to beasts of the jungle in their own tongue, I sought to imply, are not only futile but might be dangerous.

But she had learned a great many of these ready-made, paste-them-in-your-album sentences (doubtless they were memorized from a phrase book or learned by rote from a Swedish master whose identity and existence were effectively concealed from me), and in fact her accent was passable, one might almost say good. It was several days before the opportunity presented itself for her to use the next one: Jag skulla vilja ha en kopp kaffee. Garçon, en kopp kaffee for Mademoiselle! In time she might even learn to speak the cursed lingo and make up sentences for herself. Var är saxen? Where indeed were the scissors? She must have waited at least a week for this event to come by so that she could address it in Viking. We were in Quai d'Orléans and she had discovered a loose thread in my coat sleeve that wanted cutting off—a thing that I detest people doing, especially women. Or perhaps she had pulled the thread loose when I wasn't looking as the only way of utilizing number eighty-six in the phrase book. O, det var synd! (She had dropped the scissors; it was too bad perhaps but not really a sin.) And, as I remember, it was later that same evening as she poured me a tiny glass of cognac by the piano that she articulated the longest and most complicated of these linguistic Frankenstein monsters, one with relative pronouns, dependent clauses, and even a comma in the middle, and perhaps the only one of them all that had any significance: Vem som helst som har besökt Stockholm vet, att man dricker mycket akvavit i Sverige. Even the intonation was correct, our droll Hyperborean way of lilting a little upward on each syllable, and the irony that is one of our national characteristics even among the thickest-skulled of peasants. Ah, she still remembered that akvavit in Stockholm! It was as though she blamed me and the akvavit for what had happened—twenty-four hours later!—in the cottage in Finland, and by extension for everything that followed, including Stresa, but not Paris, where nothing happened. And why didn't it happen in Paris? Because she was adroit and insaisissable, slipping blithely and with a grave little non-smile out of my grasp each time to speak of theatre tickets or explore in her reticule for a chocolate which she popped into my mouth to keep me temporarily at bay. Ah, Luisa, det war synd!

•

She having at length found the tickets, we left the house on the Île, crossed the Pont-Marie on foot to rue Saint-Antoine, and went off in a cab to the Théâtre de l'Oeuvre, rue Blanche, not far from Place Pigalle. It was not a very savoury neighborhood in my estimation, but Luisa was drawn as though by a secret vice to any curious and outré event that took place in the general region of Montmartre. For this occasion she was dressed in a new manner, her fifth or sixth, I had lost count: tailored skirt, mannish jacket, and knee-length Russian leather boots. Even a tiny riding crop, which she carried inconspicuously in her left hand like a marshal's baton. For a miracle, this time she left the reticule behind. Perhaps she felt she was defended by the little whip.

In the darkness of the cab she passed me the tickets. They were fleetingly illuminated by a street lamp. *Ubu Roi,* what was that? A play, it seemed, by some ragamuffin who frequented Boulevard Saint-Germain. (I remembered explaining to her at our first meeting that I never went to plays.) There was a crush in rue Blanche in front of the theatre, and another one after we got inside. She also knew that I disliked crowds.

Finally we were seated somehow, in our own seats or perhaps in someone else's, it didn't seem to matter. There was really no need for a spectacle on the stage; the audience was enough. Men in trailing capes or long velvet cloaks with silver clasps, girls in the costume of Botticelli's Printemps, with hair to match. A woman in coarse worsted tights intended to be flesh-coloured but actually a pale orange, a purple tunic open in the front, and dirty ballet slippers; a gypsy cloak around her shoulders. In front of us was a muscular individual who seemed to be a bicycle racer: tight sweater, short coat, and old trousers tucked into his socks. Farther along in the same row a horse-faced Irish poet, and beyond him an individual wearing a headdress of Indian feathers which he refused to take off, to the indignation of the spectators behind him.

"Do you know these people?"

"Some of them."

"They are your friends?"

"No, silly."

"Then why have we come here?"

"You remember M. Lugné-Poe, the young man who comes sometimes to Quai d'Orléans?"

I supposed I did.

"Well, this is his theatre."

"Ah."

Luisa was pleased with herself. If M. Lugné-Poe came to her house, which almost belonged to the best society of the Île Saint-Louis, then that guaranteed not only the respectability but the importance of his theatre, in her eyes. (Or leave out respectability, that had nothing to do with the matter, and the importance compensated for it in any case.) As evidence that we were present at a significant event, she pointed out the eminent critic Sarcey, the theatre reviewer of Le Temps, a massive and impeccably clad gentleman who seemed too large for the seat he was sitting in. M. Sarcey seemed unhappy already; he took out his watch and glanced at it frequently, and unfurled a newspaper and read it while waiting for the performance to begin.

After some delay a crude deal table was brought out before the curtain, then a chair, then a carafe and drinking glass. Finally the author himself, M. Jarry, appeared before the curtain and sat down at the table. He began reading from a paper in front of him with a monotonous voice. He was a small man in a black suit too large for him, his face made up in the flat and blank white of a clown. He sipped nervously from the glass. It was impossible to tell what his discourse was about. Something about the tradition of the Guignol, masks, the plausibility of revolvers being shot off in the year 1000. He implied that his play took place in "Poland . . . that is to say, nowhere." At the end he bowed like a doll breaking in two and disappeared. Next a young man came out and played the overture along with his wife, four-handed, on the piano. Between the two of them they made quite a din. I was not a musician and had no opinion of this.

Finally the curtain went up. Some rather childishly painted scenery. Trees, a bed, a fireplace with a skeleton hanging by it, a window in the sky. Out came King Ubu in a pear-shaped costume. He looked around him. Finally discovered the audience. And bellowed a monosyllab obscenity, a rather amusing one I felt, if only for the way it mispronounced. I glanced at Luisa. She was sitting looking straig the stage with her chin raised, receptive but imperial, in exactly the same way as though she were listening to Chopin.

There was a second of silence, then bedlam. It was fifteen minutes or more before the play could go on. There were whistles, jeers, catcalls. Several members of the audience got up and walked out, including a gentleman who trod on our toes on his way down the row. A few objects soared up out of the pit and onto the stage; probably they were only wadded-up balls of paper. Those remaining in the audience were divided into two camps, the whistlers and the clappers. Several fist fights started in the orchestra. I began looking for a suitable exit, but Luisa was gazing upon it all placidly, her mouth fixed not in a smile exactly but in a little line of satisfaction, the riding crop lying across her knees. The Irish poet hadn't understood the obscene word and his friend was explaining it to him, of necessity raising his voice almost to a shout. In the row ahead of us the bicycle racer had climbed up onto his seat. "You wouldn't understand Shakespeare either!" he yelled at the objectors. Another voice behind us was chanting, with the repeated monotony of a machine, "It's Lugné-Pot-de-Chambre! Lugné-Pot-de-Chambre!" Some people were undecided which camp to join and were clapping and whistling in alternation; the bicycle racer was doing both at once.

The houselights were turned on abruptly, catching a half dozen or more people standing on their seats with their fists raised. The actors (there were two of them now, the pearshaped Ubu and a rather plump lady with a monobosom who had come out on the stage to see what was happening) waited patiently, looking out on the scene of tumult below them. The roles had been reversed and it was they now who were the spectators, watching the performances out in the rows of seats.

After a quarter of an hour or so of this, Père Ubu improvised a jig and fell down sprawling over the prompter's box. This accident distracted the audience enough so that the lights were turned down and the actors could continue. The Polish Army, represented by a skinny individual wearing some pots and pans, came on. Pere Ubu usurped the kingdom, ordered all the nobles to be thrown down a trapdoor, and swore by his Green Candle. For a scepter he carried a toilet brush. At the end of every scene a venerable gentleman in evening dress tottered across the stage on the points of his toes, took down a sign with the title of the scene on it, and put up another in its place. When it was necessary for new characters to enter they trooped in and out through the fireplace. Periodically the unacceptable word was pronounced:

"Mer-drrrrre!"

with a superfluous *r* that rolled on for several seconds. Each time it produced a new epidemic of shouts and whistles, and the performance came to a halt. M. Sarcey wrenched his impressive silhouette from his chair and left, indignant. Ubu, having slaughtered everybody else, now turned on Mère Ubu, threatening to shove little pieces of wood in her ears, lacerate her posterior, extract her brain through her heels, suppress her spinal marrow, and open up her swimming bladder. The bicycle racer, standing up again, shouted "Vive l'anarchie!" The people behind him stood up in order to be able to see, and this provoked a sporadic but general standing up all over the house. Luisa and I were standing up. Someone behind demanded "Sit down!" and I sat down. Luisa remained standing, and after several more shouts the beefy person behind her put both hands on her shoulders and attempted to push her into her seat. I groaned, seeing myself in the Bois on a frosty morning (it was December) waiting to receive a hole in my pancreas. I stood up again but Luisa had already turned and dealt the beefy person a sharp thwack with her riding crop. It caught him just on the side of his red neck, leaving a line that was even redder. He sat down without a word, Luisa and I sat down, and the play lurched on toward its end. Ubu was now on an ocean voyage, shouting contradictory commands to the sailors, ordering them to haul down the main bib and reach for their tonsils. The whole thing came to a climax in a kind of chorus, accompanied by the two-handed piano and an orchestra of pots, gongs, and cymbals.

No one seemed anxious to leave. Most of the spectators were still standing around under the houselights gesticulating and arguing. We fought our way out onto the street, assisted once or twice by Luisa's crop. "Canaille," she remarked quite without rancor and simply by way of commentary. Perhaps she meant the beefy-faced man who had laid hands on her, or perhaps the whole pack, with the exception of course of M. Lugné-Poe, who had been received in Quai d'Orléans. A little way down rue Blanche I managed to find another cab, and we were clip-clopping off to a cabaret that Luisa knew about on the Butte, " amusing place and some funny people." More swine no doubt, I myself. Was this the vulnerable young thing I had been obliged to to the Café Royal lest some ruffian accost her? Of course she hadn't had her riding crop then. The cab pulled up in rue des Abbesses.

It was a kind of music hall. Once inside I saw at a glance that the clientele was highly dubious. The females outnumbered the men by three to one, but they were not there to offer their charms for male approval; most of them were more interested in each other. There was an odour of talcum, perspiration, and cheap wine. Luisa was immediately recognized and hands floated up to her from a table halfway across the room. The table had quite a zoo around it. One denizen was a young woman in tight-fitting black tights and a jersey, short hair, her face covered with white greasepaint and a kind of map of intersecting black lines drawn across it. Perhaps she was part of the entertainment and would get up and do a pantomime later. Next to her was a rare creature like a tropical bird: polka-dot blouse with fuchsia borders, red wig sticking out of a canary-coloured beret, black lip rouge, spidery dyed lashes, green shadows under the eyes. This was Elka. She sat with her elbows on the table as though she owned the place, hardly bothering to look up as we sat down, and talked rapid French with a patois lilt.

"You've been dining chérie?"

"No, I seldom eat any more. It's a vulgar habit. One has been to the Théâtre de L'Oeuvre."

"Ah! La chose de Jarry.

Et c'était bien amusant?"

"Jolly."

Luisa had little more to say. Instead of paying attention to Elka, she searched around the room in an interested way to see who else was there. She and Elka were elaborately ignoring each other like a pair of strange cats. Elka eventually condescended to introduce her to the others: "Mademoiselle Hickman, a singer." This phrase seemed to me curious on two counts. First of all, it was a long time since I had thought of her as possessing a paternal origin powerful enough to confer a surname on her. Over the months she had become, in some part of my mind, the exclusive creature and product of the two old women in Quai D'Orléans, as though they had confected her out of raw materials and brought her to life through some necromancy of their own. Now was abruptly resurrected in another guise, the child of the cowboy-r who had ridden out fearlessly into the mob of howling Apaches.

Perhaps this disparity, taken in the light of the hereditary theories of M. Zola, would account for at least some of her foibles and inconsistencies. But which was it, Luisa the cowgirl or Luisa the daughter of her mother, who had struck the beefy man with her crop? There was much food for reflection here. Second, Elka's phraseology now obliged me to think of her singing as professional. Why did something in me resist this notion, something coming from below the midriff and as inaccessible to reasonable argument as it was fundamental? Jealousy? Preposterous.

As for me, nobody bothered to introduce me, but I heard someone murmur, hardly bothering to whisper, "son Suedois." *Her* Swede? Another piece of grammar with curious implications. The only other male at the table was a Peruvian, an employee of a diplomatic mission as I understood it, with oleaginous hair parted exactly in the middle and a face like a sun. His elbows were on the table too like Elka's, and he made an Incan smile.

"You perform, mademoiselle? If so I would be enchanted to come and hear you."

"There will be a recital in February."

"Till then—one can only wait. In the meantime . . ."

The devil with his pre-Columbian innuendoes. Luisa, however, hardly seemed to take notice of him. A feminine and Sapphic air seemed to pervade the place, an air of maenads. The only dancers on the floor were couples of women, and two young ladies at a table across the room—demurely clad, as a matter of fact, in blouses and long black skirts—had candidly slipped their arms about each other. Champagne came. Elka opened it—with éclat, the cork soaring across the room— and poured for both of us. Luisa and I touched glasses, her mouth set in her little well-bred and distant smile as it had been all evening.

A voice, somewhere in the depths of the room, called "Gavotte!" We were interrupted by the entertainment that broke out periodically in such places. A piano, a violin, and a set of drums played Offenbach, and two dancers cavorted into the open space in the centre of the room; there was no stage. The dancers were strong-limbed and square-jawed; the one on the left had a faint bluish shadow on her upper lip. Seizing their skirts with both hands, they kicked up their legs several times while the drum thumped punctuation, then performed the customar present-arms of their art: one foot held in the hand as far up as it wou go, above the level of their heads, they bounced like concupiscent rabbits on the other foot in time to the music. The stockings were black, the rest of the costumes white. In the masses of not very clean linen, samples of bare skin were visible between stockings and knickers. Luisa was no more perturbed by this than she had been by Ubu's monosyllable. The Peruvian caught my eye and smirked.

A drum roll. The two dancers, wearing carved wooden smiles, sprang into the air a little way twiddling their feet, and when they came down their legs split apart like broken scissors, coming to a stop stretched out on opposite sides of the floor. Applause, smoke, and more champagne. The dancers disappeared and a few lady couples took their places on the floor. Someone, probably the Peruvian, had given Luisa a long thin cigar, and now she allowed him to light it for her.

And what was the matter with me? Wasn't I enjoying myself? That was the worst of it. I was. That is, not enjoying exactly. It was a phenomenon over which I had very little control. On the one hand I found the dancers disgusting. On the other hand a kind of imaginary elastic cord established itself in my mind, without my noticing it, between those white zones above the black stockings and Luisa's businesslike form next to me in its English tweed. Now this cord gradually shortened, drawing the one image to the other. I found myself reminded of what I knew very well was under the tweed, a thought that up to then had not been appropriate or convenient because of the very tweedy briskness of her manner. This little worm prickled at me in a private place until I was exasperated. The Fiend carry off Offenbach anyhow! I pushed back my chair and announced in a firm voice that I had work to do the next day.

Elka, her tar-coloured lips fixed in a curve, looked at me and then at Luisa. "Mais tu restes n'est-pas chérie?"

Luisa hesitated for a moment, or at least remained silent for reasons connected with her own private tactics of managing the world about her. Then, with a smile quite as fixed and conventional as Elka's, she said, "No, I must go." We rose. The Peruvian started to get up and then thought better of it, putting his elbows back on the table. As we left, the Map-Faced Girl saluted in her own way: her hand raised with palm oward us, she bent down each finger in turn until it touched the palm.

The hand, like her face, was plaster-white and covered with a network of fine lines.

I handed Luisa into the cab and climbed in behind her. With an audacity, a recklessness, ignoring the risk of the riding crop in her lap, I slipped an arm under her back and pulled her toward me on the leather seat 16, Quai d'Orléans! She seemed to show no objection and the tweed shoulder even settled complacently into the niche between my arm and my chest. Once she sighed, turned the pale oval of her face toward me in the darkened cab, then seemed to change her mind and looked out the window again. The gaslights of the Grands Boulevards went by dreamily. When we crossed over onto the Île on the Pont Louis-Philippe, she stirred and became her businesslike self again. We arrived before the house on the quai with its baroque marble pediments.

That ape of an Yves was still up and let us in. Then he disappeared. Luisa led me up the broad ceremonial staircase and down the hall in the darkness. Then, at the door of her dressing room, she told me to wait. "I have to change, don't you see, dear heart."

I waited, fingering the toe of a cupid caryatid who was holding up the ceiling with the help of his companion on the other wall. In the gloom my mind quite freely generated images that were concrete enough—almost—to touch: the yellow room in Stresa, the brocade like pale peach tinged with red and gold—I took a breath, calmed myself, and looked out the window into the dark courtyard, where only a flickering oil lamp illuminated the damp reticulation of the stones. The door of the dressing room opened and Theodor appeared in his military cap and boots, buttoning the greatcoat.

"What is this?"

"I must, you see. Because only men are admitted in the place we're going."

"Place?" "The Château Rouge, in the Marais. I told you—don't you remember? It's very droll, full of voyous and sinister persons."

It was after two. The great clock in the hall below had struck while I was waiting.

"You're mistaken. I am not going anywhere."

"Please yourself. It would have been more amusing with a friend. But—"

"You're not going alone?"

"Why not?"

I could see through this sort of sham easily enough. It was only a vastly complexified and more subtle version of the tactic that had before dragged me half unwillingly from recitals to the Café Royal to fittings at Worth's and back again: the threat of some vague and unnameable peril if I was not along to offer protection. This time, still exasperated by that dumb worm of affection crawling in my vitals, I declined the gambit.

"In that case—since it's late—I'll get some needed sleep."

"Ah yes, your work—" Rather distractedly. I had lost or was mistaken; she really was going. She even preceded me a little down the staircase as though she were in a hurry, glancing back only once. We parted on the quai, the military figure going on down under the gaslights toward the Pont-Marie. I crossed the river the other way and found a cab in Boulevard Saint-Germain. Back in that leather-lined and camphor-smelling capsule of darkness (it might have been the same one) I thrust my fists into my coat pockets and clenched my jaw. The gnawing worm was taking no account of my defiance of her, my wishing her at the bottom of the Seine; it was still as vertebrate as ever. Perhaps on my way home I should visit one of the establishments provided, for reasons of hygiene. The cabman would know. Or I could have asked Theodor.

•

But these are childish disappointments, of no concern at all to a mature man of character whose two hands are firmly in control of his destiny. It is I who am in command of the expedition, I tell myself, and also the captain of my soul (Luisa is fond of reciting Henley's poem, which she knows by memory) and I can go any direction I choose through this thin whitish soup as long as it is downward. For two hours the Prinzess, with a regal dignity appropriate to her, has been descending a stairway of broad shallow steps: a half metre or so down, we throw something out, she glides level for a while, then a draft of cold air or a lazy notion strikes her and down she goes again. The guide ropes, as noted in our equipment book by Alvarez, weigh twenty-four kilos. We detach them—they unfasten with a quick-release device invented by Waldemer in case they should catch on a pressure ridge or hummock—and watch them fall to the broken slabs of ice below. The pack now resembles a large white cake which somebody has damaged through dropping. There are many gaps and cracks of black water—in places the irregular white shapes scarcely touch each other—and we must hope for luck enough to come down on the white and not on the black in this infernal checker game. Cast out something else!

"The Spiritual Telegraph?"

"No." This is irrational on my part since it is heavy and we have no more use for it. We must keep the second and lighter of Waldemer's two rifles too, and the primus, and a can of kerosene. All the tools can go, except for the old shears with the traces of red paint on the handles which we are keeping for a special purpose. Overboard with the medical kit, five kilos at least, and the wooden packing case we use as an all-purpose stool and navigation table. We are still sinking, although not so dangerously fast now. Our height, fifty metres. Stand by the maneouvring valve!

Theodor holds the valve cord ready in his hands, Waldemer prepares to leap out and hold the gondola from sliding along on this cake frosting, perhaps into a stretch of open water. The gondola touches the ice with a soft bump and rises, very slowly, a metre or so into the air again. Theodor pulls the valve cord to produce a hiss from overhead. The gondola bumps again and slants sideways, dragging over the ice. Everything in it—few enough as these items are now—tumbles to one side in a muddle. Waldemer is out onto the ice and so am I, but the gondola is not very hard to hold; the wind is light and the balloon has no pull to it any more. The great red and white globe that was so swelling and regal before now looks more like a dried fig; it droops to one side, twists drowsily, as though what it would really like to do is lie down and sleep on the ice.

This Prinzess will never take us anywhere any more. She must stay here. A dying friend; but oddly enough I find I have no more affection for her now that her usefulness is at an end. Ungrateful humanity! We will take care of the obsequies shortly. First we have a meal, concentrating on the heavier things we can't take with us: Potage Hodge Podge (a specialty of ours consisting of anything at hand thrown in), steak, a mixture of cocoa powder and tea dissolved in hot water, and hardtack with raspberry syrup. A good and nourishing dinner. Then, throwing away the pots and pans instead of washing them, we set to work constructing the vehicle that will carry us south in place of the moribund Prinzess.

The Faltboot, a clever German contrivance supplied gratis by the manufacturer, fits into a kind of suitcase. There is a complicated system of struts which must be unfolded, then the oiled-canvas cover is fitted over it. When it is done it is five metres long and weighs no more than a twelve-year-old child; any one of us can easily lift it with one hand. Onto the bottom we screw oaken sled runners, and there are three ropes attached to the bow so we can fan out like Commander Peary's dogs and pull it over the ice.

All this takes an hour. Now to the Prinzess. I climb up into the gondola and grasp the cord of the bursting valve. Putting my weight to it, I pull down three metres or more of the cord. There is a ripping sound from overhead as the stitches pull out, and a sound like a giant sigh. Quick now! There is almost no wind and the mass of red and white silk falls directly downward. I manage to drop to the ice and get away before it covers the gondola in a soft smother.

Hydrogen is odourless; that whiff of the inferno comes from the traces of the sulphuric acid the gas was made from. Taking the old red-painted shears in hand, I attack this confused mass of silk with giant-size bubbles of gas floating and oozing here and there in it. In a quarter of an hour I have cut a large rectangle out of it which will serve us as a tent. It is light, folds into a small package, and is waterproof. We set it on the ice near the Faltboot and begin selecting and piling up the other things we will take with us:

primus stove
kerosene
small saucepan
sextant and charts
compass
Faltboot
paddles
pemmican
Bovril
½ doz. misc. cans food
sugar

bacon
cocoa
Rousseau meat powder
three sleeping sacks
matches, in waterproof container
12—power binoculars
.256 Mannlicher rifle with ammunition
pair of bamboo poles, to hold up tent
1 set spare clothing, reindeer-skin

Can all this fit into that thin contrivance of canvas and struts? It seems unlikely. We set to work, experimenting with various stowage plans. The sleeping sacks are the worst problem; they are bulky. Everything finally goes in, by some miracle, and in a half an hour we are ready to leave. At noon GMT, the mist clearing a little, I manage to get a sun sight. It puts us at 82° 50' north, four hundred and fifty miles from the Pole and about a hundred and eighty from the nearest land, White Island in the strait between Cape Leigh Smith and Franz Josef Land. An afternoon's stroll, followed by a pleasant boat ride on the lake. Luisa and I have practiced for this in the Bois de Boulogne. We must remember the rules: MM. les clients are requested not to abandon their boats except in the places provided by the management. Or the deposit is forfeited by the Great Nobody.

We set out. Everybody's face is frozen; we are wrapped in various kinds of rags and cloths to keep warm. I hardly look behind at the wreckage of the Prinzess and neither do the others. All the junk, the stale hopes and dirty frying pans of our venture, is left behind. What a glory, to have no possessions but what will fit into this thin Charon's bark of canvas! We can wander wherever we want over this jumbled plain of ice blocks, the wind has no more power over us. We tug at our pulling ropes, I in the middle and my companions one on either side, and the Faltboot follows. Having referred once to the compass, I steer by watching the sun out of the corner of my eye.

As commander. I note that morale is good. Waldemer trudges along like a happy machine, bent against the rope, and Luisa is talkative.

"Do you know, there is a curious sensation. We are at the top of the world, and as we walk it turns under our feet. Like the bear at the circus walking on a large ball. But this means we will never get there. The ball turns as we walk, and we will always be at the top. Hör du mig, Gustav?"

"Ja, den är intressant."

I notice only after she speaks, and after I answer, that we are talking in Swedish. We are alone; Waldemer is only a large puffing sled dog some several metres away on our right. For some time now I have been aware of a curious sensation: that there is one more person in the party than my rational senses can account for, a ghost that melts in the air whenever I turn to find it. Now I understand it: there is a Luisa for me and a Theodor for Waldemer. The one and the other of us, looking at the slight figure in black with the shawl tied over the cap, sees or imagines something different. Which is true in all triangles of three persons, no doubt. But my case is different, because I see not only the Luisa of my own mind but also the Theodor of Waldemer's. With a little effort of the will I can make these two images merge, then separate, like the images in a badly adjusted pair of binoculars. Waldemer is dense! I had never plumbed the depth of his density before. It is the very exquisite density of intelligence. Like the density of a gas, it increases with the pressure applied to it. He is not subject to disquieting intuitions of our sort, sensations that the world is turning under his feet and so on. His insensitivity to such nuances is a quality greatly to be envied. It keeps him happy, the lucky fellow. He doesn't know that we are condemned always to remain at the North Pole.

"We will stay here forever, do you know, Gustav? We will go on walking over this whiteness and eat polar bears. It will be one long night, and we will dream in white. Nothing but whiteness and cold. And it will be pure, we will be pure, we will be the whole world."

"Provided our ammunition lasts. We have fifty rounds."

Luisa speaks slowly and forms each word with pain, not only because of the unfamiliar language, but because of the cold that has numbed all our faces and especially hers.

"We will sharpen polar-bear bones and use them to kill the others. And after we have eaten many polar bears we will become white too. We will blend into the air and become invisible. Won't that be nice, Gustav? Haven't you ever dreamed of being invisible?"

'You forget that polar bears are red on the inside."

"Not the ones we kill. They will only be dream bears. Do you think we are getting anywhere, Gustav, stumbling over these white blocks? How do you know we are going in the right direction?"

"I am steering by the sun."

"There isn't any sun just at the moment. And suppose we are going in the right direction, Gustav. What will happen then?"

"We may get to Franz Josef Land. The sealers from Tromsö call there sometimes in the summer."

"That's what I mean, Gustav. Suppose the sealers from Tromsö find us and take us back to Paris. What will happen then? I think it would be better to stay at the North Pole and go on walking and walking and let the ball turn under us. Because, Gustav, there are all kinds of circles, and if you come back and find yourself at the same place again, you're not allowed to go around again."

This childish-metaphysical style is caused, no doubt, by the paucity of her vocabulary in an unfamiliar language. The style is cryptic but quite clear, at least to me. Perhaps because I am fairly adept at cryptology, or perhaps because I myself have been thinking the thoughts she is trying to express.

"Did you know that when you came along?"

"That some circles are forbidden? Of course. It was to break the circle that I came." She turns and shifts the pulling rope to the other side, her hands beginning to tire. "The world, down there"—with no hand to point she gestures with her head—"is a hell of circles, and each one of us is trapped in a different one. Millions of circles, millions of damned souls."

"There are nine circles in hell. Do you know what the first one is, where they suffer the least?"

"Lust. Paolo and Francesca—were not so badly off, I think. But there are deeper circles. Knowledge is one. And betrayal, at the very bottom."

This, no doubt, is to consign me to my fit punishment. I help her by quoting sardonically, "When lovely woman stoops to folly / And finds too late that men betray—"

"I don't mean that. We only betray ourselves. No one is betrayed, except by himself." She tries it two ways in the unfamiliar grammar and is still not quite satisfied with the results. "If we are betrayed, it is only by ourselves." She loses her footing and slips to one knee on the glazed ice, gets up without any expression on her face grey with cold, and bends again to the pulling rope. "One way to betray yourself is to try to be too many people at once."

"How many people should a person try to be, in your opinion?"

"One, at the most. Most people don't even succeed in that."

"Whereas you and I—" She looks at me sharply. "You, Gustav, are all one thing. I am the sinner. If we were to go back—" She corrects herself. "When we come back, you will be in the first circle, I in the last."

"Say, you two. Look where you're going. Even I can tell—there's the sun over there. That sort of lighter place in the haze."

Waldemer has been doing most of the work with his pulling rope on the right, causing the Faltboot to steer badly. Our conversation is deflecting the whole expedition to the left, toward Siberia. "You fellows have been talking Squarehead for an hour now. Don't you ever get tired?"

Recalled to duty by his bluff jibes, we pitch in and do our share. The Faltboot slithers over hummocks the size of grand pianos, picks its way through gaps in pressure ridges. Setting one boot ahead of the other, at a pace of a nautical mile an hour perhaps, we progress over this junkyard and old-furniture warehouse of ice. Waldemer, still doing most of the work, grunts and emits an extraordinary amount of steam.

"Don't know what you find to talk about anyhow. Nothing up here to talk about. Probably recalling your happy memories back in Paris."

"Ah, you don't understand Swedish?" Theodor is full of mock apology for not including him in the conversation.

"Heaven forbid. I can just barely parley-voo."

"We quote poetry to each other, to pass the time."

"Poetry?"

"Dante, Goldsmith."

"Oh, bully. Save your breath to cool your mush. We've got a ways to pull this contraption yet."

•

At seven o'clock we catch sight of something ahead. We stop, and I get the binoculars out of the Faltboot to look. Through the 12-power glasses everything seems to quiver. Sometimes the white spots look round, then they elongate into pillars, move sideways, and merge one

into the other. There are four or five of them at least. I pass the glasses
to Waldemer.

He twists the focus knob, steam coming out from under the
binoculars to freeze on his mustache, which is already white with rime.

"Good. A large male. A female. And at least two good-size cubs."

The ectoplasmic effects are only tricks of the atmosphere. These
are no dream bears but creatures of flesh and blood like ourselves. For
the next hour we work our way cautiously toward them. The floes are
getting more rotten, the open leads of water more frequent, and we
progress only with difficulty. Once we are stopped by an open stretch
of water. No way to get around it; it extends off into the far distance
on both sides. It is ten metres to the solid ice on the other side. Hastily
we unpack everything from the Faltboot and launch it into the open
lead. Then, since it is only a two-man boat, Theodor crawls into it and
worms his way up into the bow, completely out of sight. Waldemer and
I then get in, pile the sleeping sacks, food, rifle, and other equipment on
our laps, and paddle across the lead to the other side. There occupants
and other contents are unpacked and the Faltboot pulled up on the
ice. While Waldemer and I go ahead to reconnoitre, Theodor is left to
repack the baggage in the Faltboot as before. Finding the bears still in
the same place, we come back and set to with the pulling ropes again.

The white spots ahead remain more or less stationary, although they
gradually assume solidity as they become larger and no longer leak out
and crawl upward into the atmosphere, or sideways into each other. At
five hundred metres we can make out the black of muzzles, and the red
stain of something they are fussing with on the ice: a seal carcass. The
large male raises his head, points it in our direction for a moment, and
then goes back to what he is doing. The bears are not educated in the
ways of men and may even doubt that we exist. We are blurry spots on
the ice, as they are blurry spots to us.

But Waldemer is cautious. He unlimbers the Mannlicher from the
baggage, we drop the pulling ropes and leave the Faltboot where it
is, and go on slowly over the ice with Waldemer in the lead. At two
hundred metres he begins bending down to take advantage of the cover
of ice hummocks, and we imitate him. When we look up again, the
female and the nearly mature cubs are lumbering off in a leisurely way,
bending their heads now and then to look behind them. The male has

turned to face us. He is quite motionless, then rears up on his haunches to get a better look. He drops down onto all fours again, and has still not retreated when Waldemer gets in his first shot at a hundred metres. A red blotch appears on his throat and he falls down, but gets up at once. The second shot takes him in the hindquarters. This causes the rear end of him to fall down, but also incites him to fresh efforts, so that he gets up and begins running, the hindquarters dragging a little. Waldemer, taking more care now and making sure of his aim, squeezes one last time the lever of his ingenious machine which will convert this dangerous enemy into butcher meat. The bear tumbles in a heap, stretches out on the ice as though he were reaching for something with his forequarters, and expires. One hind leg rises once, extends a little, then sinks slowly.

"Huzzah!"

With an exultant gesture he pushes the rifle skyward, turns his face with its sugar-candy whiskers to us, and grins. Then, catching a note of something besides elation on our own faces, he calls out to us over the ice from fifty metres away, "Hard to do a neat job with this small-caliber stuff. Have to get in two or three rounds sometimes. Should have saved the Martini."

We advance to inspect the victim. He is a big old he-bear, not really white but a pale stained yellow like dirty ice cream. The muzzle, the eyes, and the bottoms of the paws are black. The ravaged seal lies in a patch of splattered gore a little distance away, and the bear's own blood is spreading under him in a pool that becomes pink as it sinks into the porous ice. Luisa looks at it for a moment, with the detachment and slight reluctance of a schoolgirl observing a dissected salamander. Then she turns away and she and I, leaving Waldemer with his prize, trail our way back to where we have left the Faltboot.

"You were right, he is red inside."

"We always forget that. About ourselves too."

"So, the bear ate the seal, and we will eat the bear. And then?"

"You have circles on your mind today."

"I make no objection, you understand. I just want to understand clearly how everything will happen." "What happens now is that we will bring the baggage back to Waldemer, and we will make camp."

By the time we have dragged the Faltboot up to him Waldemer has opened up the bear with his hunting knife to get at the rib meat. There is not much of this, to tell the truth; the old fellow seems to consist mostly of spars. While Waldemer finishes his butcher work Theodor and I put up the tent. The bright red stripes are conspicuous on the white landscape. Our camp is a study in red, white, and black: the striped tent, the bear, the blood on the snow, the black seal carcass. Inside the tent I start up the primus and make cocoa. The primus isn't working well; the flame burns yellow and pops up and down on the burner. I adjust it to try to get the proper blue, with only partial success. Then Waldemer comes in dangling some slabs of dark red flesh. Attempts to cook these are unavailing; we don't have a large enough pan and can only hold them over the primus flame with forks. In any case they are better raw, getting cool now in the chill air and the consistency of hard ice cream. When chewed for a long time the flesh melts slowly in the mouth, turning into a nourishing essence with a taste more of strawberries than of blood, and leaving behind a certain quantity of fibers that get stuck in the teeth. It was truly an ancient he-bear, quite possibly the oldest bear in the arctic. Waldemer opines that it was probably an escaped menagerie bear. The meal is "bully," as he himself says, and we have more hardtack with raspberry syrup for dessert.

With the primus going the tent warms gradually. This makes us all drowsy after our day's promenade over the frozen junkyard, and the same is scheduled for tomorrow. All the gear from the Faltboot has been brought into the tent, and we sort out and unroll the sleeping sacks. For some reason there are only two of these. We tumble over the other things piled in the back of the tent, but the third one is not there. Waldemer even goes out to look for it in the Faltboot, letting in a quantity of cold air as he comes and goes, even though Theodor assures him that everything has been brought in.

Waldemer is bemused. "You're sure it was there when we broke camp this morning?"

"I packed it myself."

"And I recall unpacking all three of them when we came to the lead."

"It fell out perhaps when we were crossing the lead."

"Not likely."

The onus of the misdeed falls on Theodor. All three sacks were there when we came to the lead, nothing was left on the ice behind, and Waldemer now remembers piling the three of them out on the ice on the other side. It was Theodor who was supposed to re-stow everything while Waldemer and I were off scouting the route up ahead.

The sleeping sacks are identical and it is impossible to tell whose is missing. Theodor offers to go without. But there is no floor in the tent and without the sacks there is nothing to lie on but ice. Some prolonged and jocular negotiations take place as to which two of us are to share a sleeping sack. The arguments:

1. Offered by Waldemer. The Major and he have known each other the longest, they are old hunting chums and used to bedding down just any way.

2. My own, totally facetious. I am captain of this expedition and as such entitled to have a private cabin. This is not taken seriously and Theodor offers a fanfare with a trumpet made out of his hands.

3. He proposes instead his own scheme, which is based on scientific fact and is virtually indisputable. Waldemer is by far the largest of us. A sleeping sack would hardly accommodate Waldemer and anyone else. The rationale ought to be that the tandem sleeping sack should be strained to the minimum through charging it with the minimum bulk. This is constituted by Theodor himself and the Major. This thesis carries the day, and we arrange ourselves for the night accordingly.

Waldemer is deep into his sleeping sack with only the top of his head still showing, the hunting cap pulled down over it. From inside we hear, "The Major's whiskers look prickly to me, Theodor. You can come over here if you change your mind." Then there is a sigh, and nothing more from his direction. In only a few minutes he is snoring.

There are two reasons to worm one's way far down into the sack. For warmth, first of all. Even with the primus burning all night the temperature can hardly be more than freezing, whereas inside the sacks we can hope for something at least approaching blood warmth. And for protection against the light. The sun, which seemed pale outside, comes through the red and white silk as though magnified in some way in the process; the white is white as ice glare, the red is the blinding effulgence of bear blood, of fire, of the sun beating twisted on the ripples of the lake in Stresa. Down, down to escape this scarlet glare of things we have done that we ought not to have done, of things we left undone that we knew to be our duty. Did the bear ask to show us that he was red inside? He wanted only to be left alone with his wife and children. Did we debate with him like rational creatures whether his life was more important than our own? Did the Pole ask to be discovered, trampled on, soiled with our tin cans and our urine? Down, down into the darkness and warmth of the reindeer skin, another murder we have committed without willing to or ever doubting our own righteousness, like most murderers. We are nowhere, Luisa and I, everything is darkness, we are bound as though by thongs in the reindeer skin, clothing is no longer necessary in this joining and merging of two metabolisms in common warmth. In the thick bristle of my hair just over my ear I hear a murmur in Swedish: 'Vi har . . . förut.' Yes, this has happened before, and it was you who made it happen each time, fragile and ethereal, vulnerable one who must be protected in the streets of Paris, who cannot hold a bar of graphite without breaking it, it was you who lost the third sleeping sack, who pushed it into the water when nobody was looking, no doubt with that little crease of secret determination at the corner of your mouth. And yet this would not have happened, the vague notion forms somewhere in my consciousness, if it had not been for the bear. If the landscape had remained white. And then rather incongruously another lucid, scientific, and even journalistic thought occurs to me: what is happening is a very common phenomenon and yet this is a historic moment in its way, the farthest north that this event has ever taken place. Should we wake up Waldemer so that he can take a note? No, poor fellow, he needs his sleep. Four limbs are entwined somewhere down at the bottom of the sack, four others higher up near the centres of our noting intelligences. These belong to neither of us, we share the eight of them, we are a two-headed octopus hugging itself in order to stay warm and in order to know and penetrate itself, to know and receive itself, in order that its vast loneliness in regard to the sea around it may be at least temporarily alleviated. The octopus, touching at last a place of secret and hidden knowledge somewhere in its centre, vibrates with the mindless and grateful ecstasy of a saint showered with grace. And after that it is quiet, sufficient unto itself, the tentacles stirring only lazily now and then one against the other. It is safe for it here in the darkness, there is sustenance and warmth, if it ventured above the surface into that red and white light it would die, or rather separate into those two odd creatures imagined by some old Greek, incomplete, wandering apart from each other in a lonely and confused living death until at last they manage to unite once more.

"Tu es content, n'est-ce pas?"

"You are mad," I whisper back in Swedish. "Don't speak." In any case I am very sleepy.

But the voice continues. "Moi, tu sais, je n'ai pas peur de mourir. To die would not be very different from this." There is silence for a while, then the little sound, the touch of warm air, resumes now and then and brushes the chilled and half-numb outer convolution of the ear, passes down the narrow cave to the tympanum and into the shadows of the deeper consciousness. "On est dans la chambre jaune, tu sais. Le soleil se couche, tout le monde se couche, on est content." And a little later, "Tu sais, le Bois. On était content . . . le lac." What lake? The one we paddled across with half-frozen fingers because the clients are requested to abandon boats only at the places provided? But I am already far under the surface and oblivious, stirred only now and then by the warm feather touch by my ear.

"Nous n'irons plus au bois,
Les lauriers sont coupés.
La belle que voilà,
La ferons nous danser?"

My back warmed by the fire, I sit with half-closed eyes warming the cognac glass in my hands, hardly noticing what I am seeing, conscious only of sounds. The Polish cousin Gela, visiting, is at the piano. Something to one side the fashionable photographer and the aunt are talking of Dreyfus, of Wagner, of the winter, which is unusually severe and prevents one from so much as going to the Bois for a breath of air in one's carriage. "The Lac Inférieur is frozen, did you know that? We had thought of going to Menton, or to Spain, but Luisa insists on staying for her recital."

"Which is to take place?"

"In February."

And indeed Luisa is intent on this difficult task, attacking even a simple folk song with the élan and seriousness of a professional, her back against the piano, the delicate tendons at the base of her throat distended with concentration.

"Mais les lauriers du bois
Les laiss'rons-nous faner?
Non chacune à son tour
Ira les ramasser."

When she finished there was a polite but evidently sincere ripple of applause, which went on for some time. I was the only hypocrite; I struck my palms together not because she sang well, or sang badly, but because I knew nothing of music and didn't wish to be conspicuous. It occurred to me only that the choice of her song was perhaps significant, although the significance of the choice, if she was aware of it at all, lay so deep in her consciousness that it was obscured by the exquisite complexity of all her other feminine instincts, and was apparent to her, probably, only in the bluntness of the basic dilemma it posed: shall we dance or shall we gather laurels? I myself didn't dance, so if she wished to pursue the former alternative she would have to do so by herself or in the company of someone more complacent to her whims, the Peruvian diplomat perhaps or the Peninsula.

The mother, her caste mark for some reason applied to her forehead with a slight asymmetry that afternoon, not quite in the centre of her forehead, ate petit-fours while balancing—to my considerable nervousness—a cup of jasmine tea in her other hand, and informed me that Luisa's singing was "ex-kee." She seemed to be under the impression that it had been Chopin, but I may have mistook something she said. (It may have been, "Vous connaissez ce pain?" meaning the pastries.) The Vibrating Matriarch did not let me off so easily. "And so, Major" (my promotion had arrived from Stockholm by that time), "and so we can expect you in the coming summer to fly away to the polar regions, and win fame and even wealth." (I was regarded as a suitor, she was still pondering over what are conventionally called my prospects.) "I must confess that I am not quite clear as to what it is you study." (The chin, naturally, tremored "Nay, nay" through all this.) "Sometimes it is electrical undulations in the air, at other times balloons. And who are these Germans who are going to buy you a new one? Luisa tells me that you have succeeded in making it steer by pulling on ropes. You must excuse me, I am only an ignorant old woman, but I don't understand how pulling on ropes can make a balloon go against the wind."

"Go to the Canal Saint-Martin any afternoon, and you will see how pulling on ropes can make a barge go against the tide."

She might have countered that the lock-keeper had a stone quay to stand on, whereas this convenience was not available in a balloon. But this objection would have revealed some knowledge of Archimedes, and she had disarmed herself in advance through her pretence of being an ignorant old woman. It was true that she was old, also that she was ignorant, also that she was a woman. But these elements did not add up to her pretence: the shrewdness compensated for it all, and she saw through me as though I were a puppet made of isinglass. Her defence was astute, standing on grounds of social propriety rather than on knowledge of science where I clearly had the advantage. "I have never been to the Canal Saint-Martin at all. I believe it is in a working-class quarter. Do you know, Major, it is hard for us to understand why you are interested in us at all, trivial society chatterers that we are." ("Nay, nay.") "It is very flattering, of course. Something mysterious, as it were, seems to attract you to our midst. It could hardly be my old charms, and Luisa of course is engaged."

Both of us, tacitly, dismissed the notion that I could be interested in talking to the mother about pastries and Chopin.

The reference to Luisa was a clear throwing down of the gauntlet, or even tapping me lightly on the cheek with it. I was informed thereby that it is not proper for persons in my circumstances to go on indefinitely frequenting a salon where there is an eligible young lady without, so to speak, taking some steps in the conventional minuet, either forward or backward. I mustered the maximum of my sang-froid and counterattacked. I might have told her, "Madame, I can't hope to compete with the Peninsula in the area of his particular excellence," and there were subsequent times when I wished that I had. It would have demolished a good deal of her aplomb and might even have caused her to stop vibrating for a moment, with the additional advantage of ridding me of a considerable nuisance; never again would she have crossed swords and tongues with me. But it would have been ungallant to reveal Luisa's confidence. Instead, I contrived a riposte that, while almost equally telling, had the advantage that it was impossible for her to take objection to it. I told her, "I suppose it is Theodor, chiefly. I have contracted quite a warm friendship for him."

She was unperturbed. But also silent. To inform me flatly that there was no such person would have been to reveal or confess a tendency to transvestism in her niece which was inconsistent with the picture she wished to project of her household, to wit, that it almost belonged to the best society of the Île Saint-Louis. That is, it would have subjected her to the risk that I (unpredictable Swedish madman that I was) might reply, "How can there be no such person, when he has come to my lodgings, and I have gone with him to cabarets in Montmartre?" (The second of which was not strictly true, but she had no way of knowing.) And if she had said, "It is only Luisa's vapours, and it is unseemly for you to go about with her in such places, she in boy's clothing, when she is formally affiancéd to the Peninsula" (she would have called him something different of course, not even Alberto but Senõr this or Lieutenant that, I never even knew his last name)—had she done this, I say, I might have retorted with justice, "I find it hard to grasp how I have damaged the character of this young lady, since her ways are already so free, and seem to have been before I came on the scene." No, my mention of the name Theodor had demolished any possibility of portraying me, in my own eyes or anyone else's, as a middle-aged seducer bent on tarnishing the reputation of this vulnerable young thing still tremoring on the frontier of womanhood and defenceless against the machinations of a roué fresh from the vice dens of the Stockholm waterfront, and one provided with all the sorcery of a lunatic scientist to boot. My advantage assured, I was about to chase her three times around the walls of Troy when Luisa came to her rescue, and to mine too, I suppose.

"Fi donc, Ma Tante. The Major doesn't want to talk to boring old persons." (Which was perfectly true, but it needs to be said with a lilt and a flair, as in those plays by Augier that seem to be made out of meringue, and Luisa through long practice had this touch to perfection.) "Come with me, Gustavus, I have what you need, a cognac to calm you down and a black coffee to excite you again."

Instead she took me to the sideboard, found there was no cognac ("What a pity," before she had even searched properly for it), and poured me an elegant little orchid-shaped glass of something called Elixir Vert-Galant, which tasted like essence of violets. I took the bottle from her and read the label: "The most exquisite of table liqueurs, at the same time the most energetic of reconstituents and tonics. Strength, health, youth, and vigour are restored by this powerful regenerator. It is life prolonged with all its charms." To tell the truth, I had had about enough of her ironies, especially since there seemed to be no time these days even for being affectionate behind doorways and I went about constantly in her presence with an embarrassment in my clothing, as though I had left a coat hanger in there at the time of putting on my trousers. Tapping zoo lions on the nose, I wished to tell her, was a dangerous game for little girls. Instead, I returned to the tactic that was most contrary to my physical impulse, and probably to hers, and if this latter were so, then probably the most effective one. I regretted that I couldn't see her the next day, and perhaps for several days after, because I had certain investigations to conduct in the Museum of the Conservatoire des Arts et Métiers in rue Saint-Martin.

"Ah! the collection of clocks. Comme c'est charmant. I go there often. I can meet you at three, but I can only stay for an hour, because then I must go to Passy for my solfeggio." And, seeing the expression on my face, she added with a kind of amused vexation, "You won't believe I am serious, will you?"

•

She was only a quarter of an hour late; I forbore from ostentatiously looking at my watch, and anyhow I could see the clock in the courtyard of the conservatory. I passed the time by reflecting on the technical matter I had come to this place to investigate. The fact was that a certain doubt (entirely unconnected with the scepticism of the aunt) had begun to form in my mind whether a combination of guide ropes and sails was really the most effective means of steering a gas-filled airship over long distances, especially in the light of recent developments in mechanics. As early as 1883, I knew, the Tissandier brothers had ascended in a balloon provided with an electric motor and screw propeller, and in 1884, according to report, they had succeeded in stemming a wind of seven knots with this apparatus. Their project had then been taken up by the War Department under Renard and Krebs. In 1885 their fusiform balloon La France, with an air propeller at the end driven by an electric motor, had attained a speed of twenty-two kilometers per hour, or about fourteen knots. But why, the puzzle remained, had this line of investigation not been pursued further? I had several theories. One was that it *was* being pursued further, in secret, by the French military authorities. Another was that their apparatus was too heavy and the cruising range too short; the battery jars brought along to provide energy would soon be exhausted. The third was that Renard and Krebs had been on the right track but hadn't known it, like poor Professor Eggert, and had run out of funds or been too easily discouraged. The propulsion machinery of their airship, I knew, was on display in the museum at the Arts et Métiers, and it was this I had come to examine, provided with a large notebook I hoped to fill up with technical figures. I knew also that Dr. Wölfert in Berlin was conducting experiments with a similar cigar-shaped balloon but one driven by a gasoline motor. This seemed to me somewhat more promising than the Renard-Krebs design. Perhaps in the next few weeks I would have to go to Germany to interview Wölfert, or try to; he was known to be notoriously secretive and even hired a staff of private detectives to bar people from his workshops. Time was growing short, but this visit to Berlin would fit in well with a call I had to make on our estimable benefactors, Prinzessin Brauerei G.m.b.H. in Hamburg, to discuss money matters. Privately I hoped that neither of these mechanical expedients would prove as efficient as the scheme I had already devised. Motors of any kind are heavy and would require something else to be deleted from the contents of the airship. Batteries smell and are liable to leak sulphuric acid over things; gasoline motors require sparks which are dangerous in the vicinity of hydrogen. In any case, I was not as fond of machines as Waldemer was, and disliked loud noises and the smell of grease. I hoped, perhaps quixotically, to soar my way where I wanted to go in blessed silence, with the assistance only of the forces of nature. Finally, an objection which was quite romantic and which I would never have dreamed of confessing to anyone, hardly even to myself: mechanical propulsion systems involving brute force necessitated a fusiform or cigar shape in the gas envelope, and this violated my quite instinctual and affective relationship to the apparatus, one which I could not defend on any rational grounds. Sphericity was feminine and fusiformity masculine, I somehow felt, and it was necessary for the new airship to be called Prinzess III if only out of symmetry with the others, and because of the thalers provided by the loyal German brewers. But it was not only this; it was that in some obscure and yet powerfully adamant part of my mind it was settled that I, a *he,* and the airship, a *she,* were going to accomplish this feat together. Anyone else who came along or had a part in it was incidental. So gas engines and electric motors were things my private soul fiercely resisted; it was as though I were being asked to marry a creature made of iron instead of out of silk and ethereal elasticity. Still the Renard-Krebs apparatus would have to be examined. Later we would see about Dr. Wölfert.

Arrival of Luisa in a smart morning frock and paletot, immaculately gloved and hatted.

"Now don't be cross. I had to go with Ma Tante to rue de Rivoli, about a picture frame."

I was not cross; only cynical. I discounted female estimates of time entirely, by a factor of about 23 percent, and this usually proved accurate enough for practical purposes. We went into the museum without any bother about tickets—I had a pass provided by the Ministry of Commerce and Industry—and stood on the verge of the enormous and decrepit Gothic hall that until 1799 had been the Benedictine chapel of St. Martin of the Fields. It was a felicitous irony of the Revolution, I thought, to fill a desecrated church with these infernal monsters of iron that had enslaved men in the nineteenth century in place of their old masters the aristocrats; all the collection lacked was a guillotine. The first thing that caught one's eye was a Foucault pendulum, swinging with planetary slowness from a wire high overhead in the vault and shifting around its circumference by imperceptible increments as the earth turned. Luisa proceeded to explain the principle of the thing to me, with only a few inaccuracies. Perhaps she had stayed up all night, or part of it, studying some book on Foucault pendulums. She even had the mathematics right; I was impressed but only murmured vaguely, "Yes, yes."

As bad luck would have it, my use of the pass from the ministry had evoked the apparition of a curator, who insisted on accompanying us and explaining what it was that we wanted to see. I had no interest at all in Cugnot's steam carriage of 1770, or a diagram showing the coal production of France from 1789 to 1888. We came to the Renard-Krebs apparatus. Behind it was a drawing of the entire airship, showing how the propulsion machinery fitted onto the rest. Present in material form were only the motor, the air propeller, and some tangled-up wires to connect them to the battery jars. The air propeller was something of a joke; it resembled a Dutch windmill and had vanes of sailcloth. It was the motor that interested me. It was the size of a small keg of nails and probably almost as heavy. There was also a cast-iron gear box to reduce the speed of the motor, probably several thousand revolutions a minute, to one that would not rip the Dutch windmill to shreds. I inquired as to the weight of these items but the curator had no opinion. Then, as his complexion became purple with all the instincts of a curator, and he stood afraid to lift a hand against me because of the card from the ministry, I stepped over the iron chain and tested the heft of the motor. I could barely budge it, sixty kilos at least, and the gear box was worse.

I filled several pages of the notebook. The problem of weight was explained to Luisa, who suggested, "Perhaps one could make a smaller motor, which would go faster and thus be just as powerful."

I offered a brief stare, devoid as I could make it of any sarcasm. "You've hit upon it. I wonder why Renard didn't think of that."

"It would be more efficient, you see. Because the yield in mean torque of an electric motor, expressed in foot-pounds per second, is a function of the speed of rotation."

The devil you say. She had impressed the curator at least. I didn't bother to explain to her that the faster the motor went, the more its speed had to be reduced by the gears, and the larger and heavier the gear box. In addition to which Renard, being a graduate of the École Polytechnique, knew more about torque and foot-pounds than she could have learned by spending a whole month of nights over her library books. In any case, I was more interested in battery jars. Where, I asked the curator, were the battery jars? He pointed out one or two. They were cells of the Leclanché design, employing solid depolarizers of magnesium dioxide with a carbon plate. They were not exactly as light as feathers either, and it was impossible for me to find out from the curator how many of them Renard and Krebs had required for their motor. It was easy for me to make a rough calculation. The motor probably ran at something like a hundred volts, and Leclanché cells were known to produce a volt and a half each. Thus sixty-seven of these weighty jars would be required. Moreover, another rough calculation showed that, with the expected current drain, the batteries would be exhausted in something like seventeen minutes. Not enough to go from Spitsbergen to the North Pole. Hurrah! I controlled my elation only with a certain effort. Renard and Krebs were on the wrong track, and their imitators would never get farther than around the Champs de Mars on a Sunday in front of a crowd of spectators. There was still Dr. Wölfert, who didn't require any batteries—well, I would worry about one thing at a time.

I folded up the notebook, which by this time contained several drawings and diagrams and a copious collection of mathematics, most of them guesswork.

I forgot to note that about halfway through these researches Luisa had exhausted her curiosity on the subject of motors and Leclanché cells and had departed for the west wing and its collection of clocks, where I was supposed to come and collect her when I was finished. She herself was a collector of rare and curious timepieces and had several dozen in Quai d'Orléans, and had even learned something about their mechanism. This interest, which seemed a rather odd one at first, was on further reflection comprehensible and even logical, woman being God's best effort at making a clock, supposed to strike every fourth week but sometimes subject to alarming delays. I found her amid the celestial globes, clockwork figurines, and automatons of various sorts moved by springs.

"Gustavus, come and see."

"What?"

"Just come and see."

She led me to a glass case in which a small feminine figure, the size perhaps of a cat, was holding two little hammers in her hand and was seated before a musical instrument. She was indeed very elegant in the manner of the eighteenth century: pale beige satin gown with rosebuds and green trim, a beige-silver wig. "No. 7501. Dulcimer player. Automaton of Roentgen and Kintzing. Belonged to Marie Antoinette. Plays eight airs extracted and arranged from the Armide of Gluck." The satin gown came down over the stool, which evidently hid the machinery. The female attendant, charmed by Mademoiselle's own elegance in her frock and paletot, opened the glass case and set this doll going for us. The hammers descended, the airs from the previous century tinkled accurately and delicately, in rather slow tempo. Luisa clasped her hands in pleasure; she and the attendant exchanged smiles.

"But couldn't we see how she works? The dress—"

"Ah non, mademoiselle, c'est défendu."

"Gustav"—this in English—"show her your card from the ministry."

In the end I had to show her not only my card from the ministry but a ten-franc bill. When disrobed the dulcimist was wooden and complete in every way, sitting on her complicated machine of sprockets and cogs, still bewigged and slippered, holding her little hammers delicately one in each hand. Garters were painted on her legs just above the knees. At the bottom of the machine was a kind of paddlewheel which rotated in the air, like that of a music box, to prevent her from playing too fast—her metabolism.

The attendant put the dress back on the doll—(her own face was a little pink! she suppressed a smile). Luisa too seemed pleased with herself. I was surrounded by females again, who exchanged understandings around me and over my head that concerned me, probably, in some obscure way. Why had Luisa obliged me to pay ten francs to disrobe a clockwork puppet? Did she wish to remind me that musicians, however talented, had underlinen? Or was it merely the interest in clockwork of a femme-savante? I had begun to doubt that she could separate these two things in her own mind. For my part, I was less interested in the wooden limbs of the puppet than in the air paddle. Machinery, left to itself, would overrace and destroy its own ingenuity. Only air, the thinnest and least palpable of the four elements, was capable of slowing it—the same air that had dragged at Renard's balloon and exhausted its battery jars in seventeen minutes. The visit to the automaton room had only confirmed what I had earlier guessed in the ruined Benedictine chapel: it is not by striking nature with iron bars that we can hope to subdue it, only by surrendering ourselves to it and floating in the direction it wishes.

At the gate of the conservatory I offered to escort Luisa to Quai d'Orléans—a scientific ruffian might disrobe her to inspect her paddlewheel—but she had to rush to her lesson in Passy. (Which was mysterious, because the voice lessons, as I understood it, were supposed to take place in the morning.) I felt my afternoon had been well spent in spite of the fact that it hadn't commenced until a quarter after three. I decided to return on foot to rue de Rennes by way of Boulevard de Sébastopol and the Pont-Neuf. It was a clear cold day; the Seine ran like half-congealed lead, slowly, with greyish glints. In Place Saint-Germain I bought a newspaper. A government had fallen in Italy, a skyscraper had risen in New York. In Berlin Dr. Wölfert had made an ascension in his engine-driven balloon. There was an explosion in the air, the balloon fell, and Dr. Wölfert and his assistant were killed. The sun had begun to set behind the old grey pile of the church in the square. There was a chill in the street; back in my room it was warm.

22 July 1897

For four days now we have been stumbling and sliding our way across this landscape that when solid is more vertical than horizontal, and when thawed turns into soup into which we slip up to our waists. If we attempt to go by water, using the Faltboot, the water hardens into granite. As soon as we try to walk over it, it turns into water again. Under the tent, as we try to sleep, it groans most fearfully. It is always slipping, bumping, grumbling, complaining, and turning underfoot. I have lost track of the time and am convinced it is the twenty-second of the month now only because I have made little marks in my Stockholm pocket calendar each time we have camped-but suppose we have camped more than once a day? Impossible; Waldemer has his stout pocket watch, I have my own, and there are the two chronometers, Kullberg 5566 and Kullberg 5587, to verify them. But the climate or possibly the jolts we have subjected them to are not very good for these last instruments. Two or three nights ago (twenty-two minus three is nineteen, so it must have been Monday) I awoke or half awoke and heard them talking to each other in a smooth even ticking, muted so as not to awaken us.

K. 5566: "Let's speed up. Make the days go faster, bring their happy or unhappy fate to them more quickly and with less fatigue."

K. 5587: "We should go slower. That way it will be easier for them to keep up with us."

K. 5566: "Their pace will accelerate with ours."

K. 5587: "Whatever we do, we must agree. For one chronometer's time means nothing. It may be out of adjustment. But what two chronometers say is the truth, and the solar system must follow it. Thus if we speed up so will the sun and the planets..."

And so on. Their voices were unhurried, rational, leisurely, discussing all sides of the question with care. I was struck with the fact that they seemed to have our welfare in mind; this mildly surprised me, and I was also impressed that they had talked quietly so that we should have the maximum amount of sleep and be rested for the next day. When I awoke, however, the implication was that as timepieces they were no longer to be trusted very much. Certain other evidence suggests that the rate of one or the other has changed. Which one? Impossible to tell, since I can verify their accuracy only by comparing one with the other. At that time I was not as tired as I am now and I had the wit to notice that the frozen milk overhead had cleared away temporarily so that the sun and the moon were both visible at the same time. Ah! Professor Crispin. Time for a bit of higher mathematics. The method of lunar distances, which may be used not only to find one's position but also to check chronometers, has ever since the days of Gemma-Frisius been regarded as the most troublesome and difficult calculation in the art of nautical astronomy. Besides, my hands are numb, all the pens are frozen, and our only pencil has been broken so many times that it is hardly longer than a joint of my finger. But I set to it anyhow: first I cock the sextant at a horizontal angle and draw the two limbs of the sun and moon together to measure the angular distance between them. (The two orbs are approaching each other at a dizzying rate and I have to keep turning the vernier. Perhaps, I think, they will run into each other and that will be the universal end of all problems, including our own.) Then I correct for semi-diameters, enter the logarithm tables and the almanac, and begin covering one of our last pieces of paper with hen scratches.

This method, complete with mistakes and the natural inaccuracies involved in taking arcs with a half-frozen sextant, established our position at 81° 42' north, 36° 20' east, give or take a few hundred miles either way (the pencil was very blunt, my hand a numb primordial paw). Since then we have made our way more or less southward as the configuration of the half-thawed pack permitted. Franz Josef Land is somewhere up ahead and to the left, the main mass of Spitsbergen out of reach to the west. Our hands curved permanently to the diameter of the pulling ropes, we go on toiling over a landscape composed partly of white grand pianos set on edge and partly of soup. Theodor's face, as I anticipated, is not really suited to this climate. It has turned to a darkish and ironlike blue, the points of the cheeks black with frostbite. The shawl is wrapped around it completely now so that nothing shows except the eyes. But he pulls as hard as the rest of us, and as steadily, setting first one foot and then the other into the yielding and soggy ice. It is Waldemer who seems to be tiring, he that I imagined would be the strongest of us. But he makes no complaint either and seems confident that we will eventually arrive wherever it is that we are headed; he leaves the navigational details to me. He is stocky and his breath comes short; perhaps he has a tendency to asthma. When he talks—and he talks frequently, not for the most part to impart information, but to cheer up himself and us, to improve the morale of the expedition—he confines himself to shorter sentences and often waits between them, to see if he can't wring a little more oxygen out of this frozen skim milk he is inhaling into his lungs.

"If I ever get out of this . . . I know where I will spend . . . the rest of my days."

The sentences, although short, and separated by intervals of breath-taking, are perfectly constructed at least by journalistic standards; he has no pretensions as a stylist. "

The Lunatic Asylum . . . at Halifax, Nova Scotia . . ." Pause for breath. ". . . is pleasantly situated in the midst . . . of cheerful green hills, and . . . provides a very . . . English, I might say . . . comfort. I recommend it especially."

But he is fooling himself; there is no chance of Waldemer being admitted to a lunatic asylum. A single glance would be enough for any alienist to tell that he is hopelessly sane. He encounters one of the grand pianos and measures his length on the ice, and remarks without rancor, "The polar region . . . is certainly the source . . . of the idea of the stumbling block." And a little later, after a slightly more serious mishap (Theodor falls through a soft spot and goes in up to his armpits in a mixture of water and slush, and Waldemer in his efforts to pull him out does the same), he comments, "There's no hurry . . . about dying, you know . . . if we miss it this time . . . we'll always have another chance."

There are no more bears after that first one. That is, we see plenty of blurry white dots on the horizon but don't approach near enough to get in a shot. There is still a large chunk of frozen rib meat in the Faltboot; we hack pieces off it now and then and masticate them patiently to get out the red juice. Once we follow the tracks of a large male for some distance and find that, like Theodor and Waldemer, he has come to a soft spot and slipped down into the soup; so that even he is not above making mistakes in that regard. A little later Waldemer manages to unlimber the Mannlicher and plunk a seal incautiously taking a nap on a floe only a few metres from us; but the little metal bead through his lungs wakes him instantly, he flops and slithers dying to the water's edge and sinks like a rock. Waldemer is perplexed, as he always is when some mechanism doesn't behave according to his expectations. But I know the reason; the sea in July, being composed in large part of melted ice, is thin and won't support the seal, whose specific gravity is equal to that of salt water.

Theodor can't understand this point. "How can the ice melt if we are freezing?"

"There are different laws of the universe for people and for inanimate matter."

"Sometimes I think you make up these laws yourself."

"I do. And I make them work."

In spite of this talk of freezing, his clothing—the black woolen jodhpurs, the stylish military coat—exudes a steam into the calm frigid air. There is heat inside him yet, a little fire kindled with bear meat and sheer stubbornness, and in time this may even dry out his clothing. As for me, my feet are permanently wet; not even a long stay in a Nova Scotia asylum could dry them out. (That Austrian journalist who said I was either a fool or a swindler neglected to think of the third possibility, by the way: that I am mad.)

And when was this conversation? Yesterday perhaps, although because of the possibility that we have camped more than once a day such calculations are subject to wild chances of error. I firmly believe in my mind that today is Thursday the twenty-second, I have so noted in my pocket diary, and it is four days therefore since we abandoned the

Prinzess. The pack that was still relatively firm then—in that dim past—
is now rapidly assuming all the characteristics of the sea around and
under it, beginning with its liquidity. Even yesterday it was necessary to
ferry across several broad leads of open water, each time unpacking and
repacking everything in the Faltboot. For the most part, however, we
are still able to progress on foot.

Yesterday (I think it was) I saw visible ahead of us a peculiar
vaulted light stretching across the horizon, a light under which odd
things appeared, or seemed to appear. Little pieces and needles of the
horizon lifting up, squirming, and falling back again. Finally a kind
of irregular jagged line sticking up, like white saw teeth, from south-
southeast to south-southwest. Lower on the sides, a little higher in
the middle. Changing shape constantly but always there, for at least
an hour. Waldemer is watching it too. He glances at me but I go on
pulling, pretending not to notice. Faint smile forms under his mustache.
Secret. Waldemer is capable of secrets, of his own kind; usually they are
concrete, concerned with real physical or mechanical things, and they
are jokes not intended to deceive anybody. Four fifths of the time he
watches the wavering saw teeth; one fifth of the time he glances at me
to see if I've noticed them yet.

The saw teeth sometimes shift, trade places, and resume their old
form again. At one point (I'm not sure Waldemer notices) the whole
business is elevated off the horizon completely, leaving a strip of sky
underneath. This is only for a moment; it settles down and goes on with
its wavery squiggling.

"Major."

"H'mm?"

"There's, ah. Something. I'll bet you haven't noticed."

"What?"

"There's. Ah. Land up there ahead now. Not over fifty, sixty miles.
Has to be Franz Josef Land. Mountains. Nothing else that high."

"Ah." I glance ahead as though noticing for the first time. "Bravo,
Waldemer."

He is surprised I don't make more fuss over the discovery, especially
since the calculations, made by me, put us farther to the west and Franz
Josef Land far out of reach a hundred or more miles to the left. But h
leaves the navigation to me and perhaps he thinks I have known

along the mountains will be there. Theodor makes no comment. We go on pulling. Waldemer remarks that the pesky mountains don't seem to be getting any closer. We stop to examine them through the glasses. Or Waldemer does. I don't bother because I know what they are. Then abruptly, soon after he has put the binoculars away in the Faltboot, they loom much larger. Waldemer is exultant. "Not far now. For a while it seemed . . . atmospheric effects no doubt."

No doubt at all. In another twenty minutes we come up to them: some ice hummocks no higher than our knees, thrust upward by refraction into Himalayas and Sierras. We have been chasing these phantoms over the ice for two hours or more. The weak sun, shining on the ice and on the darker leads, has warmed the air slightly near the surface and converted it into a giant lens; a lens with us on the inside. Luckily Waldemer has a sense of humour. He is sheepish, knowing that Theodor will rag him about this later, when they are both less tired and in a mood for humour. We wrench the Faltboot into motion and go on pulling. I know exactly where we are, not only because of the lunar sight on the twentieth, but because of the compass in my blood: about eighty-one degrees north or a little better, White Island directly ahead at a range of perhaps fifty miles. Still a long way to go.

And Theodor or Luisa: the shawl covering everything but the eyes— the eyes luminous against the glimpsed fragments of face—which are the bluish colour of iron with traces of rust, bends against the weight of the pulling rope and plants one foot after the other in the white surface that crumbles and slips with each effort of the boots to get a grip on it. He is on my left and slightly behind me because of the geometry of the pulling ropes, so that I have to turn my head a little in order to look at him. And look at him I do every few minutes, not in order to verify anything and certainly not out of sympathy, but simply out of curiosity that this black-covered and efficient machine manages to go on functioning identically in this way hour after hour, never varying its rhythm and leaving its series of exactly evenly spaced depressions behind it in the soft crust of the ice. The right arm stretching behind it to throw its weight onto the rope, the left arm brought around the front of the chest and onto the rope to add its pull. The body at a diagonal to the vertical in the thrust of its effort, the left foot comes forward and the boot stamps into the ice to make a grip for itself. The knee straightens, the body angles downward a little more as it takes the weight, and the other boot comes forward to print its hole in the ice and wrench the body, the rope, and the weight dragging after it another forty centimeters ahead. It is slow; in an hour in this way it is possible to cover two miles if there aren't too many hummocks and ice ridges. Occasionally he slips as we all do and falls to his knees or entirely horizontally on the ice. When this happens it is our custom that the others don't stop and wait; it would mean three or four metres of progress lost. He pushes himself up with his left mitten, the pulling rope still gripped in the right, and in a moment or two catches up and is pulling again. Fifteen hours a day of this, eighteen hours a day, and if we don't rest too much we can hope to arrive some place or other before winter comes.

In any case, we don't rest very long because the cold would catch us and we would stiffen. Ten minutes is enough; we heat some cocoa on the primus and gulp it in turn from the saucepan, scalding our tongues and not caring about the brownish crust that immediately freezes on our lips and cheeks; because we spill it, like little children, trying to handle the pan in the clumsy mittens. One day—the second perhaps, or the third—we didn't rest at all but kept going, especially since the landscape on that part of the journey was composed of jumbled blocks the size of farmhouses and there was no flat space even as large as a pocket handkerchief to set the primus. The next day, the twenty-first according to the pocket calendar, we are stopped a little after eight in the evening by a broad lead that has partly frozen over. I am perplexed at first; it hasn't seemed cold enough to make sea ice. Then I reflect that there is a layer of partly fresh water on top of these leads, from melted snow or from the slow melting of the old floes, which according to Greely partly free themselves from salt over a period of time and may be melted for culinary water. The layer on the lead indeed looks like glare ice, freshwater ice. It is hard and bluish-white, perhaps four inches thick. I test it with the bamboo pole. Only with a determined stab can the stuff be broken.

What to do? The lead is a half mile or more wide. It might support our weight and the weight of the Faltboot and it might not. In any case, it is too thick for us to break our way through and cross boat-fashion. We might traverse the lead in the hope of finding a narrower place, or a stretch of stronger ice, at some other point. But it stretches away as far as the eye can see in either direction, showing no sign of narrowing. It will have to be crossed on foot.

Leaving the Faltboot behind, we venture out a few metres to test the ice. It seems strong enough to support us. It bends slightly underfoot with a rather ominous creaking noise, and a pool of water instantly collects where it has settled under our weight. But it seems elastic and we don't actually break through.

We go back for the Faltboot and set out cautiously, fanning out a little more than usual to distribute our weight. It soon becomes apparent that the ice is stronger in some places than in others. Several times we have to stop and detour a spot that is too thin and beginning to sag dangerously underfoot.

"Y'know, Major, someone should go ahead and scout out the best route. Then we wouldn't have to keep towing this blessed battleship around in circles."

A good idea, Waldemer. But who? It should be me, by all rights. But Luisa drops her towline and comes slowly toward me, stopping a few paces from me so that she blocks my path across the lead. Because of the shawl I can see only her eyes, but I know the mouth is set firmly with the little creases at the corners.

"I'm the lightest."

This is folly. I know the ice best and I am responsible for the safety of all. Besides she . . . but it has been a long time since conventions, chivalry, the ordinary hierarchies of life in the World of Cities seem to have had any significance. I am uncertain; I hesitate.

"He's right, Major. What d'you weigh, Theodor old man? Not a hundred and twenty, I'll bet. Go ahead and be careful. We'll follow."

We proceed in this fashion, Luisa two hundred metres ahead and Waldemer and I following with the Faltboot, which slips easily over this skating rink of a surface. We walk always in a film of water a centimeter or so deep, which follows us as the depression made by our weight proceeds across the ice.

We are perhaps three fourths across when I notice a peculiar—as I first imagine it—optical illusion. The ice ahead, between us and Luisa, seems to bulge up a hand's breadth or so, then in another place, a series of bulges traveling rapidly across the ice from left to right. A second later it occurs to me that seals, expecting as little as we that a lead would freeze over this time of the year, are trapped under the ice and are trying to break out breathing holes for themselves. But almost at the same instant this theory is blasted. Not far from Luisa—surely not more than thirty or forty metres from her—the ice is shattered with a dull bump or thud and an enormous black fin shoots up, followed by a glistening back the size of a hansom cab. Luisa has turned and is staring at this thing, staring across it to us. But everything happens very quickly. In another five seconds a dozen killer whales, perhaps, have broken out of the ice in a thrashing of white water. The huge hideous heads shoot vertically into the air through the holes they have smashed. One breaks out so close to us that we can see the tawny head markings, the small glistening eyes, the terrible array of teeth. They are black above, the lower parts white or yellowish-white. There is a distinctive white slash above and behind the little pig eye. They are ten metres long and weigh tons.

Believing from our shadows on the ice that we are seals, they continue to heave up and split it into fragments, thrashing the water into foam in an effort to upset us and take us into those rows of conical white teeth, in a single gulp. What puzzles them—the reason they are unable to make an end of the business immediately—is that we can move faster on the ice than seals. Luisa has turned and is slipping off rapidly to the left, away from the centre of the danger. But the whales are everywhere. An enormous black shadow, like an underwater cloud, passes almost directly under our feet, at great speed.

Waldemer and I sense the same thing almost instantly: that, against all instinct, we must not abandon the Faltboot to flee away to the left in an attempt to rejoin Luisa. The whales are sure to break the ice under the Faltboot, taking it for a large seal, and without the supplies on it we couldn't last half a day. Without a word we seize the towlines and begin running as fast as we can over the slippery and undulating ice with the Faltboot impeding us. We are attempting to make a large circle to the left and cut back toward Luisa so that we can perhaps be of some help to her. Meanwhile, we wave, indicating to her that she should make directly to the south toward the thicker pack ice only a few hundred metres away.

The ice disintegrates directly ahead of us and the black spike of a fin, two metres long, surges in the opening. A piece of ice the size of a table tips on edge, poises, and upsets. The head appears and the whale blows with a terrific roar. His breath has an odour of something rotten, of fish and death. Waldemer jerks the Faltboot to the right and I follow. The pig eyes inspect us for a moment, then the whale slowly sinks to try again somewhere else.

The near escape distracts us and for a moment—I have to admit—Waldemer and I lose our heads. We jerk the Faltboot along as best we can, skirting the many broken holes in the ice. In our concern to watch for these holes, and in foolishly looking down to glance at the black shapes shooting by underneath, we forget to keep our eyes on Luisa. When we look away to the south again there is no sign of her. A single whale rises slowly, not far from where we last saw her, opens his jaw to reveal the jagged white gleam, and settles with a sigh and a jet of steam.

We stop—another stupidity. Then Waldemer, without speaking, raises his mitten and points ahead and a little to the right. A black patch appears in the water between two floes, then something elongated extrudes from it: an arm. Luisa manages to pull half her body up onto the floe. For an excruciating time she remains thus: clutching the floe, arms outspread, her lower body still in the water. The thought of the teeth in the water under her goes knife—like through me. Everything stops in me: breathing, every nerve fibre, even my heart seems to clutch and stop. Four seconds. Five, six, seven. Why doesn't she pull herself up? She is exhausted, there is nothing to grip on the ice. There is the boom of another whale striking the ice to my left; I don't even turn to look at it.

Finally Waldemer and I come to our senses and make away rapidly in her direction. In only a minute or two we are there. By this time she is out of the water and onto the floe. The floe is not very large. There is open water all around it. A shadow goes by underneath like an express train. I drop the towline, find another floe perhaps half as large as Luisa's, and leap onto it, my momentum sending it tottering across the water like a crude raft. It sinks under my weight; my ankles are in the water. But it bumps against Luisa's floe and I scramble out onto it.

Waldemer, that fantastic fellow, has detached one of the towlines, coiled it, and thrown it in our direction. The first time I miss it. Then I have hold of the towline and Luisa and I are pulling it. We are back to Waldemer and the Faltboot. No time to attach the third towline again. Luisa flees on ahead, gesturing to right or left as she sees bad ice, and we stagger after with our load.

We are on the pack ice. Some difficulty in pulling the Faltboot up over the brink a half metre or more high. Then Luisa—doesn't collapse, simply lies down on the ice and breathes deeply, pants, while watching me out of her silent eyes.

It is important that she begin exercising immediately to thaw herself. After a while she stands up, still without saying anything. By this time Waldemer has reattached the towline. She takes it without a word. The three of us pull the Faltboot a little distance, perhaps a mile, to a place where we can take shelter behind a pressure ridge. We tumble everything out of the Faltboot with our frozen hands. The tent is up in a minute; the two bamboos push it upright, some blocks of ice hold it at the corners and around the edges. As soon as this is done Luisa collapses onto the sleeping sack without a word.

"Get out."

For some reason, perhaps sheer perplexity, Waldemer understands and leaves the tent. In a minute I have Luisa's clothes off and am rubbing her to turn the blackish white of her body to, at least, a pale pink. She is still silent, only watches me out of her motionless dark eyes. Then I dress her in the spare set of skin trousers and jacket with a hood. She is able to help with this. She crawls into the sleeping sack and closes her eyes instantly as though she were asleep. I bend over her. She is all right, her forehead warm but not hot, her breathing even.

•

I start the primus to warm the tent. Then I go outside to see what Waldemer is doing. Through the binoculars, the clever fellow, he has found a seal on the ice near a small lead a few hundred metres away, and is making for it with all the complicated skill and cunning of a born hunter. Down on all fours, the rifle concealed on the side invisible to the seal, he is working his way toward it in a simulated waddle, his arms working like flippers, legs wobbling tail-fashion on the ice. The seal is convinced. Imagining that there is a fellow of his own kind on that side, he feels safe, knowing that if a bear approaches the other seal will see it first and give the alarm by splashing into the water. So he concentrates on the other direction, turning his back to Waldemer. Who squirms on patiently, dragging the Mannlicher, to a range of seventy-five meters, where he rests his weapon on a chunk of ice and, after a long wait, squeezes the centre of it with his mitten finger. For some reason I am not aware of the sound of the detonation. The panorama itself is tiny at this distance. The seal kicks once, curls into a tight arc, and straightens again. He has no time to fall into the water or do anything else. Instantaneously he has been converted into seal meat resting motionless on the ice waiting for Waldemer, who gets up and walks toward it with an air of proud manly satisfaction.

He doesn't know that I'm watching. I go back toward the tent, which with its red and white stripes makes an incongruous effect on the frozen landscape, flamboyant and a little tawdry, a camp of bedouins in a desert of sugar candy. As I come in she wakes up, or opens her eyes, and rises a little on one elbow.

"Sleep. You're exhausted. Six hours of sleep and we must start again."

"What were those things, Gustav?"

"Just ordinary killer whales, Orcinus orca. Not common in these parts but found occasionally."

"They were trying to eat me."

"They thought we were seals. No malice in them. They were only earning their living, in the way that comes naturally."

"In that case Mr. Darwin was right, Gustav."

"I've never doubted that he was."

"I mean that we may be obsolete."

"That's what I mean." "It's the whole arrangement I don't like. B must eat A, so C can eat B. Who made the whole thing up?"

"Whoever it was, He doesn't bother much about our opinion. Close your eyes."

"If you close your eyes everything is red, and I don't like that. The insides of things are red. I don't want to know about the insides of things. The outsides of things are white, pure, clean. I like white things, Gustav. Cold things."

She goes on for some time, chattering in this toneless abstract way, almost as though she is talking not to me but to herself. I can't get her to stop.

"It's Dante again. The bottom of hell isn't fire and brimstone as people imagine. It's frozen, a frozen lake. I'd like that. I'd rather be down there frozen with Ugolino than up with Paolo and Francesca, whirling around in a hot wind. Lovers locked together so you can't escape. No chance to bathe. Imagine the smell of armpits." She laughs, in an odd cracked voice, a sound I have never heard from her before. I begin to think that she is perhaps not well. "Who are those two that go together so lightly on the wind? Conjure them in the name of their love, and they will stop."

The tent opens to a chill of cold air. Entry of Waldemer dragging his pinniped, concealing his smile of pride as best he can under his mustache. She shifts to Swedish, forming her phrases with effort so that they come out carefully if not always correctly.

"Minns du, Gustav. Do you remember that time I tried to kill you?"

"Do I? But which time do you mean? The time in the crevasse, or the time with the revolver?"

"The time in the crevasse was only a joke. That other time I meant it. But now, vet du, I'm happy I didn't. It's better as it turned out. I like it here where you've brought me, in the white world."

She seems rested now, almost content, although disinclined to move in the sleeping sack, her dark steady eyes fixed on me. Lying half propped on the bag of provisions I have given her for a pillow, her body is a shallow curve arching upward from head to foot, the pose of Goya's Duchess of Alba.

"In Paris, ser du, there was my world in Quai d'Orléans, and there was your world with your wires and sparks. I was a prisoner in my world, and you wouldn't come out of yours. And so we were enemies—do I mean fienden?"

"Fiender."

"We were fiends to each other. And here it is our world. There is nothing else. No one. Nothing but whiteness and ourselves."

There is Waldemer, but he is busy cutting up his seal, so perhaps she estimates that he doesn't count.

"Why should I have come out of my world, when it was my world that you wanted to come into? According to your own so fervent declaration."

"Don't be fiendish. What I wanted—what we wanted—was to make a world that we could both inhabit. That would be both yours and mine. And we couldn't do that there."

"And it didn't seem to me you were so much a prisoner in your own. Since you could go pretty much where you felt like it. To Stockholm. To Stresa. To Montmartre. To odd places where only men are admitted."

"Thank you, a list of my sins. Would you like to have a list of your own? But we are quarreling again."

"There you two squareheads go again. Chattering on. Must have a secret you don't want a fellow to hear about. Theodor, you caught all that Scandihoovian, I'll bet, by sleeping in the same bag as the Major."

"Must you murder that poor thing in here? It looks like a baby with whiskers."

The seal, a fine young male specimen of Phoca barbata, is turning into meat under our eyes. Unlike the menagerie bear, he is fat and seems to have only a moderate number of bones for his size.

"I murdered him out on the floe. Seventy-five metres. A single shot through the head. Not bad, if I say so myself. Now I'm making stew out of him. Which you can have for supper. If you ask me nicely in Queen's English."

Waldemer, although still jovial, is annoyed at our talking Swedish. What does he suspect? That we are what he would I I call "nancies"? He knows me better than that. Or only that we are making fun at his expense? Probably the latter.

Now he is cutting the reddish and white-streaked jelly into cubes and putting them into the saucepan, setting it on the primus, adding salt, bacon, and some broken pieces of hardtack. An aroma something like New England chowder begins to diffuse into the tent. By Thor and Freya, I still have desires! I am hungry! I wouldn't have believed it. Waldemer is a good fellow after all, invaluable. What would I we do without him? Even if he is a murderer. But at the risk of offending him I still have something to say to Luisa.

"Hör du mig, I am innocent in this thing. You had seven or eight worlds and I only one. But you bewitched me out of it, time and time again. With only a gesture of your fingers. A breath in my air. Into all those worlds of yours where I was like a dog in breeches. In Stresa, and behind all those doorways."

"Ah? An agile dog still. A clever one."

"Chow down, you two squareheads. Savvy plain English? If not I'll eat it myself."

"And the Salle Meyer, wasn't that a world of yours?"

"Ah, you are referring to my musical career."

"Why not?"

"It was such a success."

"You are such a charming person, why should you want to be famous as well?"

"Ah, tack så mycket. Be good, sweet maid, and let who will be clever."

But there is no hostility in this any more, it is a kind of a game, a casting of phrases back and forth, like those duels of old-fashioned poets jousting with lines that in any case both of them know by heart. The eyes under the reindeer-skin hood are calm, faintly ironic, if not amused any longer, at least resigned to the jest that the Great Nobody enjoys even if we don't quite as much. Looking at these eyes, I am seized with a slight vertigo of uncertainty, of the strange. Who is I she? There is something elusive and perhaps slightly supernatural about this thing she has created out of herself by sheer force of will, becoming Luisa, Theodor, nexus of erotic magnetism, femme-savante, staid Anglaise in tweeds or angry gypsy, radiating energies of love and hate that are perhaps genuine or perhaps quite synthetic and controlled, coming from a centre of volition hidden deep in some place in her that I can never know and never penetrate. For, if I keep certain places in me hidden from her, why shouldn't she do the same? To say, as I've often said to myself, that her emotions are "all on the surface" is meaningless. The surface of another human being is all we can know. I can only note, in my own sensations, that from her surface now I no longer detect either the pull of willed charm or those emanations of maenadic hatred that once seemed powerful enough to destroy both of us.

"Major's gone to sleep over his meal. Tired like all of us."

Because she has already paid me for the Salle Meyer, long ago. And I her. And how in any case should I be responsible for events that originated in her own labyrinthine and rococo but steely will, even if these events, if I am to believe the testimony of Theodor, were directed toward certain aspects of my own personality that I was somehow being asked to apologize for—my talent or alleged genius in realms where "she must leave the position of predominance to me" and "couldn't hope to compete." Ah well. Certainly I was out of it in music, but was she in? Not being God or her solfeggio master, I hardly had control over that. In short, what blame or part of blame was to be attached to me for that evening of grandiose fiasco I found it hard to fathom. Although tacitly and obliquely—and at the same time pointedly—invited, I wasn't even a member of the family party, which included the aunt, the mother, the Polish cousin, and for all I knew the Peninsula and a whole collection of Peruvian diplomats. I hadn't even, in fact, promised to come, and for all that Luisa knew in any formal and official way, it was not likely that I would be there. When the question of tickets arose I played the imbecile; not a natural role for me, but I did the best I could. "It is next Wednesday evening, you know." "It? . . . ah. It." "If you would like a ticket, Ma Tante has them." "Ah, has she?" But sins of omission are easy; I never applied to the aunt for that piece of cardboard which would have given me the privilege of sitting gratis between her, perhaps, and the lady neurologist, or the Polish cousin, in a box from which I could not escape and in which, at the very least, I would have been obliged to make noises of a conventional nature that might have been inconsistent with my view of the proceedings and certainly with my character. As it happened, this imbecility, or sin, was very wise on my part.

In any case it was not, if the truth be told, an event that caused widespread reverberations in the artistic world like the premiere of *Ubu Roi*, and probably that was not what she or anybody else intended. There were brief advance notices in *Le Temps, Le Figaro, L'Écho de Paris, Le Gaulois*. I bought my ticket at an agency in rue de Rivoli and went alone in a cab, like a spy to an enemy camp. It was a rainy night, which was bad luck. In Avenue Montaigne, in front of the hall, there were only a few cabs, and a pair of gallants in evening cloaks finishing their cigars under the marquee before they threw them in the gutter and went in. Inside, at five minutes to nine—the thing was announced to begin at nine—the long oval hall was perhaps a third full. I took my seat, which was well toward the rear. High ceiling, walls hung in thick burgundy draperies with gold trim. Some boxes along the sides, partly concealed with the same red curtains. At one end was a raised dais with a concert Pleyel sitting on it like a large black insect. The place was full of that kind of hushed and yet magnified twitter common to large rooms where an event of some sort is soon to take place. I crossed my legs I and gravely examined the program as though I didn't know what it was, still playing the imbecile.

These five-franc seats were occupied mainly by music students and other sorts of waifs from the Latin Quarter. One of them—very friendly, not to say insolent—even bent his elbow over the back of his seat to engage me in a conversation.

"Cette Hickman. Elle a du talent?"

"Parle pas francais. Suédois."

Probably he didn't believe me, because he went right on talking. "It's because, you see, they gave Casimir and me the tickets free, at the Conservatory."

"Ah, the Conservatory." I erected a painful sentence in French. "I don't know. If she has attended. The Conservatory." This convinced them that I was an imbecile, or a foreigner, which is the same thing, and they left me alone. After that they discussed the matter between themselves. "After all, one has never heard . . ." "D'accord, but if she did have talent . . ." "Certainly, but still . . ."

Entry of the accompanist, who sat down immediately, flapping the tails of his coat over the stool with an adroit professional gesture. Not very much of the chatter in the hall subsided, even when the houselights were dimmed. The student in the seat ahead of me (Gilles, as one gathered from the dialogue) explained to Casimir in a loud voice, "Non, idiot, c'est une américaine."

Luisa appeared from one side and advanced to the centre of the dais. Her gown was black velvet, with a band of white lace at the throat. Her hair was arranged in the same simple knot in which I had first seen it, at the Musée Carnavalet, and she carried a few violets in a long white ribbon. The audience to some extent stopped their chattering and rattling of programs, and there was a patter of polite applause. The accompanist made a few chords, almost lost in the large hall, and she embarked on the first item of the program.

It was "Queen of the Night" from *The Magic Flute* of Mozart, which I would describe as a coloratura aria with ha-ha's. The voice seemed thin in so large a cubic space; the ceiling was ten metres over her head. I suspected that the aria was far too high for her in spite of the extraordinary range of her voice. Still, I was not a music critic. There was one, however, sitting ten or twelve rows ahead of me where the seats changed prices. He was from *Le Gaulois* and Luisa had pointed him out to me once at a concert. Probably it was obligatory for him to come once the recital had been advertised in his paper. There were also various other recognizable characters from the Parisian musical world, even if they didn't perhaps represent its very cream: a Balkan pianist, the tenor Jean de Reszke, whom I had met once in Quai d'Orléans, and a wild-headed boy composer whose *Concerto for Larynx* had been the sensation, or scandal, of last winter's musical season. Luisa finished "Queen of the Night," there was a sound from the hall like pattering rain, and she launched into the Bell Song from *Lakmé*.

The audience seemed restive but not, at this point, in a violent or mutinous mood. After Schumann's "Frühlingsnacht" there was even a "Brava!" from a single voice. It might have been from Gilles or Casimir, but I couldn't be sure. At the intermission, however, there was a bad omen; the critic from *Le Gaulois* lurched up out of his seat and departed, exactly as Sarcey had done at the Théâtre de l'oeuvre, although probably for different reasons. Ahead of me Casimir yawned and stretched his arms. "Alors, Gilles. Tu penses?" "Je ne pense pas, je souffre."

After the intermission Luisa appeared without the flowers, slightly paler than before. The accompanist rattled off his chords and she began with some Brahms lieder. For the first one, "Die Mainacht," a note in the program warned, "O singer, if thou cannot dream, leave this song unsung." In spite of this portent the lieder, in my humble and even ignorant opinion, were fairly successful. But when she returned to opera the path was not so smooth; even I could see the rocks she was tripping over. Luisa, the man from *Le Gaulois* has fled the scene; better follow him!

But she stuck it out. She had saved her real bravura piece, in fact, for the last. This was "Charmant Oiseau" from David's *Perle de Brésil*, a confection which required the help not only of the pianist but of a flautist, a plump young man clad like his fellow accompanist in a white tie and tailcoat, who began by licking his instrument as though he were not quite sure he cared for the taste. He and the pianist signaled each other with their eyebrows. They were ready. They turned to Luisa.

The Charming Bird took wing. Luisa was pursuing it in her way and the flautist in his. The more cumbersome piano brought up the rear, like a carriage of ladies following the hunt. The main game of the thing involved Luisa making a little series of trills or la-la's that—for instance—went up and down in the shape of a tent, whereupon the flautist would attempt as well as he could to imitate this contour. Then she would make her la-la's in a slightly different way, perhaps going up but not down, leaving the coming down to the next match between voice and instrument.

$$\begin{array}{ccccc} & & & & la \\ & & & la \\ & & la \\ & la \\ \text{Luisa:}\quad La \end{array}$$

$$\begin{array}{ccccc} & & & & oo \\ & & & dle \\ & & oo \\ & dle \\ \text{Flute:}\quad Too \end{array}$$

This folly of setting herself against the precision of a metallic and finely honed instrument was her undoing. By herself she might have prevailed, or at least concluded the evening in some sort of an armistice. But this small tubular machine was remorseless. It followed her every voice-step, and when she faltered even slightly it pounced on her. Soon she was faltering more than slightly. The audience began taking an interest in the proceedings on the dais, for the first time in the evening. Husbands who were asleep were woken up, and the students grinned and nudged each other.

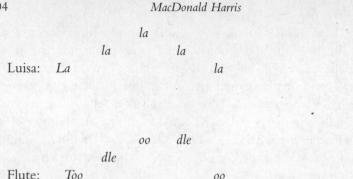

The flautist did his best. He was on her side; after all she was paying him. But he too was helpless against the fine precision of his instrument. There was no way out for him; he had to play the notes in tune. The audience, which before had only tittered, now permitted itself an outright ripple of laughter. Luisa made another of the tent-shaped cadenzas, and this time the flute, in spite of the best efforts of its operator to control it, said distinctly, "I went this way, but you went that." Luisa's voice was as it had always been: charmingly lyrical when she wished it to be lyrical, coloratura when she wished it to be coloratura, varying precisely in timbre and tone according to her will. It was only in pitch that it refused to obey her. That little force that drove it slightly up when it should have gone down, slightly down when it should have held level, was the demon of her emotions, a phenomenon I knew well from other incidents quite different in circumstances. It was the nature of her voice to rise when she was excited, to lower when she wished to convey a tone of threat. Now she was in the grip of both these forces. The flute could not have followed her even if it had been Mozart's magic one, neither could any system of notation. The more the flute reproached her the more excited she became, and the more threatening. She ended in a debacle, three notes from the tonic, in a head-voice, stopped in midair by a catch or a sob.

The applause was immediate. I had always known that Parisian audiences were pitiless and now I saw it for myself. Some clapped their hands so hard they were unable to laugh, and others laughed until they were unable to clap their hands. They rose to their feet. I with them— otherwise how could I see anything? There were only a few whistles to indicate disapprobation. Drowning them out, many bravas. Luisa's pallor was phenomenal, a medical curiosity, like a patch of brightly illuminated snow.

"A new diva!"

"Melba, it's time to retire!"

"Brava!"

"Bis! bis!"

"Charmant Oiseau! Encore!"

"Bis! bis! bis! bis!"

This chant took over the hall. Casimir and Gilles had their due part in it. I might have rapped them over the head, but I had no weapon. I ought to have brought a riding crop. Besides, by this time they had disappeared. The porter, as was customary, was waiting at the rear of the hall with a number of elaborate bouquets, including a horseshoe of carnations and lilies of the valley. These ornaments were appropriated by Casimir and Gilles, assisted by their fellow students. The porter was pushed over backward onto a chair. Luisa, who had come to her senses by this time, attempted to escape to the right. (The flautist and pianist, who should have been her natural protectors, had long since disappeared.) But she was cut off by a volley of flowers, and turning to the left saw her escape barred that way too. The horseshoe of carnations sailed through the air and struck her on the ankles.

"Bis! bis!"

"Fly again, Charmant Oiseau!"

"Brava!"

"Diva! diva! To the Opéra!"

The more respectable of the spectators, myself included, quitted the field at this point. In a box near the dais I caught a glimpse of the aunt, formidable, stoic, her chin tremoring as usual but no more than usual. Then I slipped out through a side aisle onto the street. For all I knew, the students actually carried out their promise, or threat, to attach themselves to Luisa's carriage and drag her to the Opéra. Why should I intervene? I knew nothing of music.

•

The rain had stopped; a faint breeze was rustling in the trees along the avenue and the pavements were almost dry. There were no cabs in sight and I decided to walk back to my lodgings by way of the Pont de L'Alma and the quays. It was a good distance and took me almost an hour, but it was a mild evening and the damp, faintly moving air was refreshing. When I arrived in rue de Rennes it was only a little after eleven, and the concièrge was still awake over her coffee and her copy of Le Panorama. When she was awake no one unknown to the house could ascend the stair, and when she went to bed she locked the street door with a rusty old key. I mounted the five flights, let myself in and latched the door behind me, removed my coat and hat, and put some leftover coffee on the stove to warm. Then I got out an Admiralty pilot chart of the Arctic Ocean and stretched it across the table. For some time I had been meaning to make notes on the probable winds for this region in the month of July. Now, as always when I went out to a concert or somewhere else in the evening, I was wakeful and in a mood to work for a few hours before I went to bed.

When the coffee was warm I poured it into a cup and added a little cognac to it, and set it on the table by the chart. The meteorological indications on the chart, as might be expected for so remote a part of the world, were rather meager. Still, there were a number of spidery wind symbols—circles with arrows of various length sticking out of them, to indicate average direction and velocity—in the region between Greenland and Franz Josef Land. For half an hour I happily made notes, even extrapolating the data mathematically so that I was able to draw in a few of my own symbols farther north on the blank part of the chart. Then there was a rap-rap at the door, a rather peremptory one. In the back of my mind I think I expected the concièrge with a telegram, perhaps from Waldemer in New York, otherwise I wouldn't have been so incautious as to open.

I unlatched the door enough to see who it was and Theodor pushed his way in. Before I could say a word he took a nickel-plated revolver out of his greatcoat and fired it at me point-blank. It was no joke; the sharp bang was enough to break the eardrums and there was a stench of powder. In the space of less than half a second my heart leaped twice and every nerve jangled like a billion electric doorbells: once when he fired and once when I grasped that he had missed me. I ducked to one side with my ears ringing and he fired twice more. A second or so after this there was a sound of descending glass. Probably from a picture on the wall; I didn't turn my head to look. There were still two shots left in the thing, perhaps three. I wasn't an expert on firearms but the difference in practical terms was negligible. If he kept on in his present humour, in this small room with no place to hide, he might even hit me eventually. I changed my tactics abruptly and attacked. I managed to get his wrists in my hands just as the infernal contraption went off again. A little storm of dust and grit fell down on us from the ceiling. I was surprised at the steely, fierce, and cunning strength I felt between my fingers; it was like trying to hold two angry pythons by the neck. I let go one of the wrists and concentrated on the other. By coming within a hair of breaking the thumb, I managed to pry the pistol out of the hand. It fell to the floor and, still holding one python and trying to elude the other, I bent down, retrieved it, and pitched it through the open window into the courtyard. But he wasn't satisfied; he went right on trying to tear me to pieces with his fingernails. Or let us say she now, since the weapon had become a more traditionally feminine one. This was less frightening than the part immediately previous, but even more painful. I had no more desire to be permanently disfigured than to be shot. We fell in a heap on the floor, I on top, the greatcoat and the flailing limbs underneath. For some time I tried to subdue all these arms and legs, but it was uphill work, since I myself possessed only one limb for each of his—of hers. That concièrge! Would she ever get around to sending for the police? I didn't know whether to hope that she would or hope that she wouldn't. I decided to hope that she wouldn't.

She didn't, evidently deciding that the sounds (shots, glass breaking, bumping bodies) were only from one of my experiments. And what was happening now? The nature of our struggle, it became evident after a while, had gradually metamorphosed without either of us being aware of it. It wasn't true, I reflected as I meditated in an oddly detached way on my sensations, that I possessed only one limb for each of hers. Tarnation! I swear by Great Thor in Thunderhouse that my chief concern—my only concern—was to get her subdued and to secure my own personal safety and survival, and secondarily to try to bring some sense into her fevered brain. But the very gestures of our struggle—her writhing and trying to scratch, my attempts to immobilize her limbs and defend myself—were only those that multiplied the points of our contact. Not for nothing had the nineteenth century decreed that young ladies and gentlemen were not to engage in wrestling matches while alone in lodgings. Her greatcoat had come open and the rest of her clothing, I noted in a distant part of my mind that I had for some reason kept in reserve, was also considerably disarranged. Her defence, or attack, now chiefly took the form of clutching the lower part of my face and pulling it toward her own. Our four lower limbs had now given up clashing head-on and divided up the field of encounter: hers apart to either side, mine between them. In all honesty I believed—I still believe—that I continued the pretence of struggle longer than she did. Yet it was surely not she who removed the necessary parts of my clothing; this was hardly possible since her fingers, no longer daggers now but velvet and feverish, were playing over the face pressed against her own. Her panting, her feline snarls of menace, had changed into a sound still rhythmic but something like weeping.

"I really wanted to kill you," she sobbed.

"Yes, and I really wanted to stop you."

"Then why are we doing this?"

"I don't know."

"Why wouldn't you. Answer when. I spoke Swedish to you?" she wrenched out between sobs.

I paid no attention to her questions, nor she to mine. "Why didn't you shoot the flautist? Or the music teacher in Passy?"

I didn't want. You to come. To the recital."

"Did you ever ask what I want?"

"It was all. It was all for you. Don't you know that?"

"Elixir Vert-Galant. You deserve whatever—"

'Now, oh, dearest one, now now *now now!*"

Only an inch or so from my eyes I saw her teeth grip her lower lip and a bright thread of blood spring out between them. The set teeth only gradually loosened their hold. A convulsive warm thing inside or between us still kicked now and then, more weakly and at widening intervals, like a fish dying. Her head, with a clocklike slowness, turned away from me to the right until I could see only the cheek. I was aware of the sound and rhythm of her breathing under me, not only with her lungs, but with her whole body. Inside, at the point where all the pyrotechnics had taken place, only a little spark crept ant-like now and then through the ashes. When at last, it seemed, the thirst for air in her was sated, the slow undulations spreading from her lungs to her throat, her limbs, gradually ceased.

I became aware of my surroundings again and collected myself to take note of them scientifically. Theodor's officer cap was upside down against the wall across the room. The greatcoat was sprawled in one direction, essential parts of my own clothing flung in another. Some cataclysm had evidently struck here, one that snapped buttons and tore away garments. The picture with the shattered glass, as I had expected, was an engraving of *The Wife of Poetus* in which the Latin matron was plunging a sword into her bosom and commenting to her husband, "Non dolet." Near it a chair had fallen over and was lying with four legs in the air, like a dead animal. A detail that surprised me was that the small nickel revolver was lying on the floor by the window. There were two possible explanations of this. One was that I was mistaken and it had not gone out the window after all. I was sure I had caught a glimpse of it curving through the open rectangle and downward into the darkness, but perhaps I had only been deluded by my boy's vanity about throwing things. The other was even less plausible: that the concierge had been annoyed by my throwing things down into her courtyard, which was really only a dank little well in which she kept the trash bins, had retrieved it, climbed up five flights, opened the door, clambered over our wildly convulsing bodies (oh, Major, your experiments), and set it on the floor by the window as a reproach. It was true she was a reproachful person by temperament, but she was not given to such complicated silent gestures. I picked the thing up, found out after a little fumbling how to break it open, and shook out the shiny little brass husks in the cylinder. There were five of them, all empty. Well, she had done her best. I slipped it into the desk drawer, rather furtively, with my back turned.

But she was not interested in the revolver, it was something that belonged to Theodor and it had nothing to do with her. She got up quite calmly now, even matter-of-factly and with a kind of religious simplicity, and began readjusting her clothing, the male gestures she was obliged to fall into in order to fasten certain buttons contrasting oddly with the mass of unpinned hair that fell over her face. Then she went to the sink, dampened a towel, and removed the traces of salty moisture from around her eyes and the blood from her lip. Her manner in doing all this was even and unhurried, stately, with a touch of the austere politeness she always assumed with persons with whom she chose to be a little distant, or when she preferred not to talk. It was as though the act we had just performed was a ritual of purification (now there's a strange idea, oh, dix-neuvième siècle!) which had restored to her not only her calm but her confidence, her assurance in herself that she was superior to the world around her, along with its vicissitudes and most of its inhabitants. Next in this even sequence of events she filled a not very clean tumbler at the tap and drank the contents, slowly but in a single long draught without taking the glass from her lips. Our eyes met over the top of the glass but she said nothing. Finally she went to the worktable, took up the old red-painted shears I kept there for dealing with things like cardboard and tinfoil, and began cutting off her hair just below the level of the earlobes. The hair had seemed profuse falling over her face, but there was even more of it when it came down handful by handful onto the table. Finally there was a heap of it in the centre of the pilot chart, shadowy, snakelike, faintly iridescent. Working without a mirror in this way she hadn't done a very good job. It was ragged around the edges and a little lower on one side than on the other. But it sufficed; the ends of her ears appeared under it, and when she tossed her head it flung out and then came back into place again, boy-like. With the cap on she looked the same as before except for the cut on her lower lip. The shears she put in the pocket of the greatcoat.

She came back to the table and seemed uncertain what to do with the hair; not what to do with it but what to use as a container. Finally she rolled it up in the pilot chart itself and put it in my arms, simply and modestly, with a smile, and the air of one conveying a gift. Then, still without a word (she had not spoken after she rose up off the floor), she went out the door, leaving me the hair, and taking for herself the little machine by which it had been cut off like a flower and left to die.

•

Luisa was going to Stresa, short hair and all. I was not invited. The aunt would go along and the Polish cousin, perhaps the mother. I had to go to Hamburg anyhow, to talk thalers with the brewers. We agreed to meet in Switzerland, somewhere. But it wasn't just somewhere; she knew exactly the place she had in mind. "Just by the Simplon. When I come up from Italy over the pass you'll be there. The place is called Brig, in the Valais. There's an inn. It's called—I forget what the inn is called. You can find it in the Baedeker. Goodbye."

She always spoke English now, which avoided the awkward second person in French: tu was too intimate and vous too distant, even impolite. It (vous) would have involved an awkward backing up from where we had been before, whereas tu would have indicated that nothing had changed, everything was as before. What had changed, then? I wasn't sure exactly. One thing that had changed, it seemed, was that an absolute rule or taboo of our relationship had been violated: the one that decreed that *that* couldn't happen in Paris, only in Finland, Stresa, and other far-flung corners of the globe. But *had* it happened in Paris? As the days went by I meditated on this. Perhaps not. No, it hadn't. Still, how could I reason thus, with the broken glass from the picture frame still unswept on the floor and the bundle of soft hair rolled up in the chart? I borrowed from Luisa a logic that was circular and retrograde, perhaps devious, but consoling. Since man is free, and woman also according to the aunt, we do exactly what we choose to do in this world. What we have not chosen to do does not happen. And neither of us, I persisted in believing in the face of all evidence, had willed to behave in such an irresponsible and beastly fashion, even when one of us was in danger of his life and the other defending herself against an enraged Swedish lunatic. Ergo and Q.E.D., it hadn't happened. How to explain then that I had the half-healed scars of her claw marks on my face? They were still there, on that day three weeks later when she said goodbye to me in Quai d'Orléans for the last time. If she noticed them she gave no sign. "Goodbye." That last English word—so final in contrast to the promise of au revoir or auf Wiedersehen—was spoken dryly, even with a touch of distance or dismissal. Against any risk that I might take her hand, she held both of them behind her. It was very correct. The aunt was present, observing from across the drawing room with faint denying vibrations of her head. Nay, nay! Nothing shall happen in Brig! I took my leave, seeing that this was the only thing in the house for the moment that they wished me to take.

In Hamburg I spent a week with the brewers. A pleasant time, although their notions of entertainment, involving large amounts of pigs' feet, sauerkraut and bock, tended to increase one's girth and did no good to the liver. I showed them drawings of Prinzess III, the silk for which was even then being cut by a firm in Grenoble. About the thalers there were no difficulties. They seemed to have an unlimited supply of them, guarded as I imagined by Rhine maidens in some iron-bound old chest. (But this could hardly be, I reasoned heavily, since Hamburg was on the Elbe.) The whole business was transacted in a heady miasma of hops. Herr Oberkellner, another bock for the Major! Another week of this and no balloon would lift me, nor would I care. The efficient machinery of Prinzessin Brauerei G.m.b.H. was even able to solve one of my last problems, that of the third and final member of the crew for the polar expedition. They recommended one of their own employees, a young chemist and amateur athlete named Beispiel who had, among his other accomplishments, swum the Hellespont like Byron and also rescued a dozen women and children from a sinking Elbe ferry boat in winter. (By towing them with his teeth, as I understood.) I was introduced to young Herr Beispiel and in fact he was a fine figure of a Teuton. Strong hands, thick chestnut hair, and a chest like an ale keg. There was the value of his scientific training (he was a specialist in yeast culture) and he had made at least one balloon ascension and come down by parachute, all for sport. There was a logic to this crew: Beispiel cheerful brute strength and agility, Waldemer intelligence, and I—transcendental vision perhaps, or the moral power of spirit. (The word I was groping for was German: Emporhebung.) I told him I would consider it. He, and Prinzessin Brauerei G.m.b.H., regarded the matter as settled.

After a week of pigs' feet and Gemütlichkeit, the top button of my trousers unfastened for comfort under the waistcoat, I entrained at the Hauptbahnhof for Frankfurt, Basel, Zurich, Lucerne, and eventually Brig. This proved to be a pleasant hamlet on the Rhone full of steep-pointed roofs and picturesque inhabitants. The main attraction of the place was the Stockalperschloss, an improbable castle built by some robber baron in the seventeenth century and consisting mostly of bulbous domes and watchtowers. I inquired for "the inn" and was told there were three. Following the law of averages, the second one I tried was the one where Luisa had descended earlier that afternoon. She had reserved a room for me and one for her, on separate floors as it happened. ("Nay, nay.") With her hair clipped I had half expected her to make her appearance as Theodor, but instead she was impersonating the young English lady in tweeds. The hair had been trimmed by a coiffeur in Place Vendôme, and it gave her an active-brisk-suffragist look instead of a mannish one. We had dinner according to the rustic local notions, and then she advised me to get early to bed. "I've left orders for them to knock on both of our doors" (significant detail) "at five. You have mountain clothing?"

"I have what I have on."

This was a woolen pepper-and-salt suit with knickers, woolen stockings, and sturdy walking shoes. In my room there was a cap that went with it, of the kind with two visors made familiar by Mr. Sherlock Holmes.

She looked sceptical. "Are you in good physical condition, Gustav?"

"We're only going to climb an Alp. Tourists, old ladies, and other people do it every day."

She rose from the table. "Good night." It was like the goodbye in Quai d'Orléans: friendly, correct, austerely polite. Her hands as before remained at her sides. If she had been with a gentleman she might have invited him to kiss her hand. But you know how some people are; if you offer them a finger they take the whole hand, then the arm and shoulder. I was as correct as she; I smiled like a Peruvian diplomat.

In the morning we set off for the Aletsch glacier before the sun was quite up. Luisa had found a guide, a specimen of the local fauna complete with lederhosen and strong red knees. The winding road from Brig to the foot of the glacier we covered in a sort of farm wagon with benches down the middle, so that Luisa and I sat on one side and the guide on the other. When the road ended we got out and everything was unpacked from the wagon. There were light knapsacks with blankets, food, and thermos flasks, and alpenstocks for all. Each of us wound a length of rope around the waist, to tie us together when necessary. The wagon turned and went back down the road, and we set off up the glacier. To the left and above us as we climbed was the Aletschhorn, enormously high, a sword of ice cream sticking up into the cold and absolutely clear spring morning. As Luisa strode I perceived that under the tweed skirt she wore an example of that efficient garment invented by Mrs. Amelia Bloomer, woolen as it seemed, quite smartly cut around the ankles. My salt-and-pepper suit was supplemented by a cloak the innkeeper had lent me. Already my feet were slipping in the shoes designed for walking in English country lanes.

The guide kept us entertained as we went up the glacier by yodeling in his local dialect, which involved a sound as though he were separating egg yolks in his mouth. From time to time, when he was not doing this, he made little comments. "The Herr is a little tired, yo? The Dame not. Women are strong, you know. The femelle of the sex has stronger lungs. The peasants hereabouts, you know, they drive the cows to the high pasture, but they don't take the bulls. Their lungs would collapse. Yo, yo, the woman sex is strong. My own wife—" And so on.

There may have been something in what he said. My own pulmonary system was already pounding and showing signs of distress. It was borne in upon me for the first time that I came from a flat country and that all these Alps were not really necessary in any rational and efficient scheme of constructing a planet. Still, it was not really fair. I was fat from the week in Hamburg, and she after all had the lungs of a singer; that is, even if she was not a singer artistically, she might be so regarded from an athletic point of view. She went on ahead like a blithe dryad, or did I mean Druid? It was hard to think while panting. The guide presently tied us together with the ropes, explaining that there were crevasses ahead. He knew what he was talking about, this fellow. All morning we toiled up the ice across these fissures large enough to engulf whole armies, some of them treacherously covered with snow. At noon we rested on the Obergletscher, and by five in the afternoon we were at the base of the mountain. Here we camped, or more precisely, rolled ourselves in our blankets in the protection of an overhanging crag and tried to get some rest sitting up all night, warming ourselves now and then with coffee from the thermos flasks. The guide (I never learned his name, and it is possible that in that part of the world they name cows but not sons) built a little fire for us and averted any danger that we would fall asleep by yodeling every hour or so. I believe I did sleep, as a matter of fact. For five minutes; until my head dropped sideways and touched the saw-like piece of granite I was leaning against.

At dawn, after more coffee with some sausage and bread, we set off again. And by noon, rather more easily than I had expected, we were on top of the Aletschhorn. There was a considerable view, for those interested in that kind of thing. The guide pointed out the Jungfraujoch to the north, the Matterhorn and the Dent Blanche to the south. It was cold up there and we soon left the place; there was no entertainment provided and nothing much to do. There were at least two things harder than climbing a mountain, I discovered. One was coming down a mountain. And another was crossing a glacier, either coming up or going down. Especially tied together with an alpine mountain goat and a vigorous suffragist who seeks to make some point by leaping down the crags quicker than one can follow, so that one is dragged along on the rope like a calf going to market.

"And so you" (English; the pronoun neither intimate nor unfriendly) "will be going to Spitsbergen in June."

"Yes."

"And then?"

Half sliding, avoiding disaster frequently only through adroit use of the alpenstock, I would just as soon have postponed this interrogation until later. "Northward. With a little luck. We will see."

"And how many persons will be in your crew?"

"Three."

"Ah. That's an odd number." Three was an odd number. Devil take it, this young woman was a mathematician, no denying that. "Why three, precisely?"

"Because the balloon is designed to carry the weight of exactly three persons."

"I see. And why is it designed to carry three persons?"

"Because that is the number that will be going on the expedition."

And she (over her back, giving me an encouraging little pull with the rope that almost upset me): "And who will these three persons be, pray tell?" "Myself. Waldemer. And a young man from Hamburg named Beispiel."

"H'mm. How very international. And this Herr zum Beispiel. Is he a balloonist?"

"A chemist."

"Ah. One hardly sees the logic of that. I will come with you of course to see you off."

"To Trondheim, perhaps."

"Even to Spitsbergen."

"To what end?"

"Some member of your crew might not be able to go after all. Such as Beispiel. Through illness or for some other reason."

"Not likely. He's as healthy as a performing seal."

"Still, for even a small chance of going on the expedition, it would be worth taking the trouble. And I would be useful, you have to admit that. In Sweden, after all—"

Devil take Sweden! In this system of cryptography we used for communicating with each other, "Sweden" meant the adroit way she had handled the ropes (dropping the ballast at the wrong time) and "Finland" meant—later, in the cottage. For instance, if she had said, "And I would be useful—in Finland, after all!" it would have meant quite a different thing.

"Beispiel will be very useful. He has made a balloon ascension, and he can swim while carrying children in his teeth. Besides, Beispiel means thalers. The brewers—"

"Ah, the brewers." She was scornful of material considerations, especially when it suited her. "If you want to argue that way. Why not an expedition around the Eiffel Tower instead, and you can sell sausages afterward in the Champs de Mars."

At least after that she stopped pestering me. There was total silence for an hour or two while we came back down the glacier and picked our way precariously through the crevasses. Finally, at five o'clock in the afternoon, we were out of them and onto more or less firm ice. I was tired of being jerked along and told the guide to untie us.

"Oh aber. Many more holes."

"No more holes." I untied myself and Luisa did the same. Without disputing the matter, the guide coiled up his own rope around his waist and went on a little ahead, yodeling to himself in an undertone. At the foot of the glacier, a kilometer or so ahead, we could see horse and wagon already waiting for us. A hot bath! And afterward coffee with rum, clean clothing, and a dinner in the inn. Descending a little behind Luisa and to one side, I stepped into a slight depression filled with snow, it yielded, and I fell five metres or more in a twinkling of an instant, before I had time to realise what had happened.

I was in a place with bluish light, hard walls pressing on my back and chest, the alpenstock under me, one arm over my head and the other jammed at my side. Except for a knock on one ear and a wrenched hip, I seemed to be all right.

"Gustav?"

"Here."

might perhaps grumble at Theodor for shirking and not doing his part in this respect, but in fact Waldemer has been acting very protective toward Theodor these last few days, not to say tender. This morning when Theodor went behind a pressure ridge to answer a call of nature (Waldemer doesn't even resent his wish for privacy in this matter now), he commented gruffly, "Have to take it easy on the fellow, you know. Some of us are not as robust as others."

"He's robust enough."

"Well, but . . ."

Waldemer can't express his feelings precisely. And how could he, the poor fellow? He is not in possession of the basic facts that would make him understand why he feels the way he does. Theodor gives out some sort of emanations or waves, that's all, that pass right through the clothing and make a fellow feel like taking care of him and being sure he's comfortable. Waldemer doesn't know he has instincts and he doesn't believe in spiritualism or thought waves, but in spite of himself he is a fairly subtle animal. He knows, but he doesn't know that he knows. At the edge of the ice, where we finally gave up and turned the sled into a boat, he told Theodor, "You crawl up inside the bow, old man. Have a nap up there, rest your bones. The Major and I will paddle for a few hours and then you can take your turn." When Theodor was installed in the bow, his head resting on Waldemer's ankles, Waldemer beamed jovially and seemed unwilling to meet my eye. It may be necessary to tell Waldemer the truth, in the end, in order to explain his own sensations to him and allay any fear that he is not—manly. As he would put it.

A little after seven. We have been paddling away frantically for an hour and are exhausted, but we have won. The squall will pass to the north of us. But it has left a pesky chop on the sea that doesn't make our task any easier. The island is nearer now—an oblong white mass rounded like a shield, ringed by sheer ice cliffs except in two or three places where there seem to be small shelves or beaches along the water. For another two hours we work toward it, resting only briefly because it is apparent now that there is an infernal current trying to set us off to the east, where there is no land for two hundred miles. The sea in the direction we are approaching is shallow; several large white icebergs are aground in the neighborhood of the island. As we pass one of these we can hear the groan as the swell lifts it and it grates and crumbles on the bottom. Finally, about nine o'clock, the island is abeam and we rest on our paddles.

The current has set us to the east and the island is between us and the sun. As we approach it we are enclosed in profound shadow, an immense tent of darkness extending out over the sea and gathering us into its embrace. In the swell we rise and fall very slowly. There are teeth of surf along the shore of the island, hissing and growling sleepily. There are no landing places here, but a little farther along on the east shore of the island we find an ice shelf in a tiny semicircular cove with, behind it, some fissures of bare rock showing that might serve as a ladder to climb into the interior of the island. There are swarms of guillemots and ivory gulls, whirling up with sharp cries into the air over our heads where the sun is still shining. Here we land.

We get out and draw the Faltboot up on the shelf, extract Theodor, and stand about looking at our situation. The shelf is not very much larger than a dinner table and doesn't seem excessively solid. When the confused sea left behind by the squall strikes it, it groans and complains. However, it is perhaps a metre thick. It will do for a temporary platform, but as soon as possible we will have to climb onto the plateau in the interior of the island, where there will be game and where we will have a view of the sea around in those intervals when the murky weather clears. First we set up the tent and prepare a meal: hardtack, what is left of the seal meat, cocoa, and a tin of gooseberry preserves which we pass half-frozen around from one to the other and eat with our single spoon. During this supper I feel content but somehow odd. I am conscious, so to speak, of being the object of interest of spectators, and I even glance around to see who is in the tent. The premonition or vague hallucination I have felt for several days, that there is one more of us than can be counted, has expanded now until it seems like thirteen. Where is Judas? He is at the head of the table. I help myself to more gooseberries.

"Better than a poke in the eye with a sharp stick, eh, Major?"

"I—" between swallows. "Used to gather. Gooseberries in the Stockholm skerries. When I was a boy."

"You never told me you had been a boy." Luisa too is in good spirits in spite of her ducking yesterday and her twelve hours of lying in the narrow Faltboot.

"I only was for a brief time. Then they found a doctor—who cured me. He was called Doktor Liv."

"Which means?"

"Life." I clean out the can with the spoon. To me the taste of this confection (gooseberries, not life) is deeply provocative in a way that I am not at first able to understand. It isn't the skerries, or the gooseberries themselves. It is their container, tasting slightly of copper, still shiny from the industrial machine that made it. In these few days I had almost forgotten the World of Cities. This faint tinny tang, the sharpness of bright metal calls me back to it in a way that is somehow ominous and yet at the same time richly promising: a temptation. What have I to do with that world? What would I do there, and what have I done there? Is it possible that horse cars are still clanging down the streets of Philadelphia, that cocottes and their clients are still lighting cigarettes in Montmartre? If so, it is in another existence, a quite different solar system with another sun and planets. I throw the tin away, then retrieve it and put it away with the provisions. It may serve for something or other, perhaps as a second saucepan to stew gull meat in. Our other pan was made in a factory too. The fact is that we cannot live without the World of Cities, or can live only like animals. The tyranny of the cooking pot! Without it there is no Shakespeare or Beethoven, no love of Petrarch for Laura. It is clear that for mankind it has been a long and difficult business to get where we are, and that the heritage of gooseberry tins and symphonies is not lightly thrown away. Save all these scraps of trash, then, lest we turn into polar bears.

•

After supper we decide that Waldemer will scout the cliff for us to find the best way to the top. Then, perhaps, we can all follow him and pull the provisions and even the Faltboot up after us. He is an experienced climber and looks forward to the task with relish. He slings the Mannlicher over his back—might find a snow fox up there, you know! The fissure he starts up is ideal, a classic rock climber's chimney. For the first thirty metres the going is easy, then he comes out on a ledge where he is perplexed which way to go next. I stand watching him with Luisa, or perhaps it is Theodor, I'm not quite sure. The top of the cliff, another twenty meters or so above Waldemer, is hidden in a bank of mist. Once or twice the sun gleams through openings in this veil, making dazzling white spots on the ice. Down below we are still in the chill gloom of the shadow. High above Waldemer, above the top of the cliff, the gulls wheel slowly in the sunshine.

Waldemer sets his foot on a kind of step in the rock and reaches to the left for a projecting spur. Hanging by his left hand from this, he swings outward and finds a perch on another ledge, a tiny balcony that projects out of the rock wall for ten centimeters or so over the absolutely empty air beneath it. As he does this, a gleam of sun from above catches him. The balcony is barely large enough for his two feet. His left mitten is still gripping the crag above him and to the left, the right feeling for a handhold at the level of his waist, his two feet pressed together gracefully like a dancer. The balcony breaks and he is unsupported in space.

For a fraction of a second his left hand clings to the crag, then this crumbles, the upward-stretching hand abandoning it only reluctantly. The body with one arm raised and the other extended to the side, feet still together, accelerates downward out of the gleam of sun. The speed of its racing through the shadow below is impressive. It is like a gull flashing down out of the sunlight under a cliff. About halfway down it strikes the ice wall with a heavy muffled thump. Up to this time its pose has been unchanged: one arm over the head, the other at the waist, the feet together like an acrobat or a Spanish dancer. But when it strikes the ice wall this symmetry is deranged and it turns into a rag doll, tumbling the rest of the way first with head up, then feet, then a reaching arm. This rotation seems to drive it even more violently into the ice when it hits. One shoulder touches the ice first, then the legs, which slap onto the hard surface with a second and distinct sound after the first thump. The body comes to rest with one foot in the water and the two arms stretched out over the ice. All this has happened not with dignity but with an absurd and comic swiftness, almost too fast for the eye to follow, like a clown doing something familiar at breakneck speed. The eye wishes to slow the action and understand how it has happened, what the stages of it were and the impulse and necessity of its physics, whether it was really necessary. But it is over before the mind can grasp it.

He raises his head as we come toward him. Smiles. Quickly we slip the rifle off him, lift the foot from the water, touch over his limbs with our hands. He says, "Leg." It isn't the right one evidently. He smiles again when our searching fingers find the crux of the difficulty on the left. "It doesn't hurt." The wife of Poetus–non dolet! She was either a liar or a humourist, that lady. All the blood has gone out of Waldemer's face, and although he is still smiling, the smile is like a surgical incision bent upward with retractors. We decide not to bother with splints until we have slipped him over the ice to the tent; on the tiny shelf this is only a few metres. During this journey he speaks once more: "Sorry." It is in his quite ordinary voice, even with the little clearing of the throat that he makes before speaking, as though he is apologizing to us either for falling off the cliff or for the pain we are causing him.

Then we have him inside the tent and there is something else difficult to do, turning him from his stomach over onto his back. Theodor holds the leg gently and I rotate him; he is heavy. During this he smiles with amusement at how heavily he is sweating. Found a way to keep warm in this climate, by Jove! Break your leg and you're like toast. It isn't really a warm sweat, however, but a cold one that leaves his face like milk. He needs the coats over him, all of them, and some cocoa.

"Stupid of me. Now I've made a pickle. For everybody."

"Never mind."

"Tell you what. You fellows, tomorrow. Had better just go on. Leave me the Mannlicher. In the boat, the two of you. You'll have a chance. Franz Josef Land . . ."

"Don't talk nonsense."

But he has read enough boys' adventure stories to know how to behave. In order to play the game he even has to pretend it would really work, our abandoning him and setting out over that deserted sea to the east. "Sealers there. Now and then. In the summer. You can have them. Come back and get me." He doesn't complain and he even tells jokes while we improvise a splint for him out of the rifle and some strips of silk torn from the tent. The gunstock fits neatly under his arm and the barrel comes almost to his ankle. We make him comfortable and pour the cocoa into him.

Inside the tent, in the deep shade of the cliff, there is an illusion almost of night. This is restful; the first time that watchful sun has turned away from us in ten days. It makes it colder though and we light the primus. I go outside and pile snow around the edges of the tent to keep out the wind. The rubberized silk which held the far finer atoms of hydrogen for a week will not let the slightest particle of air come through. I make sure the Faltboot is secure, wedged against the rock with the paddles inside it.

Then I go back inside and seal the flap of the tent by piling snow around it. The light that comes through the silk is thin and greyish, a light made out of shadow. The red stripes have scarcely any colour now; they have darkened to the iron of coagulated blood. This banded half-obscurity of light and dark we will call night, for our purposes. It will do. The brandy is for Waldemer. We uncork it and he lies happily with it cradled under his arm. "Cognac Fine Champagne. Very best, by George. Go first class when you go with the Major." Luisa and I unroll the other sleeping sack and get into it, with a certain alacrity, since we are coatless now.

There is no sound but the faint hush of the wind outside against the silk, and a gurgle now and then as Waldemer lifts the bottle and tilts it. Even inside the sleeping sack it is terribly cold. I turn the primus up to make more heat, and the flame goes yellow and begins to rise off the burner, making a faint popping sound. I know from experience that under these conditions the burner is inefficient and that each molecule of carbon, unable to unite as it would like with two molecules of oxygen, has to be content with a monogamous marriage with one molecule of oxygen; a slight difference statistically, but one of profound importance for us.

"Vet du, Gustav, I am not a little girl any more and I want to know. What will happen now?"

"Do you care?"

We lie quite chastely side by side, our flanks necessarily touching in the narrow sack and a common warmth suffusing the enclosed space, yet aware of each other only in the abstract play of minds and the subdued, distinct, and precise sound of voices.

"Whatever happens, I want it to happen in a way that is—how do you say—renlig—enfaldig. Nettement tu sais, without too many unpleasant details."

"As in a book."

"Not like a book exactly, but the way I have already imagined it in my mind."

"Whatever happens will happen only in your mind anyhow."

"Hör du, Gustav. Those sealers. Do they exist?"

"Which sealers?" "The ones who come to Franz Josef Land occasionally."

"They might exist."

You two. Always talking Squarehead. Discussing your love lives in Paris, probably. Might let a fellow in on it. The words are blurred now, the brandy is working. In an hour he might even go to sleep, from fatigue and through the sheer physiological efficiency of the hunter who can turn off his body when he has no use for it. He is—the idea occurs to me with the quick simplicity of a discovery—he is happy.

"And if they do exist. What then?"

"We can put our friend in the Faltboot and paddle to Franz Josef Land."

"Is it far?"

"When it happens in your mind it isn't far. Paddling, it's quite a way."

"I'm still strong, do you know, Gustav. I've rested all day. You haven't let me do my share. That's not fair. On the Aletschhorn—"

"Yes, I know."

And I have been thinking. It wasn't really because she wouldn't let me out of the crevasse that I agreed to let her go. Whether I knew it or not, it was to force her once for all out of her world, the world of couturiers and tea at the Café Royal, and into my world, the world of thought, where everything is clean and abstract. But now I know that here, the place I have brought her, is not her world and not my world, it is no world at all. It is nothing. And perhaps it is better that it should be this way. In her world or mine, one of us was always the enemy, the fool. And now the enemy is nothing. Not the whiteness and cold of a certain region of the world, even as remote as it may be, but the eventual Nothing that now gapes before us like an immense welcoming gate. But this is an enemy I have been careful to protect her from. Both of them. And they have believed me and entrusted themselves to me with a childlike simplicity—all because I have pretended to know, to be stronger than they are in my knowing, to be hard! It is important that this secret should be kept from them to the end—that there is Nothing, that no one among the angelic orders will hear us if we cry out. The other secrets—that no sealers ever come to Franz Josef Land, that it is impossible to cross two hundred miles of open sea against the wind and current—are unimportant and can be concealed with trivial lies. These are analogous to the lies I tell myself, for instance, that I am hard or that I do not care about what is going to happen.

"Hör du, Gustav. I think it was on purpose that you brought me to this place. Because it is called White Island. And I like white things. Isn't that so?"

I might tell her that sometimes she likes white things and sometimes she doesn't, and this is profound of her, and I know the reason why, but I won't tell her, because her belief that she likes white things is necessary for her now, and for what is to come.

"And are you happy here?"

"I am happy. As long as you don't touch me. And I must not touch you either. Then I am happy. I don't know why that is."

"It is because the outsides of things are white. And inside they are red."

"You mean that part of me? I don't know. I've never looked at it."

She is not fond of mirrors either. She alone, of all the women I have known, never looks in mirrors. This is something we share. She goes on: "I think it is because God is angry at us that we are condemned to be in pair. Only he—she—It—is allowed to be one. Do you know, Gustav, the Garden of Eden story is told the wrong way. We weren't two then but one, and we were happy. Then we did something terrible, told a lie or got into the jam cupboard. And He said: I condemn you to be split in two, and wander around forever looking for the other half, loving and hating at the same time. And ever since we've been trying to be one again. But that's forbidden. It's forbidden by God. It's a sin and makes us suffer."

"So there's no hope?"

"The only hope is to go where everything is very cold and white. Then this red thing inside us is chilled and we are white all through. Only the minds can touch, and they touch very gently because they don't want anything from each other. I'm tired of bodies. I have a headache. I don't know how to say it in Swedish, c'est mes époques qui approchent. I've only had this body for twenty years but I'm tired of it already. I'm glad you brought me here, Gustav."

This is a good place to get rid of it, if that's what she has in mind. It isn't really her époques, of course. The symptoms are well known to medicine: the feeling of pressure on the temples as from an elastic band or cap, weakness of limbs, gradual darkening of the vision. Lying quietly in the half darkness after she has finished talking, I imagine the atoms joining together into their silent deadly ether as thin as thought, invisible and merciful like the Grace of God itself. Two by two they steal upward from the yellow flame, clasping each other in their embrace inimical to man but not this embrace of theirs—forbidden by God, instead, it is the manifestation of His precise and infinitely complex will which never errs and which men call chemistry. Rising with a certain difficulty onto my elbow, I locate Kullberg 5566 and establish that it is ten minutes before midnight, and also note that the primus stove is working well, that is to say, it is not working well at all. (Another one of your paradoxes, Major.) To judge from the colour of the flame, it is converting kerosene to carbon monoxide at a highly efficient rate. Crispin's Axiom: machines are really of use to us only when they work defectively and produce results not anticipated by their designers. A balloon intended to go to one place takes us to another, a Bell telephone earpiece receives messages from the Infinite, and so on. I have to confess that, in spite of my technical education, I am not really much of a believer in the hope that these trivial engines will bring us bliss.

So I have not noted anything in my pocket diary about the Pole, and I have made sure that Waldemer has not kept any record of it in writing either, so that, if the nonexistent sealers or somebody else ever finds our camp, those down below in the World of Cities will not imagine that we have accomplished something significant, and Nansen or Lieutenant Peary or some other worthy person will have the honour of handing to the human race the navel of their planet on a silver platter. For me, for us, these things are unimportant. Because what does this or any of it matter, once we have opened our eyes from our sleep and contemplated at last the ultimate Nothing? Some of us are tired of our bodies at twenty, some at ninety, but we must all tire of them in the end. If man is superior to the universe, it is because he understands his predicament and is able, ultimately, to choose the means and the moment of his confrontation with it. For this, of course, strength is needed. I am happy that I have found this in myself. All modesty aside, and now that I am totally alone.

This is not to say that I am at peace with myself. Far from it! There are too many things in my head for that, too many burdens. Others have trusted in me, and I have betrayed that trust. If I did it because it was best for them, this in no way diminishes what I must take on myself. There is that betrayal, and there is this final crime of mine—and a crime it is, murder pure and simple, and what is worst of all, against persons very dear to me, not the least of whom is myself. But I have to bear these things lightly and not regard them in a sentimental way. It is a shabby Götterdämmerung in the odour of kerosene, and I am only an eccentric Swede whose hair stands on end, perhaps not even a genius, only a minor clairvoyant. What egotism! The Mental Diary has degenerated totally into these first-person pronouns. This childishness is the best argument there is against the immortality of the soul.

Something is changed. Everything is suffused with a swimming pink. My mathematical powers at least have not been impaired. I am aware of what is signified by this subtle changing of light. The sun, curving in its wolf-like lope around the horizon, has reached the point where it shines once more into our cove. I am glad that the others are asleep and not aware of this. The comfortable shadow is gone; the white stripes take the light gradually, the dark ones crawl at the edges and grow red. Midnight: altitude at the minimum, azimuth angle zero. Like a cathedral facing north our tent is aligned exactly with the meridian. This Great Window of Chartres commemorates a Passion, but it is not a holy one. The blood-glow is the sun of Stresa, it forces its way through the shutters of the closed eyelids and will allow no peace. The brocade falls, the curve of surface is a mathematical witchery of shadows. Luisa, det war synd! If this half and that half are brought together into One, it makes a fire that hurts. But she only smiles and glances downward at this most precise and unanswerable geometric theorem of her body. I float toward it and am lost in shadows, I am both the enclosedness and the enclosed, a warmth shudders somewhere at the centre of everything. This Finnish night is terribly cold. Thank God for the featherbed!